THE HAWTHORNE HERITAGE

THE HAWTHORNE HERITAGE

~

Teresa Crane

St. Martin's Press
New York

Library of Congress Cataloging-in-Publication data

Crane, Teresa.
 The Hawthorne heritage.

 I. Title.
PR6053.R356H38   1989   823'.914   88-30169
ISBN 0-312-02582-3

First published in Great Britain by William Collins Sons & Co., Ltd.

First U.S. Edition

10 9 8 7 6 5 4 3 2 1

Prologue

The sun was warm on the old woman's shoulders, and she smiled to feel it. The lake glimmered in the light, its metallic surface rippling in the gentle summer breeze. In the shimmering distance two swans, their plumage gleaming like polished silver in the sunlight, sailed in stately grace upon the waters. Behind her the docile pony stood patiently between the shafts of the dog cart.

Ten years ago she had had this seat placed here at the lakeside beside the small church of St Agatha's, and on any day that was warm enough she would escape the happy chaos of Old Hall, with its children and its puppies and its constant hubbub of noise and come to the peaceful spot. So much had happened here. So very much.

Robert had known this place. And so had Danny. Oh, yes. So had Danny.

The old woman lifted her eyes to the shining waters of the lake, remembering.

The breeze had risen a little, whispering through the trees, stirring the soft dark hair of the child who sat at her feet, his head bent absorbedly to his task.

Gabriella's grandson.

She had to smile at the thought of her daughter being a grandmother. How time had raced away with all of them. She had been born just before the century that now, like her, was in its seventies. In the past fifty years so much had changed. The railways had come to East Anglia and suddenly the world had seemed a smaller place. It no longer required a day's harrowing journey to visit London. The machines, that once had caused such bitterness and fury were now as commonplace in the

5

country as they were in the industrial cities. And the people had left, drawn from the land to those same cities by the promise of work and money.

She stirred a little, easing her back. A way of life was changing, and the heritage of the child beside her and of the children who would follow him would be very different from the one that William Hawthorne had bequeathed.

She lifted her eyes. In the far distance, over the tops of the trees at the head of the lake she could just see the peaks of the impressive roofs of New Hall. With its master dead Clara had lived in the great house alone now for ten years, childless and sour, her ambitions brought to nothing. It had been years since Jessica had seen or spoken to her. She wondered now if she had grown any wiser with the years.

'Look, Great-Grandmama – a bird! Do you see? It is a bird, isn't it?' The little boy was offering her the piece of wood upon which he had been working diligently with a small, sharp knife.

The old woman took it. It was indeed a bird, with the lift of flight in the gracefully curving wings.

'It's lovely, dear. Truly lovely.' She smiled at the pleasure that lit the serious little face at her praise. This small, talented child was her pride and her joy, and he knew it, and returned her devotion. Only she truly understood his need to create beauty, to use the as yet undeveloped skills of his hands to bring life to wood and to stone.

She held the bird as gently in her gnarled hands as if it had been alive, feeling the smoothness of the wood and watching with delight the bright and handsome face of her great grandchild. The skill of those young hands was a wonderful heritage indeed. And in the dark, shining eyes she saw another – the only heritage worth fighting for. The heritage of trust, and of love.

Part One

1810–1811

Chapter One

Jessica Hawthorne never forgot the tragic day on which her brother died.

His loss, in his twenty-second year and just three days before her twelfth birthday struck the child to the heart, her grief and shock not unnaturally intensified by the fact that this was her first unnerving brush with the reality of death. Never before had she been brought so forcibly to face the fact that both she and those she loved and depended upon were mortal, and vulnerable. That dreadful day she ever afterwards held to be a turning point, when the first unwilling steps were taken from the shelter of childhood into the perilous uncertainties of the adult world.

It had begun a day much like any other, bright with sunshine and gaudy with the colours of autumn. It was perhaps regrettably commonplace also that Jessica, before the morning sun was well up in the sky, had found herself in disgrace and at odds with her brother Giles. Soundly slapped for it and locked in her room on the nursery floor by her governess, MacKenzie, not for the first time she brooded, scowling, upon the injustices involved in being the youngest and consequently – it seemed to her – the least considered and most put-upon member of the Hawthorne family. Poor, scruffy Bran, the over-excitable culprit in her brush with Giles, had been dragged off to his own miserable confinement in the barn, and as she huddled upon the window seat of the dormer window high in the west wing of the house the dire threats that had been made against her devoted if undisciplined companion and friend worried her far more than did her own disgrace.

'I swear I'll have that damnable beast exterminated!' Giles had raged, his fair, handsome face brilliant with fury, the stableyard muck from his fall dark upon his elegant breeches. Bran, held captive by one of the stable lads, had yelped in aggrieved surprise as Giles' leather riding whip caught him viciously upon the nose.

Blinding temper had entirely ousted good sense. Jessica had flown at her brother, screeching like a street Arab. 'Stop it! Stop it! How could you? He only wanted to play – it isn't his fault if you can't keep a seat on your stupid horse –!'

He had caught her one-handed, lifting her almost from her feet, shaking her as Bran might a rat. From the corner of her eye she could see MacKenzie bearing down on them like a man o' the line, bright flags of mortification and anger flying in her cheeks, her smooth and usually iron-neat hair straggling in the wind.

'Damned brat!' Giles shook Jessica again, and her teeth rattled in her head. 'You run wild as that ill-begotten mongrel of yours!' Still holding her he swung irritably upon the panting MacKenzie. 'Where were you? Can't you keep the child under control? What's she doing at the stables at this time of day? Just look at her! She looks – like – a tinker's urchin!' He emphasized the last words with a series of fierce, neck-cracking shakes, then let Jessica go so suddenly that she almost fell.

'Steady on, Giles.' Edward, who till now had watched the whole débâcle with his usual tolerant good temper spoke, as always, mildly, calming his dancing horse, his eyes sympathetic upon his dishevelled young sister; despite being the elder of the two he had himself suffered often enough from Giles' volatile temper.

Giles did not even glance at him.

MacKenzie blushed an unbecoming scarlet, her pale and bulbous blue eyes fixed on Giles' vividly angry face. 'I'm – sorry, Master Giles –' the woman stammered, and the look she flashed at her scowling charge threatened near-murder, or worse, 'Miss Jessica is supposed to be in the schoolroom with her tutor. I left her there myself a bare half-hour ago –'

'Mr Atkinson sent a message,' Jessica said sullenly, seeing the sweet freedom that had so fortuitously presented itself being snatched from her before it had been well tasted. 'He's taken a cold and is confined to bed.'

'Wicked girl, not to come straight back and tell me —' MacKenzie slapped her bare arm spitefully hard. Edward shifted in the saddle again and was still. Jessica, sensing his sympathy yet nursed little hope of help from that direction; for all his easy-going and kindly disposition she well knew from experience that it was no part of Edward's makeup to spring to an ill-behaved young sister's defence at cost of his own comfort. He was, however, so far as she could see Bran's only chance of reprieve. She cast him a desperate look; but though his narrow, pleasant face beneath its shock of red-gold hair showed wry sympathy, he offered no positive support beyond a small grimace of commiseration.

Grimly Giles stabbed a finger at the embarrassed governess. 'Get her inside and cleaned up before Mother sees her.' He bent to dust the mud from his breeches, turned a glowering look upon the shaggy, eagerly panting Bran who, in his endearing good nature wagged his scruffy tail, sensing no danger. Jessica, paralysed with terror for him, could have cried. 'And as for that brute —' Giles said, his voice savage, 'I'll see to it that he's knocked on the head this time, see if I don't. Belle could have broken a leg —'

'No! Oh, no —! You can't kill him — oh, PLEASE —!' No effort could prevent the rise of humiliatingly childish tears.

He brushed her away. 'Lock him in the barn,' he said to the stable lad. 'I'll see to it later.'

'Giles, no!' The child's voice lifted to a distracted wail. 'Edward — please —' She turned to her eldest brother, '— please, you can't let him —' MacKenzie's iron-hard fingers, bony and cold even on the warmest day, clamped upon her thin shoulder and she was dragged unceremoniously, sobbing with rage and with dread for Bran, across the yard. Looking back she saw the big mongrel being towed reluctantly in the opposite direction, saw too Edward's face set in the disturbed and faintly puzzled look that any kind of unpleasantness always brought to it. As he caught Jessica's eye he made a small gesture, the tiniest of signals – Leave it. I'll do what I can.

Some small relief moved in her. Edward surely wouldn't let awful Giles kill Bran. But gloomily, directly on the heels of that thought came another – when had Edward, or anyone else, ever stopped Giles from doing as he wanted?

'Wicked! You're a wicked child!' MacKenzie's rage was venomous. She had been made to look incompetent and foolish, and in front of Master Giles of all people. She pinched hard as she caught Jessica's arm. 'If you die in your sleep tonight, my girl, you'll go straight to Hell, you hear me? Straight – to – the – Devil –'

The child ignored the hissed words – the threat had been used too often, and the original sting was long gone. She was concentrating the whole of her mind on willing Edward to save Bran, turning her head, pleading with wide, dark eyes that dominated a face pinched and pale with panic.

As the two brothers, followed by a mounted groom, swept past her Giles did not glance at her. Edward, however, in response to her desperate look, winked, his irrepressible smile lifting the corners of his mouth. At least a little reassured by the silent half-promise, she sullenly allowed herself to be marched like a prisoner under escort across the gardens at the back of the house – canny MacKenzie had more sense than to risk displaying evidence of such ill-temper and ill-behaviour on New Hall's immaculate front lawns with Jessica's eagle-eyed mother somewhere within the house – through the west door and up the steep and narrow nursery stairs. Once safely behind the closed door of her own domain MacKenzie vented her fury with more vindictive slapping – those cold, bony hands were as effective a weapon as any cane – before flinging open the door that led to the bedroom. 'In you go, Miss – and there you stay! Lucy – go tell Cook Miss Jessica will be requiring neither lunch nor tea. And bread and milk only for supper, if you please.'

Plump Lucy, Jessica's kind-hearted friend and confidante since babyhood, scrambled awkwardly to her feet, dropping the petticoat she had been mending from her lap. 'Yes, Miss.'

She picked up the sewing, dropped it again. MacKenzie always made poor Lucy's slow wits even slower.

MacKenzie impatiently snatched the garment from her. 'Go!'

'Yes, Miss,' Lucy said again, and casting at Jessica one terrified look of fellow-feeling she scuttled from the room and down the stairs. MacKenzie shoved the child with entirely unnecessary force through the open door. Jessica stumbled to the bed, heard the slamming of the door and the rattle of the key in the lock behind her.

She sat upon the bed, angrily rigid, fists clenched, teeth gritted against tears. She would not cry. She – would – not! She screwed her face up hard. Detestable Giles. Detestable MacKenzie. Horrible world. And poor, poor Bran –

For all her obstinacy, the last thought was almost too much for her. The tears she was refusing to shed rose burning and salty behind her eyes, all but defeating her. Stubbornly she fought them down, her face aching with the effort. 'Damnation!' she said – one of the only two swearwords she knew, culled from her frowned-upon visits to the stable-yard – and then, the need being pressing, she called upon the other one, 'Bloody damnation! Bloody, bloody damnation!' A single tear escaped. She blinked fiercely and scrubbed it angrily away. 'Bloody damnation!' she said again, but with less force, a woeful wobble in her voice. In her imagination, so real and so familiar that she could all but smell the comforting, doggy smell of him, Bran pushed his big wet nose into her hand, licked her skin eagerly with his rasping tongue. She sniffed and gulped hard, tried to suppress awful visions of what might well be happening at this very moment in the barn.

She stood up and went to the window, perching straight-backed upon the deep, cushioned windowsill – in happier moods one of her favourite spots. The nursery suite, high in the west wing, that had accommodated her three older brothers and her sister Caroline as well as the dead brother and sister that they remembered and she did not, overlooked the comings and goings of the vast three-sided court in front of the house, where the broad, gravelled drive swept in from the park

13

past manicured lawns and a pair of triple-cupped fountains to the foot of the wide flight of shallow marble steps that led up to the porticoed front door. Now in the shadows cast by the September sunshine an open carriage stood waiting, John the first footman in attendance and Brancome the coachman, impeccably turned out as always in his dark green livery, on the box. As she watched, distracted a little despite herself, John, seeing the front door open, stepped smartly forward to open the door of the carriage. Not for the first time Jessica wondered if he minded being called by a name not his own – her father, not to be put to the trouble of remembering a succession of – to him – infinitely unimportant names had years ago decreed that all the first footmen of Melbury New Hall, upon elevation to that privileged position should be called John – Jessica was certain that he did not even know, nor would he care, as for some reason she did, that this particular John's name was actually Samuel. The man stood now, servile and attentive, as Jessica's mother emerged from the house accompanied by Caroline. Gloomily jealous of the implications of adulthood and consequent privilege and freedom implicit in the scene Jessica watched them walk down the steps to the carriage. From the height from which she looked their figures were foreshortened, but her knowing eye could distinguish even from this distance her mother's regal carriage and the faultless poise of her fair head beneath the drifting plumes of her small hat. She wore dark green – her favourite colour – over the palest lawn which floated gracefully as she moved. Caroline, blessed with the striking golden looks that both she and Giles had inherited from their mother was in blue – a colour Jessica had noticed with half-envious scorn, that she had much favoured lately, ever since ghastly cousin Bertie had written a fatuous poem to her 'sapphire eyes'. At the bottom of the steps Caroline turned gracefully and spoke to her mother, and their laughter rang prettily on the autumn air. Entirely unreasonably Jessica leaned to the window and ferociously stuck her tongue out as far as it would go. Caroline, impervious and still smiling gaily stepped into the carriage and settled herself with grace upon the leather seat. Her mother, waiting, glanced about her. Knowing it impossible that she might be seen, yet still, from ingrained habit, Jessica drew back sharply from the window. She heard Brancome chirrup to the horses – Betsy and Darling, she had recognized them both immediately, even though all the carriage horses were matched bays and even Jessica's father sometimes had difficulty telling one from the other – and the big wheels crunched upon the clean, fresh-raked gravel.

Jessica drew her knees up under her chin, scowling. She supposed that her mother and sister were repaying Lady Felworth's call. Or perhaps they were going to The Limes to take a glass of wine with Mrs James Spencer. Or to Rendell's Grove to see Mrs Joyce and her three sour-faced daughters, to share tea and cakes and discuss endlessly such tediously uninteresting subjects as the youngest Belvedere daughter's latest beau, or the Hatfield girl's quite disgracefully daring dress at last week's ball at Felworth Hall (Jessica had had that from Lucy, who'd had it from Lady Felworth's laundry maid). She folded her arms upon her knees and rested her chin upon them. Who cared? Who'd want to get dressed up like a silly doll and parade round the countryside hoping to catch this eye or that? What a waste of time! She sniffed again, miserably, and moodily huddled nearer to the window. Beyond the east wing of the house, opposite to where she sat, she could see the tiled roof of the barn that was Bran's prison. The sight brought back all her fears in full force. Surely – oh, surely! – Edward wouldn't let horrible Giles really have poor Bran knocked on the head? Once again panic rose. Frantically she found herself uttering a garbled prayer,

– Please God, oh please don't let him – I'll do anything – I'll be good for ever – I'll do as I'm told, I won't steal from the kitchen, I won't swear or fib ever again – I won't listen at doors, or try to get out of going to church –

She searched her mind for other and greater sins, and was diverted for a moment by the thought that this seemed rather like the Catholic Confession of which her brother John had so astonishingly spoken. She had found that unexpected conversation memorable for more reasons than one – mainly, certainly, because she had been fascinatedly appalled at the thought of cataloguing one's every fault and misdemeanour to the judgement of a necessarily critical outsider, but, too, she had hugged to herself a secret delight at being the one to be discussing such a wicked and forbidden subject with the one member of her voluble family who rarely spoke his mind to anyone.

Guiltily she hauled her straying thoughts back to the present, MacKenzie's dour, hellfire threats fidgeting at the back of her mind. What if God were truly listening and chose to punish poor Bran for her blasphemous lightmindedness – as he had already been punished for her misbehaviour that morning? If she were going to try to strike a bargain with the Lord, she really ought to try to concentrate –

Even as she thought it a movement in the far distance of the park caught her eye, and she scrambled to her knees, hands cupped about her eyes against the reflections in the glass of the window. Yes – there she was – a briskly marching figure with an unmistakably distinctive gait that ex-Corporal Brancome had been heard to remark reminded him of his old Sergeant-Major in the North Essex.

She was off the seat and at the door in a moment. 'Lucy!' She rattled the lock with impatient urgency, 'Lucy – I know you're there – let me out! Quickly!'

Silence.

Creditably she held her patience and her temper. 'Lucy –' she wheedled, sweetly, '– she's gone. I just saw her, walking across the park, heading for the village gate. She's off courting poor old Reverend Jones –' MacKenzie's single-minded pursuit of the village's mild-mannered and ineffectual rector was an open secret, the cause of much sly amusement both below stairs and in the village. 'Come on, Lucy dear – let me out. I'll be back by tea time, I promise. She'll never know. Lucy!' Despite her best efforts her voice was rising and the words were sharp. She swallowed. 'Lucy, please! I have to get Bran away before Giles hurts him –'

Still no sound.

'Lucy!' Raging with impatience, she clenched her fists, trying to keep her voice calm, 'I know you're there!'

'She'll kill me.' Lucy's voice was doubtful.

'I'll give you a ribbon.' Jessica said, shamelessly. 'The red one that you like. And next time Cook makes some of those little almond cakes I'll get some for you, I promise –' Typically all thoughts of the half-struck bargain with the Almighty had fled her mind when the opportunity was offered to take action herself rather than relying on the no doubt well-intentioned but certainly rather more chancy hand of God. 'PLEASE, Lucy!' she begged.

She heard Lucy shuffle across the room, grumbling, held her breath as the key rattled in the lock. Then the door opened and she was out, almost knocking poor Lucy flying as she went.

'You be back, Miss Jessie!' Lucy called, anxiously. 'She'll 'ave my 'ide if not!'

'I will. I promise.' Skirts kilted above her knees Jessica was already all but tumbling down the stairs to the west door and freedom.

The barn door stood open, even from a distance Jessica could see that. Heart thumping fit to burst in her chest she ran like one pursued by demons. What if Giles had already fulfilled his barbarous threat? What if Edward had not been able to dissuade him –? Her feet tangled in the dry September grass and she almost fell, but regained her balance, ungainly arms flailing and flew on. Around the eaves of the old building the swallows were gathering for their autumn flight, twittering and swooping, wings like curved scimitars in the air. Forced by a fierce stitch of pain in her side to slow her steps she watched them lift gracefully from her approach. Edward had told her that they flew to far Africa and the sunshine. She wasn't at all sure he'd got it right, for all his three years at Cambridge. Africa seemed an awfully long way away –

The interior of the ancient building – it had stood for much longer than the great new house, built fifty years before – was dark and warm and dusty. As she hesitated at the door, adjusting her eyes to the change in light she heard movement; in the far corner a dejected head lifted, one ear cocked.

'Bran!'

The gawky bundle of bone and fur leapt ecstatically at her, despite the restriction of a hempen rope fastened to an iron ring in the wall. It was the work of a moment to free the dog, and then she was on her knees beside him, arms thrown about his massive neck, face buried in the roughness of his shaggy fur, tears of relief and reunion threatening to triumph where tears of despair had not. Frantically happy, Bran licked every inch of her that he could reach, his great flagged tail waving triumphant as a banner about them. She gave him another huge hug, dropped a quick kiss on the bony head, then jumped to her feet. 'Come on, old lad – quickly – let's find Robert. He'll help us.'

Together they fled, the slight and wiry figure of the girl shadowed by the huge dog. Beyond the barn Jessica ducked out of sight of the battery of windows on the east side of New Hall and headed towards the great woodland-fringed ornamental lake at the back of the house. A mile long and half as wide in parts, dotted here and there with tiny tree-grown islands, the lake emptied into the river very close to where Old Hall, Robert's home, lay snug within its ancient moated walls. As she ran she kept a good weather eye out for Giles and Edward, who just might choose to ride this way back across the park. The warmth of the sun was on her back, the rich smells of autumn sweet in her nostrils. Bran bounded gleefully beside her, revelling in the run, treating it all as a splendid game.

They reached the shelter of the trees on the eastern side of the lake with no mishap and no discovery; they were safe from here on. Panting, and shaking a little from reaction and relief, Jessica threw herself to the ground beneath the spreading shelter of a great old oak and Bran flopped close beside her, leaning against her, joy at their reunion easily read in his devoted, muddy-brown eyes and his one ridiculously cocked ear. Jessica scratched his head, a little absently, eyes and ears still alert. From here they could reach Old Hall easily and secretly, even though the ornamental woodlands on this side of the lake offered rather less dense cover than the heavy forestation on the other. Still fondling the dog she absent-mindedly and unsuccessfully tried to tuck the wild strands of her wiry, mouse-coloured hair back into their restraining ribbons, then drew her knees up beneath her chin, crooking her free arm about them. Slowly the uncomfortable pounding of her heart eased and her breathing steadied. From here, the wide top end of the lake at the back of the house, one of the grandest views of her home could be had. Before her Melbury New Hall stood in Palladian splendour, golden stone gleaming in the sunshine. The portico and terrace at the back of the house overlooked lake and woodland, a flight of shallow marble steps curving gracefully to the bright and velvet lawns that were invisibly divided from the park by the brick-lined ha-ha. The building, massively elegant and classically proportioned, its ranked, ornamented windows glimmering, jewel-like in the light, dominated the landscape. It had been built some fifty years before by Sir Thomas FitzBolton, the great, great-grandfather of Robert, to whom Jessica and the threatened Bran were now fleeing. The building of New Hall had been a magnificent but sadly misplaced gesture of confidence in the financial future of a family that had lived here in this green land that was the inland borders of the counties of Essex and Suffolk since the time of the Normans. For fifty short years the FitzBoltons had abandoned Melbury Old Hall, the ancient moated jumble of a house that had sheltered the family since medieval times, and gone to live in modern and punitively expensive splendour – as Jessica's family now did – in the New Hall. Unfortunately, however, the family fortunes had not been equal to the family ambitions. The extravagance of the building project itself had wrought the first financial damage – the house, designed by James Gibbs, furnished by William Kent just before his death and at the height of his fame, took eight years to complete, and the costs were crippling: even as the FitzBoltons at last took possession of their grand new home, Sir Thomas was slipping deep into debt. Unwilling, or perhaps unable, to admit to his mistake he had borrowed, imprudently and very heavily, still further, and in an attempt to reinstate the family fortunes he had invested rashly in hope of a quick return. When he died, eight years later, his son — Robert's great-grandfather — had inherited an unexpected encumbrance of grievous debt and mortgage that drove him to an unnecessarily early grave. For twenty years after that his son in his turn had clung stubbornly to grandeur, and in doing so had almost beggared the family entirely. It took Robert's father, another Thomas, a studious, unworldly and tranquil man, to solve the problem simply and swiftly. In 1798 – the year of Jessica's birth – he had sold the new house to William Hawthorne, Jessica's father, and the FitzBoltons had withdrawn, very sensibly, to Old Hall, the ancient riverside house that in the opinion of the greater part of the County they should never have left in the first place.

Now, twelve years later, it was Jessica who sat on the shores of the lake that old Sir Thomas had so recklessly excavated, a silver setting for the jewel house that had broken its builder; youngest child of a merchant family from Bristol now reaping the benefit of that ruined man's lovely vision. Few people, however, dared to or cared to mention the source of the wealth that had bought and refurbished New Hall. The Hawthornes were well-established now, here in the Eastern Counties, as had been the intention. Under the gentle, ruthless pressure of Jessica's handsome, courteous, judiciously generous and exceedingly rich parents all opposition to new money and upstart outsiders had been overcome, and if talk there still might be of a less than honourable trade, now outlawed, it was rarely within range of a Hawthorne ear. It had taken the spiteful innuendoes of Clara, Robert's sister, to apprise Jessica of her family's association with slaving. Within the family no-one ever spoke of it. Until then Jessica had had no reason to believe that the Hawthornes were any different from any other landed East Anglian family – except, perhaps, in so far as they were wealthier than most of their neighbours. She thought they belonged. Understanding and alliances had been reached. Sir Richard and Lady Felworth's elder daughter had been chosen for Edward. A Commission in the Guards for Giles, through the good offices of old General Warner of Pate's Tye, after William Hawthorne had in neighbourly fashion provided the General, who was partial to good horseflesh, with a fine black hunter. Wouldn't the fools of girls just love awful Giles in his gallant uniform, Jessica thought, sourly. A good living was being negotiated already for John, though it would be some years before he was ordained. And for Caroline a much-sought-after prize, the son of a Baronet, no less. Jessica's father was a man who liked to keep a shrewd eye on his investments, none of the fortune-hunting young blades that lovely Caroline had attracted during her first London Season had greatly appealed. In a younger sister's jaundiced eyes the match was a more than suitable one; 'Bunty' Standish had a handsome face and a pea brain, a fatuous sense of humour and no fortune of his own to speak of. Jessica was sure they would suit very well. And what of herself? She presumed, almost without thinking about it, that her parents, when they remembered her, plotted and planned her future as they did those of their older children. The problem for Jessica was that time trailed with such leaden-footed slowness that even the remote possibility of ever finding herself part of that magic and frightening adult world that she so longed and yet so feared to join seemed unimaginable. As long as she could remember everyone in her world had been older than she, busy about concerns that were none of hers, coming and going, ordering their lives – and frequently hers too – leaving her always watching and listening on the sidelines, like a spectator at a play. Always she felt like an afterthought, isolated as she was from her older siblings by several years. Nor, she knew, could she produce any great claim for their attention apart from her apparently chronic if for the large part unintentional aptitude for getting into trouble. She was neither irresistibly likeable, as Edward was, nor was she forceful and dashing like Giles. She was not beautiful, like Caroline, and if she sometimes suspected – somewhat immodestly perhaps – that she might, given a chance, be as clever as clever John, what good was that in a girl – and a second girl at that? That she was a trial to her parents she was certain. It seemed she could do little right, no matter

21

how hard she tried. Only in one particular could she always be certain of attaining the prize for which she always so longed, her father's approbation, and that was on the back of a horse. She was the most accomplished rider in an accomplished family, and was proud of it. She had ridden to hounds since she was ten and had never baulked a hedge, taken a tumble or lost the field. On horseback she shed the humiliating gaucheness that so pained her mother and became one with the animal she rode. Small as she was she could control the most fractious of beasts. But even that had brought her eventually to trouble; it having been reported to her mother that she spent more time with the stable lads than at her music and sewing. She had been cursorily forbidden the stables except for a single hour a day, between four and five in the afternoon. This arbitrary but absolute rule she had broken this morning, and beneath her terror for Bran lurked a trepidation she had been trying all day to ignore – for if her father's approval was the thing she most truly desired, her mother's cool anger was the thing she most truly feared.

She looked again at the huge, golden house, magnificent against the spacious East Anglian sky and found herself wondering why she had always so disliked it.

Bran nuzzled her hand. She wiped her green-stained fingers absent-mindedly on her skirt and scrambled inelegantly to her feet. 'Come on, boy,' and she set off at a fast pace round the lake in the direction of Old Hall, the ungainly mongrel loping at her heels.

Old Hall was a dark, draughty and inconvenient jumble of a building, its river walls damp and its roofs uncertain. It was also, to anyone with a whit of imagination, an enchanted place, the stuff of the magical fantasies of childhood. It was the Sleeping Beauty's Palace, an ogre's lair, the gaunt-walled home of an exiled prince, a fairy castle, all in miniature. Moated, steep-gabled, it was built inward-looking about a cobbled court in the centre of which stood an ancient, sweet-watered stone well. The aged brick and timber of the old buildings had been mellowed and warmed by the slow passing of time and the tall, multipaned windows glittered in the autumn sunlight as Jessica dashed across the much-patched rickety bridge that had in harder times been a defensive drawbridge. Bran, from familiar habit, led the way in a scamper, long claws clattering upon huge worn flagstones along the short dark passage that, on the eastern side of the courtyard, led to the kitchen.

'Goodness gracious me!' Mrs Williams, the FitzBolton's cook-housekeeper threw up mock-scandalized, flour-whitened hands at their sudden entrance. 'Might I ask where the fire is, Miss Jessie? And might I ask, too, what that animal is doing in my kitchen?'

'Sorry, Mrs Williams.' The apology was perfunctory. That Mrs Williams' bark was far worse than her bite Jessica had known since babyhood. 'I'm looking for Robert. It's VERY important – do you know where he is?' Another early-learnt lesson; Mrs Williams was the oracle of Old Hall that everyone consulted, including her employers. Absolutely nothing happened within or without these walls that she did not know about. Jessica eyed a tray of fresh-baked biscuits with interest, her stomach reminding her suddenly of her missed lunch, and of there being no great prospect of tea either.

Mrs Williams, small and solidly built, her hair iron grey beneath its starched white cap, the repressive sternness of her expression hopelessly belied by the twinkle in her blue eyes, turned back to her bowl. 'As a matter of fact I do. He's gone down to the old church to practise. Miss Clara chased him out of the house. Said his caterwauling was splitting her head.'

'She would.' Jessica sidled towards the biscuits and reached a tentative hand.

'Well-brought up young ladies ask nicely,' Mrs Williams said, placidly, not turning her head.

'Please – may I? I'm awfully hungry.'

'You'll spoil your tea.'

'I'm not to have any.' Jessica admitted gloomily.

The grey head turned, a kindly gleam in the astute, rosy face. 'Well – we won't go too far into the whys and wherefores of that, in case I hear something I shouldn't. Take a couple, then, and one for Master Robert, too. But not a crumb for that great beast, mind. I don't slave to feed dumb brutes like him.'

'Thank you.' The girl grabbed the biscuits, flashing a quick, imp-like smile before skipping across the room to the door that led to the great main hall and thence back into the courtyard. Like the huge kitchens of New Hall, Old Hall's kitchen was painted pale blue to keep the flies at bay, but there any resemblance ended, for the domain that was relentlessly contested by Mrs Benson, the Hawthorne's Cook General and M. Bonnard, their recently-employed almost-French chef, was vast, a series of pale caverns inhabited by an army of scurrying underlings who under stern eyes and within a hierarchy every bit as rigid as that which reigned above stairs, tended the great ranges, the hotplates, the huge open fire, the pastry ovens and the meat ovens, the churns of the dairy, the bread ovens of the bakehouse, the vats of the brewery and the ranked shelves of preserves in the stillroom. Here at Old Hall both the scale and the atmosphere were in utter contrast to the new house. The fittings had barely been altered in a hundred years, and it was inconveniently situated for the dining room, which was on the first floor, but for all that it always seemed to Jessica that this big, homely room was the true heart of Old Hall; and if the staff over which Mrs Williams ruled with despotic benevolence was a fraction of the size of the one needed to run New Hall, at least each face had a name and each servant, from Mrs Williams herself down to the lowest scullery maid, knew that the loyalty that they gave freely to the family was as freely returned.

'Tell Master Robert not to be late,' Mrs Williams called after her. 'It's rabbit pie. His favourite.'

'I'll tell him. Come on Bran.' Jessica, turning away, in swift guilt suppressed the familiar and she knew mortifyingly unworthy twinge of jealousy that contact with the small, warm world of Old Hall often brought. Stuffing a hot biscuit into her mouth she dashed through the shadowed Great Hall with its sombre panelling and tall stained glass windows that threw glimmering pools of coloured light upon the great carved staircase and the FitzBolton portraits that lined the

24

walls. Back in the sunshine of the courtyard she raced over the clattering bridge and along the narrow river path.

The tiny, age-old church of St Agatha stood almost derelict beside the lakeshore, within sound of the weir over which tumbled the lake waters into the dangerous depths of the river below. At least as ancient as the house, it had served for many years as chapel to Old Hall. Now, too far from the village and in any case too small to be used as a parish church it rarely over the past years had heard the glad and lifted voices of a congregation: the FitzBoltons and their people used the village church of St Mary's, as did the Hawthornes. The old church stood empty and neglected within a tanglewood of weeds and nettles, its stone walls dark with age and lichen, its leering gargoyles all but faceless through the weathering of centuries. Its sturdy Norman tower with its more modern spire, was a landmark from any part of the lakeside.

Jessica, over the distant rush of the falling water, heard before she reached the church the sound that told her she had found Robert FitzBolton. Clear as ringing crystal the boy's lucid tenor lifted, echoing, piercingly true. She stopped at the gate, still munching warm biscuit, and listened, Bran panting by her side, the lovely sound, muted yet clear in the darkness beyond the open door held her poised and still. Bran, knowing its source as well as did his mistress, wagged his tail expectantly. Jessica put a hand on his rough head to still him for a moment. She dearly loved to hear Robert sing. The dog with beguiling placability licked the biscuit crumbs from her fingers with a warm tongue. The voice stopped in mid-phrase, lifted again, achingly lovely. Jessica pushed her way through the sagging gate, stole along the nettled path to the open door, and was greeted by the familiar dank and musty chill that even on the warmest and driest of days pervaded the neglected place. Within the framed darkness of the doorway light fell through the narrow arches of the pale, stained glass windows on either side of the tiny altar. She stood for a moment letting her eyes adjust to the gloom. Robert stood, his back to the altar so that the faint light from the windows fell upon the finely scripted manuscript he held in his hands and at which he frowned in fierce concentration. Softly, a little tentatively, he sang a phrase, hauntingly melodic, and then repeated it, stronger and joyously full, only to falter again. He broke off. 'Blast it!' he said, mildly.

From the doorway Jessica could not restrain a small shout of laughter. 'Mind what you say in such a place, Robert! Who knows who might be listening?'

Bran, released from her restraining grip, bounded up the short aisle and nuzzled Robert, all but knocking the slight lad from his feet.

'Get off! Stupid beast!' But the protest was affectionate and Robert ruffled the shaggy ears and bent his face to the rough fur. The boy loved Bran almost as much as Jessica did. As any proper person would, Jessica thought, with dour dislike of the one who did not. Robert lifted his head and smiled at her, his sweet, brilliant smile. 'Hello. Disturbing the world as usual?'

She did not smile back, nor did she waste time in pleasantries. Thoughts of Giles had brought back all her forebodings in full force. 'Robert – I'm sorry to interrupt – but something terrible's happened – I just have to talk to you – Oh, Mrs Williams gave me some biscuits. There's one left if you'd like it. Well, almost anyway. I've only taken a bite.'

He shrugged, eyed fastidiously the grubby, nibbled biscuit she held out and shook his head. Watching as the biscuit went down in one unladylike mouthful he carefully rolled the manuscript he held and tucked it into a capacious pocket. 'Let's go outside. It's too cold to talk in here.'

Licking her fingers before Bran could get to them she followed him back out into the sunshine. He was eighteen months older than she, yet not much taller. Like her he was slight, but unlike her his slightness bespoke frailty. His bones were prominent and fragile-looking, his features delicate. His large brown eyes, shadowed still, she saw, from his most recent illness, were soft as a girl's and his skin was pale and fine. Smooth dark hair made a neat cap to his small, well-shaped head. In what could only be explained as an attraction of opposites he had been Jessica's best and firmest friend for as long as she could remember, and his going away to the

Cathedral school in London had left a yawning gulf in her life. She followed him now along the overgrown path to their favourite spot, a square stone tomb, moss-grown and weathered, its inscription long lost, that stood like a flat stone table above the waving sea of thistles, weeds and stinging nettles. Faintly the weir roared in the distance.

'How are you feeling?' Jessica had picked up a stick and swished with automatic and destructive malice at the nettles. Robert walked neatly ahead as if the rank undergrowth, that tripped and clawed at her, parted meekly at his coming. Bran grabbed at the stick, tugged happily, almost pulling her from her feet.

'Much better, thank you. A little tired still.' They had reached the tombstone. Robert vaulted, elegantly and with composure, onto it.

Jessica scrambled decidedly inelegantly up behind him and threw herself down beside him. 'I thought you weren't supposed to sing? I thought that was why you haven't been allowed back to school this term?'

He shrugged. 'I have to practise. That fool of a man! Old Margery knows more.'

'But he said that singing would sap your strength –'

Robert made a small, rude noise. 'What rot! If anything it does the opposite. I can't not sing. I can't!' There was in his voice an uncharacteristic note of intensity. She glanced at him, mildly surprised. He shrugged. 'Stupid man,' he said. 'What do apothecaries know about singing? It doesn't seem to occur to anyone that one day –' He stopped.

Her attention had been caught by a tiny, pale blue butterfly that hovered about the nettles. 'One day what?'

'Nothing. It doesn't matter. Now, come on – what brings you here looking like a waif from the poor house? What have you been crying for?'

'I haven't been crying.' The denial was automatic and half hearted.

'Of course you have.' The words held an edge of impatience but were by no means unkind. 'And your dress is torn and your boots are filthy. You'll catch it when you get back.'

She suddenly found herself, faced with the brusque, brotherly sympathy she had not in nearly twelve years ever received from a brother, blinking rapidly, colour rising uncomfortably as she fought off tears. 'Giles says he's going to have Bran knocked on the head,' she said, voice quavering way beyond control, 'and, oh, Robert he means it! He does!' Fiercely, looking anywhere but at Robert she rubbed at a mudstain on her skirt, and made it worse.

'Oh, surely not – not even Giles would do such a thing –?'

She turned her head sharply. 'He would! He will! Oh, Robert – this time, truly, he means it!'

'For heaven's sake – why?'

She scrubbed miserably at her skirt again. 'I was in the stables – I shouldn't have been there. I tried to hide when they came – but Bran saw Pasha and wanted to play – and stupid Pasha threw a fit, and Bran got all excited – you know how he does – and dashed in front of Belle, and she reared and Giles came off and looked such a fool – and, oh, you know that Giles can't abide to be made a fool of –' The words were pouring out, swift and urgent. 'And he said he was going to have Bran knocked on the head. And he does mean it, Robert, I know that he does! I'm so afraid that Edward won't be able to stop him – you know what Edward is – he can't bear unpleasantness, he always gives in – he can't stand up against Giles when he's made up his mind – and poor Bran so often seems to make a nuisance of himself – he's for ever getting into trouble, though he never means to –' She stopped, kicking in angry frustration at the tangle of undergrowth.

Robert could not help but smile a little. 'Sounds like someone else I know not a million miles from here?'

She did not smile in return, did not even glance at him.

He put out a small, sympathetic hand. 'What can I do to help?'

She turned eagerly to him. 'Please – would you hide him for me? Here, at Old Hall somewhere? He likes you; I'm sure he'll stay with you. We can pretend that he's run away – and then, after Giles has gone off to be a soldier – oh, Lord, I do hope he goes soon! – then I can say that he's turned up again – with Giles gone, no-one else will bother –'

He thought for a moment, then nodded. 'I don't see why not.'

'Oh, thank you!' In her relief she flung herself at him, hugging him. Gently but very firmly he disentangled himself. She pushed the straying hair from her eyes and smiled at him, brilliantly, her small rather solemn face transformed by the light of it. 'It won't be for long, I'm sure. I heard Papa saying the other day that it had all been arranged for Giles to take up his Commission – that means he'll be a soldier soon, doesn't it?'

Robert nodded, then cocked his head to look at her. Often he reminded her of a small, quick brown bird. 'Lucky Giles, off to kill some Frenchies and teach Boney a lesson.' His voice was dry beyond his years, 'Will he enjoy that, do you think?'

She shrugged, a little doubtfully. It had not occurred to her to think in such terms. 'I don't know. I don't really think so. I mean – I'm not sure that he awfully wants to be a soldier, but – well – that's just what he has to do, isn't it? Edward is to have the house, Giles is to go into the army and John is to join the church. It's all arranged.'

'How very well regulated your family is,' Robert's voice was light, slightly rasping, a tone that always made Jessica feel faintly uncomfortable. She eyed him warily. 'A son for the land, a son for the army, a son for the cloth. What a blessing that the fourth of the breed – what was his name? Samuel? – had the grace to die. What would they have done with him had he lived?'

'Robert!' Jessica was scandalized. 'What an awful thing to say!'

He shrugged, an odd tension holding him. Then he relaxed. When he spoke again his voice was normal, the hateful, mocking note altogether gone. 'Giles will probably be sent to Spain, I should think. Or perhaps to Portugal. That's where the fighting is likely to be, they say. I wonder what will happen? No-one's beaten Bonaparte in the field yet, though enough have tried –'

Jessica shrugged disinterestedly.

'It's incredible. He's got Rome. And Madrid. And Father says that the Low Countries can't possibly stand against him. He'll be master of Europe soon, if we don't do something to prevent it.'

'Why should we bother?' Bored, she tugged Bran's ears as he leaned against her perch beneath them. 'Who cares what happens in Spain?'

'Someone has to stop him,' Robert said, seriously. 'Or what's to prevent him gobbling us up next?'

'He's already tried.' Even Jessica knew that 'Nelson stopped him. At Trafalgar'. Young as she had been she still remembered the spectacular rejoicing that had swept the country five years before at news of that victory, to be followed so soon by mourning.

'Nelson's dead. Now it's Wellington's turn. Perhaps Giles'll come home a hero, who knows?'

She groaned, not entirely joking. 'Oh, Lord, don't! He'd be utterly unbearable!'

Robert laughed suddenly. 'You don't suppose the Guards'd take Clara for good measure, do you? That way both our problems would be solved in the same stroke!'

Jessica giggled. 'Clara FitzBolton – England's secret weapon against Boney –!'

Robert's smile had faded. Thoughtfully he dug into a mossy cleft of stone with a piece of stick. In the spread canopy of the trees above a congregation of rooks had begun to quarrel noisily.

Jessica tipped her head back and watched them as they wheeled and flew in the sunlit sky. 'She's bound to get married one of these days,' she said with beguiling incharity, 'and then she'll go off to plague someone else –'

'If anyone will have her.'

She had to laugh at Robert's tone of inconviction. 'Oh, come on, she isn't that bad! She's really very –' she stopped, uncertain, '– well, not pretty exactly – not like Caroline, that is – but –'

'Striking,' Robert said, gloomily, 'that's the word everyone uses about my sister. Striking.' They sat for a while in silence. Bran had flopped to the ground, enwrapped in nettles, and lay with his chin on his paws, watching them devotedly.

Robert eyed him. 'You'd best give me something to hold him with,' he said, 'or he'll follow you when you leave.'

'You can have my sash.' She jumped from her perch and pulled the sash from about her waist.

'Won't you get into hot water for losing it?'

She raised her eyebrows. 'The hot water I'm in already, will I notice?'

He laughed and jumped down beside her. 'You're incorrigible.'

'If I knew what it meant I'd more than likely agree with you. Can I use your belt as a collar?'

'It means very naughty indeed and open to no persuasion to improvement. Here.' He handed over his belt.

She looked up, frowning, faintly indignant. 'Robert, I'm not naughty, you know I'm not! It's just – well – things sort of keep happening –' Even she could hear the lameness of that. She flushed a little.

He grinned and bent to tie the sash to Bran's improvised collar. The big dog's tail thumped happily. Jessica hugged him, hard. 'I'll have to go. I'm supposed to be locked in my room. I persuaded Lucy to let me out. I don't want to get her into trouble.'

He shook his head, mockingly solemn. 'Incorrigible,' he pronounced again.

She eyed him with disfavour. 'If that's going to become your favourite word, then I well might stop talking to you altogether.' She led the way along the narrow path to the gate. 'When do you go back to school, do you know?'

'No.' The word was sour. 'When that fool of a quack says I may, I suppose. I'm missing all the preparations for Christmas – the best time of the year in the Cathedral –'

She glanced back at him over her narrow shoulder. 'You really love it, don't you?'

'Yes. I'll say.'

'And yet –' she drew a sharp, affronted breath as a spiteful nettle caught her arm, '– you don't talk about it very much, do you? Ouch – that hurt!' She rubbed the spot hard.

She sensed his shrug. 'How can you talk about another world? To someone who knows nothing of it?'

'You could try.' She was truly piqued at the inference of the words, and her voice was sharp. They had reached the gate. Se held it open as Robert led Bran through. 'It isn't any great secret, is it?'

She saw in the boy's dark eyes the far-away look that mention of this other life of his, the life of which she knew nothing always brought and which always infuriated her. 'No. Of course not.'

'Well, then –' Jessica stopped, cocked her head. 'What's that?'

'Horses.'

Swiftly and soundlessly she dropped to her knees beside the dog and closed a hand about his muzzle. 'Ssh!'

Like statues, they waited. From the main bridle path around the lake came the rhythmic thud of hooves, the jingle of a harness. A young man's voice lifted, and another laughed. Bran pulled against her hand eagerly, whining a little. 'Oh, hush, you! Haven't you caused enough trouble for one day?'

The sounds diminished as the riders passed. Robert let out a small, relieved breath. 'It's all right, they've gone. I'd better get the dog away now, quickly, before he's missed.'

She stood up, looking at him solemnly. 'Thank you, Robert. We'll never forget this, Bran and I, I promise.'

The swift, bright smile illuminated his face but he said nothing.

She ruffled the dog's rough coat once more, then with a lift of her hand to the boy who held him she turned and sped into the woods without looking back.

She came across her brothers' horses, tethered by the lakeside halfway to the house, next to the boathouse and tiny landing stage that their father had had constructed a couple of years before. Curious, she slipped through the trees to the lake's edge. Out by the largest island a punt slid gracefully through the sunlit water, a sparkling ribbon of gold trailing in its wake. She recognized immediately Giles' tall, elegant figure, fluently balanced, leaning easily upon the pole, driving the light boat through the water with a minimum of effort, his hair a bright halo in the sunshine. Edward, she saw, sat upon the cushioned seat, a hand trailing in the water, his narrow, laughing face lifted to his younger brother. Belle nickered a little, recognizing Jessica. The girl rubbed the velvet nose soothingly. The punt was too far away for either of her brothers to see her, she knew. She leaned against the mare's neck, patting her. The glimmering waters lapped musically against the wooden structure of the landing stage. From beneath the overhang of the bank by her feet a moorhen and her family of chicks swam busily into the sunlight. Her attention caught, Jessica watched the small fleet in delight, the little ones paddling in fussy excitement around their mother, tiny scraps of fluff upon the water. A few feet away a dragonfly swooped and hung like a great jewelled pendant upon the warm air. Forgetting her urgency, and knowing herself safe for the moment at least she wandered along the bank, losing herself in the treasures of the tranquil day. As she struck away from the water and into the woodlands towards the house she made a detour by the great chestnut tree that always had the plumpest and juiciest of nuts. The ground beneath it was a prickly carpet of green shells, the shining brown fruits gleaming like dark eyes from the litter of leaf and spiky husk. She gathered some, ate a couple, peeling away the supple skin with sharp teeth, pocketed the others to cook with Lucy upon the nursery fire. The sun had dropped quite rapidly now to the west, and gleamed in long sword-falls of golden light through the trees. Reluctantly she had to face the fact that the delight of her stolen freedom must be surrendered if further trouble were to be avoided, both for herself and for others – and if she were not to be too obviously implicated in Bran's fortuitous disappearance.

Feet dragging she turned and made for home.

Lucy, at sight of her, threw up distracted hands, her first pleased greeting dying on her lips. 'Oh, my goodness gracious me, Miss Jess! What HAVE you been doing? You're filthy! And – your dress – you've torn the hem –'

'I'll mend it, I promise. Don't fuss, Lucy, there's a dear.' She unloaded her pocketful of chestnuts onto the table. 'Hide these, and we can roast them tomorrow, while the dragon's out. She isn't back yet, is she?'

Lucy shook her head, still speechless at the sight of the wreckage of her young mistress' clothes.

'There, you see? I told you I'd be back in time. Now – quickly – help me change, then lock me back in again. She'll never know the difference. All my beastly clothes look the same anyway.' She leaned forward, whispering conspiratorially. 'Bran's safe. I won't tell you where, but he's safe.'

'No-one knows you've been out?' The girl's voice was anxious.

'No-one that matters. Now – hurry. Let's get rid of these clothes –'

It was fifteen minutes later, and a cleaned, tidied and brushed Jessica was decorously seated at her small bedroom desk reading the tract that MacKenzie had set her to study that morning when she heard a distant commotion. She lifted her head, listening. Someone shouted, a voice not quite under control. A door slammed. Voices were raised, then quieted. Unease permeated the air. Jessica frowned and went to the window. The front court was empty, the door closed. Within the house, however, the inexplicable disturbance continued. Her heart lurched a little, sickly. Had her escapade been discovered, and so soon? And – if it had – would it cause such an uproar?

She ran to the door. 'Lucy? Lucy, what's that? What's happening?'

'I don't know, Miss Jess –'

Jessica heard the nursery door open and shut. She banged urgently upon the pannelled bedroom door. 'Lucy!'

The door swung open, revealing not Lucy, but MacKenzie – a MacKenzie frighteningly white-faced and all but unrecognizable. 'Miss Jessica –'

Jessica stared at her. No denying it, here was disaster, written in distress and concern on a face not normally used to revealing either. Panic lifted, drying her mouth. Bran was dead

– Giles had found him after all – 'What is it? What's all that noise?'

'Come – sit down –'

She swallowed the lump that seemed to be growing in her throat, blocking her breath, shook her head. 'Tell me.'

MacKenzie glanced at Lucy, as if for support, but the plump, puzzled face offered no help. Unaccustomed and awkward she took the child's hand. 'There's been an accident,' she said. 'Your brother's dead.'

For a moment the words refused to register. Dead? What was the woman talking about? Who was dead? Who could possibly be dead on such a glorious, such an ordinary, day? Dead? Jessica stared at her like a half-wit child.

'Come, child. Sit down.'

She allowed herself to be led to a chair, sat awkwardly, like a strung doll in the hands of an incompetent puppeteer.

'The punt – they went too close to the weir – it went over –' MacKenzie was speaking jerkily, her voice seeming to Jessica to be small and reedy, as if coming from an impossible distance. 'Mr Giles tried to save him – you know Mr Edward was no great swimmer –'

That jolted her to agonized life. She leapt up. 'Edward? *Edward's* dead? No! There's a mistake – I don't believe it – I *saw* him – just a little while ago – he was laughing –' she crammed her hand to her mouth, stopping the words, and stared white faced.

Lucy had made a strange, small sound, like an animal whimpering, at MacKenzie's words. Now she lifted her apron to her face, sobbing, the sound loud in the terrible silence.

Jessica backed away from MacKenzie, shaking her head determinedly. 'No! *No!*' and before anyone could stop her she had darted past them through the door and was flying down the stairs as she had earlier in the day with scant regard for life or limb. This time, eyes blinded with half-formed tears, instead of escaping through the outer door she turned into the long, windowed gallery that would take her to the first floor of the main wing. In the corridor that led to the top of the central staircase she met a maidservant, crying noisily, her face blotchy. From downstairs came the sound of voices. Impelled by shock and terror she ran, almost tumbling around the curve of the wide, sweeping formal staircase.

The library door stood open. Through it she could see Giles, wet and bedraggled, a bloody gash on his blanched, dirty face, wrapped in a blanket and shivering upon the edge of the sofa. His face was agonized. 'I tried – Mother, I swear I tried! He panicked. I couldn't hold him – he'd have drowned both of us –'

Jessica skidded to a halt. From within the room came the most awful sound she had ever heard; a wordless cry of grief, no less harrowing for being stifled almost to silence before it had begun. Then, 'Edward!' Jessica heard her mother cry softly, the voice that was usually so coolly modulated ragged with savage and intolerable pain, '*Edward!*'

And, hearing it, the child knew then that the unthinkable must, after all, be true; and the world changed as she stood there.

Jessica's twelfth birthday dawned unmarked; grey, chill and building for rain. The day of Edward Hawthorne's funeral, appropriately, would see the breaking of the glorious autumn weather. The whole countryside turned out, the gentry in the blacks and greys and purples of mourning, the countryfolk bareheaded in the cold wind; the Hawthorne heir had been a fine young man, and popular. The mournful procession, headed by the splendid carriage that carried Edward's ornate coffin wound its way at solemn walking pace through the park, out onto the road and down into the village and to the church, the black plumes on the horses' heads nodding and tossing with a kind of macabre gaiety in the wind.

Jessica sat, still almost entirely numbed with shock, beside MacKenzie and opposite her brother John in the last in the line of family carriages. In the first of those carriages Maria Hawthorne sat, rigid and fragile as glass, her veil lifted to reveal a face chalk white and pared to the bone with grief, her dry eyes fixed unblinking upon the splendid box that held the mortal remains of her first-born and favourite child. She had not shed a tear; indeed, since the outcry that Jessica had heard she had hardly spoken. That Edward had always been Maria's best-loved child had never been in question – her other children had always accepted that with neither surprise nor any great envy – who could help but love blithe and gentle Edward above them all? No-one would have expected the bereaved mother to have taken this tragedy any way but badly: but to Jessica the sight of her mother's controlled face, the lovely line of bone stark and pale, the great forget-me-not eyes utterly dry and tearless, the mouth firm as always, had been the worst element in an all but unbearable few days.

The long, silent procession came at last to its destination. Jessica stumbled from the carriage and was thankful to find her small cold hand tucked firmly into John's large warm one. He half-smiled down at her, encouragingly, his eyes sad but crinkling with concerned affection. John, like the others, was very likely to forget her existence for most of the time, but at least when he remembered her he was kind. She huddled close to him as they fell into line and followed the coffin as it was carried shoulder high to its resting place. Amongst the group of people who waited already by the grave to pay their last respects she saw Robert, his parents and his sister. Robert's face was sympathetic as he caught her eye. Beside him Clara was handsome as ever in mourning black, her rather sharp features limned clear and austere in the dull light, her face still, and oddly expressionless. Watching her, Jessica remembered suddenly that just a couple of years ago, before Cambridge and before the arranged Felworth alliance, there had been some sly talk of Edward and Clara – two young people growing up together and apparently much taken with one another. Yet Clara stood like stone, tearless and composed. She surely must be feeling something?

The service had begun. Jessica averted her eyes from the coffin, closed her ears to the fearful words. She could not bear the thought of what lay within that box, nor what might now happen to it. Edward, yet not Edward, all life, all laughter, all loving fled, buried in the darkness of earth and the crawling, eating things it held. She flinched from the raw gash in the

37

ground that waited to take the coffin. Deliberately detaching herself from the unbearable proceedings she fell to studying the faces about her. MacKenzie, morbidly dour, eyes properly downcast, mouth pinched like an ill-sewn seam. Lucy, plump and good-natured, openly tear-stained. John, his quiet face softly sad, mouth set in a straight, unhappy line. Caroline, distraught, her pretty face swollen and reddened by the tears she had been shedding non-stop for days. Father – tall, narrow-faced, his red-gold hair greying a little at temple and nape but still handsome, still vigorous and the physical mirror-image of the son he now buried. Giles beside him, still-faced, the vivid life of him for the moment dimmed, the brightly handsome lines of his face drawn fine with grief and sorrow.

And yet for all his grief he lived, and Edward did not.

Shockingly, all the hostility that Giles invariably aroused in Jessica's childish breast rose, suddenly, bitterly and frighteningly forceful. Why Edward and not you? she found herself thinking. Why did he die? Why not you?

The words had been spoken, the hymns sung, Robert's voice lifting clear and heartbreakingly sweet above all. The coffin had been lowered and lay now upon its last earthly bed. William Hawthorne, face set in sorrow, dropped a handful of earth upon the remains of his son and heir and stepped back. Then Maria stepped forward, in her hand a single flower, a white rose from the gardens of New Hall. At the graveside she stood for a moment, and the lovely flower was not paler than her face. She opened her black-gloved fingers. The long-stemmed rose clung for a moment, as if reluctant to fall. Then it dropped and she stepped back. Giles stepped to her side, reaching a hand to her elbow, the eldest son now, strong and ready to serve, solicitous for her welfare. Slowly she turned her head to him.

Giles' hand dropped from his mother's arm. Composedly she turned from him, lifted her hands and drew the concealing veil over her face.

And only Jessica, her own bitterness still within her, had seen, as Giles had seen, the venom of that same question in

38

those flower-blue eyes. Why him, and not you? How are you here, when he is dead? Why did you not save him, or die with him?

With a sound as final as death itself the first spadeful of earth fell upon young Edward Hawthorne's coffin.

Chapter Two

Edward's death, inevitably, affected them all, well-loved as he had been and the king-pin of his parents' ambitions. For months Jessica found herself looking for him still, listening for the sound of his voice, the chime of his frequent laughter. The loss of her brother cast a pall upon a winter that was in any case cold and hard. The bad weather arrived like a wolf with the new year of 1811 and kept its savage grip upon the snow-bound East Anglian countryside for weeks. Abroad, despite Wellington's rapturously greeted success in Portugal, Napoleon's stranglehold upon Europe showed no real signs of weakening, whilst in a Britain isolated both economically and militarily from a virtually enslaved Europe an unstable King slipped finally and hopelessly into insanity while his foppish son devoted his time to an outrageous architectural toy in Brighton and his subjects, their jobs and livings threatened by the new machines that inventive and enterprising men saw as fortune-makers, muttered angrily and prepared for a war of their own.

Christmas at New Hall, with Edward never far from mind, was a more subdued affair than usual; for Jessica its high spot was the day that she spent with a now fully-recovered Robert and his family at Old Hall. She and Robert had together collected the holly boughs that made the old house festive, and had helped Mrs Williams to mix the plum puddings and the rich mincemeat for the pies. Amidst the gifts and the laughter, the traditional games in which the whole household joined, Mrs Williams' splendid food and the pleasure of good company she once or twice found herself altogether forgetting her sadness — a fact that brought guilt flooding when she returned to the grandeur of New Hall and to the pale, strained beauty of her mother's face. For Maria Hawthorne was inconsolable still. Not that she made great show of her grief, on the contrary, calm and composed as ever she rarely spoke of it. But it would not be eased. Edward had been her favourite, her firstborn, her darling boy and nothing and no-one could make up for his loss. Her attitude to Giles, with whom she had never had a particularly strong bond despite their physical resemblance, and who had now, willy nilly, stepped into his dead brother's shoes was distant. Surprisingly, however, Giles took no offence and showed no resentment at her cool treatment of him. Indeed he demonstrated a grace and patience far beyond any that Jessica had ever suspected he might possess. Mildly and with understanding he appeared to accept his mother's disinterest and occasional criticism and with a forebearance that seemed to his younger sister completely at odds with his character he patiently waited for Maria's grief and unhappiness to temper. More than once, however, in the stables Jessica came upon evidence that whatever his outward reaction to his mother's ill-concealed antipathy Giles' newly-discovered sweet temper was only skin deep; for after his morning ride poor Belle more often than not would stand, exhausted and whipped to a lather, her stable lad muttering mutinously at the ill-treatment of the beast. That Giles could so take out his frustrations upon a dumb animal did little to endear him to Jessica.

With his father, however, the new heir to fortune did rather better. No-one in fact could deny that in the management of the land Giles was far more adept – and interested – than indolent, happy-go-lucky Edward had ever been. William Hawthorne was a busy man, and his first interest always was the management of money. The acquisition of New Hall and its acres had been in the first place a matter of status, of recognition and respectability. However, businessman that he was he did not like to see any asset go to waste, and Giles' enthusiasm and practical grasp of the affairs of the land pleased him immensely. Giles took to the management of New Hall's estates like a duck to water. Where his brother had been happy to let things lie within months he was suggesting and implementing innovations designed to make the place both more efficient and more profitable. Land was enclosed and drained, new crop rotation systems devised. Small, uneconomic tenant farms were taken over and amalgamated with larger more productive holdings; and if families were turned from home and hearth and onto the roads and the not too tender care of the parish, it was all done with nicely expressed regret and in the name of efficiency and profit. Edward, despite his father's best efforts, had never been truly interested in anything beyond the good horseflesh with which New Hall could provide him: Giles, it now swiftly became apparent, knew enough already of the workings of the land and its tenants to make an efficient and demanding manager. He was able and energetic and had revealed in a very short space of time after his brother's death something that almost amounted to a passion for the land and possessions of New Hall. Yet still his mother's attitude remained the same – Edward was gone, and woe betide the one, however able, who thought in any way to replace him.

For Jessica those first, wintry weeks after Christmas dragged upon leaden feet. Whenever she could she escaped Mac-Kenzie's dour supervision and ran in the snow-bound fields and woods with Bran. At least out of the débâcle of Edward's death had come Bran's survival – wheedled from a still-shaken and preoccupied Giles by Jessica – and for that she could not help but be happy. But with Robert back at school she was lonely, and the weeks and months that stretched ahead to spring and to Robert's return promised to be empty indeed. Alone she roamed the woodlands, slid upon the frozen lake, rode her pony across the glittering winter ice-fields.

It was on a day late in February, with a red sun glinting fire from the ice-strung branches of the trees that she saw Clara FitzBolton riding, apparently aimlessly, in the deep woodlands to the west of the lake. Elegant as an elf-queen in her full-skirted brown velvet riding habit, the rakishly mannish cut of the jacket emphasizing the firm curve of her breasts and the slim, arrow straight line of her back Clara rode, sidesaddle, easily and well, her narrow hands in their leather gloves firm upon the reins, her head poised, glossy dark hair coiled beneath her tall-crowned hat. A hand softly upon Bran's shaggy muzzle Jessica watched from the shelter of a fallen oak as the girl's mare picked her delicate way along the frozen track. If Clara had not noticed them Jessica saw no reason to startle her with their presence – the more so since, officially, they had no business being there in the first place and Robert's sister was not the kind of person to ignore such small details. She waited until Clara had disappeared down the track before setting off in the opposite direction around the frosted lakeside; but moments later the sound of another horse stilled her movements and brought her head up sharply. Bran's tail swished, dangerously delighted. Jessica grabbed him and held on. In the distance, flickering through the trees like a shadow in the red winter sunlight, was Giles, riding Belle.

'Be still!' she whispered, fiercely, to Bran: always she kept the dog as far from Giles as was possible, knowing how swiftly her brother's temper could be aroused, and aware too that his power since Edward's death had increased considerably. Now there would be no voice to prevent him from having a worthless mongrel knocked on the head if the fancy took him – 'Ssh!'

Giles was riding purposefully down the same track that Clara had taken a short while before. Wondering a little Jessica watched him go out of sight. Had the two of them been on the other side of the lake there would have been no cause for surprise – the rides through the ornamental woodlands were sanded and easy, the views of the lake, house and river very beautiful. But so far as she knew only Jessica herself ever came to this side; the woodland was dense and wild, the paths narrow and frequently blocked by undergrowth or fallen trees and the going uneven. She had never seen either Giles or Clara here before. Shrugging she slipped a hand through the collar that the New Hall blacksmith had made for Bran, 'Come on, boy, I s'pose we'd better start back –'

They scrambled around the lakeside, slipping on frozen mud, skidding and sliding on the snow-covered surface of the

43

lake itself – this last an absolutely forbidden pastime. Cheeks glowing and fingers tingling with cold, for in her eagerness to be out undiscovered she had forgotten both muff and gloves, Jessica climbed onto a fallen log and gazed out across the magical winter iceland of the frozen lake. The vermilion sun was dipping, the air hard with frost. In the chill distance, faintly, she heard a voice calling, and then the sound of horses' hooves, drumming hard. As she slid hastily from her perch and into the shelter of the tree the two horses burst almost together from the tangle of the woodland and danced to a halt, snorting, their breath clouding the darkening air. Giles, on the bigger horse, leaned from the saddle and caught the reins of Clara's little mare in his hand. Clara lifted her head, smiling, looking directly into his face. Even from this distance Jessica sensed the challenge that fired every line of the young woman's strong face. The horses danced again, unsettled, held together by Giles' firm grip. There was a strange tension in the two figures as they leaned towards each other, an intensity that held their eyes each to the other and brought an unaccountable sense of unease to the small watcher. Then Clara lifted her riding crop, and for an incredulous moment Jessica thought that she would strike the man who had her rein: but she did not. Gently she touched his cheek with the whip, brought it in a stroking movement to his lips. As if burned Giles let go the rein and straightened in the saddle. Then with no word he wheeled Belle, dancing her upon her hind legs like a circus pony before thundering away in the direction of New Hall.

Clara laughed. Watching him go she threw back her head and laughed, peal after peal of infectious amusement. Then, leisurely, she turned the little mare and rode back into the shadows.

Jessica shivered; the wind must have turned to the north again. Hand buried in the warmth of Bran's ruff of fur she too set off for home.

A couple of days later something of a thaw set in, and with the roads and countryside fast becoming a quagmire not many souls were foolhardy enough to brave the highways. It was therefore with some surprise that Jessica, from her perch upon the nursery windowseat, saw the approach of a wagon along the sweeping drive of the house.

'It's the scotchman! Oh – I wonder if Mama would let me join them –?' So bored was she that the arrival of the chimney sweep and his boys would have been an occasion; this unexpected visit of Billy Heckford, known as the scotchman, with his silks and satins, his laces and ribbons, his battered copies of *Heideloff's Gallery Of Fashions* (far too out of date for the ladies of New Hall, but well received by the farmers' wives) and *The Lady's Magazine* was an event to rival a day at the fair.

MacKenzie shook her head repressively. 'Little girls have no business with a talleyman's frills and flounces. Time enough for that when you're grown.'

'I'm nearly thirteen. Well – twelve-and-a-half –' Jessica watched as the intriguing wagon, its shaggy little pony toiling in the slush, disappeared around the corner towards the tradesman's court at the side of the house. 'Caroline went to her first ball when she was fourteen – and she dined with Mama and Papa for AGES before that –'

'Miss Caroline,' said MacKenzie, deadly prim, 'was no doubt a different kettle of fish to a certain young hoyden I know who can never keep her face clean nor her clothes neat and tidy –'

Jessica stuck out a truly ferocious tongue at the sanctimonious back.

'– you'll be invited to join the ladies of the household when you can learn to behave and not before. Besides, your parents dine in the evening now –' the chill tone gave clear notice of the governess' unvoiced disapproval of this new-fangled habit. 'Hardly a fitting time for a child to eat –'

Jessica craned her neck, cheek pressed against the cold window. The wagon had gone. Just once, four years ago, before the advent of the detested MacKenzie she had been allowed to visit with her mother during one of Billy Heckford's regular visits, and she had never forgotten the day. Orders from

45

London – gown lengths for Mama and for a newly-grown Caroline – lace and a cascade of ribbons – little dolls, wonderfully clothed – flannel and calico for the servant girls – cotton for shirts and for shifts – handkerchiefs, bright waistcoat-pieces – the room had seemed to her an Aladdin's cave of wonders. Buttons and buckles, bright and shining, ostrich feathers, and velvet swathes. She looked down in sudden and unexpected discontent at her dowdy brown woollen dress, the skirt an inch or so too short, the high waist pinching beneath a chest that was certainly at last showing some signs of budding. Even her one good gown, the red velvet that she wore on the three occasions a week that she was taken to be presented to her parents – on Wednesdays, Fridays and Sundays in the salon after the light midday meal that was now luncheon at New Hall – no longer fitted her and was scuffed and worn at the seams. Neither had it ever recovered from an unfortunate accident with a buttered scone. For the first time she allowed herself to admit to envy for her older sister who had not only cleverly got herself born first – just about the only clever thing Caroline had ever done, she found herself thinking sourly – but whose fair grace and beauty was so enhanced by the delicate, high-waisted Grecian gowns that were still fasionable. She sighed.

'Please, Miss –' Lucy was at the open door, tapping awkwardly.

'What is it, girl?' MacKenzie, was, as always with Lucy, impatient.

'It's Smith, Miss. From downstairs.' Anywhere in New Hall that was not the nursery was, to Lucy, simply 'downstairs'. 'She says she's been sent to bring Miss Jessie to her Mama –'

'Me?' Jessica, with deplorable lack of elegance almost fell from the windowseat. 'To see the scotchman!'

Lucy's good-natured smile lit the room. 'Seems so, Miss.'

Jessica was half-way to the door before MacKenzie's firm and bony hand stopped her. 'And where do you think you're going?'

'To see Mama – you heard Lucy – she's sent for me –'

46

'And you'll attend your Mama looking like a chambermaid? Oh, no. Lucy fetch Miss Jessica's red velvet. And you, Miss – stand still whilst I brush your hair –'

Wild with impatience the child fidgeted beneath their ministrations. The red dress on, MacKenzie brushed and tugged at the mousy mop of hair with brisk disregard for a tender scalp.

Jessica hopped from foot to foot. 'Oh, PLEASE hurry! She might change her mind – or forget –'

'Smith is waitin', Miss Jessie, don't you fret.' Lucy brushed a last speck from the dress and stood back, admiring. 'There. You do look a treat. Don't she, Miss?'

MacKenzie smiled. 'Now, child. Remember your manners.'

'Yes, Ma'am.'

'Show me your curtsey.'

Rebellion raging at the futher delay Jessica bobbed a brusque curtsey.

MacKenzie shook her head. 'Again.'

Jessica took a long, sustaining breath and swept into something that at least approximated a graceful curtesy.

'Say "Good morning, Mama".'

Jessica glowered. 'Good morning, Mama,' she said, sweetly.

'Keep your eyes down, and don't babble.'

'Yes, Ma'am.'

'Right. You may go.'

Jessica turned.

'Miss Jessica!'

She froze where she stood. In heaven's name what now?

'Yes, Ma'am?'

'Under no circumstances – you hear me? – under NO circumstances – will you RUN. Is that understood?'

'Yes, Ma'am.'

'And neither will you answer back.'

'No, Ma'am.'

'Speak when you're spoken to. Hold your tongue when you're not.'

Jessica swung around, eyes ablaze, mouth open to shriek her exasperation. At the gleam of expectation in the woman's pale and bulbous eyes she stopped. 'Yes, Ma'am,' she said obediently, seething.

'Right. Now you may go.'

The salon of New Hall was in the main wing on the first floor, next to the formal dining room and overlooking the sweep of drive and the park. It was to this elegant but somewhat chilly room with its pale, ornamented plaster ceiling, its tall gilded mirrors, its gracefully proportioned windows that Jessica had expected to be taken. Instead, to her delight, the maidservant Smith led her along a vaulted picture-gallery of a passage towards what she knew to be her mother's private apartments. Almost overcome with excitement at this unexpected treat she fairly skipped at the girl's side. At her mother's sitting-room door they stopped and Smith, having first surveyed Jessica from head to toe and tucked a wiry curl tidily if uncomfortably behind her ear, knocked. Here in the private apartments the formalities of footmen and flunkies were dispensed with.

'Come.'

The room, though fairly large, was cosy, rose velvet at the windows and in the upholstery, matching silk upon the small tables and in the soft cushions that were scattered about the comfortable furniture. A fire crackled companionably in the fireplace, with its carved ornamental overmantle. Deep rugs were scattered over the polished floor and on this winter's day candles were lit, to reflect in myriad flickering images in the mirrors about the walls. Giles stood by the window, his back to the room, looking out over the park. He did not turn as Jessica entered. Caroline sat gracefully straight-backed upon a low chair, a swirling skein of glowing sapphire silk draped across her lap, her shoulders and the soft swell of her breasts fashionably exposed despite the season by the short-sleeved, almost diaphanous Grecian gown she wore. Her bright hair too was lifted and bound in the classic Greek style, fluffed at forehead and nape into ringlets that shone like spun gold in the candlelight. Jessica's mother sat at a table that was heaped with lengths and bolts of material. Beside her stood Billy Heckford, an unctuous, portly man whose moon face shone sweatily in the warmth of the room.

'Ah – Jessica –' Like her elder daughter Maria Hawthorne wore a fashionable, high-waisted gown. Her figure was slim as a girl's and the gown, black still for the mourning of her son, showed quite startlingly the pale ivory of her smooth skin. Nearly six months after Edward's death, however, still nothing could disguise the fact that her lovely eyes, blue as summer speedwell, had not lost the desperate shadows of grief.

Jessica, a little hesitantly, advanced. Her mother with a slight, faintly impatient smile held out her hand and beckoned her forward. Caroline lifted her head and smiled, vaguely. Giles still did not turn. His broad back, snugly clothed in a dark brown cloth coat that was cut short at the waist in front but hung in tails behind, fairly shrieked offence. Jessica wondered what had been under discussion before she had entered the room. Reaching her mother she curtseyed, a little unsteadily. 'Good morning, Mama.'

'Good morning, child.' Her mother returned her greeting solemnly, but there was a twinkle in her eyes. She took her daughter by the shoulders and dropped the lightest of kisses upon her forehead. 'Goodness, I do believe that you may be growing at last. Though I fear you'll always be undersized. Mr Heckford; the striped cotton, if you please –'

'Certainly, Madam.' The man, agile despite his bulk, sprang to her side, a bolt of black and yellow striped cloth in his arms.

Maria cocked an eye at her small daughter. 'Do you like it?'

Jessica, taken aback at being thus consulted nodded her head shyly.

'And the sprigged muslin, I think. You'll need something for the summer.'

Caroline looked up from her examination of a bolt of shimmering striped silk. 'Try the pale green. It will suit her colouring best, I'm sure.'

A deep blush of pleasure was mounting in Jessica's cheeks. Never in her life had she been the object of such attention. Her mother turned from her and addressed the scotchman. 'The sprigged and the green then, I think. A small gown's length of each, and the striped cotton. Caroline – you've finished?'

49

Caroline made a pretty face of indecision. 'Well the blue, definitely. And the striped – but for the spring the yellow would be so pretty – and if Bunty and I are to announce our engagement at the May Ball –?'

Her mother gave a small, indulgent laugh. 'Have it by all means. If I didn't buy it for you I daresay your father would –'

'Bunty likes me in yellow. He said so just the other day –'

By the window Giles lifted a sudden, impatient head, flicking the fair, untidy curls from his eyes, and then was still. Jessica eyed him warily, as she might a chancy dog.

Murmuring ingratiating thanks Billy Heckford packed his goods and picked up his orders.

'Ask Smith to take you to the housekeeper's room. We need some more material for uniforms, I believe.'

'Yes, Madam. Thank you, Madam –' He left.

Giles turned. 'Mother –'

Maria ignored him. 'Come here, child.' She beckoned again to Jessica who had moved a little away from her.

Quailing a little Jessica obeyed.

'Let me see – how old are you now?'

'Twelve-and-a-half, Mama.'

'As I thought. In a year or so you'll be quite the young lady.'

Jessica did not voice her own doubts of that.

'And how do your lessons go?'

'Well, I think, Mama, thank you.' Eyes downcast Jessica prayed that the inevitable question would be an easy one.

'Who is your favourite poet?'

She let her breath out in a small puff of relief and lifted shining eyes. Safe ground, this. 'William Wordsworth, Mama.'

Giles made a small, impatient sound.

Maria, real interest at last in her eyes put her head on one side, surveying her small daughter. 'Recite something for me.'

Jessica lifted her head, dark eyes half-closed in concentration, thin face intent. 'Ethereal minstrel! Pilgrim of the sky! Dost thou despise the earth where cares abound –?' She spoke the poem well; it was indeed her present favourite. Finished, and suddenly self-conscious, she opened her eyes to find her mother regarding her with quizzically amused approval,

50

whilst Caroline's blue eyes were turned upon her in sheer astonishment. Giles tapped a polished table with a long fingernail.

'Well done! So – you have finally discovered something in life beside horses? I think – yes, I really think that we must consider taking you from the nursery. There is no reason at all why you shouldn't join us at luncheon once or twice a week now that –'

'Mother!' Giles, his hard-held control suddenly breaking as he all but overturned the small table as he swung round to face her. His brilliant eyes, the exact colour of his mother's, were ablaze with anger and impatience. 'I will not be treated like this! It's intolerable! Second to talleymen and to babies! I need your decision on a matter of importance!'

The silence that fell was dire. Jessica shrank back against the table, her worried eyes moving from her brother's furious face to her mother's apparently calm one.

Maria stood. She was not a particularly tall woman, but the straightness of her spine and the arrogant lift of her head at that moment made her seem so. Her expression was icy, as was her voice. Only the slightest tremor betrayed her rage. 'You've had my decision Giles, and no amount of questioning will change it. The answer is no. Your father gave Fallows Farm to me, as a present. While it is mine the Salcomes are my tenants, and you shall not – *You shall not!* – turn them out, as you have turned others out –' Giles began to speak but she pressed inexorably on, 'I know that your father agrees with what you are doing. But in this he has promised to abide by my decision. And the answer is *no*. A thousand times. The Salcomes stay.'

Giles fisted one hand into the other, fuming. 'Mother – listen! You don't know them! They're an idle bunch – good for nothing! Fallows doesn't pay. It never will. If we take it back we can enclose the common pastures beyond –'

'No!'

Jessica, struck speechless by the raised adult voices, felt her hand taken by Smith, who jerked her head towards the door. Caroline nodded. Reluctantly Jessica allowed herself to be led away. Her mother did not even look at her, did not, apparently, notice her going. At the doorway Jessica glanced back. Giles, knowing the argument lost, was stiff with anger. 'You do this deliberately to frustrate my plans –'

'I do it to prevent a family being turned out to starve!' Her mother's voice was scathing.

'They starve already! They waste what they have – live on the charity of others –'

The door shut on her mother's answer.

'Come on, Miss Jessie.'

She trotted beside Smith, hearing her brother's raised, angry voice dying behind her, and inwardly seething.

Giles had done it again!

How dared he? Second to talleymen, he had said – and to babies! Babies! Away from the over-awing scene her own temper rose explosively. Of all the hateful, black-humoured people, why did she have to be landed with Giles for a brother? And – interrupted as she had been – would Mama even remember that she had been on the point of promising Jessica a release from the choking confines of the nursery and MacKenzie's constant and detested supervision? Jessica doubted it. Blast Giles! Blast him!

Even the thought of the sprigged muslin could not greatly console her; though by the time they had climbed the stairs to the nursery door one small bright thought had afforded her at least a gleam of satisfaction. The interview may have ended in something of a disaster: but at least this time no-one could say it had been her fault.

At first it seemed that Jessica's worst fears might be realized – for three long weeks nothing happened, and she languished, convinced that her mother's half-made promise had been utterly forgotten. A week after the scotchman's visit Jessica's parents, accompanied by Caroline, went to stay with friends in London, where the Season was in full swing. With John away at school this left Giles as the only other member of the family in residence, and the house was oppressively dull. Mrs Morton the housekeeper took the opportunity to clean the place from cellar to attic, and New Hall became a scurrying ant heap of servants with mops and buckets, scrubbing brushes and polishing cloths. Maria Hawthorne's luncheons and dinners, the morning calls and the afternoon carriage rides, all ceased when the mistress of the house was away. The weather too was dreary, cold and wet with barely a day without driving rain, and Jessica – worst of punishments! – was confined indoors. Each morning she watched enviously as her brother rode out whatever the weather on the business of the estate, and wished more than once that she had been on the kind of terms with him that might have enabled her to beg him occasionally to take her with him. Apart from those glimpses she rarely saw him; but once, surprisingly late at night, she was woken by his return. Hearing the commotion of a hard-ridden horse on the drive she crept from her bed and peeped from the window. Lucy snored, undisturbed. Below, servants hurried, cressets and torches hastily lit. Uncharacteristically clumsy, Giles swung from the saddle, abandoning Belle to a manservant. He stood for a moment, unsteady on his feet, before weaving his way up the steps to the door, brushing roughly aside a half-dressed footman's attempt to aid him. Jessica stared, wide-eyed and fascinated. Drunkenness was not countenanced at New Hall; but she had once seen one of the farm boys on Plough Monday down four pints of strong ale in quick succession and then try to walk a straight line. No doubt about it – Giles was managing no better than had that inebriated lad.

A few days later her parents and Caroline returned, and once again her nerves were strung, waiting for the summons that she feared would not arrive. Almost it had been better, she decided, when they had been away and there had been no chance of its coming. She had not and still did not say a word to MacKenzie, for fear of her scoffing.

Lucy it was who brought the news first, long before the official summons, whispering excitedly behind her hand, one eye on the door. 'Ooh, Miss Jessie – 'tis said you're to eat with the family tomorrow –'

'Who says? How do you know?' Jessica grabbed her arm.

'Ouch! Tha'ss not very nice, Miss Jess! Now you're hurting me –!' The aggrieved Lucy pulled away from her.

'Oh, I'm sorry! But – please –! Tell me how you heard?'

'Why down in the kitchen. An extra place to be laid tomorrow, they said. For the young mistress. Tha'ss what they said.'

Jessica drew away from her. The young mistress. She lifted her head. 'Thank you, Lucy.'

That evening, before going to bed, she stood for a moment before the mirror, surveying with an earnest frown her slight, nightgowned figure with its mass of freshly-brushed mousey hair. No doubt about it, her sister was the beauty of the family and had no rival here. But – if her hair were up so – she lifted her hair that still crackled from the brush and piled it untidily on her head –

'Miss Jessie! Whatever are you up to now? Into bed with you before you catch your death!' Lucy bustled in with a steaming cup of hot milk. Jessica turned from the mirror and took a single flying leap into bed. Lucy, tutting, fussed around her, tucking in the bedclothes, plumping the pillows, picking up the all-but-dismembered doll that had been Jessica's constant bed-time companion since babyhood and which had been flung onto the floor by her owner's over-energetic bound onto the bed. 'Poor Betsy-doll! Just look at her –!' She held out the doll.

Jessica lifted her hand, hesitated, and then shook her head. 'Put her on the shelf, Lucy. I really am too old for dolls now.'

With Lucy snoring on her pallet beyond the open door and the nightlight flickering comfortingly upon the ceiling she envisaged her triumph:

'Why Jessica, my dear,' her handsome father said admiringly, 'how very pretty you look! And how much you've grown! See, Maria, our daughter is quite the little lady –'

'Really, Jessica,' her father said, only faintly admiring, 'I truly don't believe I've ever seen such a little person eat so much. Has Cook stopped feeding the nursery?'

Jessica blushed to the roots of her hair and almost dropped the silver fork she was awkwardly holding. Then violently, she shook her head at the laden platter than an attentive footman was offering and from which she had fully intended to help herself to a third portion of sweet-sauced pudding. Beside her Caroline pecked like a bird. Giles, sitting opposite had greeted her civilly enough but after that had not addressed her at all. The whole conversation, indeed, had been about the London visit and to her own disgust Jessica had been too overawed to do anything but listen. And eat. Her father's remark had been the first directly addressed to her.

'The fork in the other hand, if you please, Jessica,' her mother said, quietly, 'and sit up straight, there's a good child.'

Jessica transferred the fork and then put it down with a great clatter upon the table. She straightened her back like a guardsman's, and fortunately did not see her father's hidden smile. A few moments later her mother folded her napkin and stood. 'Caroline – Jessica – we'll take tea in the drawing room and leave your father and brother to talk their business.' Gracefully erect she swept from the room. Caroline, smiling at the two men, followed, no less collected. Jessica, as she slid from her chair knocked the wretched fork onto the floor and then clashed with the footman who stood behind her as they both bent to retrieve it.

'Leave it and run along, my dear.' Her father's smile, though a shade impatient, was by no means unkind. He was a tall, well-made man, broad-shouldered and long-boned. The red-gold hair had silvered a little at the temples and cheeks of his narrow, angular face, but still the resemblance to dead Edward was remarkable. Not for the first time Jessica found herself wondering as she trailed after her mother and sister how it was that only she of all the family seemed to have missed out entirely on her parents' striking looks. Even John, if not as handsome as Giles or as Edward had been, had inherited something of the look of his father.

'– dancing lessons,' her mother said.

She started from her reverie. 'I beg your pardon, Mama?'

'I said I have arranged for you to take dancing lessons,' Maria repeated, and shook her head a little, despairing. 'Though how successful they'll be I have my doubts. Lift your head, my dear. And do try to walk more like a young lady and less like a stable lad –'

Spring came at last, and with it in the towns and cities of industrial England came the first stirrings of Luddite rebellion. In the country, however, it brought as always the fresh green of bud and leaf, the busy excitement of nesting birds. Easter Day was glorious, a promisingly bright and windy day, exhilarating and aglow with the dancing flowers of spring. Jessica attended church with her family and was then allowed to join the children of the servants and of the village in their hunt for the painted eggs that had been hidden all over the house. A few days later Robert came home, his studies and his Cathedral duties finished now for four glorious months.

'Oh, Lord, you're so *pale*! I hope you haven't been ill again? Oh, Robert – it's been so *deadly* dull without you!' Jessica and Bran danced about him as they walked through the spring-bright woodlands. 'You'll come riding with me tomorrow, won't you? I have a new pony – an absolute darling! You can ride Spot if you like – I know he's your favourite – and, Robert, I've started dancing lessons, and they're really quite fun – And I take lunch three times a week with Mama and Papa in the dining room – and oh, I've so much to tell you! Still – there's all summer to tell it, isn't there?' Without waiting for his reply she darted off, skirts lifted, Bran bounding by her side. 'Come and see the bluebell glade! They're growing already – they're going to look perfectly lovely in just a couple of weeks –!'

It took only a week or so for her to realize that Robert had changed, but a little longer than that for her to fathom exactly in what way he was different. Certainly in the few months he had been away he had altered physically, the planes of his face firmer, the softness of boyhood almost gone. But the change went deeper than that and it worried and upset her.

'You're always going off on your own,' she complained one day, 'and even when you're here I sometimes think you'd rather not be. You're in a kind of dream half the time. What's the matter?'

He shook his head. 'Nothing.'

Jessica put an arm about Bran and made a great play of stroking and pulling his ears. 'Don't you like us any more?'

'Oh, silly goose, of course I do! It's just that –' He stopped.

She turned swiftly, her face accusing. 'Just what?'

'Just – well, Jessica, you surely must see? I'm – we're – growing up. We can't just keep on doing the same things for ever, you know. We aren't children any more.'

'Well, I know that. But –' For a moment she looked lost and anxious, a child if there ever had been one, '– that doesn't mean we can't be friends any more, does it?'

He caught her hand. 'Of course not! We'll be friends for ever and ever. You know that.'

'You promise? You swear?'

He spat on his finger, slid it across his throat. 'I promise! I swear! Robert FitzBolton and Jessica Hawthorne will be friends for ever and ever!'

She smiled at that, relieved if not altogether convinced. 'Do you want to come and help me groom Spot and Dancer? You don't have to do anything,' she added hastily, eyeing his immaculate clothes and fastidiously clean hands. 'Just talk to me while I do it.'

He came to his feet neatly. 'What do you have stable lads for?'

She grinned. 'Once a week I'm allowed to do it myself.'

He pulled a disbelieving face. 'A treat?'

She wrinkled her nose at him, daring him to laugh. 'Yes. A treat.'

So she accepted his explanation and his assurances, and tried not to bring up the subject again, knowing it might irritate him. He was fourteen – almost a man – and a large part of his life was now lived away from Melbury and from her. She supposed he was right when he spoke of the inevitability of change. But still it saddened her.

'You don't seem to see so much of your friend Robert any more, do you?' Caroline asked, idly one day. It was late April, a chill lingered in the air, but the sun shone high and bright in the sky in which white clouds flew like great birds. She and Jessica were walking in the park, well wrapped against the

57

April breeze. They had been, at their mother's behest, to visit Old Marjorie, who lived alone in a cottage on the edge of the estate. Caroline swung the basket, empty now, in which they had carried eggs and butter to the ailing old herb-woman.

Jessica shrugged.

Caroline smiled, a little slyly. 'I saw him the other day. When I was visiting with Clara.'

'Oh?'

'He mooned about the place like a wraith. Didn't hear a word that was spoken to him. And didn't touch his tea and scones.' She turned sparkling, mischievous eyes upon her small sister. 'Clara declared him quite a nuisance. If you ask me –' she swung the basket, watching Jessica, 'I'd say he was in love.'

'*What?*' Jessica stopped walking and stared at the older girl, aghast. 'Robert? What are you talking about?'

Caroline tossed her head, her escaping curls flattening themselves prettily against the wide velvet rim of her bonnet. 'Well – what's so strange about that? He's a growing lad – and a handsome one, too, though a little weakly-looking for my taste. Why should it surprise you so?'

Jessica was astonished and a little alarmed to discover that her heart was pumping hard, hammering against her ribs as if she had been running. 'Of all the stupid things to say!' she muttered. 'Just because you think every man who looks at you is in love with you doesn't mean that the whole world's the same. It's ridiculous.'

Caroline took no offence. She laughed, and swung the basket high. 'You just wait, my pet. In a year or so you'll be talking from the other side of your face! You mark my words – young Robert is in the throes of his first love affair! The sister of some schoolfriend, no doubt. Or a master's daughter, perhaps. Assignations in the Lady Chapel!'

'Don't be stupid!'

She laughed again, light-heartedly. 'It might even be the sister of this schoolfriend he's going to stay with this summer –'

Jessica's heart appeared to stop altogether, then resumed its odd, lurching beat. A visit this summer? Robert had said nothing to her.

'Two months, Clara said he was going for. Seems a long time to visit with a friend he sees often enough at school, don't you think –?'

'Two months!' Jessica faced Robert, furious. 'You're going away for two whole months, and you didn't tell me?'

He made a small conciliatory gesture with his pale hands. 'Jessie, I'm sorry. I meant to – I was going to – but – the opportunity never seemed to come up –'

'Yet Caroline knows. And your family. And the whole village as far as I know –'

'Oh, come on, Jess –' Righteous indignation showed for a moment. 'You don't own me! I know I should have told you, and I'm sorry. I was just waiting for the right chance –'

She tugged viciously at a tuft of grass. 'Who is this schoolfriend, then?' She invested the noun with disdain.

'His name's Paul Aloway. He sings in the choir with me. He's – a little older. He lives in Devon. My parents thought the change might do me good.'

'I see. And –' she lifted her head, watching him, 'does he have a family, this Paul Aloway?'

He nodded. 'Parents and two sisters.'

'You've met them?'

'Yes. His father has business interests in the City and they often travel with him.'

'Are they –?' She stopped. 'What are they like?'

'Who?'

'His sisters.'

He shrugged. 'Pretty. Rather lively. One has a lovely voice. We plan some musical evenings.'

'Well, I hope you enjoy them.' Stiffly she stood and stalked away from him, leaving him watching after her with an expression half amused, half exasperated.

The May Ball at Melbury New Hall was an annual event in which, one way or another, almost the whole countryside participated. The festivities of May Day started in the village in the morning as the children danced around the decorated Maypole. An ox, donated by the estate, was roasted overnight and almost boundless supplies of ale and cider from New Hall's brewery were there to help the proceedings along. In the afternoon the fun included dancing, and games – both official and unofficial – the tossing of horseshoes, a bruising game of football, the chasing of surprised pigs and the courting of not-so-surprised village girls. By early evening, however, the focus shifted to the Hall itself as the lanes and byways filled with the carriages of the gentry from miles around as they converged on New Hall for the Masquerade Ball. This year there was added spice to the excitement, for it was an open secret throughout the county that an engagement was to be announced between Caroline Hawthorne and the Honourable Bunwood Standish.

The week before the Ball the house was in subdued uproar. Everyone, from the lowest servant girl upwards was infected by the excitement; and Jessica was no exception to that rule. Despite the fact that she had still not reached that magic age when she might attend the Masque herself she was pleased that her father had prevailed over her mother's reluctance to hold the Ball this year. Edward had been dead for nearly nine months; and sad as it was her practical mind knew that no amount of mourning would bring him back. For William Hawthorne's part, business was done each year in the smoke-wreathed library over his fine brandy whilst the ladies gossipped and the young things danced; nothing came before that. Even MacKenzie, for these pleasantly frantic few days, seemed mellower. She spent most afternoons in the village 'helping with the arrangements'. Jessica spared a wryly sympathetic thought for the Reverend Jones.

The Ball was to be held, as always, in the Long Gallery, in the west wing of the house two floors below the nursery suite. The great room, unused except for these special occasions was a marvellous sight once Mrs Morton and her army of helpers had finished their assault upon it. For days they scrubbed and cleaned and polished, until windows and mirrors gleamed, crystal chandeliers glittered like diamonds and the shining wooden floor, perfect for dancing, reflected the room's splendours like a still pool in sunlight. Chairs were brought from all over the house and ranged against the walls or clustered around small tables, where the evening's chaperons could sit and exchange scandal behind their lifted fans whilst their charges flirted upon the dance floor. Supper was to be served in the anteroom, a large room which overlooked the front court with its champagne-cup fountains. The gravel of the court and drive was raked and cleaned, the box hedges clipped, the already immaculate lawns cut and rolled until they resembled swathes of green velvet.

Jessica was everywhere, at every elbow, under every foot. Freed for a welcome couple of days from her studies – for no-one could expect her to work with such noisy excitements happening just beneath her feet – she joined in the fray with a will. In her oldest clothes she polished and she cleaned and she carried chairs from the far reaches of the house. She watched fascinated as Joey the gardener's boy cleaned the fountains, scraping out yards of clinging green slime with his net, a furrow of concentration on his usually vacant face. Traditionally the family kept from each other the secrets of their costumes for the night, but Jessica pestered so that she was allowed to see Caroline's outfit – a truly marvellous diaphanous affair of gold and blue silk sewn with ribbons and strewn with real flowers. What else could Caroline be on that day but the May Queen, the centre of attention? To Jessica's dazzled eyes she looked magnificent. A filmy train swept from her shoulders, and a gleaming gold crown woven with flowers and a golden sceptre completed the ensemble. And in Caroline's pretty ears and around her slender neck bright sapphires blazed, a gift from her father upon her betrothal, and a gentle reminder to the Baronet, in case of second thoughts, of the wealth that was pledging itself to his son.

'Oh, I do wish I were coming –' Jessica said wistfully, watching as her sister pirouetted before the pier glass, the almost transparent, clinging skirt of the highwaisted dress drifting about her. Even for masquerade Caroline had no intention of being anything but fashionable.

'I expect you will next year. How should I wear my hair, do you think? Up, like this –?' She swept the mass of her lovely hair into a pile on her head, turning this way and that to see the effect. 'Or loose – perhaps with flowers in it –?' She fluffed it out with her fingers and it lay upon her slim bare shoulders like a cloak of gold.

'Do you really think so? I shall be nearly fourteen –'

'Down I think. Everyone else will have theirs up.'

'Will you dance every dance with Bunty?'

Drawn from her preoccupation with her own reflection Caroline glanced at her sister in surprised amusement. 'Oh, Lord, no! He's an abominable dancer. And besides – we aren't married yet! He'll have to take his turn with the others.' She smiled back into the mirror. 'He'll take me in to supper of course.'

'Is that when the announcement will be made?'

'It is. Now – run along, do. I've a million things to do.'

It was the next day, two days before the Ball, that the bombshell was dropped that astonished them all and enraged Caroline to distracted, self-centred tears.

Giles had that morning formally requested an interview with his father, the outcome of which William Hawthorne announced, as surprised as anyone but not at all displeased at the luncheon table.

'– so the rogue has stolen a march on us all!' He turned to Giles. 'Not perhaps the match I might have made for you myself, my boy, but a very suitable one nevertheless. Old blood, and well respected. A FitzBolton, mistress of New Hall. Very appropriate, I must say. She's a fine girl. Has breeding. A toast, everyone – to Clara and to Giles –'

Everyone around the table was too thunderstruck for a moment to do anything but raise a glass and murmur an assent. Jessica stared at her brother. Giles and Clara! What a dreadful combination!

The storm broke later, in the drawing room over tea. Not even Caroline would dare to create a scene of any magnitude before her father. She had, however, fewer inhibitions before her mother and sister. 'But, Mama – they can't!' she wailed. 'It's not *fair*! This was to be my day – *My* betrothal! And now they want to ruin it by making it a double announcement! They'll spoil everything entirely – why can't they wait –?'

Maria was looking thoughtful, as she had ever since the surprise had been sprung. 'I'm sorry, my dear. Your brother is apparently set upon announcing it at the Ball.'

Caroline stamped her foot. 'You mean Clara is!' she snapped with a quick flash of spite, and then the tears came. 'A fine friend she turned out to be! It isn't fair. They'll spoil my betrothal – and, oh, Mama – Clara will be married before I will, and she's *younger* than I am –!' Her voice was tragic. Jessica watched with unfeigned interest. How did Caroline manage to cry without making her face blotchy and her nose run, like other people's did? Caroline dropped to her knees beside her mother, 'Oh, Mama, please, talk to Papa for me –?'

Maria shook her head firmly. 'Truly, dear there's no point. Your father won't hear of your marrying before your twentieth birthday, and that's final.'

'But that's almost two *years*! And Clara's only seventeen, and she's to be married this year –'

'What difference does that make?' Jessica asked, ingenuously, and was treated to another furious burst of tears from her sister.

'*What difference?* She's younger than me. And I'm –' she stopped. 'I should marry first,' she said, sulkily. 'Oh, I'll never forgive her for this. And to announce it at the Ball! When all along she's known this was to be MY day –!'

But rant as Caroline might – and she did – her brother was not to be moved. He had spoken to Clara's father and to his own. Both were more than happy with an arrangement that would bring back an ancient family connection to New Hall. The decision had been taken and was to be announced. That was that. The wedding was to be in October, in deference to his mother's feelings, giving a full year of mourning for Edward. Since Clara was to be married from Old Hall it was her wish that the ceremony be conducted from St Agatha's, the family's old church. The delay until October would give time to spruce the place up a little. He conveyed all this to his family briskly and in much the way he might deliver any other estate news. Jessica wondered if she were the only one to find his apparent lack of ardour peculiar. A secret courtship, successfully concluded – a betrothal – a wedding – surely even the most temperate of men – and Giles could hardly be called that – might be forgiven for displaying some emotion? Yet he betrayed nothing, behaving in an uncharacteristically contained manner. Perhaps cool Clara had influenced him with her own restraint? Or perhaps, Jessica added gloomily to herself, Caroline's self-centred histrionics at what she saw as Giles' and Clara's deliberate upstaging of her betrothal were enough emotion even for Giles?

'Did any of you have any idea?' she asked Robert as they stood watching the Maypole with its multicoloured ribbons and crown of flowers being erected on the village green.

Robert shook his head. 'It was a complete surprise. Giles simply turned up and asked to speak to Father. Clara hadn't said a single word.'

The tension between these two had eased a little in their shared astonishment at the news, though Jessica still nursed her hurt and Robert, knowing it, was awkward.

'What does everyone think?'

'Father and Mother are delighted, of course.'

'And you?'

He shrugged, grinned sideways at her. 'Me too! Anything to get rid of her!'

'It's all very well for you!'

He laughed outright at that, and she could not help but laugh with him, easing the atmosphere further. Companionably they turned and strolled towards the gates of New Hall, waving to the lodge keeper as they passed.

'Caroline's absolutely FURIOUS!'

'What about?'

'I don't know – everything! That they want to announce it tomorrow. That Clara will marry now before she does – As if it matters! What a storm in a puddle!'

He laughed. 'It'll all settle down after the Ball. You'll see.'

May Day dawned cloudy, but with gleams of sunshine promising better. Jessica was up with the lark and swallowed her breakfast bread and milk almost at a gulp. She had been given permission to spend the day in the village with Lucy and would not waste a minute. But early as they were the village was up and about before them. Upon the green the ale casks had already been broached and the smell of roasting meat from the cooking pit was mouth-watering. The fiddler tuned his instrument and everywhere there were children, dressed in their best, bells upon their wrists and ankles, dashing about like beings demented, under everyone's feet. By the time they took their places, giggling and pushing excitedly, it seemed to Jessica that most of them must be exhausted before they were ready to start. Prettily they danced, though, weaving the coloured bands into clever, intricate designs about the pole and then unravelling them, ducking and swinging in the age-old pattern of the May Day dance. When the dance was done the ox was carved, and succulent it was, with juices running. As Jessica and Lucy sat upon the grass eating their portions, wiping greasy mouths with even greasier fingers Robert joined them, neat and clean as ever.

Jessica gestured with a rib bone. 'Aren't you going to have any? It's very good.'

'I know. I've had some.'

She pulled a face. 'Then why aren't you messy?'

He laughed, and settled himself beside them. 'You're messy enough for both of us. Have you heard the news?'

'What news?'

'They say Boney's on the run in Portugal. There's going to be a battle, Father said –'

'Oh.'

He grinned at her lack of interest, reached to pick a small and dainty morsel from her bone. 'Are you staying to watch the football? Hall's playing village, over on Bonner's Field and there's likely to be bones broken –'

The day wore on in games and laughter. It was with some reluctance late in the afternoon that Jessica allowed herself to be detached from the crowd that was noisily egging on Brewer the ploughman as he chased a full-grown and indignant pig about the green and marched back to New Hall to rest.

'If you're to be allowed to stay up awhiles tonight your Mama said you was to sleep this afternoon,' Lucy reminded her scowling charge.

With bad grace Jessica allowed herself to be undressed to her petticoat and tucked into bed. In the Long Gallery below she could hear the muffled small sounds of last minute preparation; a lifted voice, the scraping of a chair, footsteps upon the polished floor.

She awoke, astonished that she had slept, to the sound of music from the room below and the sight of Lucy, beaming, with a tray in her hands. 'There, now – get that inside of you, and we'll pretty you up in your new muslin, for your Mama says you may watch the guests arrive –'

They watched together, from the top of the main stairs. Carriage after carriage rolled to a halt outside the door: at one point the waiting queue reached almost the length of the drive. Maria and William Hawthorne, splendidly robed as King Arthur and his Queen, stood in the hall beneath, meeting their guests as they arrived. Fortune tellers and Indian nabobs, gypsies and Romans, Greeks and figures from legend advanced, were greeted, and disappeared up the secondary staircase to the Long Gallery. To the watching child it was the most splendid and exciting gathering she had ever seen, and she longed almost to the point of sickness to be a part of it.

At last the flood of arriving guests became a trickle. From the Gallery came the sound of music and of laughter. Almost the last to arrive were Robert's parents and their daughter Clara.

Jessica's eyes and mouth opened together in wondering astonishment. Sir Thomas and Lady FitzBolton, dumpy, homely figures both, had chosen the roles of Pierot and Pierette, at least the dozenth couple to have done so and, Jessica had to admit, dearly as she loved them, possibly the least distinguished. Clara it was who drew the eye. If Jessica had not known herself certainly to be the only person who knew of Caroline's costume for the evening she might have believed Clara to have designed hers in deliberate opposition. For Clara, May notwithstanding, was an Ice Queen, decked in lace fragile as frosted cobwebs, glittering and sparkling, feathered with snow. Upon her piled dark hair a tall and elegantly needle-pointed crown of silver icicles added to her height and to her regal bearing. Never had she looked so handsome. As she stood, waiting to be presented, Giles appeared at the top of the stairs that led to the Long Gallery. Seeing her, he stopped, poised. Clara lifted her eyes and smiled, very slightly. Giles, a dashing and very handsome cavalier, did not. Long sword swinging easily at his side, his hat with its sweeping plume in his hand he walked slowly down the stairs, his eyes intent upon his future bride. Always graceful in his movements it seemed to Jessica, watching, that in that moment he moved like a stalking cat, tension singing in him, barely constrained. Irresistibly she was reminded of the scene in the woods. Clara had greeted her future parents-in-law and now composedly awaited Giles' approach. As he neared her she lifted a graceful yet oddly imperious white-gloved hand. For a single moment he hesitated, then took it, and in keeping with his gallant role lifted it and brushed it with his lips. Clara's mother clapped delightedly. Jessica frowned. Something, somehow, was horribly wrong. She could not explain her feeling, even to herself, she only knew in that moment that in Giles some violence lived and that Clara, far from gentling it, as was needed, thrived upon – perhaps even encouraged – it. The two were mounting the stairs together, a fine-looking young couple. Their parents, from below, watched them, pleasant pride upon the FitzBoltons' faces, a smile upon William Hawthorne's. Only Jessica, from her vantage point, saw the look that Clara turned upon Giles; sweetly barbed, purely triumphant. And only Jessica saw the flinch of pain in the girl's face as Giles' hand tightened brutally over hers, a flicker only and then she laughed, the same pealing laughter that Jessica had heard in the woods, that was then swallowed by music and the hum of voices as the pair entered the ballroom.

'Time for bed, Miss Jessie,' Lucy said, regretfully, from beside her. 'Come down to say goodnight to your Mama and Papa, and then we must go.'

Later, and for a long time, Jessica lay listening to the sounds that filtered to her ears from the rooms below. Next year – oh, please God! – next year she would be down there – dancing, laughing.

Her imagination furnished her with a silken dress, a handsome partner. Somewhere in a corner Robert glowered jealously.

Yet, oddly, the last thing that slipped into her mind before she drifted at last into the mists of sleep was a sound; the sound of laughter, mocking and musical.

Clara's laughter.

Chapter Three

At the end of May Robert left to visit his schoolfriend in Devon. The day before he went, Jessica dined at Old Hall – the meals there following the traditional fashion of dinner at midday and supper in the evening rather than the new trend of dining in the evening as Jessica's parents did – and in the afternoon she and Robert walked along the river to St Agatha's and climbed onto 'their' tombstone. Jessica drew her knees up and rested her chin on them, gloomily and in silence picking at the burrs that had attached themselves to her skirt.

'Oh, do cheer up, Jess!' Robert's voice, whilst not altogether unkind held an unmistakable edge of impatience. 'Anyone would think I was going away for ever! It's only a couple of months – I'll be back before you know it. And then it'll be harvest time – think of the fun we'll have –'

She scowled. 'It's all right for you! You aren't going to be stuck here on your own with Caroline moping and Clara lording it over everyone!' She stopped, biting her lip, then burst out, 'Oh, Robert, I do wish you weren't going!'

Robert watched her for a moment, his face intent, then he turned away. 'You're acting as if it were a hanging offence to visit a schoolfriend. Lord, your own brother's off visiting friends, isn't he? He didn't even bother to come home at the end of term –!'

Jessica, who in common with the rest of the family had in fact hardly noticed quiet John's absence shrugged peevishly and said nothing.

'You have to understand, Jessica, that you can't order other people's lives. I'm going, and I refuse to pretend that I'm not looking forward to it. I'm sorry to be leaving you, but I intend to enjoy every minute of being with Paul and his family, of seeing somewhere different –'

Shaken from her woeful self-absorption by the near-anger of his tone she cast a swift sideways look at him. 'I'm sorry. Of course you're right. And I do hope you have a lovely time. Truly I do.' Visions of Paul Aloway's no doubt charming sisters – she had a clear picture of them both as Dresden figures, fair and tiny and very beautiful – rose in her mind and, miserably she leaned on her knees again, chewing at a dirty thumb.

They sat in silence for a while.

'My father's found someone to do the church,' Robert said after a moment, his voice challengingly light in the awkward silence.

'Do it?'

'Yes. You know – clean and renovate the statues and things, so it's worthy of a FitzBolton-Hawthorne wedding.' The words were dry. 'Lord, you don't think Clara's going to be satisfied with it the way it is, do you?'

Jessica shrugged. 'Strikes me she isn't satisfied with anything. Caroline said she's already talking about the changes she'll make at New Hall when she's running the house –'

'Deer in the park and peacocks on the lawns –' Robert said.

'She's told you, too, has she? She's got some sauce your sister, hasn't she? It's Mama's business to run New Hall, after all – and will be for years yet –'

'How does your mother get on with Clara?' There was real interest in Robert's voice.

'Mama?' Jessica shrugged again. 'She likes her well enough, I think. With Edward gone Giles certainly has to marry, and she seems to think Clara as good a choice as any.'

'Wait till she has to live with her.'

'Wait till we all do!' Deep gloom had descended upon Jessica again.

Robert laughed. 'Oh, come on, she isn't really that bad!' He jumped lightly down onto the path and waited as she scrambled down beside him. 'She can actually be quite civilized when she tries –'

This was not, however, a view with which Caroline would have agreed. Her erstwhile, never more than circumstantial friendship with the other girl had failed totally to withstand what she saw as Clara's deviousness, firstly in courting Giles with never a single confidential whisper or hint to her, and then, crime of crimes in Caroline's eyes in persuading him to marry her before Caroline herself had a ring upon her finger. Over the past year, her own match made, Caroline had made too many sweetly commiserating remarks about 'poor' Clara's apparent lack of prospects to doubt the direct malice of the timing.

'The airs and graces Clara FitzBolton's putting on, you'd think she was mistress of New Hall already!' she said indignantly to Jessica, a couple of days after Robert had left for Devon. The sisters were sitting in the garden, the drowsy scents and sounds of a warm early June day about them. Not far away a young gardener clipped a box hedge, his dark eyes flickering with interested frequency to the seat where the two girls sat. Caroline, in soft lemon sprigged cotton and with a wide, ribboned sunhat shading her face was showing elaborate unconcern at his presence; but Jessica, noticing the animation with which she spoke, the slight exaggeration of her gestures, the provocative tilt of her head, was not naïve enough to suppose that the pretty performance was for her benefit. Caroline now lifted a slender arm to adjust quite unnecessarily, the ribbons upon her hat. The young man stared, openly entranced, and then, catching Jessica's caustic eye upon him, hastily turned back to his task.

'I mean – for instance – why can't she get married in St Mary's like everyone else does? Why all this sudden interest in St Agatha's? She's just got to be different, hasn't she? No common or garden village wedding for Madam FitzBolton –'

'The church does belong to them. She has every right to get married there, I suppose.' The conversation was of no interest at all to Jessica. She had collected Bran from the stables, where he lived, and he leaned now beside her. Absently she rubbed his head, watching as a sweeping skein of water birds flew overhead, gliding in a graceful ribbon of flight towards the still, summer waters of the lake.

71

'She just wants to show off, that's all. I think it's a shame – putting poor old Sir Thomas to all that trouble – I mean, it would be different if they had two pennies to rub together –' The young gardener had not glanced their way for several moments, and appeared now to be absorbed in his task. Caroline stood up, shaking out the folds of her skirt and laughing prettily. 'Lord, just look! I do believe there's a grass-stain on my dress! I must get Maisie to clean it for me –' On pretence of examining what Jessica had no doubt was a non-existent stain she lifted her skirt a little, displaying as she did so a slim ankle in a white silk stocking.

The young gardener's eyes, warm and dark, showed every sign of renewed interest. Satisfied, Caroline shook her skirt straight and turned her back on him. 'Shall we stroll down to the lake? We've time before luncheon –'

With Robert gone Jessica found that time hung heavily on her hands. Somehow, all the things she had planned for the summer – the rides, the exploration of the lake's islands, the games, lost their savour when undertaken alone. She missed Robert – missed his companionship and his dry humour, his understanding, his occasional confidences – and, oddly and extremely irritatingly she found that no matter how she tried she could not rid herself of the image of those Dresden-figure sisters. Before he had gone to Devon, and after Caroline's apparently careless but nevertheless shrewd comments she had watched him; and had been forced to the conclusion that her sister, for once, was probably right. Robert's anticipation of this trip had held a suppressed excitement that led her to suspect more than simple pleasure at the thought of visiting a schoolfriend: and she had been surprised to discover how much the thought had pained her.

The weather, however, was fine and all that could be expected of June. Every free minute she could contrive was spent in the fields and woodlands of the park. She sat one day by the lakeside, her fingers rippling the water, trying hard to dismiss from her mind a vision of Robert, in equally idyllic surroundings, paying court to one – or perhaps both! – of the

Aloway girls. And no doubt sparing not a thought for her, left here alone. Wallowing pleasantly in self-pity she pictured him, his neat dark head inclined to a diminutive, doll-like being with peaches-and-cream complexion, clean fingernails, spun gold hair and a lovely voice. She scowled at an inoffensive butterfly. That really was going too far — was it fair that the Dresden-creature could sing as well?

She lifted her head in surprise, her train of thought broken. In the distance, clear and infectious, sweet as a bird, someone was whistling, a gay and cheerfully lilting tune she had never heard before. She stood, a warning finger on Bran's muzzle, and turned her head, listening. The whistling stopped, and a man's voice took up the melody, light and true, both the rhythm and the language of the song foreign to Jessica. Intrigued, the dog a shadow at her heels, she slipped through the trees towards the path. As she stepped on to it she was just in time to see the back of a man as he disappeared where the path curved into the trees. He was swinging along briskly to the time of his own singing. Her curiosity thoroughly aroused, she followed. By the time she reached the turn in the path he had gone, but she could hear him still ahead, alternately singing and whistling, his footsteps light in the woodland litter of the path. The glimpse she had caught of him had shown a young man dressed simply in shirt and breeches, tall and broad-shouldered, though slim, his bare head black as a gypsy's. On his back he had carried a small sack. Pleased with this diversion she followed, Bran romping beside her. She would discover what right this assured young man had to walk through her father's woodlands as if he owned them. Only when they reached the river-path and she heard the creaking of the lych-gate did a disappointingly obvious explanation for a stranger's presence occur to her; surely, this must be the craftsman, or one of them, hired by Sir Robert to ready the church for Clara's wedding? She slipped around the side of the church, and, having enjoined Bran in a fierce whisper and not with over-much confidence to sit and stay, climbed the ramshackle wall and scrambled through the overgrown churchyard. It was a game now, and an exciting one, to get close to him without his seeing her. He had gone into the church, no longer whistling, but humming still beneath his breath. Like a small shadow she followed, on quiet feet, sharp eyes probing the gloom.

The stranger had moved to the altar and stood with his back to her, his head flung back as he surveyed intently the faded wall paintings. She flattened herself against a pillar, peeped round it. He swung the bag he carried to the floor, then straightened, turning, and as he did so the light from the narrow stained glass window fell directly upon his face. Gleaming dark eyes, polished olive skin, proud bright bones and a long, sweetly chiselled mouth: Jessica had never, in life, seen such a face. The features were clear cut and sharp in the shadowed light. She stared, the bright lines of that still, intent face holding her spellbound. The young man dropped to one knee beside the carved altar rail and ran a long, none-too-clean finger over the wood. Then still kneeling, he lifted his head to look up at the ancient, decaying statue of St Agnes that stood above the altar. Jessica swallowed, awkwardly. Something extremely disturbing appeared to be happening to her usually reliable insides. Her heart was racing as if she had run a long way and her stomach churned, oddly and uncomfortably. Forgetting secrecy she moved, and the rustle of it echoed in the stillness. The young man turned, surprised, coming to his feet in one fleet, graceful movement.

Without thought and for no good reason, Jessica took to her heels. Like a small, startled animal she fled, across the churchyard, over the wall and into the woods. Bran, seeing her coming, leapt to her side, tongue lolling, his great bony frame all but knocking her from her feet. The young man did not call after her, neither did he follow. She ran to the lake's edge, close to the weir where Edward had lost his life. The stranger in the church must, she estimated, be about Edward's age, and something of his build, too – tall and limber and long of leg. But there any resemblance ended, for the stranger was night-dark, and Edward had been fair as the day, and if Edward had been handsome then to Jessica's dazzled eyes the young man in the church was something beyond that. In the library of Old

Hall were books – books that had been collected by past generations of FitzBoltons at a time when such things were rare and precious – and often she and Robert had spent long afternoons poring over the treasures that those shelves contained. Her own favourite, to which she returned again and again, was an ancient, fancifully hand-illustrated book of stories of the Crusades. And of all the illustrations the one that had always most fired her imagination was the last, a picture of Jerusalem, restored to Christendom and guarded by a fierce and fiery being, a dark-faced warrior angel, arrogantly beautiful. And now, today, in tiny St Agatha's she had seen that face imbued with life; the young man in the church might have been the very model for that figure. A dark angel, fierce and sweet.

Thought of the stranger was never for the rest of the day far from her mind, and too the odd excitement he had aroused in her tingled strangely on the edge of her consciousness. He was her secret, the dark angel of Jerusalem come to St Agatha's.

The next day, as soon as she could escape, firmly suppressing her feelings of guilt at leaving the immoderately excitable Bran behind she slipped down to the church, and on finding it empty experienced a disappointment out of all proportion to its cause. Some days having passed since she had visited Robert's parents, and with the ulterior motive that someone at Old Hall might know the whereabouts and identity of her dark young man, she took the path that led along the river bank to the old house. A few hundred yards from the church she passed a row of all-but-derelict cottages that had stood empty for as long as she could remember; and there, with a strange, almost panic-stricken lurch of her heart, she saw him. He had drawn a bucket of water from the well in the overgrown front garden and, stripped to the waist, dark hair glossy and dripping, he was washing in it. Behind him the door of one of the cottages stood open. As she shrank back into the shadow of the trees he reached for his shirt, dried his face on it and rubbed his hair briskly before pulling the shirt over his head. Then, whistling again that same lilting tune she had heard yesterday he turned and walked into the house, stuffing his shirt tails carelessly into his breeches as he went. No angel this, in the bright light of day; on the contrary, even to her eyes he looked like nothing so much as a picturesque and rather disreputable young gypsy. From within the cottage she heard his voice lift again in song. Shamelessly curious she slipped through the overgrown garden and peeped in at the tiny window. In the dark little room, singing cheerfully to himself, he was busying himself as might any cottage housewife, arranging the few sticks of furniture to his own satisfaction, lighting the stove. She watched as he put the kettle on the hob and took a loaf of bread and some cheese from a cupboard. In the half-light of the room he moved like a shadow, quick and graceful, once again oddly mysterious, and again she felt that perturbing sensation, an excitement that quickened heart and pulse, as if at the approach of danger. A dauntless and confident rider she nevertheless knew the exhilarating fear of facing a risky jump, and was at an absolute loss to understand why the proximity of this total stranger should have much the same effect. She slipped away from the window and, uncommonly preoccupied, continued on her way to Old Hall.

Two days later – two days in which Jessica all but haunted both the church and the cottage in the vain hope of catching a glimpse of the intriguing stranger – John came home to New Hall. He had been visiting friends in Kent, and this was the first time he had been home since Easter. Jessica was glad to see him – if nothing else at least his presence ensured that the odd remark might be addressed to her at the luncheon table – John, it seemed to her, being the only one who ever bothered to include her in the general conversation. Approaching now his sixteenth birthday he was smaller and broader-built than either of his brothers, and his pleasant and honest face showed a calm maturity beyond his years. He was a quiet boy, not in the least given to the other Hawthorne children's impetuous habit of speaking first and thinking later – a restraint he inherited from his mother, while his looks in the main came from his father. He had been destined for the Church more or less since birth, and since, coincidentally, his own inclinations followed his father's wishes exactly the choice of career had been a happy one and his considerable strength of will, hidden as it was beneath an affable and kindly nature, had so far been used to further the family plans rather than oppose them. It would not have occurred to William Hawthorne to be thankful for this for, quite simply, it would not have occurred to him that any other course was open to the boy. John, quietly, knew differently. He was now already studying for the Ministry, and the plan was that he should follow in Edward's footsteps to Cambridge University before being ordained. William Hawthorne was determined to have a Bishop in the family: needless to say it occurred to no-one to consult with John about that. Jessica had always liked him. The nearest to her in age he had never aroused her resentment as the others so often had by treating her as some kind of half-witted inferior. In fact long before her age or understanding had justified it he had spoken to her as an equal, and if the bond between them was not as close as that she had for years shared with Robert FitzBolton, nevertheless she was fond of him, and he of her. Utterly trustworthy and always ready with a kind word, in him the easy, indolent warmth and charm of Edward had been transmuted to a rare and genuinely unselfish generosity. However not even her newly-returned brother's account of his weeks in Canterbury could draw her from her absorption with the strange young man at St Agatha's. Absently she picked at her luncheon, hardly hearing the conversation about her.

'I trust the Hely-Browns were well?' Maria Hawthorne, to be honest, often found herself forgetting this quiet, youngest son almost entirely in his absences, and was always mildly surprised upon seeing him again, though she was much too courteous to show it and would have been appalled had she realized that he knew it as well.

'Very well, Mama, and send their regards.'

Jessica fidgeted. Her morning had been a disaster – French verbs, and a deportment and dancing lesson that, for the last thirty minutes of its duration had seen her standing in a corner in disgrace, a heavy book balanced upon her head. Her neck still ached. After luncheon – providing sneaky Mr Appleday her dancing teacher had not taken it upon himself to apprise MacKenzie, and hence Jessica's mother, of what he had described as his pupil's 'scant o' grace' behaviour, an uncharitable trick that she would not for a moment think beyond him – she was free for the whole afternoon, and the sun shone sweetly beyond the tall windows, calling her. John was still speaking.

'– asked me to do them a small favour, and so of course I agreed. They have some friends in Lavenham, to whom I am to deliver a small package. I thought I might ride out this afternoon.'

William Hawthorne nodded. 'Good idea. Don't suppose you've had much exercise at the Hely-Browns', eh? Penned in the middle of Canterbury? They don't even have a stables, do they?'

John smiled a little, and shook his head. 'No, Sir. They don't.'

'Humph.' The small, sharp sound indicated clearly William Hawthorne's opinion of the bookish and theological Hely-Browns.

Maria rose gracefully. 'Jessica – Caroline –?'

The two girls rose also and obediently followed their mother from the room. Within the folds of her skirt Jessica's fingers were tightly crossed in superstitious defence against Mr Appleday's malice. Her fears, however, were groundless. An hour later she was free and, giving poor Bran, confined in the stables, a quick kiss and a promise of atonement she ran towards the lake. It was a warm afternoon, and the sun shone from a clear sky, although a dark band of cloud, at the moment not much more than a smudge on the western horizon, threatened a break in the weather.

Reaching the church she paused first to catch her breath, then slipped into the gloom.

The building was empty.

Disappointed again, and about to turn away, she stopped: the dark young stranger might not be here, but evidence of his presence and of his craft lay neatly upon a small strong table beside the altar. The statue of St Agatha, crumbling with neglect, stood there, and beside it a malet, several chisels and some other implements she did not recognize, and a bowl of what looked like clay. A stone bottle of wine stood open beside the tools. Curious, she crept forward, touched a finger to the razor-sharp edge of one of the chisels. The wooden handle was smooth and shiny with use and with the patina of age. She picked it up, appreciating even in her inexperience the lovely weight and balance of it.

From very far in the distance came the first muted grumble of thunder: and, closer, the sound of a light step upon the gravelled path.

Quick as thought she darted into the darkest corner of the nave and slipped into a box pew, its door hanging drunkenly on a broken hinge. She crouched on the floor, that was thick with dust and smelled villainously of dirt and decay.

He came from the light into the shadows, blinking. In one hand he carried a sheaf of papers, in the other candles, which he set into holders already gathered on the table and the altar, and lit. By their flickering light, his face absorbed, he studied the drawings he carried, his eyes moving now and again to the statue. Absently he reached a hand to the bottle, tilted his dark head and drank. Bottle still in hand he bent again to the drawings. Jessica watched with held breath. There in the glow of the candles once more was her dark angel, beautiful and for the moment tranquil, his face burnished by the light.

Thunder rumbled again, still distant, barely a breath of threat on the summer air.

The young man set down the bottle, lifted a hand to the statue, ran a long, gentle finger along the crumbling outlines of the saint's draped garments. Then he picked up a soft brush and began to clean the figure of dust.

Jessica, penned in her pew, watched. The young stranger was completely lost in his task, his light breathing and the rustle of his movements the only sound as he examined the worn and defaced stone. Jessica had been told by Sir Robert that it had been Roundhead soldiers who had caused most of the damage to St Agatha's, whilst hunting for fleeing Royalists after the Siege of Colchester. She did not know the truth of the story. The young man picked some clay from the bowl and began moulding it between his fingers. So totally preoccupied was he that the child was certain that if she had wished she could have made good her escape; but she did not. Enthralled she watched him, watched the play of light on the skilful fingers and on the grave and flawless face as he began to work upon the statue. Again she experienced the now familiar, though still inexplicable mixture of feelings that the presence of the young man stirred in her; excitement, an odd tenderness at the sight of the bent, absorbed head, a yearning – for what she could not say, but none the less strong for that. Quiet as a mouse she crouched, eyes wide and unblinking upon the stranger, whilst in the world outside the summer storm moved closer.

It was the storm that broke the spell. For almost an hour it had rumbled from a distance, sunshine still falling softly through the church's tiny windows to add to the illumination of the candles that flickered on the table and on the altar. It was with the abruptness of a closing curtain that the light was suddenly cut off as the stormclouds rolled across the sun. The young man looked up, frowning, his concentration broken by the unexpected darkness. Jessica heard him mutter something under his breath. Then, wiping his hands on his shirt he strode to the door and looked out. In the same moment it dawned on Jessica that if she were to have any chance of avoiding MacKenzie's wrath at wet clothes and hair she had best leave now. Under cover of an earsplitting crash of thunder she slipped from the pew and scuttled through the shadows towards the door. Beyond the young man's silhouetted figure she saw a violent and jagged flash of lightning, livid in the queer storm-darkness. The man stood for a moment looking out to where the pre-storm wind tossed wildly through the treetops then, shrugging, he turned. Jessica slipped behind a pillar, then, choosing her moment, she picked up her skirts and ran like a hare. She heard a shout from behind her, and something that sounded suspiciously like laughter, then she was gone, running sure-footed through the trees towards the park.

She had left it too late. By the time she reached the edge of the woodland huge spots of rain had started to fall, rattling through the branches above her head like flung stones. Overhead thunder and lightning crashed together and she jumped at the violence of the sound. The roiling, purple clouds echoed menacingly. The rain was coming down harder with every second, threatening a downpour to drown her. She hesitated, uncertain whether to stay beneath the trees and risk the lightning or make a dash for it across the open, rain-lashed but relatively safe expanse of the parkland. As she stood, undecided, the sound of hoofbeats lifted above the buffeting of the wind. Skirting the woodland from her right came John, grinning and waving, riding sturdy Old Jenny as hard as the staid and solid mare could manage. Puzzled for a moment as to where he could have sprung from she remembered the small bridge that crossed the river from the Long Melford Road, close by Old Hall. He must have cut across it trying to beat the storm home. Relieved, she smiled widely and waved back.

'Here –' He reached a hand. 'Hop up!'

Laughing she allowed him to swing her, light as a bird, before him on the saddle. Jenny tossed her head as the storm crashed above them again, and John clapped his heels to her side, urging her to an ungainly gallop. Minutes later, with the downpour truly upon them, they were safely in the stables of New Hall, none the worse for wear.

It was not until that night, comfortable and close to sleep, that it occurred to Jessica to wonder how it was that John, who had ostensibly set off on an errand to Lavenham had come back from entirely the opposite direction via the Long Melford Road. Sleepily she resolved to ask him the next day, but by morning had quite forgotten the resolution.

It was two days later that – almost certainly by design – the stranger caught her.

She had ridden to Old Hall to take tea with Robert's parents, and to discover if they had news of him. The short note they had received assured them of his good health and happiness and asked that he be remembered to Jessica. As she mounted

Apple, her pony, to ride home – Old Hall being virtually within the park she was allowed to ride there unaccompanied – she reflected with faint surprise that it had been some time since she had fretted jealously at the thought of the Dresden-figure sisters. She set Apple to the river path, his hooves quiet upon the grass. She hoped – sincerely now – that Robert was having a happy time. She had thought his note a little non-commital, though Clara had dismissed any worries about that brusquely – 'Heavens, Jessica, he's a boy! What else do you expect? When did you ever know a man write a civilized letter when a military note will do?'

She was approaching the church, and could make no pretence to herself that she could ride by without seeing if her stranger were there. She tethered Apple near the river and slipped through the gate and along the path. The church was empty, dark and silent. Disappointment, surprising in its depth, drew her straight brows together in a frown. She did not understand why it had become an irresistible compulsion to see the strange young man, she only knew that undeniably it had. She knew his face now as well as she knew her own, knew too his habit of singing to himself beneath his breath, recognized now the foreign-sounding tune that he most often hummed. Pausing for a moment now to reassure herself that the church was indeed empty she slipped through the shadowed gloom to the altar. The statue stood, the implements he had been using laid at her feet, as if just that moment discarded. A warning bell rang in her mind. She turned.

Silent as a cat he had come up behind her, and stood now, grinning. 'So. My little Mouse in a trap at last.'

She took a couple of stumbling steps backwards. He reached for her. Suddenly and irrationally afraid she shrank away from him, trapped by the altar rail.

The smile left his face. He shook his head. 'Don't be afraid, little Mouse. I won't hurt you.'

She said nothing.

He let his hands drop to his sides. Swift as thought she launched herself past him, but he was as quick as she. A long arm took her about the waist and swung her from the floor.

'Oh, no you don't, little one! Not as easily as that! Not until I know why you've been spying on me –?'

That cut sharply. 'I haven't been spying!' Something in the indignant tone arrested his laughter. Very carefully he set her upon her feet, his hands upon her shoulders, that dark face bent to hers interestedly.

'You haven't? Then it must have been another little mouse that I started the day before yesterday? Is the country full of them?' He raised quizzical eyebrows.

She did not answer, but treacherous colour crept into her cheeks.

'It wasn't you?'

She shrugged. His speech, like his appearance, was different from any other she had ever encountered. Clearly enunciated, the tone obviously educated, yet there was an indefinable accent there, more perhaps in the rhythm and cadence of his voice than in the pronunciation itself.

'So. It was you.' He regarded her solemnly for a moment, then let go of her shoulders and straightened. 'Perhaps – we should start again?' He waited, then as she did not respond, sketched her a small, half-mocking bow. 'My name is Danilo. Danilo O'Donnel. My friends call me Danny.' He waited, expectant.

'I'm Jessica Hawthorne.'

'Jessica Hawthorne.' He rolled the name portentiously, then smiled a smile of pure mischief that made her heart lurch in a most uncomfortable way. 'Personally, Miss Jessica Hawthorne, I think Mouse suits you better. Small, brown, and quick as that!' He clapped his hands sharply, and she jumped, then flushed again as he laughed.

He sat on a pew, patted the seat beside him. 'Come.'

Her escape route was clear. She had only to run, and they both knew it. Gingerly she perched herself beside him.

'Now, where do you come from, Jessica Hawthorne?'

She indicated a general direction with an inclination of her head. 'From the house at the top of the lake. New Hall.'

His eyes widened very slightly. 'Do you indeed?' He paused for a moment, to consider this. 'So – you are a relation of the groom?'

83

'He's my brother.' As always at thought of Giles Jessica grimaced a little, and the young man laughed.

'I see. And — may I ask —' the words were teasingly courteous, '— how it is that our paths seem to have crossed rather frequently lately?'

She kept the shreds of her dignity about her and refused to be seduced by the open invitation to laughter offered by his merry eyes and smiling mouth. 'I wanted to see what you were doing.'

'Ah.' Strangely, the answer appeared to satisfy him completely. Silence fell.

She eyed him. 'Where do you come from?'

'The cottage down the lane.' His expression was innocent.

Still she would not laugh. Neither would she be deflected. 'I mean – before.'

He nodded, accepting her question seriously for all his teasing. 'Edinburgh. And before that Lincoln. And before that London. Anywhere that folk will pay me to restore ruin to beauty.' He glanced about him.

'What did you say your name was?' In her interest she was forgetting her fright. She leaned forward, intent.

'Danny. Danny O'Donnel.'

'No. I mean —' she paused, '— the other name. The funny one.'

He laughed. 'Danilo. Danilo O'Donnel. A little strange, yes?'

She nodded.

'My mother was Italian, my father Irish. An explosive mixture, I'm afraid.' He smiled, the warmth of him like the summer sun. 'I look like my mother, and I drink like my father. I was born in Florence. I am an artist. A sculptor. But at the moment a little down on my luck. My birthday is in March, I have all my teeth and I'm scared to death of horses. There. Danny O'Donnel in a nutshell for you, little Mouse.'

She laughed delightedly. 'You can't really be scared of horses?'

'Can't I?' He put his head on one side, comically, as if considering. 'And here I've lived for twenty years thinking I was!'

84

She giggled again. 'Are you Irish or Italian?'

He looked at her admiringly. 'What a very perceptive question. I don't know. What do you think?'

Jessica considered. 'Irish I should think.'

He shrugged. 'That'll do. For now anyway.'

'Don't you care?' The child, brought up in the unthinking nationalistic pride of an English upper middle class family was astonished.

For a moment the laughter fled the dark face. 'Oh, yes, little Mouse, I care. For I am Florentine. Italian? Irish? This means nothing. But Florentine – that is to be a part of the most beautiful city in the world. To have some share in her treasures – her art, her music, her sculpture. To be at home in her squares and gardens. To be at one with her people.'

Jessica had never come across anyone with quite such a poetic turn of phrase. She was enthralled. 'Did you just make that up?'

He shouted with laughter. 'I most certainly did.' He pretended indignation.

'It was very good.'

He bowed, gracefully for all that he was sitting down. 'Thank you.'

Her mind had jumped back to the original thread of their conversation. 'Why don't you live there?'

'Ah.' In the turning of a moment again the merriment fled. He turned his head a little, looking with unseeing eyes up to where the multicoloured light flickered through the stained glass windows. Her heart lurched, watching him, seeing the sadness. After a moment, as if realizing she still awaited an answer to her question he said, 'For the moment I cannot.'

'Why not?'

Half exasperated he smiled. 'What an extremely inquisitive little mouse you are!'

She flushed, and seeing it, he laid a hand on her arm, gently. 'Ah, no. Don't be angry with me. I'll tell you. My mother was of good family, my father a penniless sculptor. The marriage – if indeed there were a marriage, I've never been truly certain –'

Jessica's eyes widened at such devastating honesty, 'was not one of which my mother's people could approve. We lived in the tenements across the river from the city, on the banks of the Arno, near the Pitti Palace. We lived with others of our kind – penniless artists, sculptors, actors, musicians – and, oh, little Mouse, what a world it was!' His head was bent to her, his eyes bright as gems in the shadows. Jessica was enthralled. 'Life was a celebration. Always there was sunshine, and laughter. Always there was wine, and music and above all friendship. Sometimes my mother would take me across the Ponte Vecchio to visit my grandparents' house. Very fine it seemed to me, with a courtyard, and a fountain and marble floors. But home was where my parents were, and their friends, and their laughter and loving –'

'What happened?'

He shrugged. 'The French came. There were disturbances. The French preach revolution. My grandparents were of the old order. My grandfather defied them. When they came to arrest him he resisted and was shot. My mother and grandmother were shot with him. Accidentally, so the soldiers said.' He paused for a moment, then added softly, 'See what happens when men of violence rule –'

The child had drawn from him in horror, her hands at her mouth. As if coming to himself he shook his head, and his voice was gentle. 'Don't grieve. There is nothing to be gained.'

'But –'

'But, yes, it was a terrible thing. A savage thing. A waste. But it is over. My father escaped from Florence taking me with him and brought me to England. He educated me and cared for me. Before death took him he taught me much, perhaps enough for me one day to be a great sculptor. I don't know. This is for the future. For now –' he spread long-fingered hands, 'I am what you see – a mender of statues, a redeemer of churches, a fighter against the decay of beauty – and yes, before you ask, I made that up myself as well –'

The mood lightened. They smiled. Then, reluctantly, she stood up. 'I have to go. Will you be here tomorrow?'

He nodded.

'If I can get away – may I come again?'

His smile was warm as the June sunshine. 'Nothing would give me greater pleasure.'

She rode home across the park, singing.

From that moment every second spent away from Danny was for Jessica wasted, and the friendship between child and young man became as firm as it was unlikely. Any moment she could snatch was spent in the church with him, and the scoldings and slappings she risked from disappearing so often from New Hall deterred her not at all. They talked of everything under the sun – of the ways of birds and the flight of butterflies, of the sound of a word and the subtlety of its meaning, of the smell of new-baked bread and the delights of clover honey. Now that she no longer hid from him Dian came too, and it was no surprise at all to Jessica that man and dog became friends on sight. Danny talked easily of his recent life, and from him she learned of the ways of a rootless itinerant artist, feckless, free and devoted to two things – the stone he worked and, always, the city in which he had been born. 'Ah, Mouse – when you are a beautiful woman you must visit her! Her young men will court you and paint wonderful portraits, and I, a penniless sculptor living in a hovel on the banks of the Arno will say – I knew her first, before her fame –' The summer rain pattered beyond the doors, and the air was chill. 'Wait till you see the golden light of sunset on the river   the tumbling red roofs, the towers and spires – it is a city of magic.'

She was enthralled. 'Is it really that beautiful? I mean – really and truly?'

'Really and truly.' He turned from the statue on which he had been working, gesturing with clay-damp hands as if to conjure the city from the dark air. 'Palaces. Churches. Tall campaniles whose bells are the music of Florence. Museums. Theatres. In the Boboli Gardens the lovers kiss and the children play, and at every turn there is a sculpture to delight the eye. Paris? Rome? St Petersburg?' He shook his head, making a small puffing noise with his mouth, 'None of them can compare –'

Her eyes widened. 'You've been to Paris? And St Petersburg?'

He smiled gracelessly, and shrugged a little. 'Not yet. But what difference? The impossible is impossible – and it isn't possible to find another city as lovely as Florence.' He picked up the stone bottle that always stood beside him as he worked and tilted his head to drink, then wiped his mouth with the back of his wrist. She watched him, as she watched the smallest of his movements, in fascination. He pointed a finger, his face almost serious. 'One day, Mouse, when Europe is free again, I shall go back. And I shall be the greatest living sculptor in Florence.'

She believed him implicitly; for Jessica, innocently, had lost her heart entirely. On the vulnerable threshold of adulthood, and until now, for a child who lived apparently with almost constant companionship, strangely lonely she had found in this warm and volatile young man a prince, the fitting subject of all her half-formed growing dreams. She listened, enchanted, and, in listening so, encouraged him to greater and more bewitching flights of fancy. As he spoke she could all but see and smell and hear the city he extolled – the wide, slow-moving river, amber ripples beneath the shadows of the Ponte Vecchio, the green hills beyond patched with olive groves and the dark fingers of cypress, the busy, colourful streets and squares, the lovely buildings. In her mind Florence became a place of mystery and delight hardly second to Paradise if Danny were there to share it. As for Danny himself – he found in the child an open, astute and receptive mind, a flatteringly attentive audience for the expression of his own dreams. Not for one moment did the young man perceive the quality of the devotion in the bright, dark eyes that watched him as he worked, nor the depths of his own influence on the child. He saw a charming and intelligent little girl, perhaps a little solemn but with a sturdy independance and a subversive sense of humour that delighted him; in short, he saw a friend, improbable perhaps, but none the less welcome for that. Not once did it occur to him to see in her the budding of adolescence and with it the pain and wonder of first love.

The communication between them was by no means one-way. Almost as interested in her way of life as she was in his he encouraged her to talk of it. She told him of MacKenzie and of Lucy, of life at New Hall, of her friendship with Robert and – finally and painfully – of Edward's death.

Danny cocked his head, listening to the distant waters of the weir. 'That must have been very sad for you all.'

'It was *awful*. Mama still cries, I think. Edward was her favourite.'

'But – now? A wedding in the family? Surely, all will be well again? Life has to go on, Mouse.'

'Hmm.' Thought of the coming wedding never particularly cheered Jessica. Even the prospect of being the chief of Clara's maids did not really ease the odd disquiet the thought of Giles and Clara always brought to her.

He cocked an eyebrow at her. 'You don't approve?' He was always interested in her opinion, having discovered long since that, child or not, her eye was remarkably clear.

It had not occurred to her to look at it in those terms. She thought for a moment. 'It isn't that. It's just – the whole thing seems so – so *odd* to me. I thought that when people were in love they – well, they held hands, and kissed and things – you know.' She had suddenly flushed bright as a poppy. 'Well, that they were *kind* to one another –'

'And they aren't?'

She shook her head. 'No.' She stopped, biting her lip in perplexity. 'I suppose I shouldn't say that? I mean – how do I know how they act when they're alone? Not that they hardly ever are – they don't seem particularly to want to be – oh, I don't know – it's just that it seems to me that something's – well, wrong –'

He had stopped working and was regarding her, surprised interest in his eyes. 'Wrong? How, wrong?'

She shrugged. 'I don't know. I can't explain. And I suppose I really shouldn't be talking about it. It isn't my business, is it?

89

Please – tell me some more about your grandparents' house in Florence –'

For several reasons, some more obvious than others, Jessica kept this new friendship very much to herself. She was as certain as she could be without putting it to the test that if her parents – or anyone else at New Hall – found out about it they would find some plausible adult reason to put a stop to it. Yet beyond that was something else; Danny, for this short time, was hers, and shared with no-one. She had never had such a private and singular relationship before – even Robert was Clara's brother, his parents' son, an approved friend of the family. And of course the very secrecy of their comradeship added spice to it. They met usually in the church, though on rare occasions she would go to the cottage where he would sit at the table with wine – which she had long since noticed with some degree of admiration he drank in copious quantities – and bread and cheese whilst she sipped at a mug of milk that somehow always tasted better than the milk she drank at home. They never seemed to stop talking. With no concession to her youth and inexperience Danny talked with indiscriminate and undisciplined intelligence of anything that came into his head; of religion, of art, of the passionate and idealistic ideas of his Republican father. That his mother had died because of these very passions had not passed him by and his general attitude to politics was cynical in the extreme. 'They're all after something, little Mouse, mark my words. Never believe any of them. If you want the truth look into the hearts of your friends –' he grinned and lifted his flask of wine '– or in the bottom of one of these –' They discovered a shared love of words that delighted Jessica, and when she shyly brought to the church a book of poetry he insisted that she read to him as he worked. For Jessica these were perhaps the happiest hours she had ever spent, reading aloud to him, stumbling occasionally over unfamiliar words or ideas, filled with happiness when he took the trouble to explain or discuss them. It was obvious that his education had been as unconventional as everything else about him. For ten years after his mother's death he and his father had moved from city to city, living always in colonies of artists, artisans and craftsmen. Inevitably these communities had grown up usually in the poorer parts of the towns but their lack of affluence and physical comfort was more than countered by the warmth, colour and variety of the life they led. Danny's father, despite his feckless inability to stay in one place had been devoted to the child and had passed on to him both his own passion for stone – and to a lesser degree the carving of wood – and his not inconsiderable store of knowledge and appreciation of all the arts. A well-educated man himself he had, until the day three years before when he had been killed in a drunken brawl in a Southwark brothel, made sure that their gypsy life did not deprive his son of learning. That there were great and intriguing gaps in Danny's education Jessica was delightedly scandalized to discover he knew nothing whatsoever of the kind of arithmetic without which, in MacKenzie's opinion, it was impossible to live – made him all the more interesting to her. Sometimes the strength of her feelings for him disturbed her. A day that passed without their meeting was a tragedy, the prospect of seeing him more exciting than anything she had ever experienced. Too young to recognize either infatuation or the growth of true passion she only knew that she could not bear the thought of being parted from him. And so she kept her secret.

July brought a heatwave. The countryside shimmered, day after day, beneath cloudless skies and a blazing sun. Dust lifted from the grassland of the park and the green was bleached from the landscape. In the fields of the estate sweat ran in dusty rivulets down the faces of the haymakers despite the protection afforded by the wide brims of their straw hats. Even the lofty, usually cool rooms of New Hall were not immune. With all the windows open the silken summer curtains hung like rags in the still air and the atmosphere was stifling. Tempers grew short. Caroline drifted about, gossamer clad and still contriving to look cool as a cucumber, declaring herself to be quite expiring from the heat. Giles' brow furrowed as days turned to weeks without rain. Even Jessica's energy deserted her a little, though nothing would prevent her regular trips to the church and Danny. He was working now on the lovely ancient wooden rood screen, his fingers deft and sure and loving as they patched and polished the ornate wood. In point of fact St Agatha's was probably at this time the most comfortable place on the estate, and it was with relief that Jessica would enter the cool dark interior and settle herself to watch Danny work.

It could not, of course, last. Such a secret, in such circumstances, was certain sooner or later to be discovered.

It happened on a blazing hot July day. There had been, over luncheon, some talk of a trip into Long Melford – Lavenham being thought too far to travel in the sweltering heat and the dust of the roads. Jessica needed some slippers and her sister, who already owned more bonnets than Jessica could believe she knew what to do with, had expressed a need for another, a need which could wait neither for the scotchman nor for an order to London. Lately she had been affecting a charming simplicity in her dress, a stylized 'milkmaid' look which suited her well – uncharitably Jessica had once or twice been tempted to remind her of the fate of Marie Antoinette not so many years before. No firm agreement had been reached about the trip however and, assuming her freedom, Jessica had collected Apple and Bran from the stables and ridden to the church. Danny looked up, smiling, at her entrance. His dark hair was plastered to his scalp and his shirt clung wetly to his body. 'I've been for a swim in the lake,' he said, in answer to her questioning look. Bran bounded to his side, flag tail wagging. Danny patted him affectionately before reaching for the stone bottle that stood on the table, tipping his head and drinking. 'It's too damned hot to do anything today.'

'You shouldn't swim this end of the lake,' Jessica said automatically. 'It's dangerous unless you're a really strong swimmer.'

He shrugged and his teeth flashed again. 'I am,' he said, modestly. He took another mouthful of wine then put the bottle down and tapped the cork back into place. 'Jessica Hawthorne – little Mouse – I hereby declare a day of rest.

I've got bread and cheese. Let's go and eat them by the river.'

She clapped her hands. 'What a lovely idea!'

He led the way outside. She took Apple's rein and, Bran trotting beside them, walked beside him down the river path.

'There's a place along here – ah, there. Will this do, my lady?'

The bank of the river here sloped gently away from the path, from which a natural screen of hawthorn hedge hid it. Downstream a willow dipped graceful, drifting fronds into the slow-running deep water. Even the grass, this close to the water, was still emerald green and untouched by drought. On the river two swans sailed, snow white and graceful.

'Lovely!' Jessica tied Apple in the shade of a tree. Bran ambled on a half dozen steps then flopped down, one eye closed, the other devotedly upon Jessica.

Danny threw himself, long and limber, upon the grass, stood the wine flask carefully on the uneven ground and unfolded the kerchief he had been carrying. Courteously he offered bread and cheese to Jessica.

She shook her head. 'I've eaten, thank you. I couldn't manage another mouthful in this heat.' She dropped down beside him, took off her wide-brimmed sunhat and tossed it onto the grass. 'Blessed thing!'

He grinned through a mouthful of bread and cheese. 'You'll end up brown as a berry if you aren't careful. Then what would your Mama say?'

'Just at the moment I don't care a fig, so there!' She laid back, staring through the still, laden branches above her to the vast, endless blue of the sky beyond. The river rippled gently and musically against the bank. Bran snored.

'Jessica? Jess-i-ca!'

Jessica started bolt upright at the sound. Danny stopped, the wine jar poised halfway to his lips.

'Jessica!'

Caroline's voice, impatient, from the path above. Jessica

scrambled to her feet. Apple, innocent traitor, lifted his head and nickered at the familiar voice.

'Oh, there you are! Jessica, really, what a dance you've led me –!' Before Jessica could move to cut her off Caroline had appeared above them, dressed in palest pink, golden hair piled beneath a wide brimmed hat that was laden with pink and white roses and was tied beneath her chin with a wide silken bow. Winsome curls had escaped confinement and strayed around her long white neck. She stood, perfectly poised, her wide blue eyes taking in the scene before her. Danny had not moved; he sat as if struck to stone. Bran lolloped to his feet and went to Caroline, sniffing her skirt, tail swishing. She ignored him. Her eyes were upon Danny.

Slowly and with grace he stood. From the moment she had appeared his eyes had not left her flushed and lovely face.

'Well, well,' Caroline said, thoughtfully. 'What have we here?'

Jessica looked from one to the other.

'Mama sent me to find you,' her sister said, addressing Jessica whilst her eyes still clung to Danny's. 'We are to go to Melford after all.'

Jessica said nothing. She stood awkwardly, hands clasped childishly in front of her, rank misery rising in her heart. She looked at Danny's lifted, burnished face, lit to angel's glory by the sun, and child though she was she saw the blinding of his eyes, saw too the expression on her sister's face as she looked down at him. For a truly terrible moment she felt as if she herself must have vanished or become invisible, for neither of them glanced at her, so absorbed were they in each other.

'It's my fault, I fear,' Danny said quietly, 'I've kept Miss Jessica talking.'

Caroline inclined her head. Her eyes flicked to her sister. 'Jessica?' she prompted gently, and her eyes returned to the dark, admiring face of the young man who stood so gracefully assured before her.

'I – oh – this is D-Danilo O'Donnel,' Jessica stuttered. 'He's restoring the church for Clara's wedding. Danny – this is my sister Caroline.'

And in the brief, telling silence that followed the introduction she knew, surely and beyond doubt, that she had lost him.

Chapter Four

Jessica's first fear – that Caroline would betray her friendship with Danny to their parents – was unfounded. Her second – that the appearance of her sister upon the scene would change and in some way diminish that friendship – was not. She was not surprised when, the next time she met Danny, he questioned her closely and with undisguised eagerness about Caroline. She did not tell him that Caroline had shown almost the same degree of interest in him. 'He looks foreign – is he?' and then, pensively, 'Florence. How very romantic. What a sly little thing you are! How long have you known this young man? How did you come to meet –?'

Danny was more direct. 'She's very beautiful, your sister.'

'I suppose so.'

'Suppose?' His eyebrows winged in exaggerated astonishment. 'Oh, come, Mouse! She's like – like a flower. No. With that hair – those eyes – she's an angel – a delicate, golden angel –'

That hurt surprisingly much. Jessica pulled Bran's ear and the mongrel cocked an injured eye at her. 'She's betrothed,' she said shortly, with truth but no charity, 'to the son of a Baronet.'

'But of course, yes, she must be.' His dark face was only a shade regretful. 'Such beauty cannot have gone unclaimed. Oh, but I should like to model her. As Diana, perhaps, goddess of the moon –'

'She was a huntress, wasn't she?'

'Yes.'

Jessica shrugged, ill-temperedly. 'Caroline couldn't hit the side of Five Acre Barn from ten yards distance.'

It was inevitable that they should meet again. Sweetly, and quite clearly with the unspoken threat of betrayal beneath the suggestion, Caroline offered to accompany her sister to the church the following afternoon. '– I'm interested to see what this young man has done. Poor old St Agatha's has been allowed to decay so – I wonder he takes it on at all –'

With resignation and no comment Jessica accepted her sister's sudden interest in things artistic to say nothing of her willingness to walk a distance that normally would have brought on a fainting fit, and agreed.

'Don't sulk, Jessica dear,' Caroline said, lightly as they walked the woodland path. 'It really doesn't become you.' She flashed a swift, enragingly lovely smile at the small figure beside her. 'Don't be afraid. I'm not going to give you away.'

'Give what away?' Jessica affected indifference.

'Oh, come now – you know as well as I. This – friendship –' the gleaming blue glance was sharp, '– is hardly one of which Mama and Papa would approve, would you say?'

Jessica did not reply.

'However –' Caroline smoothed the dainty, wrist-length gloves she had insisted upon donning despite the heat, 'I'm willing to meet the young man again and judge for myself. For this once I'm sure we can chaperon each other, little sister.' Her pretty laughter pealed through the woodland, starting a flock of small birds from the branches of a nearby bush. She was dressed in blue, a fine, ankle-length gown of pale silk, the low scoop of the neck trimmed with dark pansies, as was the bonnet that framed her face. Gloves and slippers – as unsuited to woodland walking as any Jessica had ever seen – were dark blue also, and a tiny sapphire glimmered upon a fine golden chain about her neck. She looked, Jessica had to admit, quite astoundingly lovely.

Danny obviously thought so too. After the first affectionate greeting to Jessica his every glance, his every word, every scrap of his attention was for Caroline. Poor Jessica could not have felt worse had a door been slammed in her face. Miserably she watched them. There could be no denying that they made a splendid pair, the darkly handsome young man and the slender, lovely girl, deep in conversation. Caroline was inspecting the figure of St Agatha, now completely restored, and to Jessica's astonishment all artifice, all self-conscious posing had gone. There was even the faintest charming trace of shyness in her manner as she admired the work and listened to Danny's self-deprecating account of how it had been done. From the statue they moved down the church to the rood screen, and Jessica could not help but notice that the courteous hand that Danny extended to help his guest down the shadowy altar steps lingered in hers for a full moment too long. A faint blush of becoming colour stained Caroline's cheeks, and she bent her head, apparently absorbed in the intricacies of the ancient screen.

'It's very old.' Danny's oddly musical voice echoed quietly into the silence, 'probably many hundreds of years. And in its way it's as lovely a thing as I've seen anywhere – even in Florence –' His ardent eyes were not upon the screen, but upon the flushed face half-hidden by the shady brim of the blue bonnet. Caroline lifted her eyes, her lips parted to speak, then stopped, apparently struck to silence by what she saw in the dark face above her.

Unnoticed, Jessica slipped from the pew where she had been sitting and wandered dejectedly out into the fierce sunshine, leaving them together.

She rarely saw him alone after that, and on the few occasions she did it was never as it had been before. She could not help but notice the wandering of his eyes beyond her as he waited for that other figure to appear, the lifting of his head halfway through a sentence as he strained his ears to hear that other footstep. The light in his eyes when Caroline did come, the swift happiness of his smile, cut Jessica to the heart, though she never betrayed it. For strangely, after the first wrenching unhappiness that the sharing of Danny's friendship caused her, she found herself sympathizing not only with Danny but – astonishingly to her – with Caroline too. For as the endless summer days with their evenings of lingering sunshine followed in slow succession one upon another, Caroline, under the influence of Danny's warmth and laughter, changed. In Danny's company the petulance disappeared, and the vanity, and in their place stood a clear and shining happiness whose power was impossible to resist even for one who had lost by it. To see the two of them together caused in Jessica the strangest mixture of happiness and heartache; an almost welcome pain that she was perfectly ready to endure as the payment she had to make to remain a part of Danny's life, however small. As the days moved on they met more and more frequently. It became an accepted practice that, after a little while in their company, Jessica would leave them alone together and take up station somewhere not too far away, joining them again when it was time to leave. That they met alone also she knew, for she it was who carried their messages, written and verbal. She, with freedom still that Caroline did not possess, was their link, and without realizing it was becoming as fast caught in the web of their growing passion as were they. So she acted as their go-between and guarded their secret, for nothing and nobody would make her betray Danny and if he were happy then she would do anything in her power to keep him so.

And happy he was. He sang at his work and watched for Caroline with eyes shining with content and certainty.

'Ah, Mouse – do you know I truly thought it couldn't happen to me!' he laughed one day, a brotherly arm about Jessica's shoulders as they sat on the river bank and watched the slow movement of the drought-low water. 'I've seen others struck down by love, and laughed at them for fools! Now I know – oh yes! – now I know who was the fool! Caroline loves me –' He threw back his head and spoke to the bright sky. 'Caroline loves me! And I have never known happiness before –'

Jessica wriggled from beneath his arm, and knelt beside him, her small face ferociously anxious. His words – the first open declaration of anything beyond friendship – had jolted her practical nature. This, surely, was going too far? Secret meetings and shared laughter were one thing – but love?

Caroline Hawthorne and a penniless artist? She shook her head. 'Danny!'

'Mm?'

'Danny – Caroline's engaged to be married! It's all arranged –'

He laughed. 'And can be as easily unarranged, my Mouse.'

She stared at him in doubtful silence. 'Have you spoken to Caroline about that?'

Not in the least perturbed he pulled her to him again, pushing her small nose with his finger. 'Don't worry, little one. All will be well, you'll see. How could it not be? After your brother's wedding – you'll see – all will be arranged –' He stopped, lifting his head, face alight as Caroline appeared above them on the path. Swiftly he rose and ran to her. She, smiling, waited then lifted her arms to him. He swung her from her feet, then set her down and bent a dark head to kiss her.

Jessica, unnoticed, got to her feet and plodded off along the bank, leaving them to each other.

John it was who found her half an hour later, perched upon a fallen log, shoulders hunched, in the shadow of the bridge that carried the path that led to the Melford Road.

'Why, Jessica, whatever's the matter? You look as if you've lost sixpence and found a ha'penny.' He was leading Old Jenny who hobbled painfully beside him.

Jessica ducked her head. 'Nothing. Nothing's the matter.'

He tied the lame mare to the branch then pulled himself up beside her, one knee bent, his arm across it as he regarded his small sister, his pleasant sunbrowned face concerned. 'You've been crying.'

She shook her head.

'Oh, come now – you can tell me. What's upset you?'

'Nothing.' In the past half hour, on the heels of Danny's happy confidence, she had for the first time truly thought about the consequences that might well – that would – follow any attempt by Danny and Caroline to carry their association any further than it had already gone. And had, strangely for the first time, forseen disaster. She nibbled her thumb.

He watched her in pensive silence, waiting. Solid, dependable, caring; should she tell him? At least share the worry –? The urge to confide in him suddenly was so great that it frightened her. She mustn't! He was part of that world from which Danny must be protected at all costs. Danny himself did not realize his danger she was sure, and Caroline was certainly too besotted herself to warn him. If John took her tale to Father, God alone knew what might happen. Sniffing she lifted her head defiantly. She had learned young that attack was a very fair means of defence. 'You've done it again,' she said.

He looked understandably confused. 'I'm sorry?'

'You've done it again. Gone off in the direction of Lavenham and then come back from Melford. I heard Caroline say you'd gone to visit those friends of the Helys again – and they're supposed to live in Lavenham. Now you've come back this way – the wrong way – like you did the day of the storm. What are you up to? It isn't like you to lie.'

The effect of her words shocked her. Her brother stared at her in silence for what seemed a very long time, and beneath the summer tan bright colour rose in his fair skin and then as suddenly died. Then abruptly he stood up and turned from her, staring across the river, eyes brooding, saying nothing.

'John?' She was hesitantly contrite. 'I'm sorry – I didn't mean to pry – I'm sure you have good reason to –'

He shook his head sharply, as if to clear it, ran a hand through his already tousled hair. 'No. Don't apologize. It's I who should do that.' He turned back to her, leaning against the log. For the first time she noticed tired lines of strain about his eyes. He drew a long, rueful breath. 'I make a really terrible conspirator, don't I? I can't even deceive you. It really isn't my line, I suppose –'

She watched him, puzzled, truly surprised that her self-defensive stab in the dark had produced such reaction. 'You mean – you really have been going to Long Melford when you've pretended to go to Lavenham?'

'Yes.'

She laughed uncertainly. 'But – why?'

He shook his head tiredly. 'A smoke screen. Some small

defence. In case Father had happened to enquire in Melford for the Helys' acquaintances and discovered –' He stopped.

'What?' Jessica's interest was aroused now, her misery almost forgotten. As she spoke the obvious answer occurred to her, and her eyes widened. Not – surely! – another unsuitable alliance in the family? 'John! Are you – are you meeting a young lady?'

He laughed at that, honestly, shaking his head. 'Lord, Jessie, you've been spending too much time with Caroline!'

She flushed deeply at that and half turned from him, but he did not notice. 'What then?' she asked, stiffly.

He hesitated for a moment. 'Jessica – I hate to ask it, but if I tell you – will you keep a secret for me until I've had a chance to talk to Father?'

'Of course.' She was worried by the soberness of his voice. Did everybody in the world, she found herself wondering a little irritably, have a secret? 'There – isn't anything wrong, is there?'

He shook his head quickly. 'No, no. Not wrong. Just – difficult. You see – these friends I've been visiting – they're Roman Catholics.'

She could not have been more shocked had he told her he had been meeting the devil himself. '*Papists?*'

He laughed again, but the sound had little in it of humour. 'Yes, Jessica. Papists.'

'But – why?' In common with most of the rest of the population Jessica had only the vaguest notions of the beliefs and dogmas of the Roman Church. Equally in common with the rest of Protestant England she was ready to believe without question in their perfidious involvement in any evil from high treason to the punitive price of bread. Were they not by law barred from any post of authority or responsibility on account of the subversive division of their loyalties? Here was one lesson well taught by MacKenzie; if Jessica did not actually believe that the Pope sported horns and a tail beneath his priestly garb she certainly did not doubt his rapacious corruption nor his deadly and active hostility to her country. She stared at her brother, her horror clear upon her face.

John bit his lip, fighting down exasperation. 'Jessica – listen to me. You must surely realize what nonsense is talked of the Catholic religion?'

She waited, unspeaking, her worried eyes searching his face.

'Catholic Englishmen are as true as you or I. The laws against them are outrageous and outdated. They are no more traitors than is a man who takes a different political stand from his neighbours —'

'They're foreigners.'

'Of course they aren't! The Bartletts are as old a local family as are the FitzBoltons! They simply follow the old religion — the faith of their fathers —'

'They go to Mass!' she spoke in hushed tones, generations of distrust and unspeakable rumours in the word.

'Oh, don't be silly! For the first time impatience showed. 'What do you think Mass is? Do you think we sacrifice little babies and drink their blood? Truly, Jessica, I had credited you with a little more —' he stopped.

'We?' she repeated.

He let out a long breath. 'Yes. We,' he said, quietly. 'That is why I ask you, just for a little while, to keep my secret. I have to tell Father myself that I intend to become a Roman Catholic.'

'But — you're to be a priest!'

'Yes. I am. A Roman Catholic priest, if God wills. And I pray He does.'

There was a long, speaking silence. 'Father will kill you,' she said, flatly, at last.

He chewed on his lip, shook his head. Even to Jessica his uncertainty and fear — not emotions she would have believed until now could be experienced by her almost grown-up brother — were obvious, and her heart lurched in sympathetic anguish. 'He will!' she said with urgent certainty. 'John, please! Why must you do this? You know what awful trouble there'll be —'

'Yes. I do know.' He pushed himself away from the log, moving heavily, stood for a moment, hands in pockets, looking down at her with abstracted eyes. 'I can't help it, Jessie,' he said after a moment. 'I have to. To me the Roman

Church is the true Christian Church. It isn't something I wanted to believe – it just happened. But I can't deny it. My mind, my heart – my soul – tell me the truth. I have to follow them.'

'But –'

He shook his head, silencing her.

She scrambled from the log and stood beside him. 'Don't tell him! I won't tell a soul – I promise!' The words all but fell over each other in her hurry to get them out. 'There's no reason to tell him yet. Wait for a while –' She could think of nothing but the certain holocaust of her father's rage if he discovered John's resolve. And if, beyond that, he found out about Danny and Caroline –

John shook his head regretfully. 'It's no good, Jess. I'll have to tell him, and soon. Too many people know already. If he should hear it from someone else –'

'What do you mean – too many people?' She was puzzled. 'It's only you and me – and I've already said that I –'

'No. The Bartletts know. And, more importantly, so does Clara –'

'*Clara?*' She could not hide her astonishment. 'How on earth –?'

John walked to where Old Jenny patiently stood, head down, forefoot bent. 'The FitzBoltons have friends in Long Melford. Cousins of the Bartletts. Clara saw me visiting. And guessed, I think. She asked me outright what my business with them was –'

'And you *told* her?'

He shrugged. 'As I said – when it comes to it I'm really not good at deception. Yes. I told her.'

'When?'

'Oh – a week since, perhaps more.'

Jessica's brow was furrowed. 'And she hasn't said anything? To Father? Or – to Giles?'

He shook his head. 'Why should she?'

She stared at him in grim silence. Then, 'Why shouldn't she?' she asked. Try as she might she could not believe that anything Clara FitzBolton did would be done in loving kindness or unselfish thought for others. 'It isn't like Clara.'

He smiled a little. '"Judge not that ye may not be judged",' he quoted, softly. 'Charity, Jessica. Perhaps in expecting the worst you draw the worst from her. She has no reason to betray me.'

Then she must have a reason not to. From consideration for her brother rather than in any response to his admonition Jessica did not voice the thought.

John untied the limping Jenny. 'I must get poor Jenny home. She's the reason I risked the short cut across the bridge – she fell lame as I left Melford. It would have been too cruel to force her all the way round to the Lavenham Road just to service my deceptions. So I came the shorter way.'

'And met me. John – I'm sorry I questioned you. I wish I hadn't now, if it makes you act in haste. Won't you please – *please* – leave telling Father for a while?' She laid a hand on the horse's rein, preventing him from leaving. Jenny nuzzled her shoulder. 'Just a little while?'

He hesitated.

'If you hadn't told me you'd have waited, wouldn't you?'

'I –'

'Please! For me!' Her small face was desperately solemn. 'I shall feel it's my fault if there's terrible trouble – and there will be, you know it –'

'Then what's the point of putting it off?' he asked, not unreasonably.

'Something may happen. Something may change. Oh – I don't know! But, please, John, don't tell him until you have to? At least leave it until after the wedding?'

He wavered, and she sensed it.

'Please?'

He nodded. 'All right. If it makes you feel better. I'll wait at least till then.'

And with that, guilt gnawing at her at the thought of the hornet's nest her curiosity may have stirred up, she had to be content. It was a very pensive Jessica who rejoined Danny and Caroline on the river bank later that afternoon. Though it was no great surprise to her that neither of them noticed her mood.

*

Her brother's revelation caused Jessica considerable anxiety – and by no means simply because of the certain trouble that it promised. No matter how she tried she could not rid herself of the MacKenzie-inspired image of the Papists as degenerate and soulless traitors and the Pope as the Devil incarnate. That John of all people should be considering allying himself with such outcasts appalled her. Her desperate plea to put off telling their father had been as much in the hope that given time he might change his mind than in any real belief that there might come an easier time to break the news, but somehow she sensed that this hope was in vain. With no-one to confide in her worries nibbled away in her mind like rats gnawing at a bone. In becoming a Papist, was there not a danger that John was damning his soul for ever? Should she not try to prevent that? Should she not try to dissuade him, or to ask for others' help in dissuading him? And in becoming –of all things! – a Roman priest, would he be cut off from them all entirely? Providing of course, she reflected bleakly, he survived that long once their father discovered what was in his mind! Suddenly she found she was missing Robert, more than ever. With him away she had no-one to talk to, no-one to help her. The world had changed, too quickly and a little frighteningly. She was the guardian of the secrets of others, and she wasn't at all sure that she liked it. When, for heaven's sake, would Robert be coming home?

A summons to her mother's sitting room, where a note had been delivered for Jessica from Old Hall, raised her hopes. This must surely be news of his homecoming? She broke open the seal upon the note, which had been enclosed with his last letter to his parents.

'What is it, my dear?' Her mother was watching her narrowly, 'Is something wrong?'

Dully Jessica shook her head. Damn! Damn and damn and damn – ! 'Robert isn't coming home after all.' Those Dresden-figure sisters! 'The Alloways are going to Bath to take the waters and he is to go with them.'

'He'll be home for the wedding, of course?'

Jessica glanced back at the note. 'He says he hopes to be,

yes.' Hopes to be. She was to be Clara's chief maid, in a dress of dark cream lace that even her mother had said suited her well. She had not until that moment realized how she had banked upon Robert being in the congregation, how she had anticipated his surprise at the new, grown-up Jessica as she accompanied his sister to the altar. She'd kill him if he didn't come! Damn and damn and damn!

'He's having a nice time, then?'

'Yes.' Jessica stopped, then with characteristic honesty corrected herself. 'That is – I'm not sure.'

'Oh?'

Jessica once more ran her eyes over the brief note. 'He says he's having a very nice time. But –'

'But what?' There was a faint, hidden amusement in her mother's eyes.

Forgetting herself, Jessica lifted a baffled shoulder. 'I don't know. It's hard to explain. He *says* he's happy. But he doesn't sound it.'

'Don't shrug, Jessica.' The admonition was automatic and carried no edge. Her mother stood. 'It won't be so long before he's back,' she said. 'I'm perfectly sure he won't want to miss his sister's wedding. And then you can discover for yourself, can't you? Now – run along. I have letters to write.'

By the end of July the haymaking was done and everyone on the estate was preparing for the harvest. It was with something of a shock that Jessica realized that the hay was in and the stacks built with no help from her at all. Every other year of her childhood this had been her favourite time. Though never allowed into the fields where the scythes were being used to cut the standing grass, she and Robert would sit for hours upon a gate, or in the shade of a tree and watch the rhythmic movement of the lines of workers as they stepped and cut, stepped and cut, the hay falling with almost magic precision into neat swathes behind them. From the lifting of the dew in the morning to the falling of the dew in the evening the workers laboured, with just an hour at midday for rest and food. Ale or barley-water, bread and cheese – how many times had she and Robert shared the contents of a good-natured haymaker's wallet? And how many times, enthusiastically, had they begged to help with the raking and stacking? But not this year. This year, with Robert away and her friendship with Danny to absorb her the haymaking had come and gone and she had hardly noticed its passing. The hot weather had sapped her energy. She no longer ran everywhere. Even poor Bran's exuberance sometimes got on her nerves. What was wrong with her? Even the prospect of harvest barely excited her at all. She had no great desire to run to Lower Meadow and watch as the wagons carrying the itinerant workers arrived. Each year more or less the same families came to New Hall, and many of the children Jessica had seen and played with each August for all of her short life. Last year she had looked forward to renewing the acquaintance of old friends. This year, however, an odd constraint held her apart from them, a constraint exaggerated by the discovery that the boys – and indeed some of the girls – were now old enough to be out working in the fields, whilst the other girls stayed in the work camp to care for younger brothers and sisters. It was almost a new generation of barefoot youngsters who scampered and tumbled, shrieking and screaming, about the camp. The first day Jessica bumped into a boy called Charlie Best, with whom the year before she had had a royal battle that had culminated in a bloody nose and a whipping from Mac-Kenzie, he touched his cap and grunted a grudging 'Good morning', his eyes averted; and she had acknowledged his greeting and passed on almost before she had realized who he was. The incident disturbed her. She wandered, aimless and alone, by the river, a strange melancholy upon her. In the distance Caroline and Danny sat, hand in hand, each totally absorbed in the other. With the whole estate seething with the activity of harvest their secret meetings had become both more frequent and less careful. Jessica was astonished at her sister; never before had she known her take any kind of risk – for Caroline, spoiled, pretty, rich, secure, had never been one to hazard change or trouble. A short month before Jessica would have staked her life that Caroline would never have courted disaster nor acted rashly for the sake of a penniless young man, however handsome. Yet here she was undoubtedly doing both.

Jessica sat beside the water, tossed a small twig into the current and watched as it turned and was slowly carried away by the muddy stream. Oddly, her back ached a little, and so did her head. She rubbed her forehead impatiently. Vaguely she wondered if she might be sickening for something, and for a strange, brief moment the thought of a childish illness, rest in her comfortable bed, Lucy fussing about her with pills and potions, her mother visiting, cool and sweet-smelling, was ridiculously seductive.

She straightened her aching back. What in the world was wrong with her? Why wasn't she running in the fields, as she had every other year? Why this odd depression of spirit, that was so unlike her? Her eyes turned again to where Caroline sat with Danny, laughing, her head on his shoulder, and she was filled with a sudden painful yearning so strong that she felt the rise of self-pitying tears – and there was another question; why lately, did the tears rise so easily – tears that such a short time ago she would have died before shedding? She swallowed fiercely. Her heart had started to thud, and a small, sickly pain stabbed in her abdomen. Was she truly ill? Trottie Smith, down in the village, had been just her age when she'd died last year –

Miserably she hunched her shoulders. Where was Robert? How dared he stay away so long –!

When the blood came that night she was terrified. At her small, choked scream Lucy came running.

'Lucy! I'm bleeding! I'm bleeding! What's wrong with me? Am I going to die like Trottie did –?'

'Why, bless you, no – 'tis your monthlies started, tha'ss all. 'Tis part of growin' up, Miss Jessie, an' it comes to us all.'

Jessica was still choking on frightened sobs. 'What do you mean?'

Lucy put a comforting arm about her. 'Why, little love, like I said, it happens to us all. 'Tis sent from God.'

Jessica was horribly confused. 'What is? What do you mean?'

'Why the bleeding. Once a month a woman bleeds – 'cept when she's breeding, that is –'

'You mean – everyone? You? Mother? – Caroline?' Jessica was totally astonished. 'How – how long does it last? What must I do? Why doesn't it hurt, if it's bleeding –?'

Lucy stood up. 'I'll find you some rags and make you comfortable. Tomorrow I dare say the Miss will explain.'

MacKenzie did explain. Her face blotched red with embarrassment she explained that a woman's monthly flow was a curse brought down to atone for womankind's original sin in the Garden of Eden.

Jessica, her first panic subsided, was sceptical. 'But what's it for?'

'For? I told you – it's to remind you of the wickedness of Eve! To remind you to pray that such sin does not claim you –'

'Lucy says a woman's bleeding stops when she's breeding. Why's that?'

MacKenzie was outraged. 'Does she indeed?' Her thin lips pinched to a furious line.

'Well – does it?'

'Enough of this, Miss. You've heard all you need to hear –'

'But –'

'But nothing! Now attend me! You're a young woman now – you note, I hope that I don't use the word lady?' She added, 'Once and for all your wild ways will have to stop now. You understand me?'

Cowed for the moment despite herself, Jessica nodded. She did not as it happened at the moment feel in the least bit wild. Her stomach ached and her insides felt sore.

'Things have changed, Miss.' MacKenzie folded pious hands, 'and you must change with them, whether you will it or no.'

As she stalked from the room, there was still enough rebellion in Jessica to give rise to the happy thought that, surely, if this strange event somehow marked her passage from childhood to womanhood there was every possibility that the days of governesses must surely now be numbered –?

With the weather holding well the harvest was in quickly that year, and from the middle of September, inevitably, the business of Giles' and Clara's wedding took over both houses entirely. Never had Jessica seen such preparations, not even for the May masque. Every bedroom in New Hall – and there were more than twenty of them – was opened and aired, ready for guests. The reception rooms were cleaned and polished to perfection. The kitchens were a picture of constant if controlled turmoil: every other moment, or so it seemed, Maria Hawthorne was called upon to mediate in the state of total warfare that had been declared between M. Bonnard and Mrs Benson – Mrs Benson announcing often and loudly to anyone who would listen that the French chef was undoubtedly a Napoleonic spy, and as such should certainly be shot. The argument that her rival had been resident in England for more than thirty years and regarded himself in everything but his art as an Englishman cut no ice with her at all.

At Old Hall both the excitement and the preparations were of a different nature. It was no secret that Sarah FitzBolton had been a little hurt by her daughter's break with tradition in holding the wedding breakfast at her new home rather than her old. Inconvenience and cost notwithstanding the event might have been expected to be held at Old Hall. When William Hawthorne had suggested, however, that the ball-room at New Hall might be a more suitable venue Clara, with no consultation with her parents, had accepted the offer with what seemed to Jessica quite heartless pleasure. And so, at Old Hall, there was not the bustle of expectation that there was at the newer house, though certainly some far-flung relatives would be attending and would be afforded rooms and entertainment in the FitzBolton house. Jessica, herself, as the bride's chief maid, would spend the night before the wedding at Old Hall, to be on hand for her duties the next morning. The wedding was to be at nine o'clock, and the bride, her attendants and her family, weather permitting, were to walk the river path to the church, as many a FitzBolton bride had done before. A splendid carriage, a wedding present from William Hawthorne, would be waiting to carry the newly-weds the distance to New Hall after the ceremony. Clara's dress – sumptuous white silk brocade trimmed with silver and pearls – was a lovely thing, that emphasized her slenderness and the austere grace of her carriage and contrasted strikingly with her raven hair. Yet for all its beauty, the first time Jessica saw Clara dressed in it she felt that same vague and jarring sense of wrongness that had plagued her feelings about Giles and Clara ever since she had seen them together in the woods. Standing, tall and composed, in the gleaming silver-trimmed silk, Clara lacked only her icicle crown to recreate the ice-queen of the May masque. Jessica could not help but wonder if that were an appropriate impression to be conveyed by a young bride. She showed no great excitement, no impulsive warmth or worry about the coming ceremony. Cool, collected and apparently utterly nerveless she organized her always disorganized parents, consulted with Maria about guest lists and menus, sorted and stacked presents as if a wedding were a perfectly everyday affair.

Two days before the great day Robert, at last, came home. Jessica was at Old Hall with his family to greet him, her eagerness to see him overcoming at the last moment her desire to demonstrate her absolute indifference to his long absence. The hired carriage which had met him from the stage was late.

Jessica, who had left Caroline and Danny at the church together – Caroline having with devious and graceless design assumed charge of the floral decorations for the ceremony could, for these few days at least, visit the place openly – wandered the rabbit-warren of Old Hall fighting impatience. In the lovely, ancient Old Drawing Room, hardly ever used by the family who preferred the more modern suite of rooms on the south side of the house, she knelt for a while in the great oriel window that overlooked the courtyard, watching the activity below through the old glass that yellowed and diffused the images as if she were looking through water. Then restlessly she wandered to the piano that she had so often heard Robert play, lifting the lid and striking the notes at random with one finger, listening as the sound echoed to the high, ornamented ceiling. Then, in the distance, she heard the sound of a carriage. Slamming the lid she flew from the door and down the wide, dark staircase with its ranked portraits to the courtyard. And there he was, neat, pale, collected, smiling at her exuberance.

All her carefully contrived airy speeches deserted her. 'Oh, Robert – I'm so very glad you're back –'

They had no chance to talk privately that day. With his family she heard his account of his time in Devon, the visit to Bath, the general delightfulness of the Aloway family – though try as she might as she listened to the general conversation a relieved Jessica could discover no indication of any special attachment to a particular member. It was however after supper on the eve of the wedding before she spoke to him alone.

It was the sound of the piano that drew her to the Old Drawing Room, where she had watched for him the day before. In the dark hall at the foot of the grand staircase she listened. The music cascaded, passionate and lyrical; it could, she knew, be no-one but Robert playing. She climbed the stairs, shadowed and as yet unlit, then stopped on the landing outside the door, oddly hesitant about interrupting. Then the music stopped, very suddenly, halfway through a phrase, and in the silence she heard the snap of the lid and sharp footsteps clipping upon the wooden floor, coming towards the door.

'Robert?'

He stood framed in the open doorway, small, slight, neat as a girl, his face in shadows. 'Oh, hello Jessica.'

Determinedly she ignored the lack of enthusiasm. 'We haven't had a chance to talk since you came home.'

'No.' The word was abstracted.

She ploughed on. 'It's been ages. I've tons to tell you.' The evening sun that glimmered through the huge stained glass window, into each pane of which had been inserted the ancient arms of FitzBolton and the families allied to them over the years, filled the stairwell with a strange, lucently colourful light. On impulse Jessica sat down on the top stair. 'Let's stay here for a minute. The house is so full of people there's nowhere else to go.'

Slowly he crossed the landing and in silence sat beside her, his arms loosely linked about his bent knees. She waited. After a moment he turned his head and smiled at her, the odd restraint dropping from him. 'Right. Here I am. Fire away. What's been happening while I've been gone?'

She was furious to find herself suddenly and ridiculously tongue-tied. What had been happening? The world had changed, that was all. And so had she. 'I – well – not much, really –' she found herself saying lamely. 'The – the harvest was good. And Bunty had kittens. Five of them. Bran's learned that he's supposed to drop things when he fetches them. And one of the stable boys broke a leg when he took a fall from Bellingham Lad. Father says the horse is a menace and has to be sold. I think it was the boy's own fault. I can ride the Lad without falling off.'

He nodded.

'What – what about you?'

'Me?'

'Devon. How was it? Really, I mean.'

He looked away. 'All right.'

'Only all right?'

He had to laugh at her persistence. 'Very all right. I enjoyed myself.' He hesitated. 'Paul is a very good friend, and his parents are charming.'

'And the others?'

'What others?'

'I thought he had – oh, brothers and sisters and things?'

'Oh, yes. Sisters. They're very agreeable.'

For the life of her she could read nothing into that. Exasperated she subsided into silence for a while. Then, 'Robert?' she asked, tentatively, 'can I ask you something?'

He cocked an enquiring brow.

'Do you know – that is –' she stumbled on the words, started again, 'Do you know much about the Roman Catholic Church?'

He looked at her in surprise. 'Good Lord! What a funny question!'

She did not look at him. 'Well, do you? I mean – Mac-Kenzie's been talking. You know how awful she is. Are the Papists really as wicked as all that?'

He laughed outright. 'Oh, of course not! It's all a lot of nonsense!'

She stared.

'The Church of Rome,' he said, patiently, 'lays claim – justifiably, whether we like it or not – to being the original Church of Christ –'

'But –'

He held up a hand. 'You asked me. At least let me finish. I'm no expert, of course, but I've often heard Papa talk of it. Over the years the Church became very rich and very powerful. Too rich. Too powerful. It meddled in politics. It made enemies. Many would say it abused its position; but that has nothing to do with the ordinary man or woman who follows its teachings because he or she believes that, right or wrong in its fallible human state, it is the Church that was founded by Christ.'

Her eyes were huge in the half-dark. 'If that's true, why aren't we all Catholics?'

'Because men fought for the right to worship in their own fashion. Because, in some cases, it was politic to break with Rome. Because there was money and land to be confiscated. Because good men were outraged at the thought that forgiveness could be bought with a handful of gold coins. Because Henry the Eighth wanted another wife and another alliance. Lord, Jessica, there are a million reasons! Father thinks – and I believe him – that it's possible, probable even, that England would have taken up the Protestant cause sooner or later, Henry the Eighth or no. As a nation the excesses of an extreme church simply doesn't suit us. But that's not to say that those that worship in a different fashion are wrong.'

There was a depth of puzzlement in her eyes and her voice. 'But – MacKenzie says –'

'Oh, forget what MacKenzie says!' For the first time the words were impatient. 'Use your brain! You can't sensibly believe that every Roman Catholic is some kind of seditious devil steeped in wickedness? It's utter nonsense. There are good and bad in the Church of Rome as there are in any other religion or organization. To persecute them makes no sense.'

'But the law of the land –?'

'Is wrong. It's outdated and stupid.'

'That's what –' She pulled herself up, aware of how close she had come to mentioning her brother's name. Hastily, and with real curiosity in her voice she asked, 'Well, what are the differences? There must be some?'

'Of course there are. And they're very basic. The main theological difference is transubstantiation –'

'Whatever's that?'

'Catholics believe that at every Mass the bread and the wine of Communion is turned into the actual Body and Blood of Our Lord –'

'How can that be?'

He shrugged. 'Exactly. That's what people began to ask. A miracle at every Mass? Well – I couldn't be persuaded. But I have nothing against those that are. Why should I?'

'What else?'

'Let me see. Their priests don't marry, of course. And there's the Pope. To Catholics he is the spiritual and moral leader of the world – which is fine I suppose if you have a good one and not so good if you don't. In England, of course the king – mad as he is – is head of Church and State. That's why, politically, Catholics are often suspect – there's always the worry that their loyalty to a foreign Pope will overcome their alliegance to their country. It's really nothing to do with dogma or theology. Jessica, what is all this? You've never shown the least bit of interest in religion before –?'

She shrugged, but did not answer.

He waited, watching her in the half-dark. 'Well – have I answered your question? Is there anything else you wanted to know?'

She shook her head. Then, 'Just – supposing someone – supposing I – were to become a Catholic –'

'Convert, you mean?'

'Yes. Would you say – my soul would be damned?'

'Good heavens no! But – Jessica! – you surely aren't –?'

'No! Of course not! Don't be silly. I just wanted to know what you thought, that's all. I've really no-one else to talk to. I'm afraid my parents aren't as open-minded as yours.'

He grinned in acknowledgement of that, and she smiled back, relieved to see the sudden relaxing of tension in him. 'When do you go back to school? You've missed the first part of term, haven't you?'

The smile left his face as suddenly as if a lamp had been extinguished. He turned from her, hunching his shoulders very slightly. 'I'm not going back.'

She was truly shocked. 'You're – what?'

'I'm not going back. Not to St Paul's anyway. There's no point.' He cleared his throat. The forced evenness of his tone grated the nerves.

Jessica was shaking her head, bemused. 'I don't believe it. I don't understand. What are you saying?'

He snapped at her. 'Jessica, don't you ever think of anyone's problems but your own – don't you ever see what's right under your nose –?'

That stung unfairly and she blinked, surprised and hurt.

'I'm not going back to school,' he said, slowly and clearly, 'because my voice has begun to break. I can't sing any more.'

She stared at him in silence, all words fled.

He stood up, his slight figure a shadow in the growing darkness.

'Will you – will you be able to sing again? Afterwards, I mean?'

Faintly she saw the slow negative movement of his head. 'I don't know. But somehow I suspect not. It's finished, I think. Finished.' He stood for a long moment in lonely and brooding silence before turning and walking back into the Old Drawing Room. Frozen where she sat she heard the piano start again, hesitantly, then stronger, then crashing to silence in a discord that made her flinch.

Opposite where she sat, lit by the last of the dying light, a portrait hung: an earlier FitzBolton, foppish and elegant in the style of his times, in his hands a stringed instrument that, neglected and dusty, now hung on the wall of the Old Drawing Room. Robert had told her that family tradition had it that he had inherited his voice and his musical talent from this great-uncle. Jessica had never actually much cared for the portrait,

something in the guarded eyes, the self-consciously effemin-
ate pose raising her hackles each time she saw it. 'Great-uncle
Cecil,' Robert was fond of saying, 'has a lot to answer for.'

Above her in the drawing room the piano began to play
again, softly melancholy.

She woke at dawn to the gleam of a red sunrise and the song of
birds. With her mind at rest about John after her conversation
the evening before with Robert she had slept well and was
refreshed and excited. The house was still; not even the
servants were stirring yet. Unable to lie still she sat up,
tousling her tangled hair with her fingers. In the corner of the
shadowed room hung the lovely dark cream silk and lace dress
that she was to wear that day as Clara's chief maid. She slipped
from the bed and drew back the curtains then padded across
the cold floor on bare feet to look at the dress. It was certainly
the loveliest thing she had ever possessed, and she knew that it
suited her. Carefully she lifted it from the hanger and held it to
her, peering in the long mirror. In honour of the day and her
part in it she was to be allowed to wear her hair up, beneath a
small circlet of pale roses that matched those that Clara would
carry. And Giles had given her a maid's-present of a silver
bracelet, a pretty thing that shone and jingled on her wrist as
she moved.

She drew a small, explosive breath of excitement and
danced a few steps, the dress drifting against her bare legs
beneath the short summer nightgown she wore. In an hour or
so Lucy would come to help her dress and to do her hair. Then
she was to go to attend upon Clara, to make herself as useful as
might be necessary as the young bride made her toilette. After
that would come the short procession to St Agatha's, where
Giles, the family and their guests would be waiting. Jessica
had been instructed minutely as to her duties once the bride
entered the church. Apart from keeping a stern eye upon the
two small cousins that were to be Clara's other attendants she
would hold Clara's fan, scent bottle and bouquet during the
ceremony and should help Clara remove her gloves when the
time came for Giles to place the ring upon her finger.

Traditionally the gloves then would be hers, a gift from the bride to her maid. Ruefully she surveyed her small fingers with their flat, square nails; there was never a likelihood that Clara's elegant gloves would fit that hand! She must sign the church register as a witness, and then would ride in the grand new carriage, attending bride and groom, back to New Hall and the wedding breakfast. All in all it was a heady prospect: characteristically impatient the next hour stretched endlessly. She could not – she simply could not! – sit here twiddling her thumbs until Lucy came.

She ran to the window. The brightening sky was red as blood in the east, and streaked angrily with cloud, but nevertheless the sun shone and the sky above was blue. Impulsively she pulled on her old dress and boots, threw a woollen shawl about her shoulders and slipped out of the door. Downstairs there was movement now as the house came to life; the clatter of a pail, heavy footfalls on the flagstoned floors. She ran across the courtyard, greeting a sleepy and surprised-looking maid gaily, then she was over the bridge and running along the river path. The air was exhilaratingly cool, and fresh with the first breath of autumn. In moments her feet were soaked in the dew-laden grass. The rising sun glinted jewel-like between the trees as she ran. She paused at Danny's cottage. It was shuttered and still, no smoke yet rose from the chimney. Danny was still a-bed. She skipped on, past the church and down to the lakeside. The water was a glimmering sheet of silver tinted dramatically with rosy fire. Water-birds paddled by the shore, swallows and martins, gathering for their end-of-summer flight, swooped across the glittering surface. She blinked her eyes, dazzled. A gust of wind danced through the trees, rattling the leaves that were touched already by the first flame colours of autumn.

In the distance, around the curve of the lake's shore, a movement, barely perceptible, caught her eye. She frowned, screwing up her eyes against the shifting light and shade. Then she saw it again and perceived in the dappled shadows a horse and rider. She recognized at once Belle's handsome lines, and for a moment the sun shone clear on Giles' bare yellow head.

He sat, a living statue, staring out across the bloodied, wind-rippled waters, and with a quick pang of pain Jessica guessed that he was thinking of Edward: Edward, who should on this happy day have been his younger brother's groomsman, who would have laughed kissing the lovely bride, his own childhood sweetheart. Edward, who was a year dead.

She blinked against the swift and unexpected rise of tears. The sound of the weir was muffled by the wind that gusted through the trees; the deadly currents that had taken Edward, and so nearly claimed Giles as he had struggled to save his brother, barely rippled the smooth and shining waters. Abruptly, then, as Jessica watched, horse and rider wheeled and plunged at reckless speed down the woodland path towards New Hall. The sound of Belle's hooves echoed back to Jessica for a moment, then died. Disturbed, the waterfowl fluttered and fussed, one of them squawking indignantly with what sounded like manic laughter as it paddled away from the source of the commotion.

The wind shivered again through the woodlands. Jessica pulled her shawl about her shoulders and, shrugging off sadness, turned back to Old Hall, to the cream lace dress and to what promised to be the most exciting day of her young life.

By the time they set out for the church the sun was high enough for warmth and the October wind had settled for the moment to a fresh breeze. Along the path, watchers had materialized – villagers and servants wearing white bridal favours waved and called as the wedding party passed. At his cottage gate Danny leaned, waiting. White ribbons streamed from the hawthorn that grew in the yard and he wore a huge white rose in his buttonhole. Clara smiled a little and inclined her head at the sight of the prettily decorated tree. Danny blew her an impudent kiss, and then directed another at Jessica, who blushed like a poppy. He smiled, white teeth flashing against dark skin, and her heart skipped a beat in that now familiar, achingly pleasurable way, and then they were past and approaching the church. The breeze played with the wisp of gauzy train that drifted from the back of Clara's silver headdress. Annabella, one of the small cousins, sweetly dressed in two shades of blue, a little straw basket of rose petals clutched in her plump and dimpled hand, stumbled upon the path and almost fell. At considerable risk to her own dignity Jessica grabbed her before she could sprawl full length and set her back upon her feet, righting the basket and putting a stop to easy tears. Clara did not turn; did not indeed even appear to notice the small commotion. Her head was lifted, her striking features composed. The smallest of smiles hovered about her mouth, her eyes were fixed on the open door of the church. Jessica had the notion that had the world in that moment splintered into flame it would not have prevented Clara FitzBolton from joining the man who waited within at the altar rail.

The church was packed, the whispering, shifting shadows of the congregation making the building seem even smaller than usual. As Clara appeared at the door faces turned, smiling, and the murmuring grew. St Agatha's shone, the altar decked with silver and gold, lit by a hundred wax candles, and fragrant with flowers. As the bride stepped over the threshold voices were raised in a triumphant anthem. Beside the altar rail Giles stood. He too turned as his bride entered, his face pale and strained in the candlelight. Remembering the scene she had witnessed that morning by the lake it occurred to Jessica to wonder if he had slept at all that night. Then the music died, the priest stepped forward and the ceremony, simple and straightforward, began. When the moment came for Jessica to help her brother's bride to remove her long kid gloves so that Giles might slip the ring upon her finger she was astonished to discover that Clara's hands were ice-cool and steady as rock, whilst her own were overwarm and shaky. As she fumbled with the tiny buttons on the gloves Clara, smiling that same small, imperturbable smile with calm deliberation undid each of the minute pearl fastenings and then stripped the gloves herself from her slim wrists and hands, handing them to Jessica without once taking her eyes from Giles' face. Jessica, glancing at her brother, was surprised to see that his hands, that held the ring, were trembling worse than her own. The faint, secret smile still on her lips Clara gently guided his hand

and slipped her finger through the golden circlet that made her his wife. Left to himself Jessica was certain that her usually assured brother would have dropped it. And then the bells were ringing, joyful in the rising wind, as man and wife were joined before God, till death should part them.

They rode to New Hall, to the bride-cake and the wedding breakfast, along flower-strewn paths. In the Long Gallery in the west wing a feast fit for princes was laid, whilst in the grounds outside servants and villagers celebrated the young master's marriage and the return at last to New Hall of a FitzBolton bride. Ale and wine were supplied in vast quantities – a suspicious amount of the wine French, and certainly smuggled – and the food was plentiful and good. Dressed in their Sunday best the country folk toasted the young couple and told ribald stories of weddings past. Children scrambled and shrieked, were petted and slapped; their granddams settled beneath the trees, ale glass in hand, to watch the dancing. Old Guy the fiddler, supplied with jug after jug of liquid sustenance, outdid himself, and as the gentlefolk rose from a meal that had taken a full four hours to get through the country dances were in full and energetic swing.

Jessica, her duties done and her head swimming just a little, confusingly but by no means unpleasantly, from the wine she had drunk, stood on the terrace and watched the celebrations on the lawns beneath her. Girls, bright-faced, colourful skirts swinging in the wind, danced in a circle, ducking and weaving about the clapping young men who called and shouted as they danced. The fiddler's music, infectious and gay, had even the old folk stamping in time. Around her on the terrace the house-guests watched, hands clapping, feet tapping, caught by the music and the easy laughter. A young man near Jessica, unable to resist longer, caught a village girl by the hand and swung her, shrieking laughter and insincere protest, into the circle. As if at a signal others followed, some with their own partners, some with strangers. Village boys that had been standing about the lawns, extended with great daring work-stained, roughened hands to the gentler-born girls who stood on the terrace above them. Some refused. Others, more adventurous, did not. The circle widened and split into two, until the lawns were a kaleidoscope of changing patterns and colour. Jessica, dying to join in, hopped from foot to foot. And then she saw Danny pushing his way through the crowd towards her. She held her breath. Could it be – could it? – that he was going to ask her to dance?

From behind her then she heard Caroline's voice, strangely sharp, discordant with nerves. 'No, Bunty! No! I don't want to dance!'

'Oh, come on, Carrie-oh! Don't be a spoilsport!' The Honorable Bunty Standish all but knocked Jessica from her feet as he dragged his protesting future wife down the steps of the terrace and into the dance. Caroline's face was like thunder.

Danny stopped. Jessica almost choked with disappointment. Then he came on, smiling, hand outstretched. 'A dance, Lady Mouse?'

They swung into yet another circle.

'You look – enchanting,' he said.

The roses of her headdress were shedding their petals and the cloud of her hair was tumbling about her shoulders. 'Really?' She so wanted to believe him.

'Really,' he said.

They had no breath for more. He caught her hands and swung her giddily. Above her on the terrace she caught sight of Robert, watching them, his face alight with laughter. Then the line broke and, hand in alternate hand, they danced in a great chain, the boys in one direction the girls in the other, stopping now and then and at random to link arms and swing wildly. Smiling faces passed her in a blur; blue eyes and brown, fair skin and dark. Strong hands caught her, swung her, released her and passed on. Ahead of her she saw Caroline, and as her sister turned her head she saw again the signs of fierce ill-temper. For the first time it struck her that she had hardly seen her sister smile all day. Did she really find it that hard to surrender the limelight to Clara for this short space of time? Caroline was dressed in sapphire blue, her pale skin, untouched by the summer's sun, gleamed like pearl. But there was a set and unhappy line to her mouth.

The music was slowing a little. A young man swung Jessica almost from her feet, then handed her on to another. The sun had disappeared behind a lowering cloud and the wind was cool on her burning cheeks. Danny was coming, moving up the line towards her; but no – towards Caroline. She it was he reached first, and instead of dancing past he caught her about the waist, laughing easily, and lifted her from her feet, swinging her high in the air to the delighted applause of the onlookers.

Caroline's reaction was extraordinary. As he set her gently on her feet she pulled away from him, obviously furious. He laid a conciliatory hand upon her arm. She shook it off, the angry words she shouted lost in the hubbub around them. Oblivious, the other dancers danced on. Scarlet-faced Caroline turned and pushed through the crowd, up the steps of the terrace and, without a backward glance, into the house. Danny was left looking after her; hurt, surprise and a certain anger in his face. Then a pretty girl, only too pleased, caught his hand and drew him back into the circle. Yet his eyes, Jessica saw, remained fixed on the spot where Caroline had disappeared.

Jessica, panting in a most unladylike way, her hair thoroughly and irrecoverably unpinned, found herself caught by a pair of hard hands, the face that belonged to them vaguely familiar. 'Beats trying to knock each other into fits, eh?' The swarthy young man laughed, and then she recognized him.

'Charlie Best!' she panted, close to indignation, 'I owe you a bloody nose!'

'Dance with me instead,' he said with subversive and ale-fed brashness. 'It'll be a month of long Sundays before we get another chance!'

By the time the newly-weds were ready to depart the long-threatened deterioration in the weather was almost upon them. Building clouds had obscured the sun, early darkness shadowed the landscape and the wind gusted, cold now and unpleasant. Across the empty lawns overlooking the lake litter lifted and tumbled in the wind. Small flocks of birds pecked at the crumbs in the grass and on the trestle tables that were cluttered with dishes, plates, glasses and beakers. All attention had moved to the front of the house and the carriage that waited to take Clara and Giles on their wedding trip, to London and then to Brighton to view the progress of the Prince Regent's idiosyncratic new toy and to enjoy the bracing sea air. Changed into a travelling costume of warm brown velvet trimmed with gold, Clara was radiant, poised beside her handsome husband, her hand lightly and possessively on his arm. Giles looked tired – relieved, Jessica guessed, to have the celebrations over. She had heard that a wedding traditionally was the bride's occasion; and that it was neither unusual nor unnatural for the groom to wish it past. Perhaps this was true?

The guests gathered to see them off. The courtyard was aswarm with well-wishers, and the mile-long drive lined with servants, estate workers and villagers.

Caroline was nowhere to be seen.

Standing at the top of the steps in her place of honour as chief maid, a white satin slipper in her hand, Jessica wondered a little worriedly about that. Automatically her eyes wandered, looking for Danny; but, of course, if he were anywhere it would not be here. If he were waiting to catch a glimpse of the departing couple it would be out in the windy parkland, with the other estate workers.

The matched bays pranced. The carriage started to move.

'Come on, dreamy! Throw it!' Robert caught her arm.

She threw the slipper after the carriage as, to cheers, it moved off. At her signal more slippers and shoes flew through the air. The cheering was picked up in the courtyard and rippled down the drive in a wave of goodwill.

Jessica, quite suddenly, felt very tired.

'There's more food being put out in the ballroom,' Robert said.

Guests, laughing and talking, were moving up the steps into the house.

She shook her head. 'I think I'll get a breath of air.'

He laughed. 'Plenty of that about.'

As if to underline his words a gust of wind battered them. Ladies squealed, holding on to hats and skirts. The move into the house accelerated.

The carriage had gone. The crowds strung out along the drive were heading for the gates and thence the village, where more free ale was on tap for the evening.

Jessica pushed her way against the tide of people coming into the house, down into the courtyard. Servants passed her, gossiping excitedly, called back to duty by the house-guests' renewed desire for food. She walked around the east wing of the house and out of the wind. In the park beyond the ha-ha the great specimen trees – oaks, elms and chestnuts – tossed wildly.

The gardens and terrace behind the house were a shambles. An army of servants scurried now, cleaning up the mess. She stood for a moment, idly watching them, wondering at the desolation where such a short time before had been life and laughter.

'Jessica!'

Danny's voice, soft but unmistakable, and urgent. She turned.

He was standing in the shadow of a tree. He signalled sharply with a jerk of his head. With what she knew to be an absurdly conspiratorial glance about her she went to him.

'Where's Caroline?' he asked.

She lifted her head in surprise. 'I don't know. I thought – I thought she was with you?'

He shook his head. 'I haven't seen her for two days.' He was frowning.

She shrugged, nonplussed.

He had put a hand in his pocket. Rain now hung on the wind. Jessica shivered.

'Please. Take this to her for me?' He handed her a crumpled piece of paper. 'She's angry with me, I think. I don't know why.' His dark face was intent. 'Bring her answer to me at the church tomorrow. Sir Robert is pleased with my work. I'm to stay a while longer.'

'I'll try.'

'We have plans,' he said, firmly. 'We must discuss them. Tell her she has to come.'

She nodded, hiding her disquiet. 'I'll tell her.'

He smiled his fleet, attractive smile. 'Thank you, little Mouse. I'll see you tomorrow.'

She watched him go, then looked down, sighing, at the scrap of paper she held. The excitement was over. The magic was gone. Life was back to normal, and the pretty, nearly-grown-up girl in the pretty, very-grown-up dress was a mere go-between again. The handsome prince had hardly noticed her. Glumly she tucked her head down against the wind and, ignoring the driving rain, ran back to the house.

Chapter Five

Melbury New Hall was struck to silence by the rage of its master. The household's servants scurried like frightened mice from door to door, footmen stood blank-eyed, mouths like shut traps. No voice was raised. Even the clocks, it seemed to Jessica, muffled their ticking and their chimes in the atmosphere engendered by William Hawthorne's fury.

In the dining room the family sat in a tense silence that was broken only by the chink of cutlery against china. At the far end of the table Maria Hawthorne sat, eyes downcast to her plate, face impassive. Caroline sat beside Jessica, white-faced and miserable, toying with her food. Opposite them, alone on the other side of the long mahogany table sat John, the lines of his usually open face grimly obdurate and bleak with pain. He had not even picked up his fork, and his food lay untouched and cooling before him. He had cried out just once in the course of the thrashing he had received at the hands of his father, the rest of the punishment he had born in obstinate silence, which had by no means encouraged his father to lay on the strap with a lighter hand. Jessica had run upstairs to the nursery and sat on her bed, her fingers in her ears, yet still she had felt she could hear the ghastly sound of that strap rising and falling, though common sense had told her she could not. She glanced now from under her lashes at John. He sat like a statue, eyes on his untouched plate, a faint sheen of sweat on his sun-browned skin. Beside her Jessica could all but feel the shrieking of Caroline's nerves, strung almost to breaking point.

William Hawthorne with calm deliberation cleared his plate, laid down his fork, sipped his claret, his face unreadable as he watched his younger son over the rim of his glass.

'You cannot win, John,' he said, quietly, the first words that had been spoken in the course of that awful meal. 'Accept that now, and spare us all a deal of pain. I'll see you dead before a son of mine joins the whoremongers of the Roman Church.' The last words were spoken as quietly and with as little emphasis as the first, yet something in the level tone made Jessica's skin creep.

John lifted his head in sharp protest and, despite himself, flinched at the pain the movement caused him.

His father, seeing it, nodded grimly. 'I've thrashed you once. I'll thrash you again. And again. Until you see sense, boy. Until you apologize – to me, to your mother, to your brother and sisters – for bringing such disgrace to the Hawthorne name.'

John's mouth suddenly set in the identical line to his father's. 'And is that your answer?' he asked, abruptly, deep anger sparking in his eyes. 'Is it your argument that because you are stronger than I, and think you can beat me into submission, you are right, and I am wrong?'

Jessica's stomach lurched uncomfortably; never in her life had she heard anyone take such a tone with her father. Beside her Caroline drew a sharply distressed breath and laid down her fork with a quick, nervous movement.

Colour flared in William Hawthorne's fair, handsome face. 'Argument, boy?' His quiet voice held the cutting edge of a razor. 'There is no argument! I'm telling you. No son of mine dabbles in Popery. No son of mine involves himself with a nest of traitorous idol-worshippers. 'There is no argument,' he repeated, the words softly adamant. 'I'll see you starved under lock and key before you'll shame me so.'

No-one knew how William Hawthorne had discovered about John's visits to the Catholic Bartletts in Melford: but certain it was that hearing it from an outsider had doubled the rage that had greeted John's consequent and defiant admissions. The beating had been a brutal one, and the threats of further discipline were not, they all knew, empty. Unhappily Jessica watched poor John, willing him to give in. Nothing, surely, could be worth this humiliation?

John's chin was up. He shook his head, slowly. 'No, Father,' he said.

The fine stem of the claret glass in William Hawthorne's hand cracked like a pistol shot. A footman, eyes downcast, stepped forward and took it. William Hawthorne did not even glance at him as he relinquished his hold on the shattered glass.

'No,' John said again. 'Nothing you can say – nothing you can do short of killing me – will stop me. I will be a Roman Catholic priest if it takes my life to do it.'

Face suffused, very slowly William Hawthorne rose, leaning across the table upon his hands, towering above the son who defied him. 'Brave words, sir! Brave words from a foolish schoolboy who knows nothing – *nothing!* – of what he speaks! I'll break you, boy – you hear me? – I'll break you before I see you do this. I'll see you chained in Bedlam! For that is most assuredly where you belong –!'

Even John flinched at the pitiless anger in his father's face. He bit his lip, said nothing.

'And also,' William said, more quietly, 'I'll see to it that the full force of the law is brought down upon those that have done this – those blackguards that have subverted you, turned you against your family and your heritage –'

John's fear fled. Pain notwithstanding he leapt to his feet, all but overturning the heavy chair upon which he had been sitting. 'Heritage?' he shouted, his face inches from his father's, his rage an equal of the older man's. 'What heritage? You talk of disgrace? You dare to talk of right and wrong? Oh, no Father, don't preach to me of my heritage! I want none of it. There is nothing you can give me, Father – nothing you could possibly offer – that would be worth *that* to me –' He snapped his fingers beneath his father's nose. 'Nothing! And as for persecuting those kindly souls who have helped me, that have shown me the truth – may God forgive you for the very thought. But I tell you I will not –!'

'Silence!' William Hawthorne's fist crashed upon the table, and glasses and cutlery jumped. Caroline gave a small, muffled shriek and shrank back in her chair. '*Silence* I say!'

'No!' John was as angry as his father and as far beyond reason or control. His face was chalk-white, his eyes blazing. 'You'll flog me anyway, no doubt, so I'll have my say first. Listen well, Father, for I mean every word. Beat me, starve me, chain me – oh, I know you can do all of that – but you'll not stop me! Sooner or later, unless you truly are willing to kill me, you'll have to let me go. Sooner or later I shall be free. And then I shall become a Catholic and a priest of the Roman Church, if they'll have me. And, as for all of this –' with a scornful sweep of his arm he encompassed the table with its rich food, its silver, its crystal, its fine china, 'my heritage – as you're pleased to call it –' his voice had dropped to a calm anger, his eyes were steady in his pale face. 'I spit on it. Ill-gotten gains, ill-kept. Proceeds from a shameful trade that keep us in luxury whilst those that provided it still bleed to death in chains.' He raised a shaking finger, pointing, 'Try as you may, Father, you'll never escape that. *That's* the Hawthorne heritage –'

William Hawthorne had taken two swift steps. John saw his intention and made no move to avoid it. As his father's hand crashed across his mouth he staggered, then righted himself. William hit him again, with all the force he could muster. Caroline screamed, then crammed a small bunched fist into her mouth, her breath coming in uneven sobs. Jessica's heart was thumping against her ribs. In desperation she glanced at her mother. Maria Hawthorne sat with bowed head, hands clasped tightly upon the table before her. Behind her chair a footman stood impassive, staring into space. A third time William Hawthorne struck, the back of his hand catching his son's face so hard that the boy was knocked sideways across the table. He sprawled for a moment, stunned, shaking his head. Blood marked his face, and for all his anger there was fear too in his eyes at the unprecedented rage he had provoked. His father caught him by the collar and, big as he was, hauled him upright. 'Puppy! Puking, yapping little puppy! And like the ill-mannered, ill-behaved pup you are you'll be treated, by God! You'll fetch the strap, and you'll go to the library, boy, and there you'll wait for me.' William's voice shook with the effort he was making to control it. 'You're about to learn a lesson you'll never forget, sir, I promise you.' He let go of John almost throwing him from him. 'You'll regret for the rest of your life the day you dared to cross me, boy. Now, go!'

John swayed a little on his feet. William lifted a hand. His son flinched away, putting up his hands to protect his face.

'*Go!*' William thundered.

Cowed the boy turned, his defiance fled. Slowly he walked to the door. William returned to his seat, sat down, glanced about the table. Caroline was openly crying, Jessica was white-faced and frightened. He ignored them both. 'The dessert, my dear,' he said to Maria, his voice hard as iron.

She nodded and lifted an almost steady finger to the footman.

The meal struggled on in a fraught silence that was punctuated by Caroline's sobs. At last, after what seemed to Jessica an age, Maria rose and signalled to her daughters. Thankfully they stumbled to their feet and followed her. At the door Jessica glanced back at her father in time to see him, face set to a mask of anger, pour a large glass of port, toss it back in one quick movement before striding from the room towards the library where poor John awaited him.

Miserably Jessica trailed after her mother. Once in the drawing room she caught her hand, urgent and pleading. 'Mama – please! Papa's already beaten John once – isn't that enough? Can't you stop him –?'

As she spoke they all heard the sound of raised voices – William's, deep and resonant, John's lighter and cracking with fear and anger.

Maria Hawthorne shook her head. 'Your father is the head of this household, Jessica,' she said quietly. 'It is not my place to question his decisions or his authority. And most certainly not yours. Kindly pour the tea.'

Rebellion stirred. 'But –'

From the direction of the library came a muffled shriek, and then another. The blood drained entirely from Maria Hawthorne's face. 'The tea, Jessica,' she repeated.

Caroline sobbed, clapped a hand to her mouth and ran from the room.

Jessica, aching to follow her, carefully poured the tea and for the only time she ever remembered was not reprimanded as her shaking hand spilled the golden liquid into the delicate saucers.

From the library the sound of John's torment had reduced to rhythmic, gasping sobs as already bruised flesh suffered more punishment.

Jessica looked down with blurred eyes at her teacup, praying in her innocence that John might beg for mercy, admit his sin, promise apology, reform – anything! Anything to stop the remorseless, ruthless sound of the rise and fall of the strap.

John did not. Confined to bed in a locked room for four days he stubbornly refused to capitulate. On a bread and water diet and in pain after the truly savage beatings he had suffered he grimly stuck to his guns. Threatened with further punishment he reacted by refusing to utter another word to his father. The last word had been said, his silence inferred. No brutality would make him change his mind.

No-one, not even his mother, was allowed to visit him.

'Oh, for heaven's sake, why doesn't he give in?' Jessica asked Robert miserably one day. 'He can't win against Father – he surely must know it? He'll just make things worse for himself than they are –'

They were sitting in the oriel window of the Old Drawing Room. The autumn evenings were drawing in, promising the approach of winter, and the courtyard was dismal with drifting rain; but cold as it was no-one had yet got round to lighting the fire. Jessica breathed on chilled hands and reflected a little ruefully upon the clockwork running of New Hall where by now upwards of a dozen fires would have been lit and tended by two maids whose whole duty it was.

Robert shook his head thoughtfully at her question. 'That obviously isn't the way John sees it. It must be very important to him indeed. I'm surprised, to be honest, that he should prove so strong –'

'Strong? Or stupid?' Fraught with anxiety Jessica kicked her heels irritably against the ancient panelling. 'What good is he doing? And – oh, I'm so afraid that Father will beat him again.

It was horrible!' Restlessly she slid from the seat and wandered to the piano. The lid stood open. She ran one finger sharply along the keys, producing a discordant sound. 'What I can't make out is how Father found out?'

Robert shrugged. 'Gossip. John was very naïve if he believed that he could visit the Bartletts without word getting back sooner or later. The family are known as staunch Catholics, and unpopular with some because of it. They frequently have priests staying there and quite openly celebrate Mass. Your family is one of the most prominent in this part of the country; nothing any of you do is likely to go without comment –' he stopped.

She had turned to stare at him. 'But – that's awful! You mean – people watch what we do? People who don't know us?' The thought had never occurred to her, and she hated it.

'Of course,' he said, unfeelingly cheerful. 'It's the price you have to pay for being filthy rich.'

She hunched her shoulders and turned from him. Of all the distressing things about this distressing business John's violent condemnation of their way of life had not been, for Jessica, the least. 'Well, I just wish he'd see sense so that things could go back to the way they used to be,' she said, gloomily. Aimlessly she wandered back to the window seat, hitched herself up beside him again. 'Home's not a nice place to live at the moment, I can tell you. Mama hardly says anything, Caroline keeps having fits –' She cocked her head. 'I suppose at least it's a small mercy that Clara and Giles aren't home!'

Robert laughed. 'They're in Brighton. It's cold and it's wet and no-one who's anyone is there so they're going back to London, to visit Lady Belworth. We heard yesterday. They must be there by now.'

'When are they coming home?'

He shrugged. 'A couple of weeks, I think.'

'Well John had better sort himself out by then,' Jessica prophesied grimly. 'Father's one thing – but Father *and* Giles –!' Her expression was comically graphic.

Robert looked around the room. 'It's funny, isn't it – that Clara doesn't live here any more?'

'Mmm.'

Robert stood, and stretched. 'One of the few things in life that will give my sister real pleasure, I should think.'

Jessica jumped down beside him. 'What?'

'Why, living at New Hall. She's always wanted to go back there. Ever since she was a little girl.'

Jessica stared at him in surprise. 'Whatever for? Old Hall's much nicer!'

He nodded. 'I agree with you. Clara wouldn't. Old Hall isn't grand enough for her. She's always resented the fact that the FitzBoltons had to leave the new house. She was very small when it was sold, of course. But I honestly think she never forgave Father for it.'

'More fool her. If I'd known I'd have swapped with her any time. Well, at least, as you say she ought to be happy now. Shall we go and see if Mrs Williams has done any baking? I'm starving –!'

A week later, with his wounds barely healed and still not a word spoken to his father, John climbed from his bedroom window and vanished.

House and countryside were in an uproar; and William Hawthorne's fury this time knew no bounds. At least, rumour and gossiping servants notwithstanding, John's disgraceful behaviour had until now remained a private family affair. Now the word was out, and he saw a knowing smile in every eye, heard sympathy or scorn – both to him equally unacceptable – in every voice.

When Danny asked Jessica in the midst of the commotion to carry a note to Caroline, she all but refused. The thought at the moment of being caught in the slightest wrongdoing was daunting to say the least.

'Come on, Mouse – please? I have to talk to her.' Danny was at his most charmingly persuasive. 'I haven't seen her for days! I'm worried about her.'

'You can worry about all of us if you like, while you're about it,' Jessica said, for once unimpressed. 'Honestly, it's like living on a barrel of gunpowder that's likely to blow up at any minute –!' Reluctantly, nevertheless, she took the note he held out. 'You can't blame Caroline if she doesn't come.'

'There's nothing wrong with her, then? I was afraid she might be ill.'

Jessica hesitated. 'No. Not ill. She's – upset. We all are.'

'There's no news of John?'

She shook her head. 'Not a word yet. Papa rode to Melford, to the Bartletts, but they swore they hadn't seen him. Oh, Danny – I'm so worried about him! Where on earth can he be? Supposing –' She stopped, biting off the words, turning her head, blinking, her eyes on the river.

He put an arm about her shoulders in a characteristically warm gesture. 'Oh, no, Mouse – he won't have done anything so silly! Not John. He's already shown more strength than most. He'll be all right, you'll see.'

Easily said. But as Apple plodded, head down against a blustering wind, back across the park, Jessica wondered. John had left with nothing but the clothes in which he stood. He had been gone for two full days. Anything might have happened.

In the distance, above the sound of the wind, the weir roared.

Caroline was in her room. She was sitting before her mirrored dressing-table brushing her hair when Jessica peered cautiously around the door.

'Oh, for heaven's sake, come in and shut the door! Do you want me to catch my death?'

From long practice Jessica ignored her sister's peevishness which under the stress which at the moment held the household seemed to have come back in full force. She glanced warily about the room, peered through the open dressing-room door. 'Where's Maisie?'

'I sent her away,' Caroline said, snappishly. 'The girl's as clumsy as an elephant! She pulls my hair just looking at it! If only this stupid war would end and I could find a decent French maid –'

Jessica did not bother to protest that there might be good reasons beyond that to end a war that was devastating Europe, widowing wives and orphaning innocent children. 'I've a message from Danny,' she said, shortly, and proffered the note.

Caroline stilled as if frozen, the brush poised in mid-stroke. Then very slowly she lowered her arm, her eyes on the scrap of paper her sister held.

'Well?' Jessica asked impatiently, 'aren't you going to read it?'

After a moment's hesitation Caroline snatched it and turned her back as she unfolded it. Jessica wandered to the window, which overlooked the front courtyard of the house. This was a pretty room, warm and cosy with firelight, the canopied bed draped in ivory and gold brocade, the lit candles of the branched chandelier glowing brightly. Beyond the window it was near darkness, and an autumn gale was blowing. 'I wonder where John is?' she asked, quietly, almost talking to herself.

'Wherever he is it's his own fault that he's there.' Caroline's voice was abstracted and totally lacking in any feeling. She folded the note, turned back to the mirror. On a chair by the bed was draped a dress of deep claret velvet, the matching gloves, scarf and fan ranged upon the bed, set out by Caroline's despised maid. Jessica fingered the soft material of the dress. 'I do hope he's all right.'

Caroline shrugged.

'It was awful, wasn't it – Father finding out like that?' Jessica was talking more or less aimlessly, wanting only to share her own worries, her own fears. 'Robert says it was gossip. He says that because we're who we are people watch us, and talk about us. He says we can't do anything without everyone knowing about it. Isn't that –' She jumped as her sister slammed the hairbrush violently onto the dressing-table and the glass pots and jars rattled fiercely. 'Wh – whatever's the matter?' and then 'Oh – sorry,' she added, sheepishly, her eyes on the note, 'I didn't mean –'

Caroline buried her face in her hands. 'Go away, Jessica.'

'But –'

'*Go away!*' Hysteria hovered in the barely controlled shriek.

Jessica pulled a face at the bowed golden head. 'All right. I'm going. Isn't there any answer then?'

'What?'

'To the note. Danny's note. Isn't there any reply?'

Caroline turned her head, and the expression on her drawn face struck her sister to silence. Caroline lifted the note and held it in front of her, staring at it as intently as a child that studied its first words and tried to make sense of them. 'No,' she said, 'there's no reply.'

'But Danny said —'

Caroline's hands moved convulsively, and the note crumpled. 'I don't care what Danny said. I don't care what anyone says! I'm tired. I want to be left alone —'

Jessica lifted her head sharply. 'What's that? A carriage? Who on earth can it be? We aren't expecting anyone, are we?' She ran to the window. 'Oh, Caroline, look! It's Giles and Clara! Father must have sent word to them. Oh, Lord! Giles is going to be absolutely *furious* with John —'

Caroline had joined her at the window. Beneath them Giles handed Clara from the carriage. 'Damn!' Caroline whispered, viciously, under her breath. '*Damn!*'

'What's the matter?'

Caroline shook her head. 'Nothing.'

'It doesn't sound like nothing. I've never ever heard you swear before.'

Caroline turned on her, levelling the hairbrush threateningly. 'Out,' she said, flatly.

This time Jessica did not argue.

Downstairs the new arrivals, still dressed for travelling, were already with her parents in the drawing room. Jessica slipped quietly through the door, grinning quick acknowledgement of the conspiratorial wink of the footman who stood guard by it.

'— what the devil's been going on? — Begging your pardon, Mama —' Giles added automatically. 'Father, your message said that John had run away. Run away —?'

Clara, dressed in brown velvet and smooth fur, a sweeping, elegant hat upon her dark head, stood by the fireplace warming her hands, her sharp eyes taking in everything. 'Good evening, Jessica,' she said, pointedly.

Every eye turned to Jessica who had been trying to make herself inconspicuous if not invisible behind a large sofa. She blushed violently. Trust Clara! Back in the house for five minutes, and a pain already!

'Hello Clara. Hello Giles. I saw your carriage arrive. I just thought I'd – come and say hello –' she broke off.

Giles nodded brusquely. Clara smiled. Jessica's mother stood up. 'You'll see them at dinner, my dear. Meanwhile your father has things to discuss with Giles, so run along now. Clara – a cup of tea after your journey?'

At dinner, presumably by mutual agreement of the adults present, nothing was said of John. In face of this obdurate refusal to discuss what was uppermost in all of their minds Jessica did not have the gall to broach the subject herself, though she seethed at her own cowardice. Desperately she wanted to know what was being done about finding him – what might happen to him once he was found – but her courage failed her and she ate in silence as the others lightly discussed the marriage trip.

Jessica it was who heard the faint sound of the crunch of footsteps on the gravel, that was followed by a brisk knocking on the great front door. She cocked her head, listening. No-one else took the slightest notice.

'– and is this Pavillion as much of a monstrosity as I've heard?' Her mother was asking, as if the foibles of the man who ruled England as Regent for his mad father were the most interesting subject she could possibly wish to discuss.

'Indeed it is, Mother-in-Law –'

The door opened, and the head footman entered and made his silent way to the head of the table, where he bent to whisper in William Hawthorne's ear. Jessica saw the blood rise in her father's face, and then drain away leaving it bleached of colour. He stood up. From the hall below the sound of a familiar voice drifted, loud in the silence that had fallen about the table.

With no word William strode from the room.

'And was the weather really so bad?' Maria asked, politely, the hand that held her delicate glass shaking almost imperceptibly.

'It was dreadful,' Clara said. 'It rained all the time.'

'And Lady Belworth? She was well?'

'Wonderfully. I don't know how she does it at her age. She was to have given a ball for us next week.'

'Mama,' Jessica said urgently, 'that's John's voice.'

Maria surveyed Clara with unseeing eyes. 'Really? How very kind of her. What a pity you had to leave –'

'*Mama!*' Unable to contain herself longer Jessica leapt to her feet, 'I'm sure I heard John!'

Maria said nothing. Giles pushed back his chair and stood up. 'If you will excuse me, Mama?'

Maria nodded without looking at him.

The women watched as he left the room.

Jessica could not bear it. 'Mama! Please! Can't we at least go and see if it's him?' she begged, tears standing in her eyes.

For a moment she thought that her mother would refuse. Then Maria lifted a finger to the footman who stood behind her and he stepped to her chair, pulling it back so that she could stand. 'Come,' she said.

The room led on to the spacious landing from which the great curved staircase swept to the marble-floored entrance-hall below. Here Jessica and Lucy had stood to watch the guests as they had arrived for the May Masque. She stood in the same spot now, leaning over the ornate banister. Below in the hall, facing his father and Giles, stood John dressed in poor and ill-fitting clothes, his face thin and strained. Beside him stood an imposing figure – tall, thin, with a dark, aesthetic face that was dominated by a beak nose, wearing unfamiliar garb that Jessica took to be that of a Catholic priest. In his quietly folded hands he carried a broad-brimmed hat. The skirts of his soutane were mud-stained.

'– if you aren't out of my house in ten seconds –' her father was saying, levelly, his rage on tight leash, '– I'll take a horse-whip to you. How dare you, Sir? How dare you cross my threshold? You, I have no doubt, are the one who has subverted my son –'

'No,' John said, hoarsely.

His father did not even glance at him. '– And yet you have the gall – the impertinence to –'

'Please.' The stranger held up a long, narrow hand. His quiet, pleasant voice was placating. Yet, oddly Jessica thought, William Hawthorne fell to silence. Even the watchers on the landing could feel the quiet power of the man's presence. 'Mr Hawthorne, I understand that you are angry – hurt – outraged, even. It was wrong of John to run away as he did. It solves nothing. I bring him back to you –'

'No!' John cried again.

'I bring you back your son,' the stranger repeated, gently and inexorably, 'so that we may discuss what troubles us. I would suggest there are arguments you have not considered –'

William recovered his voice. 'The law will hear your arguments, Sir. And the law will not take a light view of this – !'

'Father –!' John pleaded.

'Shut up, John!' Giles, standing beside his father, glowered at his brother. 'Haven't you caused enough trouble?'

The stranger lifted his head, and again Jessica was struck by the commanding aura of the man. 'I fear that you are right, of course. The law of the land is on your side; sadly it always is when it come to matters of Holy Mother Church. But Mr Hawthorne I entreat you, for your son's sake – for his happiness and for the good of his soul; what of God's Laws? What of His claims upon us?'

'Claptrap!' Giles snapped.

William raised a hand that enjoined silence. He and the strange priest studied each other for a long, level moment.

'Do you know your son?' the man asked, at last, quietly. 'Do you know his strength? You'll never break him. Who, ever, has broken you?'

There was a strange moment of silence. Then, 'Come,' William said, brusquely, and turned, leading the way upstairs. The priest, the boy and Giles followed. The women drew back as the odd little procession passed. Jessica caught John's eye and his attempt at a reassuring smile failed miserably. He passed his mother with downcast eyes. 'Attend the ladies, Giles,' William said, quietly and in a tone not to be questioned. 'We'll not be long.'

As the library door closed behind them Maria unclasped hands that had been white with tension. 'The food will spoil,' she said. 'We'll dine without your father –'

It was nearly an hour before the strange conference was done, and the rest of the company by then had given up any pretence of eating and had retired to the drawing room and the teapot, though Giles had resorted to the brandy bottle.

Jessica, hearing the library door open, jumped up. 'They're coming!'

'Sit down, please, Jessica.' Her mother's admonition was not unkind, 'We will discover soon enough what is to happen.'

Reluctantly Jessica sat, picked up the ill-executed sampler she had been struggling with.

'Please, Father,' – John's quiet voice filtered through the open door. 'Do I have your permission to say goodbye?'

There was a moment's quiet. Then, 'As you wish,' William Hawthorne grunted.

Maria rose as her son entered the room and faced him coolly.

'Father has agreed that I may go with Father Peter,' the boy explained quietly. 'It's what I want more than anything. I'm sorry, Mama. Truly sorry.'

Maria said nothing.

John stepped to her and his lips brushed her cold cheek. She did not move to embrace him. He hesitated, as if to say something further, then shook his head slightly and turned to where Caroline sat. His sister averted her head and neither moved nor looked at him as he quickly kissed her cheek in farewell. Clara offered a hand, gracefully. To Jessica's surprise she was smiling, very slightly, a small, secret light of pleasure in her eyes as she looked at John's bowed head. Giles ignored John's tentatively proffered hand, turning from him in deliberate insult, saying nothing, tossing back the last of his brandy in a swift, angry way. Hurt in his face John shrugged, and turned to Jessica who, uncaring of the proprieties, launched herself at him, flinging her arms about his waist, burying her head in his chest. 'Oh, John!' her voice was desolate and wobbling with tears. 'I wish you wouldn't go!'

He held her tightly for a moment, stroking the mass of her

hair, then gently he put her from him. 'I must, Jessie. Please try to understand. I must.'

Mute with misery she stepped back and watched him as he walked past his father to where Father Peter waited, calm faced, by the door.

'Understand,' William Hawthorne said, coldly, to his son's back, 'that this is the end. There will be no going back. You are no longer my son. Not now. Not ever. You have no birthright. You'll get not a penny nor a brick of mine.'

John stopped, then turned, shaking his head, his face sad. 'Father – and father you'll always be, admit it or no – will you never see? I don't want your money. I never wanted it. You have tonight given me the only thing I have ever wanted, and for that I thank you from the bottom of my heart. Please believe that I'm sorry to have caused you so much distress.' He glanced at his mother's still face, then turned abruptly and left the room, the priest's dusty skirts swishing in his wake. Profound silence followed their going. Giles, in a sharp release from tension, stormed to the window and stood nursing his empty glass looking into the darkness. William extended a steady hand to his wife, who as steadily accepted it, and together they left the room. Jessica wondered if she imagined the extra brilliance of her mother's blue eyes.

Caroline clicked her fan nervously upon her velvet-clad knees. 'Well, thank heaven for small mercies. Now perhaps we can all get back to normal.'

Clara had joined her husband at the window. She touched his arm lightly, and he turned. She tilted her head and smiled, that strange, small, secret gleam of pleasure once more in her eyes. 'Poor misguided John,' she said, gently. 'We must all pray for his happiness, mustn't we?'

It was less than a week later that Jessica began to realize that matters were far worse between Caroline and Danny than she had first believed. The meetings that she witnessed between them were no longer the joyous affairs they had been. Certainly Danny still watched for Caroline with intent and anxious eyes, certainly he still hurried to her side when she appeared, but his manner was strained and, alone with Jessica, he often fell to brooding silences. Then one day she came upon them quarrelling violently. Caroline, on seeing her, turned and fled, tears streaming down her face.

'Caroline!' Danny shouted after her, his voice a mixture of anger and entreaty, 'Caroline, come back! It does no good to run away –!' But on she ran, and Danny with no word had brushed past Jessica and gone into his cottage, slamming the door behind him.

Caroline kept to her room for a day or so after that, pleading a migraine, and Jessica did not see her until, upon answering a summons from her mother she entered Maria's small and elegant sitting room to find Caroline already there, perched sideways upon the deep windowsill gazing in brooding silence out across the park where the last brazen colours of autumn blazed like fire and the leaves skittered across the grass in the breeze. Her sister did not turn as she entered the room, but her mother looked up from her embroidery with a small, welcoming smile. 'Ah – Jessica. You've brought the book?'

Jessica nodded shyly, offering the book of poetry that she carried for her mother's inspection.

Maria waved a white hand. 'I leave it to you, my dear. Start with your favourite, if you wish. Mr Wordsworth suits my mood well enough this afternoon. Caroline – ring for some tea, would you? Now, Jessica, let us see if MacKenzie's grudging praise of your reading talent is justified –' Her mouth quirked in a small, surprising smile and her glance was almost conspiratorial. Astonished, but more than happy to oblige her mother in this, the only ladylike pursuit in which if she did not actually excel at least she could hold her own, Jessica settled upon the stool next to her mother and opened the book at a much-thumbed page. The next hour passed very pleasantly. She had a true love of poetry, and could communicate that as she read, the lovely rhythm of the words singing in her mind as she spoke, the imagery firing an imagination already, according to MacKenzie, woefully inclined to the romantic. After a while her mother laid aside her needlework and took the book, and in her low, well-modulated voice read

extracts from her own favourite work, Milton's *Paradise Lost*.
Jessica was enthralled, John Milton's command of the poetic
language conjuring for her another world, of fiery angels,
mystic landscapes and searing emotion.

'– Now glowed the firmament/ With living sapphires:
Hesperus that led/ The starry host, rode brightest, till the
moon/Rising in cloudy majesty, at length/ Apparent Queen,
unveiled her peerless light –' Maria stopped.

Jessica, absorbed, her eyes upon the glowing depths of the
fire, looked up in surprise at the sudden silence, then saw, as
her mother had a second before, that Caroline who for an hour
or more had sat staring from the window contributing little or
nothing to the conversation had bowed her head to her hands
and was crying desperately and silently, her shoulders shaking.

'Why, Caroline – my dear – whatever is the matter? Are you
ill?' Maria, concerned, laid aside the book and went to her
daughter, laying a light arm across the narrow, heaving
shoulders.

Caroline did not lift her head, but her sobs redoubled.

'Caroline?' Maria's voice had sharpened and was edged with
worry. 'Come, child. What is it?'

'I – have to speak to you –' The words were muffled, broken
by sobs. 'Oh, please, Mother, I have to! I fear I shall go mad –!'

'Oh, come now!' Firmly Maria lifted her daughter's chin and
looked into the lovely, tearful face. 'What can possibly be that
bad?'

Caroline pulled away from her, crying distractedly. 'Send
Jessica away. Please! Oh, please, Mother – I *have* to talk to
you. Alone!'

Maria hesitated, frowning. There was no doubting Caroline's distress, nor the fraught edge of hysteria in her voice. She
turned to Jessica, who had come to her feet and was staring at
her sister an odd, half-concerned, half-wary expression on her
face. 'Jessica –' her mother was faintly apologetic, '– you see
the state your sister is in. It's best that you should go.'

Jessica stood a moment longer, desperately and fearfully –
and unsuccessfully – trying to catch Caroline's eye.

'Please, Jessica.' Her mother was gently insistent.

'Very well, Mama.'

'Good girl. I'll see you at dinner. Do wear the brown velvet. It suits you very well.'

'Yes, Mama.'

Caroline sobbed on, frenziedly, her face buried once more in her hands. Jessica cast her one, ferocious look. 'Caroline –!'

'Best you should leave her to me, I think, Jessica. Off you go.' The slight sharpness in her mother's tone brooked neither argument nor any further delay. Reluctantly Jessica left.

Outside, with the door not quite shut, she stopped. In this private and more informal part of the house the corridor was empty. In suspicion and fearful distrust she leaned to the door, listening. She heard her mother's quiet, soothing voice, then Caroline's, lifted hysterically, the words all but indistinguishable in the wild sobbing that accompanied them. Jessica strained her ears. '– Oh, Mother, the disgrace! I shall die! I know I shall! I can't have it! I won't! Oh, I wish I *were* dead – and the child with me! I've been so afraid! Afraid to tell you – to tell Father – oh, Mama, please! Don't let him beat me – don't let him beat me as he beat John! I couldn't bear it! I couldn't –!'

Maria's voice murmured again, low and sharp.

'No! Of course not! How can you think it!' Caroline was all but screaming, entirely out of control. 'He forced me! I swear it! It was horrible! He hurt me – and I was so afraid – so ashamed – I couldn't tell you! I couldn't. And now – oh, God! I'll kill myself, I swear I will –!'

'Caroline!' Maria's sharp voice carried clearly to the all but paralysed child hidden beyond the door. 'Calm down! Caroline!' There came the swift and unmistakable sound of a slap. Caroline drew a gasping breath and for a shocked moment was silent. 'Now.' Maria's voice was grimmer than Jessica had ever heard it. 'Begin at the beginning. Tell me everything.'

Jessica leaned against the wall. Her heart was beating painfully and the blood rushed uncomfortably in her ears. There was no doubt in her mind as to what Caroline was doing

– nor what the consequences for Danny would be once the squalid story Caroline was sobbing out so pathetically and so treacherously to her mother was carried to her father. That Caroline would save her own skin at the expense of Danny's she had no doubt; yet in that awful, blank moment she could see no way to stop it. No-one would listen to her, of that she was sure – confronting Caroline with her lies would do nothing but harm.

As she stood, trembling and irresolute she heard sudden movement within the room, and once again her mother's voice came clearly to her. 'Stay here. I'll see your father at once. You'll have to face him later – but once he hears the truth of it be assured he won't punish *you*.' The emphasis on the final pronoun was grim. 'For now, I'll see him alone.'

Hearing the brisk, hurrying footsteps Jessica gathered her wits enough to duck into a nearby open doorway. She caught the briefest glimpse of her mother's face, bone-white and outraged, as she passed and then she was gone and Jessica flew back to the sitting-room door, throwing it open with a crash fit to tear it from its supports. 'What have you done?'

Caroline was sitting in an armchair, her face blotched, sobbing into a sodden rag of handkerchief. She jumped, startled and afraid, at her sister's precipitate entrance.

'*What have you done?*' Jessica was across the room and was upon her, shaking her. 'You're wicked! Wicked! What have you told her?'

Caroline, face blazing, wrenched herself from the younger girl's grip. 'Go away! *Go away!* This is all your fault –!'

'You've told her something awful about Danny, haven't you? You've told lies about him, haven't you? *Haven't you?*'

'Get away from me!' Caroline pushed her hard, and she almost fell. The hysterical tears had started again. Jessica stood for a moment staring at her sister in disgust and dislike before whirling and running from the room, following the direction that her mother had taken. If her father were out – if there were just some time to warn Danny –

She heard her father before she even reached the main wing of the house. 'Giles? Giles! Here, to me! At once!'

Jessica flew to the top of the stairs. Down in the entrance hall her father, his face grim with anger, was struggling into his riding coat assisted by a frightened-looking young footman. '*Giles!*'

Giles, his face the picture of astonishment was standing halfway up the stairs. 'Father? What is it?'

William looked up and never, not even in facing John's defiance had Jessica seen such a distortion of rage upon his face. 'Fetch the gunroom key. Get four men together. Tell Jessup to saddle half a dozen mounts. Hurry.'

'But what –?'

'Do it. I'll tell you as we ride. We've vermin to hunt.' William took his riding whip from the quailing footman and slashed in furious impatience at a small marble table. 'The gunroom key, Giles! Hurry, I say!'

Jessica ran. Fighting tears of terror she ran on slippered feet along the corridor to the west wing, almost bowling over an astonished maidservant as she turned a corner. At breakneck speed she tumbled down the stairs and out into the cold and darkening afternoon, dashing to the stables her feet winged by fear for Danny. She hardly felt the cold that struck chillingly through her thin indoor gown nor felt the sharp stones that cut her feet through slippers thin as paper. As she reached the stables Apple lifted his head, blowing warm affection and Bran launched himself at her all but bowling her over. 'Oh, no – Bran you can't come! Stay! Bran – stay!' Frantic she shrieked the word at him. The dog's ears drooped. 'Down!' Her hand was entangled in Apple's shaggy mane. There was no time for saddle or bridle. '*Down!*' she shouted again at the dog. Bran, dispirited, fell back upon his haunches. She jumped and swung herself onto the pony's warm, smooth back. Fortunately at this time of day the stables were quiet, though in the distance she could already hear the sound of raised voices and running feet. Her heart in her mouth at their closeness she guided Apple out of the stable yard and set him at a flat run across the park.

Danny was in his cottage, as she had guessed he would be with the early darkness closing in. Before the labouring Apple had fairly stopped Jessica had flung herself from his back and was pounding at the door. 'Danny! Danny, open the door!'

The door swung back and Danny stood there, blinking in astonishment. 'Jessica! What in the world –?'

She wasted no words. 'Father's coming! And Giles! They've got guns! Danny, they've found out! About you and Caroline –she's told the most terrible lies – they're going to kill you! You have to get away. Hurry –!'

He stared at her. Shook his head.

'Danny!' She was frantic. 'Don't you hear me? Caroline's told them –! They're coming here with guns –'

'Told them? About the child? But yes – we knew she'd have to, now –'

She shook his arm fiercely. 'You don't understand! She lied! She said the most terrible things about you. And Father believes them. And now he's coming with men, and guns – oh, Danny, you've got to get away –!' She was crying now, tears streaming disregarded down her cheeks. 'Oh, *please!* – *hurry!*'

He stepped back, shaking his head. 'No – Caroline? She wouldn't –!' He stopped, baffled incredulity in his eyes.

'She did! I heard her! She told Mother that you – forced her – that you hurt her –'

'Oh my God,' he said.

'And now they're coming, with guns. Danny, you have to get away. You can't face them. They'll kill you!'

'She – said that? That I'd – forced her? – *hurt* her?'

His face was white as paper. She could not look at it. 'Yes,' she said.

He shook his head, shock still holding him. 'But – there must be a mistake. A misunderstanding. We were to leave together. Tomorrow –'

For the first time Jessica noticed the bare tidiness of the hut, that was usually such a living shambles. A small bundle of clothes lay upon the table. She shook her head fiercely.

'*Caroline!* Oh, Danny – are you mad? Caroline won't come with you. She never would.'

But I would. Oh, I would. Anywhere – The words echoed wildly in her heart, unspoken. Unwanted.

He was still struggling with disbelief. 'But she said –'

She all but screamed at him. 'Will you stop arguing? They're coming! Now! They're coming with guns because of the lies that Caroline has told them. Danny, she doesn't want your baby. She told Mother she wished she was dead, and the child with her. I heard her!'

He stood for a single moment longer, and then, at last galvanized into action he turned moving swiftly to the table and grabbing the bundle that lay there. 'Money,' he said, his voice suddenly sharp and clear, 'I'll need money –' He went to a drawer and took out a small bag that clinked as he dropped it into his pocket. Then he ran back to the door where Jessica waited. Faint hoofbeats sounded, and a man's voice lifted distantly.

'It sounds as if they're going to the church first,' she said, more calmly than she could herself believe, though her voice trembled and her stomach roiled with sickness. 'You've a few more minutes. Take Apple. He'll carry you. But hurry!'

He shook his head. 'No. I'm better afoot. That beast would unseat me in a hundred yards – and if they caught me there'd be a hanging charge to my name if I were riding your horse. Anyway, I'll not embroil you further. I'll get down to the bridge and slip across country to Sudbury. There's a coach leaves for London –'

'No! They're bound to look there when they realize you've gone. Go further afield before you take a coach!'

He nodded and turned to go. Then, swiftly, he turned back and hugged her fiercely, hurting her with the strength of his arms, his cheek pressed hard against her hair. 'Thank you, little Mouse. God keep you.' He turned his face in her hair and she felt the pressure of his lips. 'Bless you,' he said, and then he released her and was gone, fled into the darkness of the woods. And with him fled the last vestiges of Jessica Hawthorne's childhood. She had saved him, her dark angel, but in doing so she had lost him. She would never see him again.

Dully she remounted Apple and trotted him back through the woodlands towards the park and the great house.

Part Two

1815–1817

Chapter Six

Waterloo.

The word was on everyone's lips.

Waterloo.

Near this small and hitherto unheard-of village in Belgium that until that mid-June day of 1815 could never have dreamed of such lifelong notoriety, Napoleon's might, at last, had come to nothing. In England and all over Europe the bells rang jubilantly for victory, and in every town and village Wellington's success was fêted. Melbury was no exception. Seventeen-year-old Jessica Hawthorne, deceptively demure and slight in pale green silk and a large, shading bonnet sat with her mother in an open carriage on the edge of the green and smiled with unaffected delight at the village children who danced energetically around a hastily-erected Maypole.

'What a good idea to have just red, white and blue ribbons! It makes a very patriotic show, doesn't it, Mama? – Mama?' she prompted, turning her head to look at her mother.

Maria Hawthorne's preoccupied gaze was fixed not on the dancing children, but upon her husband who was engaged in conversation with a group of men on the far side of the green. Jessica's eyes followed her mother's, and her smile faded. The past months had seen a marked and frightening change in William Hawthorne, and although, almost as if in conspiracy, no-one openly spoke of it those nearest to him were both acutely aware of it and even more acutely apprehensive of what it might betoken. And in the past weeks his physical decline had accelerated. His handsome, ruddy face had lost its colour, his large, spare frame shed weight that it could ill-afford. Despite all his efforts it was sometimes impossible for him to disguise the fact that he was in considerable pain. Suddenly grey-faced he would turn from the company, or leave a room with no excuse and no explanation, leaving behind him a concerned silence that was laced with uncertainty and question. With terrifying and savage rapidity a vigorous man was wasting away before their eyes, and no amount of frightened self-deception could disguise it. Only last week Jessica had ridden up to the house in time to see Mr Jeffries, the family physician – who was only called in times of dire need – deep in conversation with her mother at the top of the steps. As she had pulled her mare to a sharp standstill the man had doffed his hat, grave and unsmiling, before bending briefly and solemnly over Maria's slim hand and mounting to his carriage. Her mother's face as she had watched the carriage drive away had brought Jessica's heart to her throat in a sudden spasm of panic. What could the man have said to produce such naked grief in one whose emotions were almost always masked? For the past week she had tried desperately not to remember that look, not to watch her father, not to see that which it was becoming impossible to ignore. William Hawthorne's pain grew worse by the day, and his constitution, once so robust, could no longer fight it. He stood now, leaning heavily upon a stick, talking to Squire James, a local Justice of the Peace, whose own face showed a politely disguised shock of concern.

The music and the rhythmic sound of the bells the children wore jigged on.

'Your father is dying, Jessica,' Maria said, suddenly and quietly, her voice strangely distant as if she did not herself believe the words she spoke.

Jessica sat, rooted in shock.

Across the green her father doubled over, coughing, his face a distortion of pain. The Squire stepped to him, anxious hand outstretched. William waved him impatiently away, fought for breath, then straightened. Try as she might, Jessica could not speak. Her throat appeared to have closed up altogether. She turned stricken eyes to her mother.

Maria nodded. 'It's true. You see it is.' Then, 'I'm sorry,' she said softly, 'I should not have told you in such fashion. I had

156

not planned it so. I just –' she shook her head in an odd and uncharacteristically perplexed fashion '– I just had to tell someone.'

'Does he know?'

Maria nodded. 'Yes.'

'And yet – the Ball tonight? And – all this –?' Jessica spread her hands, indicating the revelry around them.

'But of course.' Faint reproof edged her mother's voice. 'A great victory must be celebrated. The people expect it.'

Jessica swallowed protest. She had known, she realized now, without being told, for the past few days at least. What difference did it make after all that the unthinkable had been put into words? Her mother was right. Life went on. And William Hawthorne would have been the last to deny it.

'Do you know – how long?'

Her mother shook her head. 'Not long.' Then, 'I believe,' she said, her voice still calm and low, 'that we should send word to Caroline.'

Dumbly Jessica nodded. Caroline – for the past four years the future Lady Standish – rarely visited New Hall since her marriage, for all that Standish House was a mere twenty miles from Melbury. Her 'illness' four years before and her 'recuperation' at a small and exclusive clinic somewhere in the south of England had been a five minute wonder in the neighbourhood, and if anyone had had suspicions none had ever dared voice them aloud to a Hawthorne. On her return to health a visit had been paid to the Baronet, the obliging Bunty's equally obliging and penurious father, the upshot of which had been a swift and in the circumstances a remarkably quiet wedding. In the wake of these celebrations Standish House, whose fabric had been crumbling for nigh on a hundred years, had received extensive repairs and renovations. A year after her marriage Caroline had dutifully produced the son and heir that Jessica was certain had been part of the bargain, eighteen months later another and so, the Standish line safe, everyone was apparently happy. Jessica had never found herself able to take to her two fair, dull-eyed nephews whose small round faces were unremarkably regular and chinless as their father's. She could never see Caroline without wondering; did she never dream of a sharp, dark angel's face? – of a shock of black hair – gleaming, laughing, graceless eyes? Did she never think of the child, conceived in love, denied in terror and cowardice, to whom life had been so brutally denied? Jessica never asked – rarely, indeed, ever spoke to her sister if she could avoid it. The betrayal had been too great. As much by luck as by design Jessica's part in Danny's escape had never been discovered. She would not at the time have cared if it had been – her father might have beaten her half to death and she would have counted it a worthwhile bargain – but now she was happy that to this day no-one at New Hall knew of her friendship with Danny. For it still to be a secret somehow kept the magic untarnished.

She had no idea where he might be, had no hope ever of seeing him again, but yet hardly a day passed when she did not think of him, did not think of that lovely, bitter-sweet summer of his coming, of those days before Caroline had taken him from her, and then discarded him.

And now, remembering that summer, another face came to mind.

'Mama –?' she asked, hesitantly, 'Should we not – try to contact John –?'

'No!' The snapped word brooked no argument. 'Absolutely not. I forbid it.'

'But –'

'John made his choice, Jessica,' her mother's voice was even. 'May God forgive him for it, for I have not and neither has your father. No, child, we shall not send to John.'

She knew her mother well enough to know there was no arguing with that tone. 'Do Clara and Giles know?'

'Not from me.' The words were cool. Her mother cast her a swift, veiled look, then turned back to the scene before them.

Jessica sighed. Even before her father's illness life at New Hall had been far from comfortable since Giles' and Clara's return after their marriage. The battle, politely vicious, between her mother and Clara for control of the household had been – Robert had declared, only half-joking – an affair only slightly less cut-throat than that between Napoleon and Wellington. To Jessica, caught between them, that had been all too shrewd an analogy; she, like many of Wellington's men, had become adept at keeping her head down and staying out of trouble. In various ways, some more devious than others, Clara had brought her innovations to New Hall. By appealing prettily to her father-in-law she had her peacocks, that now strutted the lawns of New Hall, their raucous cries mocking any who did not care for them. As Maria did not.

By relentless pressure, charmingly applied, she had introduced to the house the new and fashionable habit of eating the family dinner early so that a later 'company' supper might be enjoyed. It seemed to Jessica that never an evening passed without its card game, its theatrical pleasantries, its musical entertainment, over which activities the new young mistress of the house presided, sparkling and graceful. The carriages bowled to the door at six and rarely left before midnight, except of course during the Season, when she and Giles rented a London apartment and New Hall was left in peace. The small suite of rooms that Maria had had decorated and furnished for the newly-weds had within six months been entirely re-furbished to Clara's taste and inclination. Giles, so forceful with everyone else, so stubbornly set upon his own way, seemed incapable of standing against his wife in the smallest thing. In everything it seemed her wishes were paramount; yet time and again, still, Jessica sensed that strangeness between them, a barbed tension bordering on violence that to her bore little relationship to love or affection. And for all her relatively small triumphs, Clara, Jessica suspected, was not a happy woman, for she had signally and publically failed on two counts; for all her efforts she had in no way succeeded in usurping the quietly-wielded power of her mother-in-law, nor had she produced a child. Seated beside her mother, struggling to adjust to the devastating knowledge of her father's coming death as the village celebrated the freedom of Europe about them it came to Jessica with something of a shock that the first of these failures was about to be rectified. With William

Hawthorne dead Giles would be master of New Hall. And his wife its mistress.

She looked down at her hands, which still small, square, decidedly inelegant were clasped in her lap. Tears were burning suddenly behind her eyes.

Her mother's lace-gloved fingers lay upon hers for a moment, gently and with sympathy. 'Come. We should go back. There are preparations for tonight still to be made.'

For Jessica the Victory Ball, so much anticipated, was ruined before it started. Try as she might she could not take her eyes off her father. He played the perfect host, upright, courteous, dauntlessly attentive to the ladies, an unfailing part of the camaraderie of the men. Yet his face was ashen and his loss of weight horribly obvious in the immaculate dark dress suit that hung upon his gauntness, a mockery of times past.

Her card was full – it always was, though she had no illusions as to the reason for that. She bore with harassed equanimity the efforts of the younger local gentry to convince her – and her rich parents – of their eligibility as they galloped with more or less skill and enthusiasm around the ballroom floor, her usual amusement at their often less than polished efforts to gain her attention on this occasion totally lacking. Her relief when Robert, with whom there was no necessity to play silly games, claimed her at last for an energetic polka was palpable.

'Well,' he said, grinning, as he led her onto the floor, 'I suppose it will occur to me next time to book the supper dance three weeks in advance? Such a popular young lady you are these days –'

'Oh, don't be silly.' She was a little brusque, her eyes upon her father as he steered the overweight Lady Felworth around the floor. 'We both know that I'm the only Hawthorne left on offer. That's got to be worth a few dances, hasn't it?'

He missed a step in the dance, cocked a surprised eyebrow. 'So sour on such a day?'

She bit her lip. 'Robert, I need to talk to you. I really do. Are you hungry? Do you mind skipping supper?'

He shook his head readily, his eyes curious. 'Surely not. But I'm engaged with the Honorable Lady Mary –'

'And I with the young Mr Mowbray. I'm sure they'll suit each other very well. If I can arrange it – will you meet me on the terrace when the others go in? I really can't face the thought of food.'

'Of course.' His eyes searched her face. 'A problem?'

She nodded.

The music lifted, bizarrely lighthearted, and the breathless dancers, smiling and perspiring, whirled past them.

With a diplomacy worthy of her mother she freed them both. They met on the terrace, the cool air a benison after the crowded, foetid atmosphere of the ballroom. She leaned beside him at the balustrade, looking towards the lake. The full, glowing moon threw shadows in the park.

She stood in silence, trying to marshal words, and failing. 'How's Oxford?' she asked, at last.

He turned his head to look at her, quizzically certain that they had not forgone supper to talk of Oxford University. 'It's pretty good.' At nineteen he was of no more than medium height and still slim as a girl. The neat, dark cap of hair and the equally neat regular features were reassuringly the same as they had always been. Whilst others of her acquaintance had, with the onslaught of adolescence, produced violent and awkward changes as disturbing to them as they were to her, Robert had maintained that fastidious collectedness that for Jessica held the uncomplicated attraction of long familiarity. Their affection for each other had in no way dimmed. He was still the trusted companion of her childhood; her other, more reliable and less passionate self.

'Father's dying,' she said.

He drew breath in a long silence. 'Yes,' he said, and the soft compassion in that one word almost drew the tears again. 'I guessed.'

She swallowed. 'Is it so obvious, then? Does everyone know?'

He turned, his back against the stone balustrade. The light from the house caught his face and she saw the pain and the sympathy. 'Yes. I would imagine so.'

She made a small, choking noise then lifted her head to look up into the star-strewn sky. 'What will we do without him?'

He shook his head, gently and in silence.

She closed her eyes, took several deep, even breaths, fighting off anguished tears.

His small hand covered hers, firm and warm. 'It's awful, Jess. Of course it is. But these things happen. It will happen to you. To me.'

She nodded.

'He's very brave,' he said quietly. 'Very strong. I admire him greatly. I think you have to follow his example. If he can face it, so can you.'

She tried to speak, and could not. In the warm night she trembled. The arm he laid about her shoulders was brotherly and loving. She leaned to him, miserably. Softly and with no words he laid his cheek against the mass of her hair. Behind them the music had started again, garishly cheerful.

'Jessica?' Her mother's voice, quietly, behind her.

She pulled away from Robert, sniffing. 'Yes?'

'Our guests are waiting.' The firm words were not unkind, but Maria's gaze was steady and uncompromising. 'Lady Felworth was asking for you. You should speak with her.'

Jessica ducked her head. 'Yes, Mama.'

As she moved away, Robert made to follow her and was detained by a light touch on his sleeve. 'She must not be allowed to break, Robert,' Maria's eyes were on a level with his own. 'Not yet. Afterwards –' she paused, '– afterwards she will need your friendship. For now she must stand alone. As we all must.' Calm and beautiful she turned and walked back into the brilliance of the ballroom, her back straight as a lance. Robert watched her go, an odd mixture of emotions on his face.

'So *there* you are!' Lady Mary Bentley, flushed and perspiring in inappropriate red velvet had appeared beside him. 'Really, Robert FitzBolton, times have come hard when a girl has to search out her partner –! Think yourself lucky that I'll dance with you at all –!' With a firm grip and a dangerous gleam in her eye she steered him forcefully back to the dance.

*

Three days later William Hawthorne rode out to inspect the summer wheat that Giles had planted on a fertile stretch of newly-enclosed land, and a mile from the house he collapsed. They brought him home upon a cottage door, wrenched from its hinges to provide a stretcher. His face was a death's mask of pain. For twenty-four hours he lay struggling for every breath, the last of his obstinate strength of will the only thing that kept him alive. He died in the darkness of the second night, his family by his bedside. Caroline, sobbing hysterically, was led from the room by her husband. Jessica stood by her mother, dry-eyed and exhausted. On the opposite side of the vast testered bed stood Clara and Giles, side by side but not touching each other. Giles' eyes were fixed upon the still face of his father, drawn even in death into lines of mortal pain. Clara's unfathomable dark eyes lifted to her husband's face. And almost Jessica was ready to swear that she smiled.

The battle began the very day after William's death.

'Purple drapes for the dining room, I feel. Not black. Black is so very –' Clara paused, delicately, '– depressing, don't you think? I'll tell Mrs Benson. And perhaps, Mother-in-Law, you might let me have a list of guests who might expect to eat with us? I must know the numbers if I am to discuss the funeral meats with Chef this afternoon –'

Even in her grief, Jessica fumed. Her mother, her face set in an iron mask of composure, her eyes shadowed with pain acquiesced to this overriding of her authority with more grace than Clara deserved – yet Jessica sensed the stirrings of anger and wondered if Clara really believed that Maria Hawthorne would so easily surrender her place and her influence.

The funeral was huge; the whole county and half of London were there. Jessica struggled through it with a strange sense of unreality. Surely it could not be true that her handsome, forceful father could be dead? Sometimes, absurdly, she found herself listening for his voice, looking for his red-gold head above the crowd of mourners. It was hard to accept that such vivid life could have been extinguished.

She sat before her dressing-table late in the evening of the funeral, the tears of the day still reddening her eyes, her exhausted sadness a dull ache in her head and in her heart. Lucy brushed her hair gently. The windows of the room high up in the west wing were open to a balmy night. On her sixteenth birthday, with MacKenzie triumphant in her final capture of the unfortunate Reverend Jones and her schoolroom books packed into a trunk in the attic, Jessica had begged to keep the nursery suite as her own. Her mother had been surprised; all the family suites – her own Yellow Suite, William's very masculine rooms, Giles' and Clara's small suite – were in the east wing, and it had been assumed that Jessica would take the Blue Rooms, three small rooms on the top floor above Giles' and Clara's. But Jessica was adamant. She wanted the nursery suite, and she wanted Lucy to go with them. She ignored Robert's shrewd teasing about little girls who did not want to grow up. Stubborn as any of them she dug her heels in; and half-exasperated, half-amused her mother had given in. Jessica loved the familiarity of the little rooms – refurbished and refurnished to be sure, but still comfortably and reassuringly hers – loved even their isolation from the rest of the family's accommodation. And Lucy was a friend, utterly reliable and devoted, even if as Clara frequently and caustically pointed out her skills as a lady's maid were limited. So, Jessica had been known to retort sharply, were her own skills as a lady.

'I'll bring you a posset, Miss Jess,' Lucy said now, gently. 'T'will help you sleep, maybe.'

'Thank you, Lucy.' Jessica, sighing, rubbed her eyes with the back of her hand. 'It's funny, isn't it – I don't think I believe it even now.'

Lucy nodded knowingly. ''Tis the shock. You'll get over it, Miss Jess. Quicker than you think. You'll see.'

'And Mama?' Jessica asked, more of her own reflection than of Lucy. 'Will she?'

'Why bless your heart of course she will. You mark my words. Now. Into bed with you. I'll go and get a nice warm drink –'

Too tired to sleep Jessica lay in bed watching, as she had so often watched as a child, the flicker of the nightlight upon the bedroom ceiling, and wondered for the first time and faintly uneasily how this horrible upheaval would affect her own life. For it suddenly came to her that her brother Giles was now the head of the family and as such presumably had the disposal of her hand in marriage. There had been in the past, Jessica knew, some approaches to William Hawthorne, none of which, thankfully, had met with his approval. She did not know why she did not share Caroline's eagerness to marry before she was eighteen; she only knew that, as with so many other things, she did not. Would Giles be as scrupulous for her welfare as her father had been? Or would he simply be so anxious to get her off his hands that he would hand her over, bag and baggage, to the first man who bothered to offer? Her father had left good provisions for a dowry – who in heaven's name might that not attract once the mourning period was done? Just before she slipped at last into uneasy sleep she resolved to speak to her mother on the subject; Maria, hopefully, would not see her youngest daughter, gauche as she still might be, married off to an old man with grown children – or a young one with no brains and less money like the fatuous Bunty Standish –

Maria, however, it soon became apparent, had worries of her own.

Two days after the funeral – Jessica later grimly came to wonder how she had left it so long – Clara made her first real move to claim her place as undisputed mistress of the household. Jessica came to breakfast that morning a little late – breakfast was served at ten and she always walked in the park with Bran, weather permitting, before joining the family for this first meal of the day. That morning Bran – a rather more staid Bran now, his puppy exuberance somewhat tamed, but still as accident-prone as ever – had chased a duck into the lake and on emerging had shaken himself happily, covering Jessica from head to toe in flecks of mud and slime. Consequently on arriving home she had to change her clothes before making her way to the breakfast-room.

Clara's voice, sharp and clear, stopped her in her tracks

outside the door, '– is perfectly obviously my right as your wife and mistress of this house. You must move in to your father's rooms, of course – and the Yellow Suite must be mine. Your mother will see that, I'm sure. She can move into our rooms. They're perfectly adequate for a woman alone. You'll arrange it –?'

Giles muttered something.

'I beg your pardon?' Clara's voice was icy.

'I said – yes! I'll speak to her.'

'Good.' Jessica could hear the cool smile in her sister-in-law's voice. 'And I'm quite sure she'll understand.'

'Yes,' Giles said, flatly, 'I'm sure she will.'

A knife chinked quietly onto a plate. 'I really must go,' Clara said, 'I am expected in Lavenham for a meeting of the Committee for the Relief of Mendicants. You'll be in for luncheon –? Why, good morning, Jessica –' Clara's dark brows climbed in surprise as she swept past Jessica, who stood hesitating at the door. 'Whatever are you doing there, my dear? Eavesdropping?' and she was gone, smiling.

Jessica glared after her, then erupted into the room where Giles stood, hands in pockets, in characteristic pose, glowering out of the window.

'Giles!'

He did not turn.

'*Giles!*'

He swung his head. 'Eat your breakfast, Jessica,' he snapped ill-temperedly. 'And be quiet.' Steaming silver dishes of eggs, bacon and kidneys sat upon a side table.

Jessica ignored them as she ignored her brother's words and their dangerous tone. 'Giles – you can't! You *can't* turn Mama out of her rooms – not yet –'

He turned back to the window.

'Giles, answer me!' Jessica was livid. 'You can't do it! It's too cruel! Those rooms have been hers ever since Father bought the house. At least give her time! You can't let Clara just turn her out –!'

'Oh, for God's sake! You make it sound as if Clara's throwing her out into the park!'

'As she would if she could!' Jessica snapped back without thought, then drew back as Giles swung on her. 'Giles please!' she pleaded. 'Don't you think that Mama has enough to contend with at the moment? You can't be so heartless –!'

'Leave it, Jessica.'

'I –'

'Leave it, I say!'

She subsided, biting her lip. Giles' handsome face was set in anger, though whether with her, with Clara or simply through being so dragged into the squabbles of women Jessica could not tell. 'It really is none of your business,' he said after a moment in quieter tone. 'Leave it to me.'

And with that for the moment she had to be content. But it was by no means the end of the affair. She rode that afternoon in the park and came back to an odd air of tension about the house. The maid who relieved her of riding hat and whip glanced at her surreptitiously as she did so, a curious gleam in her eye. 'The mistress –' she stopped, flustered '– that is the older Mrs Hawthorne – asked to see you when you came back, Miss.'

Jessica stared at her. 'The older –?' She stopped. The *older* Mrs Hawthorne? Was this more of Clara's malice? 'Very well. Thank you.'

She heard the voices before she reached her mother's sitting room – her mother's shaking with uncharacteristic rage, Clara's cool as cucumber and utterly calm. '– then I'm sure you'll see reason. After all, if Giles is to have the adjoining suite it's obvious that these rooms should be mine –'

'And they would have been!' Maria's voice cracked sharply across the words, 'if you'd had the courtesy – the decency! – to wait! I'd have given them to you Clara, in time. Or if I had been asked. But, by God, you shall not demand them as a right!'

'But it is my right.' Clara's voice was level and reasonable. 'You know it is. Really, Mother-in-Law, you surprise me – such an exhibition is not worthy of you. There cannot be – I have to insist that there will not be – two mistresses at New Hall. You must understand that, and so must everyone else.' The words, beneath the calm, were steely. As Clara spoke she turned, and caught sight of Jessica, standing struck to silence by the door. 'Really, there you are again, Jessica, hovering by a door!' she said, mildly malicious. 'A quite reprehensible habit, you know.'

Jessica flushed deeply, and pointedly ignored her. 'You asked for me, Mama?'

For a moment Maria looked at her almost absently before pulling herself together with an obvious effort. 'Oh – yes, Jessica. I'm sorry. I had forgotten. Other things intervened.' The words were biting.

'I could come back later if you'd like?'

'No, no.' Maria put slim fingers to her forehead for a moment. 'It's quite all right.' She lifted her head then, her eyes direct and challenging upon her daughter-in-law, 'Clara was just leaving, I think.'

Clara smiled. 'So I was.' She nodded to Jessica, and to Maria. 'Jessica. Mother-in-Law. I'm sure you'll see the good sense of my suggestion when you've had a chance to think about it.' She left the room quietly.

Jessica stood, watching her mother. Maria shook her head, slowly, her eyes upon the closed door, suddenly calm. 'I should not have lost my temper. I – should – not!'

'With poisonous Clara an angel would be hard pressed,' Jessica said gloomily, and was surprised by her mother's sudden, genuine laughter.

'That's true.' Gracefully erect Maria sat upon a small velvet upholstered chair, waving to Jessica to do the same. 'Have you heard my new title?' she asked, bleakly humorous.

Jessica eyed her a little warily, uncertain of this swing of mood. 'The older Mrs Hawthorne?' she ventured.

Maria nodded, straightfaced.

Jessica nibbled her lip, and then at the grim gleam of laughter in her mother's brilliant eyes she could not help but laugh herself. 'It's ridiculous!'

'Of course it is. And that's how we must treat it.' Maria sat in thought for a moment. Then, 'Ring for tea, my dear, would you? And send to Mrs Benson to say I wish to see her at four.

If I am to vacate my rooms then at least some of my furniture will vacate them with me.'

Jessica stared at her, aghast. 'You're – you're going to let Clara have them?'

'But of course.' Her mother's voice was even. 'She is right. These are the rooms of the mistress of the house.' She moved her head a little to look directly into Jessica's eyes. 'She will, however, regret the manner of her acquiring them. I do assure you of that.'

And at the perilous glint of rancour in those sapphire eyes Jessica suddenly did not doubt it. As she moved to the bell she found herself wondering if Clara realized who and what she was taking on; for if the war in Europe were over at last, only the first skirmish had been fought in the battle for New Hall.

Unexpectedly the next, and inevitable clash came not through a matter pertaining to the household but through a change of policy on the estate in this case instigated by Giles but certainly encouraged if not actively suggested by Clara.

The Game Laws were – as was to be expected in a country still more or less entirely ruled by the landed gentry – punitive. Not a bird could be taken, not a fish nor the smallest game except at risk of prison and the treadmill – or at worst transportation for the culprit and consequent destitution and starvation for his family. It was forbidden for anyone apart from the squire and his eldest son to carry a gun on the land except by express permission. In common with many other landowners William Hawthorne had never invoked the full force of the law upon his own people; upon New Hall land the owner was the law, and his was the hand that dealt it. Let a stranger be caught on Hawthorne land with a gun, a cudgel or a noose and the orders had always been clear; to Melford and the officers of justice he would be marched and the law could take its harsh course, and welcome. For the locals, however, as long as no large-scale operation was suspected, a beating from the gamekeeper and the threat of worse should the offence be repeated had long been regarded as sufficient punishment for the loss of the odd partridge or pheasant. Often a blind eye had been the order of the day, as long as such leniency was not abused. It was with horror, therefore, that Jessica learned of the arrest and threatened prosecution of a lad she had known since childhood for the taking of a hare. Perhaps unwisely she took her distress to her mother.

'Mama, Jem has two sisters and a sickly mother – his father died, you remember, in the epidemic last year? – who'll surely starve if he's transported. The new gamekeeper took him last night – badly injured they say – and has already delivered him to the Justices in Melford. There must be a mistake –'

'How was he injured?'

'I don't know. It's said by a man-trap, but that can't possibly be – there are none on New Hall land. His sister came to me – we've known each other since we were children. She says they've been told they are to leave the cottage – Mama, where can they go? What will they do? We must do something –'

Her mother stood up. The severe black she had worn since the death of her husband suited her. Certainly it added a formidable aspect to her slim, arrow-straight form. 'Come.'

They tracked Giles down in the Estate Office behind the stables. He looked up in more than half-exasperated surprise at the interruption. 'Mother? Jessica? What are you doing here?'

'We wish to speak with you, Giles.' Maria's tone was uncompromising.

Ben Black, the estate manager, a ruddy-faced, bulky man in his early forties who had scrambled to his feet as they had entered the room took the hint readily, to a glint of approval from Maria.

'I was just going. I'll see you tomorrow, Sir, with those reports.'

Giles nodded briefly. 'Very well.'

The man left. Giles steepled his fingers before him. His face was bland, his eyes cold. Jessica had no doubt at all that he knew their errand. 'Well?' The word was polite enough, but not encouraging.

Impulsively Jessica opened her mouth to speak. Her mother held up a commanding hand, and with unthinking obedience she fell to silence. 'I should prefer to sit, please Giles,' Maria said gently reproving, 'and so I am sure would your sister.'

The natural high colour in Giles' cheeks darkened a little. 'Of course.' He came out from behind the desk and drew two chairs forward. Jessica perched impatiently upon one, her mother settled herself with equanimity and grace upon the other. Giles returned to his own chair behind the desk and waited, warily.

'It seems,' Maria said at last, 'that an error of judgement has occurred. I think that one of our employees has been – a little overzealous. I'm sure the matter can be speedily rectified.'

Giles said nothing.

'A lad – what was his name, Jessica?'

'Landry. Jem Landry.'

'Ah yes – Landry – it seems he's been taken for poaching and has been delivered to the Justice in Melford?'

'He was hurt too – badly his sister said –' Jessica burst in, not able to keep quiet.

Unperturbed, Giles nodded. 'He was caught in one of the new traps. That's what they're for.'

Jessica stared at him. Even Maria appeared for the moment bereft of words.

'A *man*-trap?' Jessica gasped. 'On our land?'

'That's right.'

'But – Father always said –'

Giles stood up and the muted violence in the action cut off the words almost before they were spoken. He leaned forward on the edge of the scarred and littered desk, his weight turning his knuckles white. 'Father is dead,' he said, the words clipped and precise, 'New Hall is mine. As he intended. You – both of you –' he added with emphasis '– know Father's feelings and intentions in this. That the house and the land and the management of it should pass from eldest son to eldest son. Not to a damned committee!' The suppressed violence had for the moment silenced even Maria. 'Mother – New Hall is your home. It will always be your home. But you have to accept this

– I am a man! And New Hall is mine! I'll run it as I see fit and I *will not* have you interfering in that. Is that *clear*?' On the last word he hit the desk violently with his fist. Jessica jumped. Maria did not even blink. 'The Game Laws are there to be used.' Giles' voice had calmed a little, 'And I will use them. I will not have the tenants taking my game. They have to learn that. They were warned. The boy Landry was taken, red-handed. He pays the penalty.'

Jessica jumped to her feet, pleading. 'But, Giles, please! His mother – his sisters –! They are to be turned out of their home! He's hurt – isn't that enough? He must have had the fright of his life! He will have learned his lesson – and the others too, I'm sure of it! Please don't do this! If they transport him – Giles, it was only a hare –!'

Stone-faced Giles resumed his seat. 'No.'

'You say we know your father's feelings and intentions,' Maria said her voice quiet, 'well let me say this, and I dare you to deny it. This was never his intention! That his people should be trapped – transported –? Their families turned out into the road? Never!'

'He ruled his way,' Giles said, evenly. 'I rule mine.'

Jessica looked in desperation to her mother; and even she was taken aback at what she saw in the spare, lovely face as Maria Hawthorne looked at the man who was, to all intents and purposes, her only surviving son. Giles held his mother's eyes for a moment, then sat back, looking down at his clenched hands.

'No,' he said.

In silence Maria stood and left the office with no backward glance. Jessica trailed after her. At the door she turned, beside herself with a frustration of fury and distress. She lifted a small finger, pointing. 'The day that Edward died –' she heard herself say in a voice she barely recognized as her own, '– was a bad day for everyone. Everyone but you!'

His chair rocked violently as he leapt to his feet. '*Get out!*'

She ran.

The situation, as it was bound to, went from bad to worse.

Within the house Clara, finding something to be desired in some of the older servants' attitude to the new order of things simply and without consultation dismissed them and hired others from farther afield who were too pleased to find work to find fault with the young mistress who had provided it. Maria, the recipient of desperate appeals, could do nothing but provide good references – which Clara had refused – and a guinea apiece to soften the blow.

Jessica seethed, and was ignored. 'I'd like to hang, draw and quarter your sister!' she told Robert furiously as they strolled the banks of the river on the day before he left to go back to university. 'She's awful! And getting worse! And as for Giles –!' She lifted hands to heaven, words deserting her.

Robert smiled a little, sympathetically. The early tints of autumn once more tinged the leaves, but the day was warm with just the softest of breezes to ripple the water. A dragonfly darted, poised and elegant, glinting metallically in the sun. 'Perhaps you should get married,' Robert said, teasingly.

He might have suggested that she throw herself in the river. '*What?*' She spluttered.

'Get yourself married off.' The sideways glance he threw her was not altogether laughing. 'Then you could move out and leave her to it. You must have thought of it?'

She said nothing.

'Jessie?'

She shrugged and averted her head. 'Don't be silly. There's plenty of time for that.' She had never told him – had never told anyone – of the strange feelings of panic that assailed her at thought of marriage. She watched Caroline, a docile doll obeying her husband as she had her father with no thought but what she might gain from it, and she could not bear the thought of becoming like her. Worse, she watched Clara and Giles, and hated and feared that undercurrent that she sensed between them. Weeks before she had come across them unexpectedly in the drawing room, quarrelling. The cause of the quarrel she had not known, but she had heard Clara taunt her husband, seen the strange, wild light in her eyes, the challenge in her face as Giles had lifted a hand as if to strike her. But he had not. Instead he had reached for her, and dragged her to him, kissing her with a fury that had been worse than violence. Jessica had fled, had sat upon her bed in the old nursery shivering as if with fever. Was this what marriage was? If so she wanted none of it. 'It's all right for you,' she said now, miserably. 'You're a man. One day Old Hall will be yours. Oh, Robert, how I envy you! I wish I were a boy! I wish I could come to Oxford with you tomorrow!' She laughed suddenly, forcing gaiety, 'We could share a room! And I'd torment the life out of you and stop you from studying!'

He said nothing. She glanced at him and was surprised when something close to a flinch of pain flickered upon his face. 'Why, whatever's the matter?'

His face rearranged itself into a swift smile. 'Nothing, you goose,' he said, and laughed; and Jessica was too preoccupied with her own problems to hear the falseness of the sound.

The real storm broke after an uneasy two weeks of peace when a small deputation of estate workers, bleak-faced and embarrassed, respectfully requested an interview with Maria Hawthorne; an unprecedented occurrence.

Jessica was with her mother in her small sitting room, perched in the window seat, a book open on her lap when the group were shown in, caps clasped in their hands, booted feet scuffling the carpet uncomfortably.

'Good morning, Mr Arkwright,' Maria addressed the obvious leader politely, concealing her surprise, 'You wished to see me?'

'Yes, M'm.'

Maria waited.

'Tha'ss – tha'ss Mr Giles, M'm. We – we wondered if you'd 'ave a word, like, with 'im –'

'Oh?' The expression on Maria's face had sharpened infinitesimally at her son's name. 'In some particular aspect?'

'Yes, M'm. That is –'

'Oh, get on with it, man,' someone muttered from the back of the group.

Poor Arkwright flushed like a beetroot. 'Tha'ss like this, M'm,' he said in a rush, 'Mr Giles is cuttin' the wages. Cuttin' them to the bone. We can't live on what he wants to pay us, an' tha'ss a fact. The little 'uns'd starve, that they would –'

There came a murmur of agreement from the others, a small growl of outrage that stirred the hairs upon Jessica's neck, though there was no overt hostility within the group.

Maria had lifted her head, frowning. 'Mr Giles is cutting your wages?'

'Yes, M'm. By more than half he says. I tell you, M'm – we can't live on that –'

'No.' Briskly Maria stood. 'No, of course not. I see that.' She paused for a moment. 'Might I ask – why have you come to me?'

There was much shuffling of feet and clearing of throats.

She nodded grimly. 'You've already spoken to Giles.'

'Tried to, M'm.'

'And?'

The man shook his head, almost puzzled. 'He threatened to have us thrown out, M'm, for a bunch of trouble-makers. He says the estate can't afford to pay the wages –' His tone clearly indicated what he thought of that for a story. '– He says that the parish will make up the difference. But, M'm, you know they don't make it up to a livin' wage – Mr William always said –'

'Yes. I know what Mr William always said.' Maria paused for a moment. Then, 'I'll speak to my son for you,' she said quietly, and lifted a hand to stem their muttered thanks, 'That doesn't mean I'll get anywhere. On the contrary,' the words were edged with bitterness. 'But I'll try.'

'Thank you, M'm. Thank you kindly.' They shuffled out, pushing and shoving at each other in their eagerness to get out of the unfamiliar and to them obviously uncomfortable environment of the house.

Jessica closed her book with a snap and laid it aside. 'He can't do that. Surely he can't? Father always said that New Hall would never use the Speenhamland system! We've never sent our people to the parish for poor relief !'

Her mother sighed. 'That was your father. We're dealing with Giles now.'

'But he knows as well as we do that the relief only makes up the wages to barely above starvation level.'

'He knows also,' Maria said quietly, 'that very many farmers in the southern counties use the system to line their own coffers and force the parish to feed their people.'

Jessica shook her head violently. 'But it's immoral! It pauperizes the people! Not even Giles would do that!'

Her mother did not reply.

Giles' fist slammed the table and silver cutlery jumped. 'I tell you Mother, I'm tired of your interference! This is none of your business!' He levelled a long accusing finger. 'Clara's right. You try to keep me at your apron strings! When Father was alive you never tried to interfere with the running of the estate!'

'When your father was alive,' Maria returned with calm asperity, 'there could never have been any question of cutting the workers' wages by half.'

'The war is over, Mother. Food prices are falling. There's a depression coming in agriculture. Profits are going down –'

'By how much?'

He ignored the sharp question. 'If we are to restore our profits we must do as others do – use the supplementary system –'

'Abuse it, you mean!'

Giles sat for a moment, fists clenched upon the dining-table, head down like a baited bull's as he forced control upon an all but uncontrollable temper. When he lifted his head his face was a mask of calm in which his brilliant eyes, so like his mother's, blazed with rage. When he spoke his voice was absolutely steady. 'Understand this, Mother. I will not discuss estate matters with you. My decisions are not open to your questions or to your criticisms. New Hall is your home, and of course always will be. But I have to remind you that your presence at this table is at my sufferance. I will not tolerate your interference –' He stopped as, very collectedly, Maria laid down her fork and stood, the footman behind her hastily stepping forward to move her chair.

'In that case,' Maria said, quietly and clearly, 'I no longer choose to eat at –' her scathing glance moved from her son to his wife and back again, '– your table. From now on I shall take my meals in my own rooms. No, Jessica,' she added gently as her daughter started to rise, her usually pale face flushed with anger, 'You will remain, please. This is not your quarrel, and I would not make it so.' And in the utter silence that followed her words she turned and left the room.

'Damn!' Giles in a frustration of fury buried his fair head in his fists.

Clara laughed quietly, the heartless, beguiling, tainted laughter that Jessica so hated.

'*Damn!*' Giles said again.

Maria kept to her word. In months she did not eat with her family, neither if she could help it would she set foot in any part of the house but her own small suite of rooms. To Giles and to Clara she was invariably civil but always cool. With Jessica she refused to speak of the quarrel, was adamant that her daughter should not take sides. She had made her gesture, there was nothing else she could do. Giles went ahead and cut the wages; and on the estate and in the village the effects began to show.

Jessica hated it all. She hated the atmosphere in the house, could not face the workers, who had known her all of her life and whom she had considered without thought and in the true sense of the word her friends. She did not now begrudge them their resentment against her family, but that did not ease the hurt or the embarrassment.

This year it had been planned that she should spend at least part of the Season in London. With no word spoken it was understood that the hunt for a husband was on. Jessica kept her own thoughts on that subject to herself. Her mother planned to take an apartment near Hyde Park, it now being out of the question that they should share a house with Giles and

Clara as had been originally intended, though to keep up the fiction of a united family much of the entertainment would be shared. As autumn wore on, damp and melancholy, Jessica submitted with little grace to sessions with dressmakers, sessions with hairdressers, sessions with the makers of dancing slippers. She did not want to go. Yet neither did she want to stay. As melancholy as the weather she wandered the parkland with Bran, isolated in that half-world between childhood and adulthood, unhappy about the present, confused about the future.

It was upon one of these aimless expeditions that she chanced across an old woman and a child plodding up the drive from the village. She watched them, frowning. The woman was decently if shabbily dressed, a threadbare shawl about her grey head to keep out the mist of drifting rain. It was the child who arrested the eye. His face beneath the bright, dripping hair was sweet as a summer's day, his brilliant smile as he looked at Jessica tugged at her memory and at her heart. It had been a long time since she had seen such a smile. The sapphire eyes were merry and trusting. He was better dressed than the woman, his shoes stout, his coat of good and sober cloth. Bran licked his hand and as the boy chuckled delightedly the dead lived again. He was perhaps eight or ten-years-old. His hair was bright as marigolds in sunshine.

'Can I help you?' Jessica addressed the old woman uncertainly. She could not take her eyes from the child, who was playing now totally unselfconsciously with the dog.

'Yes.' The old woman was short of breath, and her colour was not good. 'You can tell me if the lady of the house is at home?'

'Yes. That is – I'm not sure if you mean my mother or my sister-in-law?'

The shrewd old eyes were thoughtful. 'Not the young one,' she said at last.

'Then it's my mother you're looking for?'

The grey head nodded affirmation.

The child shouted with laughter and ran with the dog.

'Come on, boy! Come on! Oh, look, Gran! He's just like old Tim!'

Even his voice held that light, pleasant timbre that Jessica remembered still in Edward's. 'I'll take you to her,' she said.

Chapter Seven

The child's name was Patrick; and he was Edward's son.

'I don't believe it,' Clara said, flatly, her voice tightly controlled.

'Then you ignore the evidence of your eyes.' Maria's words were cold. The child sat, all but lost in the depths of a leather armchair, his eyes moving uncomprehendingly from one face to another, ill-concealed anxiety making the soft lips tremble. Impulsively Jessica crossed the room and perched on the arm of his chair, smiling reassuringly at him. The child smiled back, a little wanly, the blue eyes understandably wary. Straight-backed upon a chair by the library's tall window sat the elderly woman who had brought him. She looked exhausted and far from well, but her eyes were calm as she studied the faces about her.

'Oh, the child is his,' Clara conceded. 'A byblow. A bastard. He isn't the first and he won't be the last. It's this talk of a marriage that I dispute. It's palpable nonsense.'

'I am assured it happened,' Maria said quietly.

Clara glanced in disdain at the woman by the window. 'And the proof?'

'— is evidently in Cambridge. In the church register and in the testimony of the priest who married them.'

'You surely aren't taking her word for that?'

Maria made an impatient gesture. 'Of course not. I have already sent an urgent message to Sir Charles Sanders, our solicitor. He will be here within the week. In the mean time —' Maria surveyed the faces about her calmly, '— I intend to visit Cambridge myself to make preliminary enquiries.'

Clara lifted her head sharply, frowning, her expression

quarrelsome. But as she started to speak Giles, who had until now barely said a word, said suddenly, 'Be still, Clara.'

She turned angry eyes upon him, and he shook his head. 'Be still!' he said again, his voice tense.

Clara took a sharp breath. 'If you think I'm going to sit by whilst a chit of a child –'

For a moment it looked as if Giles might strike her. Ignoring the onlookers he caught her wrist and hauled her to her feet where she stood, unafraid, glaring, equally as angry as he. 'This is Edward's son!' Giles said, the words grating harshly. 'Look at him! Edward's son! There's no doubt!' His fingers still in painful grip on his wife's wrist he swung to look down at the frightened child. 'Edward's son!' he said again, very quietly.

'Edward's bastard,' Clara snapped.

'Perhaps. Perhaps not.' Giles let go of her wrist and his hand dropped to his side. 'I'm not sure that it matters.' The words held a weary contempt that to Jessica seemed directed as much at himself as at Clara.

Clara stared at him incredulously. 'You aren't going to accept this? You aren't going to give up all we've done, all we've fought for, for this – this brat?'

Maria was watching them both narrowly, making no attempt to interrupt or interfere.

Giles' face was like granite. 'If the story is true – if Edward did marry this girl secretly – if the child is legitimate – then we have no alternative.'

'And if he did? A runaway marriage – Edward was under age! A student!'

'That would neither invalidate the marriage nor affect the legitimacy of the child,' Maria put in, quietly.

Beside herself Clara swung on her. 'Oh, you're enjoying this, aren't you? Well let me tell you this –' she stepped forward, rage bringing colour to her clear-cut, striking face, '– if you think I'm going to be cheated of my rights you can think again, Mother-in-Law! And if you think that I'd trust you – you! – to go to Cambridge alone to verify this story then you must be mad!'

Maria drew herself up, her face a mask of chill outrage. 'I beg your pardon?'

Clara was beyond discretion or control. 'Do you think I don't know that you'd do anything – anything! – to get your hands on this house again –?'

'Are you suggesting that I conjured the boy out of mid-air?' The calm voice was icy, 'Are you – can you be? – suggesting that I could possibly be party to some kind of conspiracy? Beware what you say, Clara.' She turned to her son. 'Giles. Please control your wife. She's behaving like a fishwife.'

Clara was trembling. 'I won't let you do this,' she said. 'I won't!'

'Clara, be quiet.' Giles turned abruptly and took two long strides to the table upon which stood a decanter half-full of brandy. With a jerky movement he poured himself a glass and tossed it back in one movement.

'Giles –!' Clara began, impatiently.

He spun on her, levelling a finger. 'Quiet I say!' and the dangerous force of the words struck her for an unexpected moment to silence. Giles poured himself another drink. Then he strode to where the old woman sat, watching him. 'You say that my brother married your daughter nine years ago, whilst he was a student at Cambridge?'

'Yes. The child is nearly ten years old.' There was neither servility nor fear in her voice.

'And his mother is now dead?'

She nodded. 'Yes.' There was a small silence. The woman looked at Maria. 'He was a handsome lad, your boy. Handsome, and kind – or so he appeared. He and our girl seemed made for each other. And then –' She paused for a moment, shaking her head, her face bitter. There was another moment of quiet. 'When Anne told her father, he all but killed her. He couldn't stand the disgrace. The shame. He threw her from the house.'

'She was breeding?' Giles asked, bluntly.

The woman nodded. 'She was desperate. She went to your brother's rooms. She took his razor and she cut open her wrists.'

Jessica made a small, stifled sound. No-one else stirred.

'He found her. Just in time. He swore he hadn't known about

the child until then.' Jessica remembered Edward – gay, warm, lovingly impulsive. What else would he have done in such circumstances but marry the girl?

'They loved each other.' The woman was looking down at her clasped hands. 'Anne didn't want your money. She didn't want anything to do with you. She wanted him. She wanted a father for her son.'

'And so – you say – they married?'

'Yes. He warned her that the marriage would have to remain a secret. At least until he came of age.'

'And she didn't mind that?'

'Mind? Of course not.' The woman lifted her head, looked Giles in the eye steadily. 'I keep telling you. She wanted none of this. None of it. She wasn't stupid. She understood. If he'd brought her here what would have happened? Would you have accepted her?'

Clara was staring in clear disbelief.

'She had a house and she had some money. She had her child, who she loved more than anything else in the world. Even when she realized that his father would probably never openly acknowledge their marriage – even when she began to suspect that one day he would find some reason to deny it, she would never even consider coming to you. She was afraid of you. She knew that the least that would happen if she came to you was that she would lose the child. She knew enough of the ways of the gentry to be sure of that. And at the worst she feared you'd find some way to disprove the marriage, to make of her boy a bastard.'

'But you've brought him to us now?'

She shrugged tiredly. 'Needs must. She's dead. And I'm dying.'

Jessica heard the sharp intake of the child's breath beside her. She put out a hand and he took it.

'The money's gone. There's no-one to care for him. She came to me at the last. Now I bring him to you, for the alternative is the Parish, and we all know what that means. God will watch how you deal with him.' She fell to silence, her breathing heavy and difficult. Her eyes were on Maria.

'He's Edward's son,' Maria said. 'We'll deal with him well, I promise you.'

'This is absurd!' Clara spun on her heels and marched to the door. 'Have you all taken leave of your senses?'

The child watched her with fearful eyes, his hand clutching Jessica's. She squeezed it reassuringly.

'Edward's dead!' Clara snapped, and the words were for Giles. 'Dead! And nothing can bring him back. New Hall is yours by right. Fight for it! Or by God, I will!'

Giles was upon her in a movement of such violence that the child clutched at Jessica's hand, frightened. Giles grabbed his wife's shoulders, shaking her savagely. 'By Christ! One of these days I swear I'll —'

'Giles! Clara!' Maria's command cut like a knife.

Giles let go of his wife and swung to face his mother. Clara rubbed her arms where he had bruised her with his grip, breathing heavily. There was a long tense moment of silence. Then Giles caught his furious wife's arm and propelled her through the door, slamming it behind them.

Jessica was watching her mother. Maria sat still as stone for a moment, her eyes upon the closed door, and in them a gleam of something close to triumph. Jessica could stand it no longer; sick at heart she forced a smile, bending to the child. 'Do you like marzipan?'

Wordless he nodded.

She stood up briskly. 'Then follow me. I know where Cook keeps her secret store!' She was well rewarded by a brilliant, tremulous smile before the child followed her to the door. As she opened it she glanced back. Her mother had moved to the window where she stood beside the other woman, a reassuring hand upon her shoulder. Tiredly the sick woman looked up, and Maria smiled. Deep within Jessica some unease moved. She turned away, holding out her hand to the boy. Trustingly he took it. And, troubled, she found herself wondering how long, in the hostile and suspicious atmosphere that had invaded her home his innocence could last.

The next day Maria, accompanied by Patrick's grandmother,

left for Cambridge. The boy stayed at the house, cared for by a happily fussing Lucy. He cut a subdued and pathetic little figure, the immediate uncertainties of his young life quelling spirits that Jessica suspected might under more normal circumstances be cheerily high. She spent the first morning with him, walking in the park with Bran after breakfast and then taking him up to her own rooms to see if she might find in the schoolroom trunks something of interest to keep him occupied – and out of Clara's way – for the rest of the day.

'Poor little mite,' Lucy said. 'All alone in the world at such an age!'

Jessica had had a lifetime to accustom her to the apparent omniscience of servants; it did not surprise her in the least that Patrick's circumstances were apparently already common knowledge in the household.

'Strange business, though – Mr Edward being married, like –?' Lucy cast a look of tentative enquiry.

'We don't know that he was,' Jessica said, briskly. 'And there again, we don't know that he wasn't. That is what must be established.'

Lucy, busying herself about the bed, allowed herself a small uncharacteristically mischievous smile. 'No doubt about the other, though, eh?'

Jessica looked at her, puzzled.

'Two peas in a pod,' Lucy said, nodding knowingly. 'Every-one's sayin' it –'

Jessica sighed, knowing she should reprimand the girl: but to what purpose? Gossip and rumour must be flying about the house like dust. There was no way to stop it – no way either to prevent it spreading further. Such a choice morsel, no doubt suitably embellished, would be County property in no time. Who could blame Lucy for being intrigued? She bent over the trunk, rummaging amongst the well-worn books of her childhood.

'You'll be goin' to see Mr Robert, I expect?' Lucy asked, conversationally.

Jessica straightened in surprise. 'Robert? Of course not. He's at Oxford.'

Lucy shook her head. 'Bin home for two or three days,' she said. 'Not bin well, so Mary Baldock says. Talk of him not goin' back.'

'Surely not?' Jessica's brows furrowed.

'So Mary Baldock says.' Lucy quoted Old Hall's kitchen maid as an unimpeachable source.

Jessica hefted a book in her hand. 'I wonder why he didn't send to tell me? Yes – perhaps I will pop over there. This afternoon.' She looked in sharp concern at Lucy. 'He's ill, you say?'

Lucy shrugged. 'That's what they say. Though Mary said he seems all right to her. Just a bit down, she thought. It's all that learnin' if you ask me. Enough to put anyone under the weather.' And with that gem of wisdom she left, her arms full of bed linen.

Jessica rode to Old Hall after luncheon. She found Robert in the Old Drawing Room, hunched into a chair, staring into space.

'Robert? Whatever's wrong? Why didn't you let me know you were home?'

He turned his head, his reverie broken. 'Oh. Hello Jessica.'

She was taken aback by the look of him. Always pale, his skin now had an odd, unnatural translucence and was drawn across bones so fragile-looking that they might have been made of glass. 'You look awful,' she said, with the childish directness of close friendship.

'Thanks.' He smiled a little.

'Whatever's wrong?'

He shrugged. 'I haven't been all that well.'

'All that well? You look –' she stopped. 'What is it? What's wrong with you?'

'Nothing.'

'But –'

He lifted an impatient hand. 'Nothing now. Jessie, don't fuss. I've been unwell. Now I'm better. Just – a bit tired –'

She watched him, frowning, not sure how far to trust his reassurances. 'How long are you home for? The rest of term?'

'At least that. Possibly for good.'

'For good! But Robert – why on earth –?'

'Jessica, please!' His voice held a grating edge of nerves. 'I asked you not to fuss! I've been ill. I'm all right now. But it may be better if I don't go back to Oxford. I don't know yet. Now. I'd like to talk about something else, if you don't mind.'

She surveyed him for a moment longer, her eyes still worried, then, shrugging a little, she plumped into a chair opposite him, by the fire. 'Well, there's certainly something else to talk about!'

He listened to her story with astonishment and gradually reviving interest.

'Edward's son? His legitimate son?'

'So it seems. So the old woman says. And – oh, Robert, when you see him, you'll believe it! You remember the picture in the dining room? The one of Edward and Giles as children? Patrick is the image – the very image – of Edward. It's quite astonishing. And he's such a sweet little boy –'

'I doubt my sister thinks so.'

Jessica sobered, 'No. She doesn't.'

Robert shook his head. 'Trouble, trouble and more trouble,' he said, quietly. 'Keep out of it, Jessica, if you can. Trouble like this is like the rising of a flood. It can drown anyone who's near.'

Unsurprisingly Robert's words proved all too prophetic. As they waited for Maria's return and for the arrival of Sir Charles Sanders the family solicitor, trouble did indeed appear to be rising like a flood in the house. Clara's mood was foul. And Giles, apparently abandoning his duties on the estate, had to all intents and purposes so far as Jessica could see given up eating in favour of drinking. He was seldom sober. His and Clara's angry voices, raised sometimes but equally often fiercely and implacably quiet echoed in the rooms and corridors of the great house. Late on the afternoon of the second day after Maria's departure Giles stormed from the house, setting his horse at the drive like a cavalry charge. Jessica watched him go from her window high in the west wing. In a Christian attempt to keep Clara from Patrick she had had the child installed in a small room near hers, to motherly Lucy's delight. Over the past days Jessica and Patrick had become wary friends; but his heart was given to Lucy, and hers to him. Jessica could not bring herself to blame him. Though he said nothing she was sure he understood all too well what was going on, and at least part of what hung on its outcome; and she, for all her efforts must for the time being anyway be ranked with the enemy in the child's sensitive mind. Lucy carried no such stigma. As Jessica watched her brother gallop wildly down the drive and wondered wearily what new crisis had triggered such a departure she could hear Lucy and the child laughing in the other room as they played a simple card game that involved much shouting and slapping down of cards.

Giles did not return for dinner, which in accordance with the new order was served at six o'clock. Clara sat, frigidly silent across the table from a Jessica who after a few desultory attempts at polite conversation gave up and ate in silence also. She was glad to escape to her rooms after a brief and barely civil farewell from her sister-in-law. Outside the wind was rising. In no way unhappy with the solitary comfort of her small, familiar sitting room she settled back before the fire. Patrick was asleep in his little room along the corridor and Lucy, who for so many years had slept beyond Jessica's own open door had, on the understandable plea that the child was restless in a strange house, moved her own truckle bed into the boy's room where she sat now, within call, sewing and watching the sleeping child. Jessica had reassured her of her own capability of putting herself to bed when the time came; the thought of an uninterrupted evening's reading was bliss. With a small sigh of relief at the peace of the moment she reached for her favourite book.

Ten years before, with Europe still at war Augustus Von Kotzebue had travelled through Italy, describing in detail her lovely countryside and the treasure-houses of her cities. Jessica had discovered the book some two years before; parts of it she knew almost by heart – 'the view of Florence, with the surrounding hills and the houses dispersed on them would be accounted by many as unparalleled –' It had been counted so, she remembered, by Danilo O'Donnel, her Danny, who had sown within her the seeds of a love for a city she had never seen. As she picked up the small book it fell open at a well-worn page. A Florence she had read about so often that she felt as if she knew every street, every church, every sculpture in every gallery, waited in those pages. Smiling, she settled down to read and to dream. The glow of the fire was transmuted to the warmth of a southern sun. Narrow streets, smiling people, the centuries' store of lovely things – her head nodded, and, sweetly, she slept.

She jumped awake stiff and cold and for the moment completely disorientated. The fire had collapsed to ashes, and those candles that had not died altogether were very low. It must be very late indeed. She stretched her legs gingerly, that had been tucked beneath her and were now painfully cramped. She could not place the sound that had awakened her until it came again – the quiet scrape of a restless horse's hooves upon the gravel of the drive below. Flinching at the pain in her legs and her stiff back she got up and went to the window. In the flickering light of the wind-blown cresset by the front door she saw Giles' horse standing, head down and blowing, a still, shapeless shadow slumped on his back. As she watched the animal danced again, eager to be rid of its burden and safe in a warm stable. Giles – for he it most certainly must be – did not stir. The horse moved again. This time Giles lifted his head, painfully. He was lying sprawled full length upon the horse's neck, arms dangling limply on either side. God only knew how he had stayed in the saddle this far. Jessica reached for a shawl. She saw her brother, swaying perilously, try to lever himself upright in the saddle, saw him pitch over and disappear from sight. The horse tossed its head and danced dangerously. Flinging her shawl about her shoulders Jessica ran from the room.

She encountered no-one in her flight through the house. The world, it seemed, was sleeping. But as she reached the landing above the entrance hall, in which two wall-mounted candelabras threw their elongated, dancing shadows, she stopped. The

189

front door had been opened by a sleepy footman. Giles leaned in the dark opening, his hat gone, his greatcoat muddy, his hair tousled. His fair face was flushed with bright colour. Almost at the foot of the stairs Clara stood poised, dressed in a froth of virgin white lace that hid her slim body from throat to ankle. Her face was still and pale as marble, and venomous with anger.

'Thank you, Frederick. That will be all.' Her voice was savagely quiet.

The footman, long past curiosity or question in the matter of his master's behaviour, mumbled a goodnight and left. Giles swayed, his handsome face lifted defiantly to his wife.

'Where have you been?' The question was icy.

'Drinking,' Giles said, and grinned belligerently.

'I can see that, fool!'

'Mind your tongue, woman.' Giles was undoubtedly and barbarously drunk.

Clara took a step down, towards him. 'You're disgusting!'

He laughed, as if truly amused. 'Then we make a good pair, my dear. But then, we always did. Two cats in a cage. Two – disgusting – cats in a cage,' he corrected himself punctiliously.

From where Jessica stood, unseen, on the landing above she could see Clara's hand trembling upon the smooth wood of the sweeping banister. 'How dare you speak to me like that?'

He too stepped forward, tilting his head further, the candles shining full on the perilous blaze of his face. 'Well, how dare I?' he asked, softly, of the ranked portraits that lined the walls. 'How dare I speak so to the woman who blackmailed me into marriage – who sold her body and her soul for – this!' He flung out his arms as if to encompass the house and its contents.

Clara stood like a stone, watching him.

His voice grated on, bitter and uncontrolled. 'Whore!' he said. 'WHORE! Are you satisfied now? Are you enjoying your ill-gotten gains?'

'At least I didn't kill for them,' she said, flatly and clearly, pure contempt in the words.

He stood as if she had struck him.

'Did you hear what I said? I said –'

'I heard what you said.' There was violence in the quiet voice. He was advancing on her slowly.

'– at least I didn't kill for them,' she repeated, inexorably spiteful.

He stopped. 'I didn't kill him,' he said. 'You know I didn't!'

'You didn't save him. You stood, and watched him die. Where's the difference between that and murder? You let the boat drift away from him. Knowing he couldn't swim. You left him. Deliberately left him to drown when you could have saved him. I saw you. You know that I saw you!' The momentary silence that followed the fierce words was terrible. 'Oh, yes, Giles Hawthorne,' Clara said softly, 'you killed your brother.'

'No!'

'And I say yes! You know it, and I know it, and I dare you to deny it, you coward! Why else did you marry me but to still my tongue?'

For a moment Giles bowed his head, his shoulders hunched. Clara descended the last couple of steps into the hall. She was smiling now, a small, excited smile that brought a sudden feeling of nausea to Jessica's stomach. She tried to move, to retreat from this nightmare, and could not.

'You killed your brother for New Hall.' There was a taunting in Clara's manner, like a child that tormented a wild dog for the fearful excitement of it. 'And you were willing to take me to prevent me from telling what I saw that day. Don't complain of your bargain now! Don't dare! I'll not give up this house! It's mine by right! And FitzBoltons will inherit it, as they should!'

He lifted his head and stared at her. 'You'll do as I tell you, Giles,' she said, and this time there was no doubt that the taunt was deliberate.

'Bitch,' he said, flatly.

She moved closer to him. As she moved the froth of her nightgown drifted and her naked body gleamed in the fitful light. She did nothing to cover herself. Giles clenched and unclenched his big hands, trembling. 'Bitch!' he said again, quiet violence threading his voice.

Her eyes glinted. 'Hit me!' she said, a fierce excitement in her face. 'Hit me, damn you!'

He did. He hit her, hard, open handed across the face.

She laughed.

Jessica turned, her hands to her mouth.

'Again! Hit me again, you pig!' Clara's voice was husky with excitement.

With a choked sob Jessica turned and ran, blindly.

Behind her, Clara laughed again, clearly for a second before, suddenly, the sound was smothered.

Jessica could not get up from bed the next morning – could not face a world so suddenly tainted and awry. She had slept hardly at all, and her heavy-eyed pallor easily convinced a worried Lucy that she was in danger of fever and needed rest and care. She lay like a doll, or like a small sick child, staring at the ceiling, in her head the endless repetition of that dreadful scene, the endless echoes of the terrible words.

'– you killed your brother for New Hall,' Clara had said, '– and you were willing to take me to prevent me from telling what I saw that day –'

And Jessica believed it, could not help but believe it in face of Giles' anguished and guilty reaction. She lay in silence and utterly alone. In whom could she confide such a secret? The thought of the grief such knowledge would afford her mother was unbearable. John was gone – lost to them all by William Hawthorne's intransigence. Jessica had not the first idea where he might be or how to find him – and for the first time she understood that even a part of that might be laid at Clara's door. Clara's silence, her covert encouragement of John's Catholic leanings had not been for his benefit but for her own. Edward dead – John disowned and disgraced – Giles the only son left, the Hawthorne fortune his and his alone. No wonder Clara had done nothing to discourage John!

Jessica tossed uncomfortably in her bed.

'Here, my love –' Lucy supported her head and held a small spouted cup to her lips. 'This will help you sleep, poor lamb. Drink it down – tha'ss right –'

She sipped the drink, sank thankfully back onto her pillows.

'Jessie?' A small bright head had appeared at the door. 'Are you sick?' Patrick's face was drawn with worry.

She tried to smile, tried to ignore the stab of pain that the sight of the child brought. 'I'm all right. I'll be better soon.'

'Are you sure?' He advanced uncertainly to the side of the bed, his wide eyes searching her face. With a pang she realized that in all probability he had watched his own mother die, and very recently. He never spoke of her.

'I'm sure.' She put out a hand, and he took it. 'Do you want to take Bran for a walk for me?'

His face lit like a lamp. 'Oh, yes please! May I?'

She nodded. The sleeping draught Lucy had given her was taking effect. Her eyelids drooped. The marigold shine of the boy's hair in the light from the windows blurred as if seen through tears. Somewhere very deep within her a resolution began to form. Giles had let Edward die. This was Edward's son, legitimate or otherwise. Somewhere here was justice – and Giles, she suddenly thought, remembering the scene in the library, had probably been the first to see it. She tightened her hold on the child's hand a little. 'Patrick?'

'Yes?'

'Do you like it here?'

He hesitated for only a moment. 'Y – yes.' He could not keep the doubt from his voice.

'Would you like to stay here?'

'I – think so.'

'If you could have rooms of your own – books to read and toys to play with – Lucy to care for you – Bran to play with –?'

He nodded vigorously. 'Yes.'

'A pony?' She persisted. 'A pony of your own?'

His eyes had widened.

She closed her eyes, letting the relief of drug-induced sleep seep into her exhausted mind. She felt the child's hand slip from hers, heard him leave the room quietly. Distantly, hatefully, those words rang again in her ears '– you were willing to take me to prevent me from telling what I saw that day –'

She slept at last.

She woke, heavy-eyed and unhappy late in the afternoon. Her sleep had been haunted by dreams she did not wish to remember, and the worst nightmare of all – the truth – crouched waiting for her as she awoke. But one thing had come to her, one small grain of comfort. She was not, after all, entirely alone. Robert was home. Robert would help her, as he always had. Robert would know what was best to be done.

The thought once lodged she wanted to act upon it. She threw the bedclothes back just as Lucy came quietly into the room. 'Goodness, Miss Jess! What do you think you're doing?'

'I'm getting up. I have to see Robert.'

'Oh, no you don't!' Firm hands pushed her back. 'You'll catch your death, the state you're in!'

'You don't understand, Lucy – I have to see him. At once!'

Lucy shook her head. Slow she might be, but her mind once made up was not easily unmade. 'Over my dead body you'll go out there! Ha' you seen that weather?' The afternoon was bleak and threatening. The wind gusted still, rattling the windowpanes. 'The very idea!'

Jessica, truly distressed, sucked her lip and fought against childish tears. The thought of clear-headed, dependable Robert had come like a ray of light in a dark world. She had to talk to him. She could not endure the long hours of another night solitary with her grim discovery. She had to talk to someone. 'Lucy – please! I can't explain, but it really is important. I have to see Robert.' In her agitation she had caught the older girl's hand. 'If I send a note, will you make sure he gets it?'

Lucy patted the hand that clasped hers. 'You know well I will. I'll fetch paper, and a pen.' At the door she stopped, and turned. 'My head's like a sieve! I forgot to say – Mr Giles sent to ask after you and to ask if you'd be joining them at dinner this evening?'

Jessica actually felt the blood drain from her face. Panic rose, choking her. The mere thought of facing those two – of ever having to face them again – brought a lift of physical sickness. 'No!' she said, and then again, 'No! I don't want anything!'

Lucy nodded placidly. 'I'll let them know in the kitchen. They'll send up a tray.'

'Yes. Thank you.' Jessica laid back on her pillows. Robert. She needed Robert. 'Bring the paper and pen, Lucy. And – please – hurry?'

It was early evening when he came. A tray had been sent up, and sent back untouched. Von Kotzebue's little book, usually a solace for all ills lay upon Jessica's lap, fallen open at the pages that she usually perused so eagerly. She had insisted on dressing and had resolutely refused Lucy's offer of another sleeping draught. Remembering the desperation of the note she had sent she swung between certainty that Robert would come this evening and equal certainty that he would, very sensibly, decide not to brave the darkness and the bad weather but come in the morning. Guiltily she remembered that he had not been well. Supposing he came, and in coming made himself sick again? Frowning, she nibbled her thumb and glowered into the fire.

Lucy drew the curtains and lit more lamps to dispel the darkness. Usually Jessica loved the atmosphere of this little sitting room with its small windows and sloping ceiling, but tonight she found it oppressive. She wished she had gone to Old Hall. Perhaps she might have persuaded the FitzBoltons to let her stay there? Perhaps she might never have come back? She knew the thought was childish, but that was what she wanted – the need that was growing: to get away. For ever. She shifted in her chair, staring into the flames, her mouth a set and unhappy line.

'You've not eaten a thing all day –' Grumbling good-naturedly Lucy moved about the room, plumping pillows, straightening curtains, fussing with the fire. '– you'll not get better if you don't eat, Miss Jess, I'm tellin' you that. A chill's what you've got, I reckon – feed a chill, starve a fever, that's what they say –'

Jessica did not reply; indeed she barely heard the words. Somewhere in a small corner of her mind the first germ of an idea had stirred. An outrageous idea. But yet –

Abruptly she stood up and peered into the mirror that hung above the mantle. A small pale face looked back, freckled faintly still despite all Lucy's efforts with lemon juice and pastes. Her eyes weren't bad. Her hair was awful. Exasperatedly she poked at it with a finger. It resolutely refused to curl smoothly and so the fashionable short styles – that of course suited Caroline as if specifically designed for her – were completely out of the question. The only way to keep it under control at all was to scrape it into a bun at the nape of her neck – and even then it flew like mousey wire about her head the moment she moved.

Lucy had stopped her fussing and was watching her in surprise. Jessica bit her lips as she had seen Caroline do, to redden them. 'Lucy? Am I very ugly?'

Lucy laughed outright. 'Why bless you, no–!' She stopped as a shadow moved in the doorway. Jessica jumped, and sudden colour rose in her cheeks.

'Robert! You – startled me!' She turned and held out her hands. 'I'm sorry to have brought you out on such a night. But I had to see you – and Lucy wouldn't let me out! Thank you so much for coming!'

He advanced into the light. 'How could I not? I never read such a desperate plea! What's happened? Have the French after all landed on the Suffolk coast?' The walk across the park had brought colour to his cheeks and the wind had ruffled his neat hair. She had never been so thankful to see anyone. He took her proffered hands and, whimsically, carried them to his lips.

She smiled a little, and blushed again. Lucy was watching her narrowly.

'Lucy – take Mr Robert's coat. And bring something – Robert, what would you like? Something to warm you?'

He shrugged lightly, slipped neatly from his greatcoat. 'A glass of wine would be more than acceptable.'

'A glass – a bottle – of wine.'

'Yes, Miss.' Lucy hovered by the door.

Jessica looked at her sharply. 'Off you go, Lucy.'

'Yes, Miss.' She left, leaving the door ajar.

Robert chuckled a little. 'Your mother hen doesn't trust me.'

Jessica turned away from him to hide the deep colour that she knew had risen again in her face. 'Don't be ridiculous,' she said, lightly. She settled herself, straight-backed in one of the small armchairs, waved him to the other.

He sat forward, elbows on knees, face suddenly intent. 'Well, now – what is all this? What's so desperate as to bring me through wind and rain to a distressed damsel's side?'

She shook her head. 'It isn't funny, Robert. Truly it isn't. It's awful.' She paused. 'I had to talk to someone. Had to talk to you. I've got something terrible to tell you. And something – something very important to ask you.'

He leaned back, his eyes concerned and questioning despite the lightness of his manner. 'Well here I am.'

She indicated the still-open door. 'Wait. Wait till Lucy's gone.'

He lifted a hand and nodded agreement. They sat in silence as Lucy reappeared, bearing a tray upon which stood a bottle of wine and two glasses. She was puffing a little from the stairs. She put the tray down with a clatter. 'There'll be murder done between me and that Frenchie one of these days, just mark my words. I nearly had to fight him for it, that I did!'

Jessica smiled. 'Thank you, Lucy.'

Lucy hovered.

'You can go and see to Patrick now.'

'But –'

'Lucy!' There was exasperation in the word. 'If I need you I'll call. I want to talk to Robert privately.'

'Yes, Miss.' Grudgingly she left, closing the door behind her.

Robert poured the wine and handed Jessica a glass. She held it, not tasting it. To her surprise he drank his thirstily and poured another. She waited for him to sit down. Faced with the moment words had suddenly deserted her.

'Now then,' he sat down, watching her, 'tell Uncle Robert all about it.'

She told him, carefully and with restraint, not looking at him, watching instead the dance of the firelight in the depths of the glass she held in her shaking hands. Once or twice her voice almost failed her, and she struggled to control tears. As faithfully as she could she repeated word for word the conversation she had overheard, tried to describe the scene as she remembered it. After a first, small shocked movement he remained very still and quiet, not interrupting, saying nothing to ease the fraught silences when once or twice she choked to speechlessness. By the time she finished she could not despite her best efforts control her tears.

'God in heaven,' Robert said, simply. Then, practically, 'Drink your wine. Just a little.'

Trembling uncontrollably she tried to obey, but the wine slopped over the side of the glass and spilled onto the fine wool of her gown like blood. Gently he reached and took the glass from her.

'What am I to do?' she asked, desolately. 'Oh, Robert – what am I to do?'

He knelt beside her, supporting her, an arm about her shoulders. 'Poor little thing,' he said, softly. 'Poor little Jess.'

She was sobbing now. He held her gently until the crying eased. Eventually she pulled away from him, dashing a hand across her eyes. 'I'm – I'm sorry. I didn't mean to cry.'

He sat back on his heels, his face sombre. 'Who can blame you? What a pickle, eh?'

She nodded. 'I don't know what to do.'

'No.'

She looked at him, her tear-streaked face woebegone. 'I can't stay here! I can't! I can't face them – can't bear to see them –'

'Will you tell anyone? Anyone else, I mean?'

She shook her head in desperation. 'I don't *know*! Oh, Robert – you can see that I can't tell Mama? It would kill her! And anyway –' she stopped.

'They'd deny it,' he finished.

'Yes. I haven't any proof, have I? And – what could Giles actually be accused of? He didn't save Edward. Well, we all knew that, didn't we? What we didn't know was that he acted deliberately. That would surely be impossible to prove?'

He nodded.

'There's just one thing.'

'Yes?'

'Patrick. If there's any justice in this world then that marriage will be proved. If there's any doubt – any doubt at all – that Giles will accept it then I'll tell him.'

'Tell him what you heard?'

'Yes.' Her face was set in stubborn lines. 'I may not have proof, and he may be able to deny it. But it would make life very unpleasant for him if I told what I heard, wouldn't it?'

'There's little doubt of that.' Robert's voice was dry.

'If I told Mama, she'd move heaven and earth to disinherit Giles, and he must know it.'

Robert nodded.

'So at least if I have to I can use it as a weapon. For Patrick.' She hesitated. 'For Edward.'

He nodded. He was watching her with a small glint of surprised admiration in his eyes.

She rose and walked to the fireplace where she stood looking into the flames, her arms folded across her breasts. Then she took a long, slow breath and turned. 'I'll have that wine now.' Her smile was weak, but it brought an answering one from him. He handed her the glass. Steadily she took it, and as steadily drank. 'Thank you for listening.'

He smiled and shrugged the thanks away, gracefully. Then he looked at her. 'You said you had a question?'

Abruptly she turned from him.

He smiled. 'Well? Fire away.'

She shook her head. 'I can't.' Her voice was faint, all her calm again deserting her.

He surveyed her back, puzzled. 'Why ever not?'

She shook her head again.

He stood, and taking her by the shoulders turned her to face him. She ducked her head. Her face was fiery. She would not look at him. He laughed, perplexed. 'Jessie? What is it?'

'An – idea I had.' She struggled with the words. 'A stupid idea.'

'Try me.'

She shook her head.

'Jessie, please – what is this?' Faint exasperation was in his voice.

She lifted her head, an odd mixture of determination and desperate uncertainty on her face. 'Do you think I'm ugly?'

'*What?*' Almost he burst into laughter, but the serious look on her face deterred him.

'Do you?'

'No! Of course not! What an idiotic thing to say! Is that your question?'

She ducked her head again. 'Not – not exactly.'

'Then what?'

She hesitated a moment longer then bravely lifted her head to meet his laughing eyes. 'Would you marry me?'

The laughter fled his face. The hands that had held her shoulders dropped to his side. Before he turned from her she saw the look in his eyes, and flinched from it. Humiliation flooded her. She clasped her hands tightly before her to still their shaking. 'I said it was a stupid idea.' The trembling of her voice betrayed her.

He shook his head, helplessly. 'Oh, my God!'

'It doesn't matter. Truly it doesn't. I just thought – we've been friends for so long – and – and I told you – it was a stupid idea. Stupid.' She could not stop her tongue. She could hear the hysterical lift in her voice. She clamped her mouth shut.

In the silence a wild gust of wind battered the small panes of the window.

Robert was standing, head bowed, leaning against the armchair. In the quiet she could hear his breathing. 'Please, Robert, don't be upset,' she said at last her voice childishly small in the silence. 'I – I don't mind. I don't blame you –'

He shook his head, slowly. 'Stop it, Jessica. You don't understand.'

'I do – yes, I do. And I'm sorry –'

He spun to face her, caught her hand. 'No! I tell you, you've nothing to be sorry for. It isn't you. It's me. I – Jessica if I intended to marry anyone – if I thought I could marry anyone – it would be you. I promise you that. But –' he stopped.

'What?' She was truly puzzled.

That he was fighting a battle with himself was nakedly clear upon his face. At last, painfully, he said, 'Sit down, Jessica. Let me try to explain. As best as I can, at any rate. You deserve that at least.'

A little shakily she sat. He remained standing, half turned from her. There was a long and difficult silence.

'Robert, please —' she ventured at last, 'What is it? What's the matter?'

He lifted his head. 'First of all,' he said, his voice low and clear, 'I have to tell you that I lied to you. About the reason why I shan't be going back to Oxford. It isn't by choice. I've been sent down.'

Shock held her silent for a moment. Then, 'But — Robert! Whatever for? Whatever did you do?' She could not for a moment imagine Robert involved in any kind of wrongdoing.

His head lifted, sharply and somehow proudly. His face was grim. 'Nothing!' he said, 'I swear to you, Jessie — nothing! It was a misunderstanding! A — a horrible misinterpretation — by people who — who simply won't — or can't — see that we are not all the same. That we don't all conform to their narrow-minded idea of what we should be. They dirty everything they touch!' The words were bitter.

She said nothing for a moment. She sensed in him a pain, and a sudden violent anger that confused and just a little frightened her. This was not the Robert she knew. She reached and pulled a chair forward, closer to the fire. 'Come. Sit down and tell me about it. Everything. Please, Robert.' She added as he hesitated, 'You have to tell me now. You can't stop.'

He moved slowly to the chair, perched tensely on the edge of the seat. For the space of several breaths he stared into the fire, collecting himself. When he spoke his voice was quiet and strained, and he stumbled over the words. 'I think you know that — that I've never made friends easily? I don't — I'm afraid that on the whole I really don't like people very much. I find most of them coarse — uncaring — insensitive —' He fell to silence for a moment. 'I can't stand it,' he said at last, quietly. 'I think — I think there must be something wrong with me. I'd rather be totally alone than forced into the company of — of people who trivialize — brutalize — the most beautiful things in life. But then — sometimes — maybe just a few times in a lifetime – you do meet someone different. Someone who feels as you do. Someone who understands. And – when you meet someone like that the bond you form is very special. It is – an association of souls. A refuge against a horrible world. It's love, in the true sense of the word.' He stopped talking for a moment, sunk in thought. Then he sighed deeply. 'Paul Aloway was a friend like that. At least – I thought he was. I don't know how I would have survived my schooldays without him. But – he changed. He said that our friendship was childish, and must be put away with other childish things. I think in the end it – it embarrassed him, even.' His voice was bleak. His hands were clasped before him, the right thumb rubbing nervously upon the left. Jessica, oddly, found herself watching the compulsive movement, unable to look away.

'At Oxford –' Robert continued after a moment, 'I at last found another friend. Another – special friend. We were closer even than Paul and I had been. Sebastian was –' He lifted his head and, shocked, Jessica saw the glitter of tears in his dark eyes, '–he was the most wonderful person I have ever known. Intelligent. Sensitive. Understanding. But – they couldn't leave us alone, of course. People – were jealous of our friendship. They – said things about us –' A deep flush of colour was rising in his face. He could not hold her puzzled eyes. He looked down at his clasped hands. 'They said we – were more than friends –' he stopped.

For a moment, nothing registered. Then, very slowly, the words made a horrible sense. Sheltered she had been, but her reading had been extensive and even in her innocence she had picked up a smattering of information, mostly more confusing than otherwise, about certain unnatural sexual practices. She looked away from him, chewing her lip.

'It wasn't true!' His voice was suddenly passionate, 'Jessie, I swear it wasn't true! Sebastian was my friend – my true friend. We were brothers of the soul. We cared for each other. We shared things. We thought alike. Our friendship was the most wonderful – the most sacred thing I have ever possessed. I don't understand how people can be so – destructive! So horribly filthy-minded!' He ducked his head abruptly, knuckling his forehead.

She waited a moment. Then, 'Didn't you tell them?' she asked.

He lifted his head. 'Of course we did. They didn't believe us. They preferred to believe the filthy lies that people told about us.' He laughed, suddenly and harshly. 'Which just shows how little they knew of us. If they had only known –' He pulled himself up.

'What? If they had only known what?'

He hesitated. Then, 'You do realize,' he asked quietly, 'what it is that I'm trying to tell you? What – what accusations were made against us?'

She nodded, albeit a little uncertainly. 'Yes.'

He shook his head. 'They tried to make out,' he said, his voice grimly controlled, 'that we – Sebastian and I – had a – a sexual relationship. Nothing – nothing! – could have been further from the truth. The truth is that this was one of the things that drew us together. One of the things that we agreed upon utterly. We both found the –' he hesitated, avoiding her eyes, '– the very thought of physical love – repulsive.'

She was struggling to understand. 'You mean – all of it? I mean – men and women too?'

He nodded. 'Yes.' Tensely he flicked with one thumbnail at the other. In the silence the clock ticked loudly. Jessica frowned, trying to assimilate this strange piece of information. Robert made a sudden, small violent movement. 'I can't help it! I hate the thought. It disgusts me. People would say that was unnatural. But what could be more unnatural than that – that horrible act –' He made a small grimace of distaste.

She sat in silence for a moment, still frowning. 'I really don't think I understand,' she admitted at last.

He lifted helpless hands. He looked suddenly tired. 'Why on earth should you? How can you be expected to understand something that I can't entirely explain to myself? I only know that it's so. When I was a child –' He stopped, and Jessica, puzzled, saw the quick lift of embarrassed colour in his face again.

'What?' she asked. 'What about when you were a child?'

'Nothing,' he said. 'Nothing important. I only know that I can't stand for another person to touch me.' It was obvious that that had not been what he had started to say. He rushed on. 'When – when I stayed with Paul Aloway – you remember?'

'Yes.'

'His sister – the elder one, Chrissie – she liked me. She kept – touching me – trying to hold my hand. It was horrible. One day – in the garden – she kissed me.'

'And?'

'I was sick,' he said. 'All over her dress. It was awful.'

She stuck her thumb in her mouth and nibbled at the nail.

He was sitting tense as a drawn bowstring. 'Women – all of them – frighten me. The way they look at you –' He glanced at her and saw the expression on her face. 'Oh, no, Jessie! Not you! You're different. You're my friend. Don't you see – that's just what I've been trying to tell you! Sebastian understood. We had a name for what we had – we called it –' he hesitated, then continued half-defiantly, 'we called it our passionate friendship. But that didn't mean that we did anything wrong! It didn't. We were as close as brothers. Closer.' His face was alight now, suddenly soft with the shadow of remembered love. 'We shared everything. Every single thought. And then they dirtied it.' He closed his eyes as if at a spasm of pain. 'It was the very fact that he was of my own sex that made our friendship possible.' He said after a moment, his voice intense, 'There simply cannot be that kind of relationship between men and women. Women want to touch, and to whisper. To kiss, and to –' He trailed off and Jessica detected the faint shudder that shook him. 'The Greeks understood,' he said. 'They knew about unsullied love. They didn't drag everything down to the level of the gutter. But the English? Who would expect them to understand the purity of Platonic love? They accused us, and they shattered what we had. I'll never forgive them. Never. If they wanted me back, I wouldn't go.'

'What will you do?'

He shook his head. 'I don't know. But – you do see – why I can't marry you?' His voice was suddenly tired. 'I'm no use to you, Jess. I'm no use to anyone.'

'Don't say that!' She reached a hand to his. He drew back from her, very slightly, avoiding her touch. She nibbled her lip. 'Robert – please, don't say such silly things. It isn't true. You're the best friend that anyone ever had. I hate them for what they've done to you! It isn't fair!'

For a fleeting moment she thought he would smile. 'No,' he said, 'it isn't. And it isn't fair that my parents believe they have an unnatural son –'

'No!'

'Oh, yes. And who's to blame them?' He shook his head. 'I suppose in a way they're right. And you – what about you? Jessica, poor Jessica – you send to me for help and what do I do? I simply add to your problems by bleating about my own troubles, that are nothing to do with you –!'

'Of course they are,' she said, sturdily.

He smiled.

'It's because we're friends that I needed for you to come this evening.' She paused for a moment. 'It's because we're friends that I asked you to marry me. Silly, wasn't it?' She smiled a small, watery smile. Silence fell. Then, 'Or was it?' she asked in a voice that was barely audible against the sound of the wind.

She saw him stiffen and turn his head sharply towards her. Her eyes held his. 'Was it?'

He shook his head. 'Jess – I don't think you understand –'

A slow conviction was growing. She interrupted him. 'Robert – don't you think that – perhaps you need help as much as I do? I asked you to marry me because I wanted you to help me. But – but don't you think that I might be able to help you too?'

He said nothing, but shook his head bemusedly.

'You're serious – about not going back to Oxford even if they allow you to?'

'Absolutely. How could I go back after what's happened – after the gossip, the rumours –?' His voice was bitter. 'Conviction by rumour is all but impossible to refute. They don't need proof. They can sack me on suspicion with no questions asked.'

'Suspicion that would be confounded if you married,' she said, quietly.

He became very still, watching her.

'Doesn't it make sense?' The confidence of youth, that sees no obstacles that cannot be overcome shone in her eyes. She in truth had only understood a part of what he had told her, but she had recognized another troubled soul, and the attraction was magnetic.

He shook his head. 'Not for you. You don't understand what you're suggesting. Jessica – you can't marry a man who can't –' he stumbled over the words, 'who can't love you as you deserve.'

She pondered that. 'The way Giles loves Clara?'

Some understanding flickered in his eyes. 'It doesn't always have to be like that.'

'No of course it doesn't. Look at Caroline and Bunty. There's a love-match if ever there was one.'

'Jessica –'

'They aren't even *friends*! At least we'd start with that! Robert, I have to get away from here. I have to! The only way I can do that is to marry. My portion from the estate comes to me when I marry, and not before. I'm penniless without it. Where would I go? What would I do? And you? – You have as much a need as I have to get away from here. We could help each other. And I'm sure in time you'd learn to – to –' she stopped, fiery poppies of embarrassment in her cheeks, 'to love me,' she finished, determinedly.

'And if I didn't?' His eyes were very tender.

She shrugged a bravado shrug. 'It wouldn't matter. So long as we were friends.'

'You make it sound so easy.'

'It is.' She would not admit to her own misgivings. She could not.

He stood watching her, chewing his lip.

'I've quite a bit of money coming. We could go away. You could study music. Abroad. We –' She threw in her trump card with a casual touch that might have done credit to a hardened gambler, 'We could go to Italy.'

'Your mother –'

'– would be very happy to have me off her hands, thank you. Look at me. Hardly cut out for the routs of London, am I? What about your parents?'

'They'd be delighted. More than delighted.' His tone was heartfelt. For a week the look in his mother's gentle eyes when she had looked at him had flayed him.

'Well then.'

The strain was lifting from his face. Against all good sense and reason her persuasive enthusiasm was winning him. He shook his head. 'I shouldn't let you do this.'

'Try to stop me.' She grinned an urchin smile that lit her tired, tear-stained face to devilry.

'God Almighty, Jessica,' he said.

'It strikes me,' she said, collectedly, 'that He has very little to do with what goes on around here. Will you do it?'

He stood for a long moment, the decision in the balance. Then he stepped to her, hesitated for just one short moment before gently lifting her small face in his hands and brushing her hot cheek very lightly with his lips. It could hardly have been called a kiss, but it was, she thought, a start. His mouth was dry and cool and utterly passionless. She liked it. There was no violence here. No threat. She let out a long, sighing breath of triumph. He lifted his head. 'Jessica?'

'Yes?'

'Will you marry me?'

She hesitated for one mischievous moment. It was like the games they had played a hundred times before. Then, 'Yes,' she said.

Chapter Eight

'Well –' Gravely, yet with the faintest gleam of amusement Maria Hawthorne looked from Robert to Jessica and back again, '– so, willy-nilly I am to acquire a new son-in-law as well as a new grandson?'

'If you'll have me. I've decided not to return to Oxford, and my parents have agreed,' Robert said, adding evenly and without glancing at Jessica, 'I think perhaps that I'm not suited to the academic life.' They had approached Maria together on her return from Cambridge. Their own decision firmly taken they had both been eager to gain her consent as soon as possible. For three days Jessica had talked and reasoned, her determination growing with every objection that a still-worried Robert had put up. Now, for both of them, it had become the thing that each most wanted from life; to marry, to escape, to start anew.

Maria nodded, accepting the explanation at its face value. As a matter of fact I think it an entirely suitable match, and one of which Jessica's father would have approved.' Her astute gaze moved, reflectively, to her younger daughter. 'Though you do seem to have taken matters into your own hands to a quite extraordinary degree.'

Though the reproof was mild, Jessica flushed a little. 'I'm sorry, Mama, but –'

'But you're as headstrong as the rest of the brood and will have what your heart is set on despite the conventions.' There was, unmistakably, open and tolerant humour in the words. Jessica, at last, allowed herself to relax. The thought occurred to her that whatever her mother had discovered in Cambridge it had evidently not displeased her. Maria folded her long, pale hands in her lap and tilted her head enquiringly. 'And may I ask if you've gone so far as to put a date to the event?'

'As soon as possible,' Jessica said without thought and before Robert could open his mouth.

The fair head shook. 'Oh, no.' Maria's voice was absolutely firm. 'No, no, no, Jessica! No daughter of mine gets married with the indecorous haste of a fallen scullery-maid! We'll have no talk of hasty weddings, if you please. Unless, that is –' she added, voice and eyes suddenly steely as she fixed her gaze on Robert, '– there is need for such haste?'

Jessica's mouth dropped open.

Robert flushed deeply and painfully, but he kept his composure and his voice was even. 'No, Mrs Hawthorne, I assure you there is not. Only Jessica's and my eagerness to get the thing done.'

She held his eyes for a moment then, satisfied, she laughed a little. 'Lord, lad – you make it sound like having a tooth pulled!' Lightly she turned to Jessica, 'Springtime, my dear,' she said, firmly. 'You'll marry in the spring. And that's my last word on the matter.'

Jessica knew better than to argue. Disappointed, but relieved to have met so little opposition where there might have been so much, she nodded, accepting the decision with as good grace as she could muster. 'Very well, Mama.'

Robert stood. 'Thank you, Mrs Hawthorne. You've really been more kind than we deserve. You won't regret it, I promise you. I'll take good care of Jessica.'

Maria inclined her head with a smile.

'Now, if you don't mind, I'll go to my own parents.'

'They don't know yet?'

He shook his head. 'We wouldn't say anything to them until we'd spoken to you. But I know they'll be delighted.' He smiled one of his rare, warm smiles that lit his serious face like sunshine. 'They already think of Jessie as a daughter I know. That we should marry will be more than they dared hope for, I think.' Jessica caught the double meaning of that at the same moment that Robert himself did, and looked away quickly from the sudden painful flicker of guilt that she saw in his face

He bent over Maria's hand. 'Thank you again, Mrs Hawthorne. May I perhaps beg Jessica's company at Old Hall for supper this evening? I'm sure my parents would love to see her.'

'But of course. And some time soon – next week perhaps – we shall all get together for a celebration supper. I'll call on Lady Sarah tomorrow.'

'Thank you. I'll tell her.' Robert turned to Jessica and formally bowed over her hand also. It was all that Jessica could do not to explode into laughter at the sight of Robert FitzBolton, with whom she had had more stand-up fights than she cared to remember, kissing her hand like a courtier. 'I'll ride over for you at three,' he said.

She grinned at him, mischief in her eyes. How many times had she ridden to Old Hall alone? And Robert hated riding. 'Thank you,' she said demurely, and searched his eyes for the glint of fun that must surely be there at this grown-up charade. But disconcertingly she found none. His face was strained and sober. Her own smile faded a little. She watched him, neat and erect, as he left the room, a small furrow between her brows.

'Well, my dear,' her mother said mildly as the door closed behind him, 'I suppose I might have known you would make your own arrangements and not wait for any plans I might have had?'

'Oh, Mama – you aren't angry? Not really? You said yourself that Papa would have approved. And – oh, you must know how I hate it all – London, those silly balls, those awful, mindless young men –'

Maria laughed gently and shook her head a little. 'The arrogant condemnation of the young!'

'Oh, I didn't mean it to sound like that. You know I didn't. I suppose they can't all be as bad as they seem. It's just – there's something so awful about it all – it's like a cattle market! This one has such-a-fortune, that one doesn't –! Robert and I have known each other for ever. We're friends. We're good for each other. Isn't that a better reason for getting married than land, or title, or money?' Her voice was impassioned.

Maria eyed her indulgently. 'Some would say so. Some not. Your sister for example –'

'I'm not Caroline!' Jessica snapped too sharply, and then blushed a little at her own presumption as her mother's brows lifted.

There was a short silence. Then 'No,' Maria Hawthorne agreed, thoughtfully, 'That you certainly are not.'

Jessica fidgeted uncomfortably, looked down at her hands. Her thumbnail was ragged and broken. Valiantly she resisted the urge to nibble it.

Her mother watched her. 'Tell me, my dear,' she said at last, making no attempt to disguise the gentle hint of amusement in her voice, 'Is it the latest modern trend that the word love should not be mentioned?'

Jessica's head snapped up like a startled hare's. 'What do you mean?'

Maria shrugged a little, elegantly; but there was real and mildly amused curiosity in her eyes. 'You talk of friendship. Of being – what was it? – good for each other. Robert talks of getting the thing done as if he is to have a broken bone set! I have to declare myself a little confused by a young couple ready to face parental rage and disapproval with arguments of such practical good sense!' She made a small, oddly self-deprecating grimace. 'You make me feel an ageing romantic!'

Jessica said nothing.

'Why, when William asked my father for my hand –' Suddenly Maria's still-lovely face was distant, the sharp blue gaze soft. She laughed, quietly, the sound a mixture of amusement and sadness, '– I was dramatically poised to kill myself had his suit been refused!' She drew herself back from the memory, eyed her daughter with a bland and half-exasperated humour. 'I'm filled with admiration! I'm perfectly sure that such level-headed arguments as yours would have swayed my father more than all my passionate declarations of undying love!'

She was teasing, and Jessica knew it. Yet there was that small, sharp edge of curiosity in her voice and something uncomfortably perceptive in her words. Jessica suppressed a faint twinge of – what? Regret? Dissatisfaction? With what? She had what she wanted. She would not look further. 'Of course we love each other,' she said. 'That's why we're getting married.'

The pause was infinitesimal. 'Of course,' her mother agreed, her voice tranquil, but her eyes were still questioning. 'So –' she continued after a moment, brightly, '– the wedding will be in the spring. April, I think, don't you? The daffodils will be out, and the celandines. You'll be married at St Agatha's, of course, and then – what? With the wars over at last you could take a marriage trip to Europe before settling at Old Hall. It will be nice to have you so close –'

It was only later that the quite astonishing motherliness of that struck Jessica. At that instant, taken unawares, she stumbled a little over her reply. She had hoped that this subject, much discussed between herself and Robert over the past few days, would not be broached until later. 'I – we –' she stammered, 'that is – well, we haven't exactly –' she stopped. Then said in a determined rush. 'We're going to live in Florence. To begin with, anyway.'

Very slowly Maria turned her head. Her face was an absolute picture of astonishment. '*Live* in *Florence*?' She said it as if the very idea were an outrage to nature.

'Lots of people do, Mama,' Jessica said, and was rewarded by a coolly unamused lift of her mother's brows.

'Those unfortunate enough to be born there, perhaps,' Maria said.

'There's quite an English colony, actually,' Jessica stubbornly held her patience. 'Artists – writers –'

'Quite.'

Jessica ploughed doggedly on. 'Robert is going to study music. He's written to a teacher – quite a famous one – hoping he'll take him.'

'May I ask to what purpose?'

'He wants to be a composer.'

There was a long, pained silence.

'A – composer,' Maria said at last, as if she had only that moment come across the word and could not begin to imagine what it meant.

'Yes.'

'I see.'

'I don't think you do. Mama – please – it really isn't such an outrageous idea. We both know that sooner or later Robert will have to come home to take over Old Hall and the farm. We're both ready for that. But it'll be ages yet – and in the meantime why shouldn't he do the thing he most wants in the world? I have my portion that will come to me when I marry, and Robert has a little money from his grandmother. We can manage perfectly well for a couple of years. Mama, you surely must know how he feels about his music? It's his life. He can't sing any more, and he's honest enough to admit that his talent for the piano isn't strong enough for him to perform publicly. But for the past year or so he's been writing music – his tutor at Oxford said it was good –'

'I'm sure he was an expert. Wasn't Robert studying English Literature?' Maria's voice was acid.

Jessica ignored the sarcasm. 'He deserves the chance. If we go to Florence, he'll have the chance to study – to discover if he really can compose –'

'And if he can't?'

Jessica's small mouth set. 'I'm sure he can.'

Her mother sighed.

'All right! If he can't, then he can't – but at least he'll have tried. We're young and we have a little money. Why shouldn't we live in Florence for a while?'

'Yellow fever?' her mother suggested, tartly. 'Typhoid? And supposing you have a child? What then?'

Jessica felt painful colour rising. She ducked her head. 'It's no good, Mama, we've made up our minds. We're going to Florence. For a couple of years at least.' Through the window she saw a rider, bright bare head windblown, galloping across the park towards the house. She turned her eyes from the sight of her brother. 'We want to get away,' she said, softly, but with determination like steel beneath the quiet.

With a whispering rustle of silk her mother rose. 'Well, you'll do as you wish, I daresay. Though I must say I find it extraordinary that you should choose voluntarily to live – for however short a time – amongst heathen Papists who will no doubt knife you in the back as soon as look at you – however –' she stopped her daughter's half-formed protest with a lifted hand, 'if that's your wish then far be it from me to stand in your way. After the wedding you will be Robert's responsibility. I –' she paused, and her face softened. 'I shall have new responsibilities of my own.'

Jessica lifted her head, interested, and pleased to change the subject. Something in her mother's face told her the answer to her question before it was asked. 'The marriage is proved? Edward *was* married?'

Maria folded her hands. Her face was composed, but her eyes glowed. 'So say the Parish Registers of St Margaret's in Cambridge. So says the priest who married them. Sir Charles is there now – but yes, I believe it. Edward married Anne Stewart when he discovered that she was carrying his child. Patrick is legitimate.'

Bereft of words Jessica let out a small, unladylike whistling breath at the implications of that. 'So – Patrick is Edward's heir?'

'I believe so.'

'And – Giles?'

'We have to leave that to Sir Charles,' Maria's voice was collected, her eyes suddenly as hard as the jewels with which they had so often been compared. 'The situation is complicated, certainly. We'll see. Now, my dear, we have arrangements to make – there must be a formal announcement, of course – perhaps a small entertainment for our close friends? I do somehow assume that you don't want a great fuss made –?'

The change of subject was determined; with grace, though consumed with curiosity Jessica accepted it and dutifully turned to a discussion of her betrothal party.

'But – what will happen, do you think?' she asked Robert later that afternoon as they rode at Robert's demure pace across the park. 'If Patrick is legitimate, and Edward's heir, then surely it means that New Hall is his?' The late autumn afternoon was crisp with a hint of winter despite the sunshine that gleamed fitfully through the branches firing the leaves that remained on the trees to gold.

Robert shrugged. 'I really don't know.'

'And what will happen if Giles – and Clara! – fight it?'

'God only knows. The legal battles could last for years. Litigation like that has been known to break families of greater fortune than yours. If it goes to Chancery it could be years before a decision is given –'

'And the costs could be crippling,' Jessica put in soberly. They had both heard of such things. 'Oh, Lord, Robert, I do wish we didn't have to wait until spring to leave. There's going to be the most awful trouble. I know it.'

'I wouldn't be surprised.'

'Six months,' she said. 'Six months, and we can marry and go. France – Switzerland – Austria. And then – Italy!' Her small face was suddenly lit with brilliant excitement. 'Just imagine it, Robert! We're going to *live* in Florence! We can do as we please! No-one to say Jessica this, and Robert that, and Jessica the other! Oh, it's the biggest and best adventure we've ever had!'

He reined in his placid horse and looked at her, smiling. Jessica's mount danced beside him, as ardent and lit with life as its young mistress. 'You haven't asked me what my parents said.'

Jessica giggled infectiously, like a child. 'Oh, Lord! I quite forgot! Were they horrified?'

He shook his head. 'They were delighted. They said that you were probably the best thing that ever happened to me.'

'Bless them!' she said, delighted.

'I think they're probably right.'

Startled and gratified she opened her mouth, could not think of a single appropriate word to say and shut it again, blushing. He reached a hand and she took it, leaning easily with the movement of the horse. 'It's all going to be all right,' she said, 'I know it is. You're going to be the most famous composer in the world. And we're going to live in Florence. We're going to live happily ever after, you'll see.'

And in that golden November afternoon with the fire-colours of a Suffolk autumn in the trees and the bracken, she believed it. She was eighteen. She was marrying Robert, her dear Robert, always her true friend. She would be free of New Hall, and its malevolent antagonisms. Nothing could go wrong now.

Smiling they rode on hand in hand through the woodland.

Clara and Giles quarrelled constantly; never publicly but with a quiet and vindictive force that seemed to reach right through the house and poison the very air. In company they were frigidly correct with one another; only God and they knew what went on in the privacy of their rooms. Jessica shuddered to think.

On Sir Charles' return from Cambridge a family conference was called in the library. The solicitor was a fleshy man in late middle age, pink jowled and small-eyed, with his hair curled and clubbed back in the outdated style of his famous barrister father. He stood before the fire, hands behind his back, sober-faced and portentious with all eyes focused upon him. Giles and Clara sat side by side on a sofa, not touching, Clara's full skirt drawn tellingly away from contact with her husband's long legs. It was as if neither could bear to touch each other. Giles was very pale and, Jessica would have sworn, stone sober for the first time in days. Clara sat like a ramrod, her head lifted, her eyes sharply intent upon the lawyer's face, her mouth a straight, bleakly determined line. Maria sat in a leather armchair, apparently poised and relaxed, her hands calm upon her lap. Yet there was an air of tension about her and the blue eyes were veiled and completely expressionless. Jessica sat on a stool near her mother. Caroline – her figure uncomfortably bulky in advanced pregnancy, her pretty face petulant as ever – sat beside her husband, who had been dragged very reluctantly from the prospect of a good day's hunting, on the sofa opposite Giles and Clara. Caroline looked bored and Bunty – as always, Jessica thought – slightly blank. He was plainly out of his depth before a word had been spoken. Patrick was not there and, surprisingly, neither was his grandmother Stewart, who had been installed in comfort on

Maria's orders in one of the estate cottages. Jessica wondered if she were too ill to attend. Her condition had been growing steadily and obviously worse over the past few days.

Sir Charles cleared his throat. 'There is no need, I think, to go into the background of this meeting –?'

'None at all, Charles.' Maria spoke crisply, 'We all know why we're here.' So just get on with it, said the small, impatient lift in her voice. Jessica smothered a smile.

'Er – quite –' The man was for a moment thrown from his stride, but soon regained it. 'I stand before you to offer you my considered opinion and, if you should ask it, my advice upon the quite extraordinary circumstances that appear to have arisen here –' Sir Charles was every inch upon his dignity.

Clara made a slight, irritated movement of her head.

The big man rocked on the balls of his feet, hands still clasped behind his back, eyes on the high, ornately plastered ceiling. 'As you all know, at Mrs Hawthorne's request I made a visit to Cambridge, to the parish of St Margaret's, for the purpose of enquiry into the validity of a marriage claimed to have taken place nine years ago between Edward Hawthorne, deceased son of this house and Anne Stewart, daughter of Joseph and Isabel Stewart, and the consequent legitimacy of the only fruit of that union, the child known as Patrick Michael Hawthorne –'

Clara shifted again, and for once Jessica was in sympathy with her. Despite her own efforts and the importance of the occasion she found it almost impossible to concentrate on the dry, expressionless voice. It was easy to see why Sir Charles had not found it possible to follow in his illustrious father's footsteps. Jessica watched Clara for a moment, wondering what was going on in her mind. Then her eyes moved to Giles. He was leaning forward, his face intent. Here was one member of the group whose attention had not wandered one jot. Her mother too was watching Sir Charles. She had moved forward a little in her chair and the white hands showed a small, regular pulse of movement as if by some independent will of their own they refused to be still.

'– and on this initial evidence I am forced to the conclusion that there is every likelihood that the claim could be proven. The Parish Record is quite clear. The priest, though old now, and very frail, actually identified the miniature of Edward that I showed him. And – perhaps most telling of all –' Sir Charles had all their attention now, and he knew it. He paused for dramatic effect, rocking on his heels again, 'I have discovered a witness.' He paused again. Clara drew a sharp breath, and was still. Maria moved a little in her chair. In fact a small frisson of movement seemed to ripple around the room. Sir Charles continued soberly, satisfied with the sensation his words had caused, 'A young man who actually attended the wedding and is ready if necessary to swear so. A fellow student of Edward's who thought the whole thing, so he tells me, a great jape.' He eyed his audience one by one. 'A young man of title,' he added as if this fact were enough to prove the case on its merits alone.

'So – are you saying –' for all her efforts Maria's voice shook a little, '– are you saying that you believe that Edward *was* married? That Patrick is his legitimate son?'

'I'm saying,' the man was predictably ponderous, 'that in my opinion there is good ground for believing so, yes.'

Clara shook her head. 'No!' The word snapped from her almost reflexively. Sir Charles did not look at her.

Giles stood. Maria's fierce eyes lifted to him. The room seemed to Jessica suddenly to be invested with a nerve-stretching tension. The lawyer faced Giles frankly. 'My opinion of course has no force in law. You may fight it.'

'Sir Charles –' Maria began, but courteously and firmly he held up a hand to stop her. In the way of his kind he would say what must be said and nothing would stop him.

'Anyone with an interest in the case may challenge both the marriage and the child's legitimacy in the courts. However –' another pause '– I have to warn you that in my opinion that is a course only to be taken after much advice, and a very great deal of consideration and thought. Once the case goes to Chancery –' he shook his head, 'the costs can be inestimable, and as for the time before a decision might be reached –' He spread pudgy hands expressively.

218

'We won't fight it,' Giles said, very clearly.

Sir Charles was already continuing. 'I would suggest that anyone who decides to contest should perhaps consult –' he stopped. 'I beg your pardon?'

Every eye in the room was on Giles.

Maria stood to face her son. He looked at her steadily. 'We won't fight it,' he said again.

Jessica saw the slight movement of her mother's shoulders, the convulsive clenching of her fists before they relaxed by her side. 'You mean that?'

'I do.'

Clara was looking from one to the other as if she could not believe her ears. 'Giles!' she said, sharply.

Giles looked down at her. 'We're not contesting it,' he said, voice and eyes like ice, 'and that's an end. This is Edward's son. New Hall is his.'

'Are you mad? Or drunk?'

'Neither.'

'You'll throw away our home – our livelihood – our children's future –?'

'Oh, come now, Clara –' Maria was sweetly conciliatory, '– you know very well that no-one would see you flung from the door penniless, for heaven's sake! Your children – when they come –' her smile was barbed '– will be quite safe, I promise you. Giles will be needed to run the estate. Patrick's a child, after all, and I'm an old woman –' neither her tone of voice nor her bearing gave any credence to that. 'He'll need a man to guide him.'

Giles turned from her. 'I said nothing of that.'

Inexorably pleasant, Maria continued. 'I thought perhaps Tollbridge Farm might suit you both very well? For I do assume you'd rather have a home of your own? It's a nice old house, and the land is good. The estate would of course bear the cost of any improvements you might care to make before you move in –?' She had thought about it. Planned it to the last detail. Her triumph was made more complete by her good-mannered determination not to show it. Clara glared at her.

Giles said nothing. His face was bitter.

Clara stood, facing him, her head flung back to look him in the face, her hands clenched to fists at her sides. 'Fool!' she said, very quietly. 'You fool, Giles Hawthorne!'

He blinked, and was still. Clara's eyes were dark pools of contempt. She stared at her husband for a moment longer. Then, with surprising dignity, she turned and left the room.

'Well,' Maria said, quietly and with finality in her voice, 'that would seem to be that, wouldn't it?' She faced her son, honestly. 'Thank you, Giles. This is more than I dared hope. I know it isn't easy for you.'

Giles' already pale face whitened further. The handsome bones stood out like blades against the fine skin. A muscle in his jaw throbbed. He said nothing.

His mother laid a hand upon his arm. 'And – you will help us? You'll stay and manage the estate? You're so very good at it – I know how you love it –'

He jerked his arm from her touch as if it had burned him. 'I – don't know.'

'Please?'

His mouth tightened a little. 'I'll think about it,' he said, stiffly.

Maria nodded, satisfied with that. She turned to Sir Charles, 'You'll take care of the legal complications for us? You'll continue the enquiries – and there must be –' she shrugged, airily and prettily, 'documents and deeds and things?'

He nodded. 'Of course.' His small eyes flickered warily to Giles' taut face, 'And – if I might suggest –?'

'Yes?'

'An agreement. A legal agreement. That at no time in the future will anyone contest the boy's claim –?'

'Oh, for Christ's Sweet Sake!' Giles burst out, 'I've said it, haven't I? I've said it! What more do you want?'

'Giles –' His mother stepped towards him.

He stared at her, a bright and bitter glint in his brilliant eyes. 'Oh, go to hell!' he said, quietly and savagely. 'The lot of you! *Go to hell!*'

Maria froze. He strode past her and through the door, slamming it behind him to shake the house to its foundations.

Maria stood absolutely still for the space of perhaps a dozen heartbeats.

'Well!' It was the first word that Caroline had spoken, and she spoke it with some force, 'Of all the ill-mannered – beastly – ways to act! Really! I sometimes wonder what on earth this family is coming to!'

Maria bowed her head and passed a hand wearily across her brow.

'Not on,' Bunty agreed, solemnly. 'Absolutely not on.'

Maria eyed them both in mild despair, then turned to Jessica. 'Ring for John, would you Jessica?' she said with remarkable calm. 'I think we should tell Cook there'll be just the five of us for luncheon –'

Apart from Clara, Jessica was perhaps the only person in the house who did not, grudgingly or otherwise, admire Giles for the difficult and apparently unselfish decision he had taken. Maria was gentle with him; she had her way, she could be and was generous. Only Jessica knew what lay behind her brother's brusque rejection of his mother's advances. The same thing that had lain behind his decision not to contest Patrick's claims as Edward's son. The same thing that lay between herself and her brother like a barrier of steel, though he did not know it.

Guilt.

She had no doubt at all that this was the key to Giles' behaviour. Patrick's coming must have seemed to him – as it had seemed to her – divine retribution. The meek would inherit the earth – literally – and the wicked would not profit from their wickedness. She could not feel sorry for him. He had allowed Edward to die. If not for him, Edward might have been here now – laughing, self-deprecating, winding them all around his smallest finger, glorying in the handsome child his son had become. Oh, no – Jessica felt no admiration. She watched with no compunction and little pity as Giles, his marriage a shambles and his aspirations ashes took refuge in the bottle and in the dubious charms of the less respectable village girls who were all too eager to oblige the tall and handsome young man they all still knew as 'the young master'. She was young, and she was unforgiving as only the young can be. She watched Giles' attitude to Patrick like a hawk.

She and Patrick had become friends. He was, as she had suspected, a lively youngster, and as each day advanced so did his confidence. Oddly enough as she got to know him better more than once she surprised herself comparing him in character not with Edward, but with Giles. The living picture of Edward yet he had Giles' restless recklessness, his single-minded confidence in himself, his determination to run faster, climb higher, be better at everything than anyone else. He was a charming child and popular as Edward had been with all who came into contact with him. Lucy would have died for him, and most of the rest of the staff – particularly, Jessica noticed with amusement, the females – took risks with their own safety and security more than once to prevent the wrath of his elders descending upon his bright head after one or other of his more outrageous pranks. He put pepper in the spice jar. He might have burned the house down with a home-made firework hidden in the log-stack for the great kitchen fire. He climbed one of the great elms by the park gate and Charlie Best broke his arm trying to rescue him. And through it all he danced and smiled and apologized always with grace; and escaped with a whole skin. Surprisingly Jessica, with the others, adored him – surprisingly because after one defection – Lucy's – came another, Bran's. The dog took to following the boy like a shadow. Jessica could not find it in her to resent it, though she could not deny a certain pang of pain. The dog, though getting older, was in no way a reformed character. He yearned still for the excitement of a rabbit-hunt, or the exercise of a gallop across the park. With her new preoccupation with Robert and Old Hall, and the preparations to be made for the wedding she had little time to indulge the dog as she once had. In a way she knew it was a good thing – she would be leaving soon now, but Bran would not pine. Nevertheless it was not easy for her to say, one squally winter's afternoon when sleet and hail hurled itself at the windows of the house, 'Would you like to have Bran for your own?'

The wide eyes regarded her, startled, and with slow-dawning pleasure. One of the boy's great charms was that he never expected nor took for granted the favours that life and his own blithe character brought to him. 'You mean it? My very own?'

She nodded. They were sitting by the fire in the library. Jessica, always fascinated by books, had been delighted to discover that somewhat unexpectedly Patrick – whether from inclination or a simple desire to please, she did not know – apparently shared her passion and had enthusiastically embarked with her on the task of sorting and indexing the books that had been bought or otherwise garnered in the nearly seventy years of the house's life. It was something she had always planned to do, and this last winter at home offered her the perfect opportunity to do it.

Patrick sat back on his heels. His face was a picture of delight. 'I do love him very much,' he said.

'I know. Or you wouldn't get him!' Jessica briskly entered a title and an author and snapped a heavy tome shut. 'After I'm married Robert and I are going to live abroad for a while. Bran can't come with me. I need to leave him with someone I can trust.'

'You can trust me! I promise! I'll look after him for ever and ever!'

She put out a hand to ruffle his hair. 'I know you will. That's why I'm giving him to you. The bit of him he hasn't given to you already himself that is!'

'Oh no!' His face was concerned. He shook his head vigorously. 'He's your dog! You should see the way he watches for you when I tell him you're coming! He'll never love me as much!'

She smiled. 'Perhaps. He'll soon forget me, I expect, when I'm gone.'

'Of course he won't!' He jumped to his feet eagerly, 'I'll talk to him about you *every* day. And – I'll read your letters to him, and let him smell them! You are going to write lots of letters, aren't you –?' He stopped as if a whip had cracked. He stood absolutely still for a moment, looking into the shadows by the door, then very quietly slipped behind Jessica and stood, tense as a drawn bow, his hand clenched on the back of her chair. She lifted her head. Giles stood, silent and swaying, by the open door. 'Christ in heaven,' he said, drunkenly and dangerously equable. 'Isn't there a single square inch in this bloody house where a man can be on his own?'

She stood up, tidying the books. 'It's all right. We'll go.'

Giles walked carefully to the table where stood the brandy and the glasses and as carefully poured himself a drink. He sank into a deep armchair before the fire and nursed the glass, his haggard face in shadow. Jessica eyed him suspiciously. '*You* don't have to go,' he said, 'but send the brat away, will you? I surely don't have to be afflicted by him every corner I turn?'

Jessica's mouth tightened. Before she could speak Patrick grabbed her hand. 'It's all right.' Eyeing Giles' still form warily he sidled around the chair and fled.

Jessica stacked her books. 'That was entirely unnecessary.'

He shrugged.

Just the sight of the handsome, slouched body triggered in her a terrible animosity. The childhood dread had gone; he had no power over her now. Only a dislike that verged on hatred remained.

With a sudden movement he tilted his head and drank the brandy at a swallow. Then he got up, walked to where the decanter stood, picked it up and carried it back to his chair.

'Don't you think you've drunk enough?'

He laughed. 'No. Not now. Not ever. There isn't enough.'

'You'll kill yourself.'

He lifted one derisive shoulder.

She walked determinedly to him. 'Giles?'

'Mm?'

'I want you to promise me something.'

He poured the brandy, steady as a rock; not a drop spilled. 'Oh?'

'Don't make his life a misery.' As you did mine. She did not add the words, though she might have.

There was an instant's dead silence, then he barked harsh laughter. '*I* make *his* life a misery?'

'Yes.'

He contemplated the brandy, then lifted the gleaming, forget-me-not eyes. 'Why shouldn't I?'

She fought an awful rage. 'Because it isn't civilized. Because it isn't his fault, what's happened. Because he's been through enough and he doesn't deserve more.'

He laughed, a sharp crack of a sound that held no humour at all. 'Deserve? Who gets what he deserves?'

She could not hold her tongue. 'Perhaps you have,' she said, quietly.

That shook him. He lifted his head, staring at her. 'What do you mean?'

'I think you know.' She was shaking. She wanted nothing but to get away. She turned from him. Like a steel clamp his hand closed on her wrist.

'Tell me,' he said, very softly.

She shook her head.

'*Tell me!*'

She swallowed almost painfully, and stood mute, caught like a bird in a trap. To struggle would be useless, and she knew it.

'How have I got what I deserved?'

She would not look at him.

'*How?*'

The words were there, trembling on her tongue, shrieking to be let loose. You killed him! You killed Edward!

He shook her again. 'Tell me!' His eyes were blazing, his rage was feeding on his frustrations and his drunkenness and there was no stopping it. 'Open your mouth, damn you! Tell me what you mean!'

She shook in his strong hands like a doll. His fury terrified her. Yet, pushed to it, her own anger, her own disgust, her own hatred could match his, and more. 'I heard you!' she whispered, 'I heard you both! You killed him! You let him die –!'

He let go of her as if she had stung him. Almost she fell, but regained her balance and stood, shaking and sick with rage, tears of grief burning in her eyes.

'What did you hear? When?'

'You and Clara. The night you came home drunk. I saw you fall off your horse outside and came to help –' She almost choked at the irony of that. 'You quarrelled, down in the Hall. I was on the landing.'

'Well, well.' His smile was wholly a sneer. 'What a sweet little sister I have. You make a habit of eavesdropping on other people's conversations, do you?'

'I wasn't eavesdropping. I couldn't help overhearing –'

He laughed, quietly and unpleasantly.

She stepped away from him, and he let her go. They stood watching each other. Measuring each other.

'And what have you done about it?' he asked at last, pleasantly.

'Nothing.'

'You've told no-one?' His eyes had narrowed.

She hesitated for a second. '– No.'

'Why not?'

'How could I? It would have killed Mama, and done no good. Nothing will bring Edward back, will it? I – didn't know what to do –'

'So –' he was regarding her coolly, 'You ran to your pretty little friend Robert and he is to marry you and take you from the Ogre's castle?'

The hateful perception took her breath away. 'Yes.'

He smiled.

'You're wicked,' she said.

'Perhaps.'

The gall of him stung her to anger again. 'Well, listen to this, Giles – for as surely as I'm standing here I mean what I say! I haven't told what I heard. That doesn't mean I won't. If I hear of unkindness to Patrick – if you dare to make him frightened, or unhappy – then I swear I'll tell!'

'I'll deny it.'

'That's as may be. But there's plenty who'll believe it. We both know that.'

He looked at her for a long, slow moment. 'Well, well,' he said, 'so the Hawthorne spots come out at last. Very well, little sister. You have a bargain. And may you rot for it.'

She could take no more. On trembling legs she turned and walked, straight-backed from him, closing the door very quietly behind her.

It was a long, hard winter, deep in snow from January on and with a flaying wind that it seemed must be whipping across the flatlands of East Anglia directly from the frozen spaces of Russia. As the bad weather dragged on through an early Easter, April seemed an eternity away. And yet then, suddenly, it was upon her and with it the first song birds, the buds and blossoms of spring and the happy turmoil of her wedding.

She awoke on the day to sunshine; surely, oh, surely a happy omen after these past bitter months, she thought as she jumped from bed and ran to the window on bare feet. Outside her window birds sang and fluttered in the ageless rites of mating and nesting, out in the park beneath the trees the daffodils that carpeted the ground bowed their pretty heads to the sun. She took a deep, deep breath and stretched. It was here at last. The day of her freedom.

'Why, Miss Jess, whatever do you think you're doin'?' Lucy, flustered and sleepy-eyed bustled into the room clucking like a disturbed broody hen. 'Back in that bed with you, this minute! Tha'ss still too cold to be runnin' about with next to nothin' on, sun or no sun!'

Laughing Jessica turned and ran back to the high bed, leaping onto it like a child, bouncing into the feather mattress. Her wedding dress hung on a wooden dummy by the window, the sun sheening the ivory silk with gold and glimmering on the tiny pearls that patterned the skirt like light gleaming on water. For weeks she had longed for the day she would wear it; even Caroline had conceded at the last fitting that it suited her 'tolerably well' and had declared that to see her baby sister looking so positively grown up made her feel quite ancient. The veil lay beside it, covering the chair on which it lay like a froth of sparkling mist. 'What time is it?'

'Only just past seven. You've plenty of time yet.' Lucy was

plucking at the dress gently, straightening the folds of the sweeping skirt. 'My, this is just the prettiest thing I've ever seen, you know that?'

Jessica hugged her knees, her eyes shining. 'I think so. Oh, Lucy – just think – by this afternoon I shan't be Jessie Hawthorne any more. Not ever again. I shall be the Honorable Mrs Jessica FitzBolton. And one day – oh, years I know – but one day I'll be Lady FitzBolton! Doesn't that sound funny?'

'Everything you do's funny.' The young voice came from the doorway. 'Funny-Bunny-Jessie! *That's* what your name *ought* to be!' Patrick shrieked with laughter and dodged as Jessica with sure aim flung a pillow at him. Then he danced into the room, grinning. His hair was tousled, the leather of his boots dark and stained with damp. 'It's a lovely day. Bran and I have been out already. You should have seen him make the rabbits run!'

Jessica swung her legs off the bed. 'You'll be the death of that poor old dog.' She had long since become accustomed – even pleased about – Bran's attachment to the child. When Patrick's Grandma Stewart had finally succumbed to an inflammation of the lungs in early January the boy had taken strange consolation in the companionship of the dog. At a time when no-one else could console him the two had trudged the parkland and the lanes, and in solitude Patrick had recovered his spirits and come through his grief. Since then the two of them had been all but inseparable, and Jessica had no qualms about leaving them so. In fact she had few qualms about leaving anyone or anything at New Hall. Over the past few months the thought of this day had become the thought of freedom and happiness. She had not spared a thought as to whether the first was possible or how the second might be achieved. The one would follow the other as day followed night – 'and they lived happily ever after' had become almost a password between herself and Robert. For Robert too, with the decision taken and the arrangements made had taken his cue from Jessica and come to see their marriage as a solution to all problems. Jessica's enthusiasm, her boundless optimism, her refusal to admit to any possibility of failure had infected him

228

like a fever. To his delight he had been accepted by Maestro Pietro Donatti as a pupil, with such help and guidance, surely, even Jessica's rosily-painted pictures of success were not too far-fetched. They had rented an apartment not far from the Ponte Vecchio from June and for an indefinite time thereafter. Like children they had plotted and planned, like children they had created a world of their own where problems existed only to be surely overcome. Like children they assumed that to wish something was to make it so. They had not once discussed Robert's problem nor its possible effect on their marriage; like children they had shut their eyes, pretending the serpent in their Eden did not exist.

Lucy shooed Patrick from the bedroom, clapping her hands and flapping her pinafore as if she were herding geese. Laughing still he went, swearing he was off rabbit hunting with Bran. Not for anything would he have admitted how much he was looking forward to wearing the satin suit that had been made for him for the occasion, as one of Jessica's attendants. Royal blue and trimmed with oyster silk, it made him look a young prince and he knew it. He also knew its likely effect upon pretty little Betsy Morris, the new dairy maid. Jessica was not the only person looking forward to this day, and with good cause. . . .

She enjoyed, with intent, every single moment of it. She did not – she would not – let the smallest second pass without savouring it. She wallowed in the perfumed bath that Lucy and another maid prepared for her. She enjoyed the long and complicated process of dressing her hair – a task undertaken on this special day by her mother's new and extremely chic French maid whilst Lucy stamped about the room ostensibly tidying up but actually registering her chagrin and disapproval by making as much noise as she reasonably could without actually drowning the conversation. When it was done Jessica peered in pure pleasure at the small, oval face crowned by a mass of artfully piled and curled hair in which pearls glimmered like tiny stars. 'Oh, how clever! I can never make it stay up like that!'

'I'll show you, Mam'selle –' The girl smiled at her delight.

'See – you place the combs so – and so – and the pins – so –' She demonstrated deftly with her own hair. 'You'll soon learn how – and see how it suits the little face and the big eyes – la-la! The young M'sieu will be pleased I think!'

It did indeed suit the little face and the big eyes – and the young M'sieu was most certainly pleased. When at last, dressed and perfumed and feeling like a princess in a fairy tale she drove with her mother, Giles and Clara through the spring woodlands to St Agatha's she saw it in his eyes as she joined him at the altar, her small hands full of spring flowers, her eyes shining her happiness. Strangely, of the ceremony itself she remembered very little later. The church was cool, and lit by the shafts of sunlight that cut like golden sword-strokes through the high, narrow windows and dimmed the light of the altar candles. As she stood beside Robert and uttered obediently the appropriate responses her eyes were upon the smiling statue of St Agatha, and in her heart, suddenly and with a clarity that astounded her, she saw the dark angel-face, never forgotten, the skilled, strong hands that had worked upon that statue, that screen, this altar rail –

She was going to Florence. She – the child who had sat enthralled at the tales of an enchanted city – was going herself to live there, to see the wide, muddy Arno and the spired and gabled city, to watch the children play and the lovers stroll in the Boboli Gardens –

'You may kiss the bride.'

Robert's hand, gentle upon her arm, brought her from her reverie. She lifted her face, alight and glowing as if at some vision. He hesitated for one second, then his lips brushed her cheek. She smiled at her husband, brilliantly and took his arm to walk the dark aisle to the glory of sunshine beyond the open doors. The light dazzled them as they stepped into it. Then they were surrounded by laughing well-wishers, kissed and patted, Robert's hand shaken. The bells pealed joyfully, silencing the birds.

Then, 'Good God!' someone said, 'Whatever is the child doing?'

Heads lifted. Necks craned. Silence fell. 'Oh, my God!' Maria said, white-faced.

Out of the window of the tower high above them a small, brilliant figure had clambered and was making his dangerous way around the narrow, crumbling ledge that edged the decaying battlemented tower. In one hand he held a small bundle. Seeing he had caught the attention of those below he waved, blithely and at risk to life and limb. A shower of small stones sprayed from beneath one of his feet. Someone shouted. Maria put up a sharp, imperative hand. 'No! Be still! Don't distract him!'

In tense silence they watched as the child crept along the ledge, clinging like a bright-coloured fly to the weather-rotted walls. Jessica swallowed noisily. More stones scattered. Patrick stopped for a moment, testing the ledge, then moved on again more slowly. For what seemed an age they watched him, until at last he reached the gap in the battlements he had been making for and with a lithe twist of his body was through it and disappeared from sight onto the tower roof. There was a moment's dead silence, then murmurs of relief and laughter began to ripple through the crowd, to gain in volume as from the tower two great silken silver streamers were suddenly unfurled to ream in the wind.

'What the —? Oh, look! See what it says! "Jessica" and "Robert"! What a little tinker that child is! He surely can't have realized the danger —?'

'Giles. Send someone for a ladder.' Maria's voice was calm, her face sheened finely with perspiration.

Over the battlemented tower a small face appeared, marigold head gleaming picturesquely in the sun. The laughter grew, fed by relief. A small hand waved, casually. Many of the ladies plucked lace handkerchiefs from their sleeves and waved back. Someone started to clap. Patrick grinned like an imp of Satan. The silver streamers cracked gallantly in the breeze. The applause was taken up by more of the crowd and again Patrick waved. Perhaps the prank had been successful enough for him to escape the whipping he knew he well deserved. Perhaps not. He did not care. Jessica was smiling at him, wagging a playfully admonishing finger. He did not look at Maria.

They left that afternoon for London, where they were to spend a few days before starting off on the adventure of the longer trip through France and Switzerland to Italy. There were some tears shed, and some shaken heads. There were quietly-spoken predictions that the young people would be home where they belonged well before the end of the year. There were a few who watched in envy. Jessica, dressed elegantly in dove-grey and fawn travelling suit, her face aching from her constant smile waited by the carriage as Robert fought his way through a back-slapping and hand-shaking crowd to her side. The steps of the house were crowded with family and friends; behind them were ranged the servants, from the steward and the butler to the smallest maid. Jessica, lifting her hand for a special wave, saw tears on poor Lucy's face and for the first time found herself swallowing frantically against an enorm-ous lump in her throat.

'One more kiss! One more kiss!'

Rice flew, and flowers.

'One more kiss!'

She lifted her face. Awkwardly, his own face fiery, Robert bent and pressed his mouth to hers. And with shock she felt, through the contact of her hand on his arm, how his body flinched from hers.

Smiling gaily she climbed into the carriage and settled herself in the far corner. Robert sat beside her, a foot's distance between them. After a second, tentatively, he reached out a hand and after only a moment's hesitation she took it.

And so they sat, like well-mannered children at a party, their hands linked on the seat beside them as to cheers the carriage rolled off down the drive, the horseshoes that Patrick and the stable-lads had tied to the rear axle spinning and clattering behind them.

Part Three

1817–1823

Chapter Nine

The mules stood like statues, patient as time in the blazing sun. The Appenine air shimmered with heat. In the hazed distance of the green and golden vale of the Arno the terracotta roofs and gleaming domes of Florence nestled within their surrounding walls.

Jessica breathed the scented and dusty air and fixed her eyes, narrowed against the brilliant light, upon the distant city.

'– the view of Florence, with the surrounding hills and the houses dispersed on them would be counted by many as unparalleled –'

If she had ever doubted, at this moment those doubts were put to rest; so far as she could see, those that would describe it so had been right. In the past three months she had ridden through the flatly fertile fields of Belgium and visited the fairy castles of the Rhein, she had walked the flowery mountains of Switzerland and the verdant tracks of the Austrian Tyrol. She had seen Bruges and Brussels, Strasburg, Munich and Vienna and had wondered at them all. Yet this first sight of the city that she had dreamed about for so long and travelled so far to see could not have struck her with more freshness or force had she been transported here by magic, with no comparisons to make.

The last couple of weeks had been, perhaps, the most tiring of the trip, and for more reasons than the obvious. It had taken eight days to travel the three hundred miles from Vienna to Trieste, travelling in a well-sprung but tediously ponderous *diligence* that had skirted through the foothills of the distant mountain ranges to the shores of the Adriatic Sea. As they had descended the hills into the town she had seen for the first time the lush colours and vegetation of a warmer climate; dark cypress trees and silver-pale olives, fig and peach trees, stony slopes of broad-leafed vines. The Adriatic, a silvered, almost waveless mirror to the blue sky, had startled her as much as anything she had ever seen, so different was it from the rough grey northern seas that were all she knew.

They had stayed a couple of days in the busy commercial town before taking a barque to Venice – a coasting vessel that plied between the two ports carrying goods and, of secondary importance, passengers. The accommodation had been adequate but basic, and the trip made difficult by a sudden squall that had to his chagrin reduced Robert to wretched seasickness. In Venice the weather had been unseasonably cold and by now, with their goal almost in sight they had been anxious, each for their own reasons, to push on. Yet they had been reluctant to bypass such a famous place altogether, so for two days under grey skies, huddled into greatcoats and scarves they had explored the canals and tiny, winding streets, the palaces and churches, were astounded by the almost wanton profusion of precious things the decaying city held – like an old, old woman, Jessica had thought, hoarding her treasures in a dilapidated house where in the darkest corners the brightest masterpieces might be discovered.

On the day they had left the city heading for Padua the fickle sun had reappeared, and had shed its golden southern warmth on the rest of the journey. The voyage across the lagoon from Venice had been leisurely, the cruise up the canal to Padua, the boat now drawn by patiently plodding horses, uneventful. The banks had glided by, picturesque with pretty villages and villas. Bare-legged, brown-skinned children had raced gaily to the river-side to wave. From Padua, using coaches driven by that tough breed of men known as the 'vetturini' they had travelled across the flat and fertile valley of the Po via Verona, Mantua and Modena, and thence to Bologna, where the horses had been exchanged for mules and they had set off into the towering and beautiful Appenines for the last stage of their journey. The past night had been spent at a mountain inn famous neither for its food nor its comfort but rather as being the scene of the particularly gruesome murders of several travellers some years before. Annabel Romsey, a travelling companion ever since Vienna, had delightedly declared it quite the most barbarous place she had ever encountered and had chattered about it constantly and with shattering single-mindedness ever since. Standing here on the sunlit heights that overlooked the domes and spires of Florence the subject still engaged her.

'– one would think, truly, that they might improve such facilities, now that Europe is at peace and so many English are travelling – it's quite outrageous that civilized people should have to contend with such squalor! Whatever were the French doing all the time they were here, do you think? Quite the least they might have done might have been to make travelling these mountains more agreeable –'

Jessica shut her ears and her mind to the light and pretty voice, as she did to the assenting and solicitous murmur that she knew it would inevitably produce from David, Annabel's very new, young and besottedly devoted husband. She moved away a little further from the group – Annabel, David and Robert – and to the crumbling edge of the road. From the arid-looking, sunbaked ground tiny-flowered herbs sprang in amazing, shrub-like profusion, perfuming the air. In the still mountain silence the sound of the bees busy at the flowers was loud. No bird sang. The city shimmered, waiting, in the distance.

Behind her the *vetturino* grumbled in scolding tones to his mules, who shifted a little, and the heavy coach's wheels cracked on the stones of the road. Over these past weeks she had stood so in many strange places, heard many such sounds, strange to her ears and exciting because of that, seen many such beautiful sights, and had, until Vienna, loved it all.

Until Vienna.

'– I'm absolutely certain that I've been bitten by something beastly. David, darling – is there not a patch on my cheek? I shall be mortified if there is –'

David laughed, indulgently, 'No, no, my love. Truly not, believe me. Your pretty little face is sweet as ever –'

Jessica flinched. Did they have to talk to each other like characters in one of the worst of Caroline's insipid romantic novels?

'Good heavens, Jessica dear –!' Annabel had raised her voice a little. 'Whatever are you doing over there and without your parasol? You silly thing! You'll *die* of sunstroke! To say nothing at all of ruining your complexion!'

Robert leaned into the coach, then came towards her, neat and elegant as ever despite the intense heat, stepping quietly over the rutted road carrying her parasol. 'She's right, Jessie. You really must be careful. This isn't the sun of a summer's day in Suffolk.' His voice was meticulously courteous and sounded, in her ears at least, as distant as the city upon which she gazed. Their fingers did not touch as she took the parasol from his hand. She found herself thinking, briefly, of their laughter on the Dover packet when the wind had taken his hat, of the smothered, childish giggles when in Bruges they had totally mistranslated a menu and had to struggle through an enormous meal they had not intended to order. Oh, yes – there had been laughter at first, and warmth, something more than the careful good manners they now both devotedly employed and which, admirably as it fooled the world, did nothing to disguise for themselves how disastrously their relationship had changed.

Since Vienna.

'Well –' David was jocular, '– are we going to stand here all day looking at the place or are we going to get on down there?' He put a hand to his ear in an exaggerated listening pose. 'I hear the call of a good meal and a very large, very cool bottle of vino!'

'Oh, you!' Annabel pushed him, squealing like a child with laughter. 'What a beast you are! You think of nothing but your stomach! Well –' she convulsed into sudden giggles '– almost nothing!'

Jessica turned away abruptly. If only – if only! – they had never met these two! If only they had never gone near Vienna!

She clambered into the close atmosphere of the rocking coach, hampered by her long, clinging skirt, suddenly aware of the oppressive heat and of the sweat that uncomfortably slicked her body. As she settled into her corner the sun glinted through the drawn blind, striking into her eyes, dazzling her with a rainbow prism of colour. She closed her eyes, drawing a long breath. No. To blame these two was not fair. If it had not been Annabel and David Romsey, it would have been, sooner or later, someone else. If it had not happened in Vienna, it would have happened, sooner or later, somewhere else. Why hadn't she known that?

Giggling and teasing, Annabel and David settled themselves opposite her, their hands linked upon the seat between them. Robert, having seen everyone and everything safely stowed aboard, neatly followed them, slammed the door crisply shut and settled collectedly in the other corner, as far from Jessica as space would allow.

The driver yelled, the whip cracked, and the coach, lurching, started down the mountain road.

They had met the Romseys on the famous rampart walk of Vienna, and the meeting at first had seemed fortuitous to them all. The month had been June, and the weather had been kind. Jessica and Robert had found themselves enchanted both by the city and by its people. The journey until then had been every bit as exciting and as pleasurable as they had dared to hope. They planned now to stop for a week, or perhaps two, to catch their breath and to experience the pleasures of a city that could well be counted as one of the gayest in Europe. Their guesthouse was situated in a small square not far from the ramparts. In the tree-shaded platz a tiny, elaborate bandstand stood, and each evening the promenaders were treated to the light and lilting music of Vienna. As in every other square and boulevard of the city there were pavement cafés serving coffee and chocolate as well as more intoxicating beverages, and specializing in the creamiest and most delicious confections that Jessica had ever seen, let alone tasted. They visited the inevitable museums and art galleries, they strolled the boulevards and parks, and each day, late in the afternoon, they walked the ramparts, as did most of the rest of Vienna, enjoying the cooling breezes and admiring from the high vantage point the splendid buildings and neatly patterned, colourful gardens of the city.

239

It was on one such walk that Robert, with commendable presence of mind, trapped a gaily-flowered straw hat that was bowling at a merry pace towards the steep drop of the rampart wall.

'I say! Thanks awfully! I'd never have got to it!'

They both turned in surprise at the pleasant and extremely English tones.

'Er – vielen dank –' the young man stammered, grinning. He was tall and fairish with regular features, flushed now with the exertion of chasing the hat. His clothes were well-cut and he carried a gold-topped cane. Hurrying behind him came an extremely pretty girl, trim in pink and white muslin, her dark head hatless and her equally dark eyes alight with laughter.

'Oh, how priceless! I knew I should have put a pin in it! Thank you!' she directed a sparkling smile at Robert. 'I'm afraid I don't know the words in German,' she added with blithe and somehow endearingly absurd honesty.

Robert smiled, and bowed, handing the hat. 'Think nothing of it. Neither do I.'

They stared at him. Jessica giggled. The girl in pink lifted an astonished and laughingly accusing finger, 'You're *English*!'

'– as boiled mutton,' Robert agreed, solemnly.

The young man thought about that for a moment, then threw back his head in laughter. 'You've been to France –'

'Belgium, actually.'

'– where everyone thinks –'

'– that the English eat nothing but boiled mutton –'

'– and drink nothing but bad beer!'

'Quite.'

Smiling, each pair looked at the other for a moment, delighting in the unexpected and slightly silly pleasure of the moment. Then the young man bowed a little, gracefully. 'David Romsey,' he said. 'And this – ' disarmingly he blushed faintly, and the girl, nibbling her lip in sudden shyness dropped her eyes, '– is my wife, Annabel.' As he said it his eyes were drawn as if by a magnet to the flower-face that lifted smiling to his. Unexpectedly Jessica, watching them, felt an odd tightening in her chest, a strange small stab of something remarkably like physical pain, that constricted her heart and interrupted the rhythm of her breathing. She had never seen two people look at each other so, openly and unreservedly. They exuded love, it tangled them like the gay ribbons of the Maypole, its bright patterns weaving about them in some way that was like a magic shield against the rest of the world. For no good reason she found the warm intimacy of that look painfully disturbing. She slipped a hand through Robert's arm.

'I'm Robert FitzBolton,' Robert said. 'This is my wife, Jessica.'

They murmured their 'How d'ye do's'. Then, 'You're staying in Vienna?' David asked.

Robert nodded. 'At the Brathoven Guesthouse.' He pointed to where the roof could be seen through the trees, 'Over there, in the Konigsplatz.'

Annabel, in the graceful act of putting on her retrieved bonnet let out a small shriek of astonishment. 'I don't believe it!'

'We're there, too,' David said. 'What an amazing coincidence!'

'It couldn't be —' Jessica asked, laughing, 'that you're following Mr Blenkinsop's excellent itinerary from *Travels in Europe*?'

'The very same!'

They all laughed.

'The mystery is solved,' Robert said. 'Who could travel Europe without trusty Blenkinsop?'

'David calls it "The Honey-Moon Book",' Annabel confided, giggling infectiously, 'for truly we've met so many other newly-wedded couples in the hotels we've stayed at —' She stopped and looked, innocent-eyed, from Robert to Jessica.

Laughing, Jessica nodded, satisfying the other girl's artless curiosity, 'You've just met another.'

'Oh, how splendid!' Annabel clapped her hands like a child. 'We must see more of each other! The wind has ordained it! It blew my hat right into Robert's hand, just so that we should meet! Now — to start right away — why don't we go to that wonderful little café on the Baumstrasse — have you discovered it yet? – and have some of that perfectly wicked *kasetorte* and a cup of chocolate? I vow –' she added confidentially into Jessica's ear, slipping her hand into the crook of her arm, '–that I am becoming quite addicted to the wretched stuff!'

And that was the beginning. Within a day the two young couples had become inseparable; strolling together, shopping together, taking their meals together. It came as some mild surprise to Jessica that vivacious Annabel seemed eager to be her friend. 'David's such a dear, and I do adore him so – but oh, how I miss my sisters and my friends! Do you not?' Perhaps fortunately giving Jessica no opportunity to reply she chattered on. '– Men are quite wonderful creatures, I know, and I would never dispute it, but truly even the best of them can sometimes be so deadly *dull*, don't you think? My mama says it's because they have never learned the art of gossip –' she giggled happily '– and do you know I believe that she's right? Oh, how I've missed my dear gossips!'

During the days that followed she certainly, and to Jessica's amusement, made up for their lack. 'I don't think I've ever known anyone talk so much!' she said, ruefully to Robert one night as they prepared for bed. As was their invariable custom she was undressing in the bedroom, whilst Robert used the dressing-room that adjoined, though the door stood open between them. 'Yet she's so charming – I just can't help liking her.' She buttoned her nightgown to her throat and climbed into the huge bed, burrowing comfortably into the feather mattress.

Robert, somehow managing to look more dapper in his striped nightshirt than most men appeared in full dress came to the doorway, smiling. 'Me too. She ought to be tiresome, but somehow she isn't.' He moved about the room turning out the lamps one by one, and lighting the night candle that stood upon the table. In its uncertain light Jessica saw him cross the room and slip with no sound and barely any disturbance into his side of the bed.

She turned her head, looking at him. 'Good night.'

He lifted himself upon one elbow, leaned to her. She felt the soft, cool brush of his lips on her forehead. 'Good night. Sleep well.' He made to turn from her. This was the pattern of their nights. He slept, still and quiet as death, with his back to her on the far side of the bed, never moving, never touching her. On impulse now as he drew back she slipped her hand into his and brought it very softly to her lips in the darkness. 'Thank you, Robert.'

The hand rested in hers for a quiet moment, then was gently removed. 'For what?' The words were as gentle and as careful as the movement.

'Oh – I don't know. Just thank you.' Restless, she tossed on her side, then turned on her back again. Her eyes were used now to the gloom and the night candle cast dark, steady shadows upon the ceiling. She could see a rabbit with rather short ears, and a castle with a dragon flying towards it. She closed her eyes, opened them again. They simply refused to stay shut. She studied the shadows again. The rabbit was not a rabbit. It was a camel with two big humps. 'Robert –?' she whispered, quietly, '– are you asleep?'

He did not reply. As always his breathing was deep, even and peaceful. Yet, oddly, she was certain that he too was awake. She resisted the sudden urge to shake him. The floorboards of the room above creaked. David and Annabel were preparing for bed.

Jessica shut her eyes, tried to wipe her brain free of thought.

Something thumped on the ceiling. Jessica could almost hear Annabel's irrepressible giggle. The guesthouse was old, and soundly built, but yet noise travelled, particularly down through the floorboards. 'You have the room beneath us, don't you?' Annabel had asked, amused and confidential over their *kasetorte* that afternoon whilst the young men had been deep in discussion of Mr Windham Saddler's feat of crossing the St George's Channel in a balloon. 'Thank goodness for that, anyway!' She spluttered with shameless laughter, ducking her head and covering her mouth with her small hand, mischief in her eyes. 'At least I don't suppose we disturb you – I mean –' she stopped.

Jessica looked down into the creamy froth of her chocolate. 'Disturb us?'

Annabel suddenly blushed a fiery red. 'Don't tease, Jessica! You know what I mean!' She exploded again into laughter. 'That wretched bed squeaks like an ungreased cartwheel!'

Jessica smiled woodenly. Annabel, convulsed at her own daring and with a wary eye on her more conventional spouse had leaned forward and pitched her voice for her friend's ear alone, 'I don't think it will ever be a problem for anyone else – David says the hotel's likely to need a new bed by the time we're finished with that one –!'

Jessica now, alone beside her apparently sleeping husband, determinedly closed her eyes again. They had today visited the Augarten, an elaborate public pleasure garden that had been laid out by the Emperor Joseph II in 1775 and that Robert had said was much like the gardens of Vauxhall in London –

Silence now, broken only by Robert's quiet breathing. She relaxed a little, then tensed again. Above her head it had started, as she had known it would, and had prayed it would not; faintly at first, the very echo of movement, delicate, rhythmic, horribly and shamingly disturbing.

Robert did not stir.

Grimly she forced her eyes shut, turning her mind back to the gardens, to the peace and the birdsong as they had walked beneath the linden trees that had spread their green canopy between them and the brilliance of the sky –

'– honestly!' Annabel had giggled as they had strolled in the dappled shade '– aren't men beasts really? David simply cannot resist – well, you know! I must look an absolute *wreck*! I'm getting absolutely *no* sleep!'

She did not look a wreck. In fact she looked radiant, and she must have known it. What she did not know was the humiliating depths of Jessica's ignorance.

The noises from the room above were stronger, more urgent. Jessica slipped her hands carefully from beneath the covers and pushed her fingers into her ears, as she had done as a child when she had wished to cut herself off from a disagreeable world. Yet through the booming rush of sound it produced in her head she felt it, felt the ruthless, rhythmic energy that seemed to pulse through her with her blood. There was a strange heat in her body. She clenched her fists and lay as rigid as death, staring into darkness as she listened to the sounds of their lovemaking.

It seemed an age before the noise stopped, leaving in its wake an unquiet silence that rang with echoes. Jessica lay quite still, the terrible and somehow obscurely shameful excitement that those sounds produced in her, night after night, raging at the very core of her body, burning in some part of her that she had barely known existed. Her breathing was quick and shallow, as if she had run a distance, and her heart pounded. With enormous effort she relaxed, filling her lungs slowly and carefully. Upstairs someone walked across the floor and clearly she heard Annabel's murmuring voice, sleepy and tender.

With an abrupt movement Jessica turned on her side and buried her head beneath the feather counterpane.

Robert breathed gently on.

The next day she surprised Robert at breakfast by asking, more brusquely than she had intended, 'Don't you think it's time we started to think about moving on? We've still a fair way to travel.'

He glanced in mild astonishment from his engrossed study of a month-old English newspaper left by some previous traveller. 'Leave Vienna? But I thought you liked it here?'

'I did – do –' she corrected herself hastily. 'It's just – as I say – we still have a long way to go. We can't afford to stop here much longer, can we, if we're to get to Florence before the real heat starts?'

'Oh, there's plenty of time.' His eyes had drifted back to the paper. 'David and I were talking about it yesterday. He agreed that if we leave next week we can stop in Venice for a couple of days and still make Florence by mid-July.'

She looked at him, frowning a little. 'We?' she asked, carefully.

He nodded, turning a page. 'Didn't you know? They're heading for Florence as well – only staying for a couple of weeks, but we thought it would make the journey more agreeable if we travelled together.'

The sudden, convulsive grip of her fingers upon the handle of her teacup spilled some of the hot liquid into the saucer. 'You didn't mention it to me.'

'I didn't think it necessary. You like them, don't you?' His voice was faintly and reasonably surprised, 'I thought that you and Annabel got on so well? It must surely be pleasant for you to have female companionship?'

'Yes – yes, of course – it's just –' she stopped.

For the first time he lifted his head and looked directly at her, his brows drawn to a dark, puzzled line. 'What? Jessica – is something wrong?'

Miserably she shook her head.

'Don't you like Annabel? Has she done something to upset you?' He was truly concerned.

'No – no! Of course not! I suppose – I was just looking forward to being on our own again.' Even in her own ears that sounded lame.

He laughed a little. 'We've got the rest of our lives for that.'

She swallowed. The tea slopped in her saucer again.

'Good Lord, what a mess you've made!' Robert laughed good-naturedly, 'I'll call the waiter. You need a clean cup –'

The day was warm, close and thundery. They lunched, the four of them as always, at an open-air café in the park, served by waiters and waitresses in Tyrolean national costume that the unrepentantly amused Annabel said made them look like the clockwork dolls they had seen in the tourist shops. 'David, darling, you really must buy a pair of those little leather trousers before we leave. They'll show off your wonderful legs to perfection! And one of those dinky green hats! Good Lord, they do look like – what are those little Irish fairies called?'

David smiled indulgently, though the irreverent mention of his legs had brought a slight blush of colour to his fair skin. 'Leprechauns, I think.'

'Of course.' Annabel fanned herself vigorously. 'My goodness, it's hot! Why don't we go to the ramparts? It's bound to be cooler there.'

They strolled, as they habitually did, with the two girls in front, Annabel's small hand tucked firmly into Jessica's crooked arm, the young men behind. Jessica could hear their voices, deep and pleasant, in idle conversation.

'– so why Florence?' David was asking, 'I don't pretend to be any kind of expert – far from it – but it's hardly the centre of the musical world, is it? Why not Venice? Or Rome?'

'Jessica particularly wanted to go to Florence. And it happens that there's a teacher there with whom I should like to study. Signor Donatti – Pietro Donatti. He was one of Rossini's tutors at Bologna. He retired a couple of years ago, to Florence where he was born. He only takes a few pupils – mostly English –'

'Oh? Why's that?'

Robert laughed, quietly and self-deprecatingly. 'Signor Donatti has a passion of his own. English Literature. Which just happens to be what I studied at Oxford – so he didn't enquire too deeply into my musical accomplishments –'

'Jessica, I declare! You aren't listening to a word I say!'

'I'm sorry.' Jessica smiled at the mildly indignant Annabel who smiled swiftly back and leaned her head conspiratorily close.

'I wanted to ask you something.'

'Oh?'

Annabel nodded, her face suddenly solemn. 'It's very – personal. I hope you won't be offended?'

Jessica laughed, intrigued. 'I shouldn't think so.'

'It's –' Annabel fiddled self-consciously with the lace trimmings at the shoulder of Jessica's dress. 'It's not something that a lady is supposed to talk about – but – I am most abysmally ignorant of such things and I just thought that you might be able to help me –?'

'If I can.' Jessica was astounded. What in the world could this gay and confident creature not know that she, Jessica, might?

'It's –' Clearly the other girl was uncomfortable. She glanced over her shoulder to where David and Robert followed, deep in their own conversation. 'I just wondered – oh, dear, I really don't know how to say it!'

Jessica waited.

'You and Robert –' Annabel began afresh, 'you've been travelling for some months?'

'Yes.'

'And you mean to stay in Florence for some considerable time?'

'Yes.'

'So –' Delicately she picked at the lace again, 'You aren't – anxious to start a family yet?' The last words came out in a self-conscious rush.

Jessica could not have been more taken aback had the other girl grown fangs and bitten her. 'Er – no,' she said. 'I suppose not.'

'I just wondered if you knew – that is, just before I came away a friend told me there were ways – you know – to prevent –' she mumbled to a stop, and then, as if finally impatient with her own embarrassment lifted her face and looked Jessica full in the eye, '– to prevent conception,' she said, clearly and softly. 'I'm afraid of becoming pregnant whilst we're travelling. Two of my cousins died in childbirth, you see, and the thought frightens me no matter how hard I try. Why – just before we left England poor Princess Charlotte died – and she was the king's favourite daughter! If it could happen to her –' She sucked in her lip. 'Well – out here – anything could happen, couldn't it? Even if we tried to get home – well, who knows what that might bring on? Mama had three miscarriages in two years, and she travelled no further than Richmond! I attempted to speak with her about it before we left home – oh, Lord above, you just should have seen her face! –' Despite her embarrassment the merriment that always seemed to hover just below the surface broke through and glimmered in her eyes, '– and all she would say was that if I were lucky – *lucky*, mind! – David would be gentleman enough to abstain from the "animal desires" that might – well, you know – cause such a thing to happen. As if poor David were the only one to have anything to do with it! I didn't know then what monstrous rubbish she was talking, of course – I wasn't yet married, and didn't understand. But I declare she spoke of the thing as something to be avoided or endured, like

248

toothache or the ague! It truly frightened me at the time – but then – David, dear David showed me differently –' her eyes softened and she squeezed Jessica's arm hard, 'Oh, Jessica, is it not marvellous to be loved? Did you know – could you guess – that it would be such a wonder?'

Dumbly Jessica shook her head.

'I know it's considered unladylike – though why it should be I really can't imagine, for after all here we all are, and we all came by the same road, did we not? Why should it be right for men to find pleasure in the act and not women? Whoever started the nonsense that it is only the men who enjoy it?' The spark of mischief was back in her face, that died a little at recollection of her dilemma. 'But, oh Jessica, it's the women who have the babies, and I'm frightened of that. Aren't you?'

'I haven't actually thought about it.'

The other girl's eyes widened. 'You mean that? It truly doesn't worry you? The thought of it happening far from home – far from your family –?'

Jessica shook her head. Desperately she prayed for an interruption to this uncomfortable conversation. In the sultry air she felt a runnel of sweat trickle unpleasantly down her back.

Annabel's mouth had dropped a little in disappointment. 'So – you don't know of anything? Anything to – prevent it happening?'

Jessica shook her head again.

The other girl straightened up, sighing philosophically. 'Oh well. I'll just have to hope for the best, I suppose.'

'Couldn't you –' Jessica ventured, and stopped, clearing her throat.

'What?'

'Couldn't you – take your mother's advice? I mean – if David knew how you felt –'

'What?' Annabel squealed with incredulous laughter, 'Oh, Jessica, don't tease! I'm serious!'

Jessica smiled weakly.

Annabel regarded her, faint astonishment in the candid dark eyes. 'Could you?'

Jessica was once more reduced to a wordless headshake.

'Can you imagine it? Goodness, they'd have to lock me up! It's dreadful of me, isn't it?' She was suddenly uncharacteristically serious, 'But, oh Jessica – if he touches me – looks at me – I'm wild for him. Isn't it disgraceful?'

'Of course not.' Jessica's voice was gentle. Beneath the other girl's gay bravado she sensed a true anxiety. Brought up to believe the joys of the body to be a purely male preserve Annabel's awakening had not, Jessica suspected, been without the penalty of guilt.

'I wonder if it will always be like this?' The pretty voice was pensive, 'I mean – when we're old? I pray so. I truly do.'

Jessica said nothing.

Faintly in the distance, thunder rolled.

'I think there's going to be a storm,' Annabel said.

Against her will she found herself watching them. She watched the touch of their hands, the almost unconscious movement of their bodies towards each other, the warm secrets in their eyes when their glances met. She watched the teasingly provocative way that Annabel lifted her face to her husband, small teeth glimmering in a smile that brought answering laughter to his eyes – laughter, and something else, a strangely dangerous gleam of excitement and of challenge. She sensed Annabel's suppressed excitement when her young husband took her hand, or touched her cheek. Sensed it and, she realized with something of a shock, envied it deeply.

'You're very quiet?' It was early evening. They had dined and were about to set out for their evening stroll around the Konigsplatz. The band was already playing, liltingly light and pretty music that floated upon the warm air like brightly coloured bubbles.

'I'm all right.'

Robert shook his head. 'It's the weather. It will storm, I think. A walk in the air will do you good. Ah – here come the others –'

She took his arm and they joined Annabel and David under the trees. A small, too-warm breath of air shivered the leaves and was still. Jessica was suddenly and somehow shockingly aware of the warmth of Robert's arm through the thin material of his lightweight coat. Her shoulder rubbed his. She leaned to him a little.

Annabel was laughing at something he had said. David had an arm about her waist. The band struck up again. A passing couple nodded, smiling, and the man courteously lifted his hat.

Jessica slipped her hand more firmly into the crook of Robert's elbow. She turned her head to look at him. The neat dark hair curled a very little into the nape of his slender neck. The line of his jaw was sharp and fragile. She could see a small pulse beating softly beneath the skin.

David was talking. '– and so I said to the fellow – "Good God, man, what do you take me for? A Lord of the Realm? Two guineas, you say –?"'

'And he got it for one.' Annabel cut in pertly, obviously heading off a lengthy story she had heard often before. 'Wasn't that clever of him?' She lifted a hand and tweaked his nose. He growled and pretended to bite her finger.

Robert laughed softly. The flat, handsome planes of his face were lit and shaded by the coloured lanterns that were strung in the trees. Suddenly a flood of tenderness lifted in Jessica, so unexpected and so intense that it brought an absurd sting of tears to her eyes, an awkward lump to her throat. She wanted to lay her head upon his shoulder, to trace the delicate lines of his face with tender fingers, as she had seen Annabel do with David.

'Well –' David had stopped, swinging Annabel close to him and dropping a light kiss upon her cheek, 'anyone for a nightcap?'

Robert glanced at the bemusedly silent Jessica and shook his head. 'I think not tonight. Jessica is tired, I believe. An early night will do her no harm.'

Annabel pulled a droll face and chuckled a little.

'It's the weather,' Jessica said. 'I have a headache.'

'Of course. Off you go, children.' Annabel beamed, making no pretence at belief. 'We'll see you tomorrow. Darling David – are you going to treat me to just one of those wonderful chocolate cakies –?'

'You'll get fat, you little pig,' he said.

'All the more to cuddle!'

They walked off, squabbling fondly, and crossed the square that was still busy with people. With Robert's hand on her elbow Jessica climbed the steps to the guesthouse and then the single flight of wide stairs to their room, which was large and comfortably furnished and looked out onto the square. The atmosphere was very close. Robert opened the curtains and threw open the double doors onto the balcony. Music and a babble of talk and laughter rose. The ceiling was gay with coloured light. 'Is that too noisy for you?' He was solicitous, as always.

She shook her head. 'No.'

'Would you like me to get you something? A glass of water, perhaps?'

'That would be nice. Thank you.'

He left the room. She walked restlessly to the window and stood looking down into the square. She could see Annabel and David sitting at a table in the shadow of a tree, their chairs drawn close together. As she watched Annabel broke off a small piece of the cake she was eating and lifted it to her husband's mouth. He took the cake with his lips, nibbled her fingers, kissed the palm of her hand.

Jessica turned away.

She took off her hat and gloves and tossed them on to a chair. Kicked off her slippers, not caring where they landed.

The door opened and Robert came in carrying a glass which he put on the table by the bed. She watched him in silence, watched the neat, graceful movements, the turn of the small, handsome head.

'Would you help me with my buttons?' She turned her back to him, looking over her shoulder.

'I'll ring for the maid.'

'Oh, no – please don't. It's so embarrassing to be waited upon by someone who doesn't understand a word you say. Please – won't you do it?' Despite her best efforts her voice was forlornly cajoling, the voice of a child begging a favour from an adult.

252

'Of course.' He was as always unfailingly courteous. She felt his fingers, light and competent and totally impersonal upon the small buttons that fastened the back of her dress. 'There.'

'Thank you.'

Light from the swinging lanterns danced upon the wall.

'Shall I close the shutters?'

'Oh, no! It's so very hot – so very close –' She turned. He had not moved. She stood not a foot from him, her head tilted to look into his face. 'Robert –?' she whispered, her voice almost lost in the music and laughter of the world outside.

Infinitesimally the sharp lines of his face tautened further. He did not move.

'– please – couldn't we – couldn't we try?' She could not believe what she was saying, nor the sudden fierce note of pleading in her voice. With no thought she let the dress slip from her shoulders to the floor and stood before him in her petticoat, flimsy for the heat, the fine material, damp with perspiration, clinging to her breasts and hips. 'Couldn't we – shouldn't we – just try?'

He stepped back from her, putting out a hand as if to ward her off. She caught it in both of hers, carrying it fiercely to her lips. 'Robert – please! I'm your wife –!' She fought the rise of tears.

He had frozen where he stood, his hand taut and still in hers. Very slowly she drew it to her breast. He did not move. The involuntary brush of his curled fingers against her nipple made her tremble. The teat hardened, standing against the damp cloth of her petticoat. She moved instinctively, arching her back, rubbing the small, sharp, sensitive point of her breast against his hand. Pulsing warmth flooded her belly and the secret places of her body moistened. She made a small sound.

'Christ!' The agonized violence of the word pierced her consciousness like a needle. He snatched his hand from hers.

'Robert –!' Hands outstretched, she stepped towards him.

'No!' He pushed her, violently, the action almost a blow, one arm crooked before his face as if to ward off the very sight of her. '*No!*' His face was convulsed. 'She did that! She made me do that! God in heaven – I should have known it! You're no

253

better than she was! None of you are! She made me touch her —!'

As she staggered from him she stumbled upon the hem of her petticoat, dragging it from her shoulders, baring her breasts. She recovered her footing and swung to face him. The revulsion in his face, lit by the demonic lantern light, stopped her like a flung stone. Yet she stood, and in pride would make no move to cover her nakedness. 'What are you talking about?' she asked.

His face was rigid with disgust. He lifted a finger, pointing. 'Slut,' he said. 'She was a slut, and you are too. I thought you were different, but you aren't. You're the same as all of them. A slut —!' His voice was trembling uncontrollably.

'Who? Robert — who are you talking about?' She was desperately confused.

'Who?' His eyes gleamed in the light, his voice was suddenly soft. 'Why the girl — the woman — who made me suck her dugs before she would give me my supper. An eight-year-old boy. The woman who would make me take down my breeches for the birch and then —' he could not go on. His face had turned sickly pale.

She crossed her arms over her bared breasts, staring at him. 'A — a *nursemaid*? Did that?'

'And more. Do you want to hear more?' He was beside himself with rage and revulsion. She could see his trembling from where she stood. 'She'd make me put my fingers in her. Wet, and hot! Disgusting. Disgusting!' He retched. She took a step towards him. He backed away from her, his eyes wild.

'Robert, stop it,' she said, the calmness of desperation in her voice. 'This is nothing like that. I'm not her. I'm Jessica. Your wife.'

He had calmed a little, but his voice still shook. 'You're all the same. All of you.'

She made her voice gentle. 'You don't mean that.' Very slowly she reached a hand towards him. He jerked back.

'Get away from me. *Get away!*' He knocked her hand aside, violently.

The violence frightened her, but she hid it, trying to keep

reason in her voice. 'We should *try* Robert – we should! For both our sakes.'

'No.'

'Please!' She was surprised to discover that tears were sliding unchecked down her cheeks.

'*No!*' He tried to brush past her, making for the refuge of the dressing-room. Without thought she caught at his arm. With a sudden savage movement he tore himself free of her, and as he did so, whether by ill luck or design she could not tell, his hand caught her sharply on the side of her jaw, knocking her head back painfully and sending her spinning from him to land on hands and knees by the bed. He cried out, in anger and despair. She heard his swiftly-moving footsteps and the slam of the dressing-room door. Heard the turning of the key in the lock.

She lifted her head. 'Robert? *Robert!*'

Silence.

She staggered to her feet and ran to the door. 'Robert!'

'Go away,' he said. 'Please, just get away from me.'

'Robert –!'

He did not speak again. Half an hour later, exhausted, she gave up her tearful pleading, left the door and stumbled to the bed. Outside the music played, cruelly gay. There was no sound from the dressing-room. She crawled into the bed like an injured animal crawling into its lair, and there she lay, the silent tears shining on her face whilst beyond the open windows the world danced and laughed and took its pleasure.

In the distance the thunder rumbled, but the storm stubbornly refused to break.

The custom-house by the city gate was an officious and fly-specked shambles, a vexation after the lovely drive down through the terraced vineyards of the mountains with the tantalizing vision of the spires and roofs of Florence growing closer at every turn. A swarm of slovenly-uniformed police, soldiers and officials presided over the chaos, that seemed rather more designed to prevent the flow of traffic into the city than to facilitate it.

'Oh, for heaven's sake!' David's fair face was flushed with exasperation and the heat of the afternoon, 'We'll be here till next week at this rate!'

Robert put his hand into his pocket and Jessica saw the gleam of silver. 'Wait here a moment.'

A scant half-hour later a hired carriage, lighter and blessedly cooler than the heavy coach in which they had travelled from Bologna, was bowling down the Via St Gallo towards the centre of the city. The road was wide, straight and smoothly paved with the huge flat stones which graced almost all of the main streets of Florence and which made travelling in the city less of a penance than the cobblestones most city-dwellers were used to. Impressive buildings lined the way, façades by Michelangelo and Raphael jostling shoulder to shoulder with the more ancient frontages of the early medieval city. So much had Jessica read of this place, so often had she studied its layout, with its Roman grid of straight streets, its piazzas, its palaces, its numerous churches, that she felt an odd but reassuring sense of recognition, as if, far from being a stranger in a strange city, she were returning to a familiar and much-loved place.

'Look – oh, look! The Cathedral! Isn't it splendid? – And the Baptistry! Oh, Annabel, do look –!' Jessica breathed. The mass of buildings gleamed in the light, the brilliance of their colourful marble façades blinding in the sunlight. The slender *campanile* towered to a flawless blue sky. Enthralled, Jessica twisted in her seat, leaning through the window as they passed through the great square. 'Just look at the gates of the Baptistry! Even from here you can see how wonderful they are –!' She drew her head in and turned back to Annabel. 'They're by Ghiberti – I knew someone once who said they were one of the wonders of the artistic world –'

Annabel smiled wanly. She was hot, she was extremely tired, and she had seen enough cathedrals, baptistries and campaniles over the past weeks to last her a long lifetime.

They were in the narrow via Calzaioli now in the old, crowded part of the city and moving towards the river. The Romseys' hotel was on the far side of the river, by the Pitti

Palace, whilst the apartment that the young FitzBoltons had rented was in the via Condotta, not far from the ancient piazza del Gran Duca, where stood possibly the most famous and most certainly the most pictured place of Florence, the Palazzo Vecchio. Most of the FitzBoltons' luggage had been sent on and hopefully awaited them at the apartment. The trunk that had travelled with them through Europe had been left at the custom-house for later collection, for both had decided, to their travelling-companions' amazement, that their first approach to their new home should be afoot. They consequently took their leave of Annabel and David at the city end of the Ponte Vecchio, promising to meet at the Romseys' hotel for dinner a couple of evenings later. Jessica stepped from the carriage into the dusty heat of the afternoon, raised her parasol against the sun's glare. The greenish-brown river moved sluggishly beneath the ancient bridge, slapping softly against the stone pillars that supported the structure and its huddled fringe of picturesquely dilapidated houses. A dog chased in the shallows, where a woman with tired, rhythmic movements slapped the garments she was washing against a stone, and in the centre of the wide river, summer-low, a boy waded, the water no higher than his thighs. The midden-smell of it assaulted Jessica's nostrils. In an alleyway running down to the river washing hung like dispirited flags, unstirring in the hot air. She hardly noticed as the carriage drew away, with Annabel waving bravely and very slightly tearfully from the window.

Frowning a little Robert studied the map he carried, then pointed. 'There, I think. It isn't very far.'

She nodded. Since Vienna conversation between them had not been easy. She could not look at him without remembering with a flush of almost unendurable humiliation the bitter shame of that night. It had never been mentioned between them, but they had been like strangers since, polite travelling companions who shared nothing but the accident of travel. It was a relief, she discovered now, to be free of the company of the Romseys, for at least that meant that they were free too from the need for pretence. She laid her fingers lightly upon the arm he courteously proffered, barely touching him, and from habit neither spoke as they walked into the shaded canyon of the via por Santa Maria, for neither had a thought to share with the other.

Until they walked, unsuspecting, from the short, darkly-shadowed street into the wide and sunlit space of the piazza del Gran Duca.

As one they stopped, staring. On the far side of the L-shaped square the bulk of the great, fortress-like Palazzio Vecchio, square-built and imposing, dominated the place, its incongruously slender, crenellated tower, strangely elegant, reaching like a pointed finger into the blaze of the sunlit sky. Two colossal sculptures stood before the palace and more glorious statuary adorned the great ornamented Loggia which stood at right angles to the ancient palace. A huge white fountain, one of the few in this city where public fountains were oddly rare, played in the square. But even at this distance one object drew the eye and stopped the breath. Michelangelo's *David*, one of the master's greatest works, stood gleaming in the sun before the palace – huge, the stone smooth as a boy's skin, unbelievably and beautifully lifelike.

With no word they both moved towards it, drawn as if by a magnet, Jessica folding her parasol as she went. At the statue's foot they stopped, looking up in awe at the smoothly sculptured muscle and bone, the gallantly lovely face. Enormous as it was it would have been no surprise had the figure moved and breathed, lowered the sling it carried, stretched, smiling, in the sunshine. Danny had spoken of it in such terms to Jessica. And she, in innocence, had believed he exaggerated.

'It's the most beautiful thing I've ever seen,' she said.

Robert nodded, blinking.

'How – how can it be so huge, and yet so lifelike? So utterly perfect?' Faced with this shared wonder, all constraint between them had fallen away. She spoke not to the man who had refused and shamed her but to the boy, the friend of a lifetime with whom she had shared so much.

'Genius is beyond the bounds of the normal,' Robert said.

'That's what genius is. Like Mozart. Or Haydn. Genius is – has to be – larger than life.'

An odd catch in his voice made her glance at him. The sharp glitter of tears in his eyes made her turn hastily from him. They stood for a very long time, looking at the statue, studying in thoughtful silence every last lovely detail of the figure. Through her fingers Jessica could feel the strung tension of Robert's body. The slender arm she touched was taut as steel beneath the elegance of his lightweight coat.

'Jessica,' he said at last, his eyes still upon the statue, 'we have to talk.'

Panic rose. She shook her head.

'I hurt you.' He spoke with difficulty. 'I'm sorry. I wouldn't do that for the world.'

'I know.'

'It was unforgivable.'

She said nothing.

'It was – you took me by surprise –'

'It doesn't matter.' Her voice was high, threaded faintly with nerves. 'Don't talk about it.'

'We have to. We can't go on like this.'

She remained silent for a moment. Then, 'How else?' she asked, her voice bleak.

Still he did not look at her. His pleasant voice was controlled now, quiet and firm. He might have been discussing still the genius that had produced the masterpiece that stood before them, beautiful, perfectly formed, and as far removed from the paltry emotions and troubles of man as it was possible to be.

'I'm sorry – but I have to say it – you knew, before we married, how I felt about –' he paused, cleared his throat, '– about physical love.'

'Yes.'

'But you didn't understand. And that was my fault.'

She shrugged, wearily. Despite the sun she felt suddenly chilled. 'Robert – please – I truly can't see there's anything to be gained by talking about it –'

'There's everything to be gained.' He swung to face her, took her by the shoulders, forcing her to look at him.

259

She lifted her head, looked him in the eyes, asked the question that had haunted her since that night. 'What you said – about the woman – the nursemaid – it was really true?'

She felt the tremor that ran through his body in the hands that held her. 'Yes.'

'I'm sorry. It must have been horrible for you. Couldn't you – couldn't you stop her? Couldn't you tell anyone?'

He laughed, a dry, unpleasant sound. 'Do you remember being eight?'

She did, all too well. She nodded.

'Then you'll remember how easily intimidated you are by an adult. How easily threatened.'

'Yes.'

'And –' he smiled, the familiar, rueful smile, 'I wasn't a very brave little boy. I was never like you.'

'I'm not brave.'

'Oh, yes. You are. You always were. It is what I have always admired most in you. Oh, Jessica, can't you see? You were always blind. You looked up to me because I was older. But – you were the brave one, always.'

She shook her head. The sun, lowering to the west, gleamed through a tracery of stone and glittered in her eyes.

'I don't feel very brave now,' she said, and turned from him.

In the silence that followed a clock struck, closely followed by another. Somewhere, distantly, a bell tolled.

'Jessica,' Robert said. 'Listen to me. You are my wife. For better or for worse, you are my wife. You agreed to that. I'm sorry. I'm sorry that I am as I am. I'm sorry for what happened. I'm sorry I was weak enough – cowardly enough – to accept the sacrifice you offered when I knew that you didn't know what would be involved for you. I despise myself.' It was said evenly, almost unemotionally.

She turned her head, watching him, the wide brim of her hat shading her small face.

'It's done,' he said. 'But –' he hesitated, painfully '– it can be undone.'

She frowned in question.

His face was like stone in the sunlight, with less of life about it than the blank-eyed David who stood above them. 'You could have the marriage annulled,' he said, quietly. 'No court would deny you.'

She stared at him. 'You'd – do that?'

He nodded.

'But – Robert – what would that mean for you? What – what would people think? They'd – they'd be sure to say the most awful things. It would kill you!'

In the silence a pigeon strutted at their feet, pecking crumbs. A gaily-dressed girl, dark hair glossy, olive skin smooth as silk swung past, a basket of flowers on her arm.

Jessica shook her head. Her eyes were bewildered. 'No!' she said.

'Think before you say that. I might not always be so – courageous.' His mouth twisted bitterly upon the word.

She turned from him, staring at the feet of the statue. 'No. I couldn't. I couldn't!' Her vehemence surprised herself. She pressed a hand to her forehead.

There was a very small silence. 'Why not?' Robert asked, very softly.

'I – don't know.' But she did. Somewhere within her the lump of ice that had been her heart since that night in Vienna was melting. The pain she had locked within that ice flooded her. She almost cried out with the force of it. She knew that to do as he offered would be to hold him up to public ridicule, and possibly worse. The Oxford scandal would be dredged up, and that could destroy him. And that was something she could not – would not – be a part of. He was, after all, still Robert. Still, despite all, her lifelong friend. And for that, still, she could not help but love him.

'Why not?' he asked again, gently persistent.

'Because –' she struggled, and stopped.

Very gently he turned her again to face him. 'Because you're my dear little Jessica,' he said. 'My good friend. Sister of my soul.' He lifted a finger and touched her lips, the tenderest of gestures. She blinked rapidly against the scald of tears. Tiredly she leaned to him and softly he held her.

'What can we do?' The words and the tone of her voice were that of a bewildered child.

For a long time he did not answer but stood, his arm about her, his head thrown back as he looked at the sculptured glorious boyhood of innocent David.

'I don't know,' he said, honestly. 'But – Jessica, life isn't a child's puzzle, with one easy answer, that someone else will give you if you can't find it yourself.' He turned, smiling a little, and took her hand, drawing it companionably into the crook of his arm – a gesture that a few short hours before she would never have believed possible. 'Don't let's say any more for the moment. For now –' he smiled down at her, 'well, at least we've broken that beastly silence and are friends again. That will do for now, won't it?'

Bemusedly she nodded.

He indicated a small street that ran into the square not far from where they stood. 'Our new home,' he said, smiling, 'is somewhere over there if I'm not much mistaken. Shall we go and find it?'

Numero 3D, via Condotta, was a surprise, and a delightful one. Though now much-neglected it had once been the reception rooms of a small palace. Marble-floored, ornately-ceilinged, the rooms, though smaller, were as splendidly proportioned as any in New Hall. As the swarthy, ill-tempered-looking caretaker threw open the vast double-doors that led from a landing at the top of a wide, dark sweep of staircase that must once have seen the grandeur of palatial comings and goings Jessica gaped like a child.

'Good Lord!' Robert said.

Tall shuttered windows led to a balcony that overlooked the narrow street. Ornate, fly-specked mirrors reflected, floor to ceiling, the slatted golden shafts of the setting sun. The furniture was ramshackle and barely filled the place, and the sorry curtains hung in ragged holes. In the centre of the gracious but empty reception hall their trunks stood stacked, a small lonely island in a sea of smooth marble.

Robert turned to the man. 'Thank you, *Signor*. This will do very well.'

The man grunted but made no move to go.

Jessica cocked an eye at Robert who reached into his pocket. The gnarled fist closed over a small coin – a *paoli* – and without thanks the man turned and left.

Jessica, all tiredness forgotten, danced a few steps. 'Robert – this is magnificent! And at such a rent! We can buy furniture, and curtains, and it will be truly beautiful! And Mama thinks we're starving in a garret!'

Robert strode to the tall windows and flung them back with a clatter. Slanting golden sunlight streamed into the room. The walls were painted with idyllic hunting scenes, the hunting party in the gay clothes of three hundred years before, a palace in the distance, pennants streaming gallantly from its towers. Amongst stylized trees and flowers the stag reared, unafraid, frozen in lordly defiance of the puny hounds that snapped at his heels. The cobweb-hung ceiling was ornately gilded. Jessica clapped her hands. 'A palace! Our very own palace!' She turned to him, laughing, and stopped, struck to stillness by the expression on his face.

He reached for her hand, smiling. 'That's the first real laughter I've heard since Vienna,' he said.

She flushed. 'Don't. Don't talk about it. We're here. A new start. We don't have to talk about it.' He held her hand a moment longer, studying her face, his eyes serious, then stepped back, letting go her hand.

Jessica ran to the window and looked down into the street. Carts rolled by on the smooth, flat paving. A horseman, bravely dressed in red and blue glanced up, caught her eye and bowed gallantly from the saddle. In her excitement she smiled shyly back, and was rewarded by the gleaming flash of white teeth. Children shrieked along the road, playing some game of battle, the unknown liquid tongue of Tuscany echoing in her, rattling from the high walls and closed shutters of the narrow street. A spired church stood at the corner, ornate and graceful. *Florence*. She was in Florence at last.

Robert joined her and stood leaning, his narrow hands upon the wrought iron rail of the balcony, looking down. 'Florence,' he said. 'At last.' And was surprised and pleased at the soft sound of her laughter.

Chapter Ten

Almost the first thing that any newly-arrived English traveller to Florence discovered was that the well-established British colony in the city fell into two distinct and utterly inimical parts. Into the first – the society that revolved about the Residence of Lord Burghersh, reputed to be the most popular Ambassador in Italy – the young FitzBoltons had easy entry, their way already prepared by judicious letters to various family and business contacts. The Romseys as well had brought letters of introduction – indeed, since Annabel's second cousin's husband was cousin only once removed from Lady Burghersh herself they were even better connected than were Robert and Jessica, and all four young people were assured of that immediate and unqualified acceptance that, oddly and to the favoured few, only such a closed society can offer.

The second group of British exiles, however, proved in their own way to be more exclusive, for doors here were not so easily opened by money or by social connections; on the contrary such things could prove a positive disadvantage when approaching the artists, writers, musicians and their acolytes who were centred upon a house on the via del Corso not far from the splendid Cathedral Square of the piazza del Duomo. Between these two groups there was no love lost, their common language and heritage serving rather more to divide than to unite them. To the established society of monied and influential expatriates who dined regularly at the Embassy with the Ambassador and his Lady, who frequented the boxes of the theatre and the opera with the Grand Duke and his family, who drove in fine carriages or rode imported English hunters with imported English hounds at their heels along the leafy avenues of the Cascine, their less conventional compatriots who frequented the elegant Palazzo owned by Sir Theodolphus Carradine on the via del Corso were a frank embarrassment, to be ignored if possible and dismissed with confident scorn if not. A bunch of penniless and scruffy artists with a known collective addiction to cheap wine and radical politics contributed no great service, in the eyes of the Establishment, to the name or reputation of their country. That the apostate king – or, as sly tongues would have it, queen – of this alternative society should be a renegade from their own ranks did nothing whatsoever to encourage friendly relations between the two groups. And that Sir Theodolphus, last, elderly, utterly amoral sprig of a well-founded Buckinghamshire family, cared not a fig for any opinion but his own did not greatly help matters. Bravado in the face of censure might have been understood – even possibly secretly admired – but total and honest indifference to the disapproval of a righteous world was not to be endured; and so Theo Carradine, wicked old libertine that he quite truly was, was *persona non grata* with his own kind. To the struggling and sometimes literally starving young artists that he gathered around him, however, he was food and drink and a roof above their heads. For the price of a little entertaining conversation there was good company, good food and good wine to be had, the loan of a few *paoli* for next week's rent and pretty young things of either sex ready and eager to please the good friends of their good friend Theo. There was always a meal and a bed for anyone, on one condition – convention was Theo Carradine's sworn first enemy, his second boredom and his third self-righteousness. Anyone suspected of being tainted with one or all of these deadly sins was politely shown the door and invited not to return. For the rest, there were, quite simply, no rules. Small wonder that almost the first words that were spoken to Jessica over the dinner table at the Embassy a few days after their arrival concerned Theo Carradine and were words of warning.

'– it's always just as well to be forewarned, my dear. For – is not Mr Fitzbolton about to take up the study of music? Very creditable, of course, and I'm sure he must be enormously talented but – one must always be careful. This is not London. One never can tell with whom one might come into contact –'

Jessica found herself reflecting, with fleeting amusement, that the speaker, a florid-faced matron whose enormous bosom rested upon the table like a pudding upon a shelf, might have been speaking of the possibility of contracting some awful contagious disease. '– Not that such personable and – normal – young people as yourselves are likely to hold much interest for Theo –' The red lips pursed sanctimoniously. 'How such a man, born to such privilege, can have fallen so low is beyond me. Utterly beyond me.'

Jessica had her own reasons for being interested in what she had heard of Theo Carradine and his coterie of penniless British artists. 'You know him?' Something about the easy use of the Christian name had alerted her.

Her informant flipped a pudgy, scandalized hand. '*Knew*, my dear, knew. No-one – no-one who is anyone, you understand – *knows* Theo Carradine these days.'

'But – you did know him?'

'Oh, yes. Quite well, in fact, in our younger days. His people were friends of my parents. Lived not far from us in the country, so the two families used to spend quite a lot of time together. His father mastered the most wonderful pack of hounds, I remember. Many a happy day I've spent following them. Not Theo, though. The man never could keep his seat. Simply could not stay on a horse –' She spoke with a kind of smug satisfaction, as if nothing she could say of the man after that could possibly be as bad. 'Even then he was a bad lot. Always has been. How the Carradines came to whelp such a runt I'll never understand.'

Jessica was intrigued. 'Is he really that bad?'

'Worse, my dear. Much, much worse! The man is pernicious!' Liking the word she repeated it fiercely, rolling it on her tongue, her chins wobbling fiercesomely. 'Pernicious! And is really not a fit subject for civilized table talk.' She dismissed Jessica's obvious interest out of hand. 'Now, tell me – the

Suffolk Hawthornes, you say? It seems to me that I may have met your parents – and your sister – don't you have a very pretty sister –?'

A week or so later the Romseys left the city to continue on their tour, with tears from emotional Annabel and on Jessica's part a guilty trace of well-concealed relief. Much as she liked them, their blissful relationship had sharpened her nerves intolerably, as had the need for pretence in their company. Even a little removed, as they had been these past two weeks she found their constant, happy presence a strain. What that revealed about her relationship with Robert she did not care to think too deeply about.

Robert, meanwhile, had begun his attendance at the teaching studies of Maestro Pietro Donatti, studying the *pianoforte* and – more importantly to him – composition. He was delighted to discover in the Maestro a kindly and intelligent man, patient with his pupils and unhurried in his ways. Robert was no musical genius, and he knew it, but that did not prevent him from feeling passionately about his music. For all of his younger years it had been his life. Desperately now he needed to discover and nurture some talent that might replace the glory of the one of which he had been so cruelly deprived. His voice had been his treasure, and it was lost. Without it he was nothing. His dream was that in creating music for other voices the treasure would be his again, this time to keep for ever and to pass on to others. Maestro Donatti, a pleasant, easy-going man, semi-retired and finding endless pleasure in discussing his own passion for the works of William Shakespeare with an intelligent and well-educated young man did not see the necessity to destroy that dream. And so, at least for now, Robert was happy and occupied and his heart was hopeful.

Not so Jessica's.

It was a month after their arrival in the city and two weeks after the departure of Annabel and David that she first honestly admitted to herself both the magnet that had drawn her to Florence and the utter idiocy of believing she might find what she at last forced herself to acknowledge she had come to seek. She stood one day upon the busy thoroughfare of the Ponte Vecchio and stared disconsolately at the broad, muddy waters of the Arno. The bridge's fourteenth-century creators had, even so long ago, left a gap in the buildings so that passers-by might gaze on the lovely view of the river and its valley. The first time she had stood here she had been enchanted, and every word that Danny had spoken about it had rung in her ears. Now she hardly noticed it. The weather was very hot, the sun blazed from a brazen sky. The river smelled appallingly. The gold and silversmith's shops of the Ponte Vecchio were thronged with customers. Crowds pushed and jostled on the bridge. The *lungarnos* too – the built-up banks of the ever-flooding Arno – were alive with people. She must have been mad ever to think of finding Danny here! To think for a moment that it might be possible to find one person, one individual, in this teeming city of tens of thousands of souls! And someone moreover who might anyway never have returned here in the first place. She had nothing but instinct to suggest that he had, not one shred of evidence beyond a private conviction that with war-torn Europe at peace at last Danny O'Donnel would have made for his personal Mecca with all speed. – 'One day, Mouse,' he had said in the cool darkness of St Agatha's, 'when Europe is free again I shall go back. And I shall be the greatest living sculptor in Florence –'

Since she and Robert had arrived they had explored Florence street by street, building by building. They had marvelled at Ghiberti's Gate of Paradise, been captivated by the beauty of the *Pieta*, and dazzled by Botticelli's lovely *Spring*. They had visited the Duomo and the Baptistry, and climbed Giotto's famous Campanile. They had been to so many churches and basilicas, so many galleries, palaces and museums that Jessica found it difficult to remember names and geographical placings. They had strolled in the Boboli Gardens with their great walks and fountains, had ridden the shady avenues of the Cascine, that ran by the broad slow waters of the Arno, passing the time of day with other riders and carriage parties for all the world as if they had been in Rotten Row. And yes, as Danny had said, as she had known it must be, Florence was the most wonderful of cities.

But in the teeming streets, the long, cool galleries, the sunlit parks, the shadowed churches not once had she seen the face for which she had constantly looked. Of course not. Foolish even to have harboured the hope.

What had she expected? That she might one day have been strolling the via Calzaioli and Danny would step, smiling, from the crowds? That she might stand gazing at the *Pieta* and he would appear at her elbow, her dark saint, the dark angel come whole to life?

The dreams of a child – embarrassing in a grown woman.

And if he did – she asked herself with ruthless common sense – then what? What could she possibly expect from him? She was a married woman, and he – who knew what he might have become? Who knew what he had been to start with? The Danny O'Donnel she remembered so well was probably more a product of her childish imagination than of real life. Stupid to hope. Stupid to carry with her that memory, like a talisman –

Blindly she turned from the river and all but bumped into a smiling young man sho stood just behind her. Slick black hair, shining black eyes, teeth gleaming pearl-bright against an olive skin.

'Oh – I'm sorry –' Instinctively she side-stepped, trying to pass him.

Smoothly he moved with her, blocking her way, talking rapidly.

She shook her head. 'I'm sorry. I don't understand.'

His smile widened. His hand was on her elbow, very firmly. His eyes discomfited her. Hot already she flushed uncomfortably, trying to shake herself free.

He spoke again, very fast and low. The intimacy of his voice frightened her suddenly.

'Please! You've made a mistake! Let me go –!' Temper rising with her fear she wrenched her arm from his grip so fiercely that he let her go. She turned and began to hurry through the crowds. To her horror he followed, still talking, pushing through the stream of people by her side, keeping pace with her until he could catch at her arm again.

Anger and fright came to her aid. She spun on him savagely. 'Let me go!'

A few passers-by turned. One of them smiled. No-one stopped. Most ignored the scene, intent upon their own business.

'Get away from me!' She pushed him, hard.

He staggered a little. The smile had gone. Dark, furious colour lifted in the handsome face. He snapped something, his voice vicious.

She shook her head. 'Go! Go away! Or I'll – I'll call the police. Police! You understand? Policia!' she shouted, helplessly italianizing the word and hoping she'd got it right.

He sneered unpleasantly but at least made no move towards her. She turned and hurried from him. Her heart was pounding horribly. Sweat slicked her skin and soaked her clothes. At the corner she had to glance back. He stood where she had left him, a look of Latin disdain on his face. Seeing her backward glance he made a brief, graphically obscene gesture. Scarlet with shame and fury she all but ran to the via Condotta. She let herself in through the great, peeling outer doors and ran up the sweeping staircase to the doors of their apartment. At least it was cool here, cool and shadowed, the marble floors striking cold through the thin soles of her slippers.

She let herself in to the apartment.

Bars of sunshine, unnaturally bright to northern eyes striped the walls and ceilings, reflected blindingly from the mirrors. Despite the closed shutters it was hot and stuffy. She opened the shutters. Heat and dust lifted from the street, seeping into the room like smoke. Even the smells were foreign; alien.

She was trembling violently.

She went into her bedroom – in the privacy of the apartment she and Robert made no pretence of sharing a room – and threw herself onto the bed, fully clothed, staring up at the dirty, peeling, ornately plastered ceiling. As she did so a sudden vision of New Hall's cool and lofty ceilings blurred her eyes. The view of the parkland that could be had from every window, green and graceful, spread with the shade of its magnificent trees, the silvered lake glimmering through distant woodland – all at once she could see it so clearly that she might have been there. In her mind she whistled to Bran, set off, ankle deep in cool grass, richly green, towards the lake path and Old Hall –

But no. New Hall was no longer her home. Bran wasn't even any longer her dog. She was no longer a child. And Robert was no longer her friend. He was her husband.

And she was in Florence, that seemed suddenly a strange, outlandish and hostile city, looking for a man who in all probability no longer existed either. If he ever had, that dark angel to whom a lonely little girl had so totally and passionately given her heart.

Wearily she turned her hot face into the pillow, and let the miserable tears come.

When Robert came home she was still lying in the darkened room, dressed in a loose robe, one arm flung across her face.

'Jess?'

'I'm here.'

He came to the doorway. 'Are you all right?'

'I had a bad headache this afternoon.'

'Should I get you something? A cold drink? A cup of tea?'

'Tea would be nice.' She was listless.

He went into the kitchen calling as he went. 'I've some news that will cheer you up.'

'Oh?'

'I mentioned to the Maestro this afternoon the trouble we've been having with the maid –'

Pietra, the girl who they had virtually rented with the apartment was the equally surly niece of the surly caretaker. She was slovenly, and affected stupidity. Jessica was also certain that she stole, but lacking the language did not know what to do about it. She sat up, plumping the pillows and leaning on one elbow. 'And?'

Robert came back into the room. Not for the first time Jessica marvelled at the fact that not even the heat and dust of

Florence in high summer could apparently ruffle his neat, cool good looks. 'And – it seems he knows just the girl for us. The daughter of one of his own servants. Her name is Angelina. She cooks, is utterly trustworthy, clever with money – and she speaks English!'

That galvanized her. 'What?'

'Apparently she worked as a nursemaid for several years for an English family who have now returned home. She comes with excellent references.'

'Will she be able to control Pietra, do you think?' Jessica was doubtful.

'Of course she will. The girl sounds like a paragon. Exactly what we're looking for. Doesn't that make you feel better?'

She nodded, a little sheepishly, the depression of the afternoon lifting a little. 'It will certainly help to have someone who speaks English.'

'That's not all my news. Wait. I'll get the tea.' He went back into the kitchen to reappear a few moments later with two steaming cups. He handed one to her then sat on the bed. 'We've been invited to supper at the via del Corso!'

She shook her head, puzzled. 'The via –?' she stopped, 'You mean – the Carradine man? That they're always talking about at the Embassy?'

He laughed. 'Sir Theodolphus Carradine. The very same.'

'But – how? We don't know him. And – well – should we, do you think –?'

'Of course we should!' It came to her suddenly that Robert, uncharacteristically, was very excited. There was a faint flush of colour in his face and his dark eyes sparkled. 'And as for the how – yes, you're right, I don't know him – but there's a young man who attends the composition classes in the afternoons who's a good friend of his, and he's invited us. This evening.'

'But – can he do that? I mean – it doesn't seem right? Shouldn't we wait for a proper invitation –?' She knew how stupid that sounded as soon as she spoke. Yet something about Robert's unwonted excitement obscurely disturbed her.

273

'Jessica, haven't you listened to a word that's been said about the man? Theo Carradine doesn't issue "proper invitations". You come, and if you interest him you stay –'

'And if you don't?'

He shrugged.

She looked at him in mild astonishment. 'You really want to go, don't you?'

'Yes.'

'Why?'

He stood up, moving restlessly. 'Look – we came all the way to Florence to escape the restraints and conventions of England. And when we get here – then what? The people at the Embassy – the people we dine with – the people we ride with – they might just as well be our parents, our brothers, our sisters, our cousins! The via del Corso is where we'll find the kind of people we've come to find – artists, writers, sculptors –'

She did not for a moment answer. The first thing she had thought when she had heard of Theo Carradine and his coterie of artists was that if she were to find Danny anywhere in Florence it would be most likely to be there –

Robert had walked to the window and thrown open the shutters, stood leaning on the balcony rail looking down into the street. 'Of course if you don't want to come I wouldn't dream of insisting. I'm quite ready to go alone.' She frowned a little, watching the slight, slim back. It had almost seemed to her that there had been tentative hope in his voice.

'I'll come,' she said.

The façade of 17, via del Corso was imposing. Marble gleamed in the evening light and tall, ranked windows shone in the late sunshine. The massive, iron-studded door stood open and, faintly, from somewhere within the house, came the sound of music and laughter. There was no-one to be seen.

Jessica hesitated at the open door. 'Should we?'

'Of course.'

Still faintly reluctant she followed him. The grand entrance hall in which they found themselves was deserted. Massive and ornate double doors at the end of the room were closed and fastened. A great white staircase, its balustrade finely carved with fruit and flowers swept to the landing of the next floor, from where came the sound of music and voices.

'I do suppose,' Jessica said, her laughter rather more nervous than she cared to acknowledge, 'that your Arthur has the right to invite us here?'

'Jessica, for God's sake!' It seemed to her that Robert's sudden snappish tone held even more of nerves than had her own laughter. She looked at him in surprise. He stood poised at the foot of the stairs, looking up, every line of his face and of his body tense with a kind of eager and nervous expectation.

She joined him, and they started up the stairs. 'What's he like?' Jessica kept her voice very casual. 'Arthur, I mean? Do you know him well?'

'Not very, no. We met a couple of days ago at the Maestro's. He's –' he hesitated, 'he's rather fine actually. One of those people who can turn his hand to anything. Or perhaps I should say his brain. He's a fine Greek scholar. And a writer too. He's had poems published.'

'Oh?' Rarely did Robert speak with such intensity and enthusiasm. Jessica glanced at him from the corner of her eye.

'He met Lord Byron last year. Byron praised Arthur's poems. It was a turning point in his life, he said.'

'In what way?'

'He said – he had never believed in heroes before.'

'And Lord Byron changed his mind for him?' The words were a little dry.

'Yes.'

'Perhaps that had a little something to do with his lordship liking Arthur's poems?'

'No!' The word was irritated. 'Arthur isn't like that! Jessica – just wait till you meet him, and you'll see –'

She made no comment, but paused to look down on the great chandelier that hung in the stairwell, glittering like a glass waterfall.

'And when you hear him sing –'

She looked up in surprise. 'He sings too? Goodness, he is a

275

talented lad, isn't he?' she said, lightly. Irrationally, but profoundly, this unstinting admiration for the unknown Arthur was disturbing her.

'He could sing professionally if he wanted. He's been approached.' He was waiting, impatiently, for her to join him.

'Why doesn't he?'

'He wouldn't prostitute his gift so. Theo Carradine wouldn't allow it.' He turned and started up the stairs again.

She hitched up her skirts and scuttled to catch up with him. 'Singing professionally is prostituting yourself?' she asked, curiously.

'For some people, yes.'

They had reached the landing. The music had died but the sound of talk and laughter drifted from behind a pair of tall double doors that stood a little ajar.

'And Arthur's one of those people?' She could not, somehow, let the matter drop.

'Yes. He is.' Robert's tone was utterly uncompromising, and in no way amused.

'Well,' she said, not disguising the doubt in her voice, 'I look forward to meeting him –'

She did not have to wait long. As they stood, hesitant, on the threshold a tall blond young man, languidly handsome and dressed in open-necked silk shirt and beautifully cut trousers that were tucked with casual elegance into soft leather boots advanced on them, a long, white hand held out in greeting. The fair hair was Byronically tousled above a wide brow, enormous grey-blue eyes were fringed with improbably long and dark lashes. 'Robert! You came! How perfectly splendid! I did so hope you would – I came straight back this afternoon and searched out that reference that we were –' he stopped, apparently only just at that moment aware of Jessica. He waited, politely.

Robert's normally pale face was flushed with faint colour as he made the introductions. 'Jessica – this is Arthur Leyland. Arthur, I'd like you to meet –' the hesitation was tiny and telling, ' – Jessica.'

'Robert's wife,' she said, sweetly, and was herself surprised at the mild malice that had undoubtedly prompted the words. She offered her hand.

Arthur took it and bowed a little, gracefully. Unreasonably but with certainty, she knew she would never like the man.

'Why Robert, you dark horse,' he was saying, beautifully arched brows lifted, 'you didn't tell me –'

Robert said nothing.

There was a small, unaccountably difficult silence. Then Arthur stood back, smiling, for Jessica to pass into the room. 'Do come along – I'll introduce you –'

He led the way into the most exquisite room that Jessica, New Hall notwithstanding, had ever seen. Obviously one of the original state rooms of the palace it was huge and cool, marble-floored, the high ceiling restrainedly ornate, the frescos on the walls delicately beautiful. The windows were tall and perfectly proportioned, curtained with a material so fine it floated on the evening air like a cool mist. Gilded mirrors reflected from all angles a dozen or so perfect pieces of marble sculpture, all of the young male human form, and – most surprisingly to Jessica, who had never seen growing things used so indoors, a perfect jungle of plants and shrubs. Planted in tubs they had been used to create small, pretty arbours of privacy. Somewhere at the end of the room a fountain played. Everywhere there were couches, tables and chairs, most at this moment occupied, each piece of furniture gracefully in keeping with its setting. Another enormous glittering chandelier ornamented in the Venetian style with delicate coloured glass flowers hung in the centre of the room, and candles that were being lit upon the tables and about the walls were in candlesticks and sconces of the same style. Silver was everywhere – silver plate, tiny silver figures, silver urns and vases, even a collection of little silver thimbles adorned a small glass shelf. Jessica had grown up with opulence tempered by her mother's good taste at New Hall; but never had she come across anything so breathtakingly and imaginatively beautiful as this.

Arthur had led them to a table where sat three young men.

'Here we are – Richard, Georgie – and the one with the scowl's Stuart. This is Robert and – ah –' he hesitated, seeming quite genuinely to have forgotten Jessica's name.

'Jessica,' Robert put in quietly.

Arthur smiled a charming smile. 'Of course. Jessica.'

Jessica smiled shyly and hastily prevented the three young men from scrambling to their feet. They all looked, if a little Bohemian, reassuringly normal bearing in mind the stories she had heard of this establishment. Richard was small, dark and intense-looking and had paint stains in his hair and on his clothes that looked as if they had been there for some considerable time. Georgie was a large and friendly-looking young man with hands like hams and an engaging smile, while Stuart was scruffy, thin-faced and rather sombre-looking. Unlike the picturesque Arthur their clothes were of the cheap workaday type. All three held glasses in their hands and there was a large jug of wine and more glasses upon the table.

Georgie gestured. 'You'll join us?'

'Thank you –' Jessica began, but Arthur was quicker.

'What a perfectly splendid idea. Jessica – you don't mind if I steal Robert from you for just a moment? There's something I particularly want to show him –'

She hesitated, looking at Robert, not happy to be abandoned quite so soon.

'Only for a moment,' he said.

She nodded. 'Of course.' She watched them walk away, already deep in animated conversation, Arthur's artfully tousled blond head bent to Robert's dark one.

'A glass of wine?' Georgie asked, and it seemed to Jessica that she caught a galling spark of sympathy in the friendly eyes.

'Yes,' she said, composedly. 'Thank you.' And had to prevent herself from drinking it in one gulp.

She spent a remarkably pleasant half hour in their company. Richard and Stuart, she learned, were artists, Georgie was studying sculpture. None of them, upon her casual questioning, had ever heard of Danilo O'Donnel. And between them, they assured her, they knew everyone there was to know in

278

Florence. They were not backward in assuaging Jessica's curiosity regarding her unknown host.

'Old as Methuselah, rich as Croesus, wicked as the Devil, and as partial to the lads as any old dame I've ever come across –' Stuart eyed her a little slyly.

She did not bat an eyelash. 'He seems very generous?'

'Oh, yes. If he feels like it he'll give you the top brick off the chimney.'

'And if he doesn't?'

Richard laughed a little ruefully. 'Steer very clear. He can be absolutely vicious.'

The other two nodded sage agreement.

'He sounds charming, I must say.' She laughed, a little nervously.

'He's all right.' Georgie tossed back his wine and planted the glass firmly upon the table. People had started to drift past the table towards the far end of the room. Georgie tapped the side of his nose with a huge, dirty finger. 'If I'm not mistaken I smell food. Coming?'

Jessica shook her head, unwilling to forsake the safety of her secluded seat. 'Not yet, thank you.'

Richard stood. 'You don't mind if we do?'

'Of course not.'

He smiled an engaging smile. 'It's the first square meal in days!'

She smiled back. 'Please. Don't let me stop you. I expect Robert will be back soon.'

She remained in her seat, sipping her wine, watching people as they strolled past the table in twos and threes. For all the notice anyone took of her she might have been entirely invisible.

Where was Robert?

The crowd seemed to be at least three-quarters male, predominantly down-at-heels working artists or students. A few wantonly beautiful youngsters of both sexes drifted like rapacious butterflies about the room. The women in the main were very young, very pretty and very Italian-looking. She felt entirely out of place.

The room emptied. She sat for a while alone. Then, with a quick, overdetermined movement she tossed back the last of her wine and stood up. If Robert were not going to take her to dine, she would take herself.

At the door of the equally exquisite dining room, however, her nerve failed her. About the room were dotted small tables at which groups of people sat, talking and laughing. A long table, all snow-white linen, crystal and silver, held platters of delicacies of all kinds and a vast regiment of wine bottles. At a large table in the centre of the room sat an elderly man, his face rouged to a terrible parody of youth, skinny as a waif but with the paunch of Bacchus, a huge grotesquely curled and powdered wig framing the equally grotesquely painted face. He was presiding over a slavishly laughing group of young men and women. This, no doubt was her host. There was no sign of Robert.

Jessica fled. She slipped back through the statues and the jungle of plants to the table where she had sat with Georgie and the others, and which had taken on the aura of a haven. With a small sigh of relief she sank onto a sofa. As if by magic a flunkey appeared, costumed in ivory silk, a powdered wig only a little less ornate than his master's on his head. 'Wine for Madam?'

She hesitated. He took her silence for assent and handed her a glass. She took it.

'Thank you.' She sipped the cool liquid. The hum of laughter and conversation from the dining room rose and fell.

Where was Robert?

Perilously quickly she finished the glass, and in a moment the servant, hovering behind a palm, had refilled it. She stifled a small, hysterical giggle. At this rate Robert would have to carry her home –

Robert! Where was he, damn him? It really was too bad of him to abandon her so. He had not been, so far as she could see, in the intimidating dining room. Slightly unsteadily she set her wine glass on the table and stood up. He must be somewhere.

She found him at last in an arbour by the fountain, screened from the room by a curtain of greenery, seated beside Arthur at a small table. An almost untouched bottle of wine stood before them. They were talking animatedly and did not notice Jessica's approach.

'It's there, oh yes, it's there –' Arthur was saying, his fair face intense, the grey-blue eyes glowing ' – and someday someone will find it –'

'But how?' Robert was totally absorbed, his eyes riveted to the passionate face.

'By using the *Iliad* of course! It can be done, Robert! It will be! Troy will be found, I know it! Oh, God! I'd give an arm to be the one! Imagine – just imagine being the one to prove that Troy did exist! That the *Iliad* is more than just a poet's fantasy!' The two young men were as unaware of Jessica's presence as they were of the handsome marble centaur that pranced through the crystal screen of the fountain's dancing water. She stood for a long moment, watching them, incapable of breaking in on that magic circle of intimacy that surrounded them. They did not want her. Nobody wanted her. She turned and walked away, fighting a sudden surge of self-pity and loneliness that tightened her chest and brought the ridiculous sting of tears to her eyes. People were beginning to wander back in from the dining room. No-one took any notice of her. At the far end of the room a heated argument had broken out. The candle-lit air was heavy and hot, laden with the stink of perspiration, perfume and wine. A group of rowdy young men were coming towards her, pushing and buffeting each other like a pack of unruly and ill-trained young puppies. She backed away, flattening herself against an enormous carved door, which gave a little as she leaned against it. She turned her head. Through the narrow opening she sensed rather than saw a cool dark room, blessedly empty. Giving herself no time for thought she slipped through the gap and pulled the door closed with a sharp click behind her.

She stood still for a moment, letting her eyes adjust to the dimmer light. She was in a library, as different from the room she had just left as it was possible to be. No ostentation here, no glamour, no glittering chandeliers or artfully arranged effects. Tall windows, open, led out onto a cool and shadowed balcony. The room was large but comfortably proportioned and its walls were lined with books. Books too lay upon the beautifully carved desks and lecterns that were placed in convenient positions about the room; books open, books closed, piles of books, books in boxes, books on shelves. On the floor were soft rugs of oriental design glowing with jewel-like colour in the illumination of the few lamps that threw their patches of golden light across the rich, gold-tooled leather of the volumes' covers. Large comfortable armchairs and two enormous sofas completed the furnishings. At the far end of the room a great marble fireplace, empty now, a gilded mirror gleaming above its mantle, spoke of warmth and comfort on a winter's day. The room was utterly quiet, utterly peaceful. Even the sounds of talk and laughter that percolated faintly through the wall from the gathering next door failed to disturb it.

She walked quietly across the room and out onto the balcony. It overlooked not the street but an inner courtyard of the house, two floors below. Elegant and vine-grown, its seating and statuary was of marble, as were the two small fountains that sent their cool music rising to her on the warm air.

She wandered back into the room, moving about the shelves, stopping now and again at random, picking out a book or sometimes simply touching, wonderingly, an expensive tooled leather spine with a gentle fingertip. She had never in her life seen such a treasure-trove of learning. Even her small experience told her that this room held a small fortune in books – books of every description, every age and what looked to be every language in the world. Lying open on a table, lit by a heavily shaded lamp, was a huge and wonderfully illustrated tome with Arabic script as decorative and beguiling as the birds, beasts and flowers that embellished it. Absorbed she studied it, enchanted by its colourful beauty, though afraid to touch it or to turn a page. On another table she found upon a small shelf a collection of books which caught her eye with their faint familiarity. A little more confidently she picked one out and carefully opened it; and was transported with soul-shaking suddenness to the ancient library of Old Hall with its smoky fire and its great mullioned windows, its dark oak panelling and the sound of winter's wind buffeting the walls. She moved closer to the lamp, studying her find. So entirely rapt was she that she did not hear the soft opening of the door; only the sharp click of its closing started her guiltily from her dream and almost made her drop the precious thing she held.

'Well, well – what have we here?' The voice was light and sharp, dry as the parchment of the ancient books about them. The old man's skinny legs, encased in old-fashioned breeches of pale pearl grey, were bowed, the satyr's paunch even more noticeable on his skinny frame as he stood, leaning heavily upon a gold-topped cane, peering at her, frowning.

She regained some small part of the breath that had deserted her in her fright. 'I'm – sorry,' she managed, and put the book down as if it had suddenly become red hot. 'The – the door was open – I – I came in here – to –' Idiotically her voice slid to nothing.

He stumped to the table and with a mildly testy movement pulled the quite ridiculously ornate wig from his head and flung it down. His own hair was wispy and wild about a vast bald pate. ' – to get away from that?' He jerked his head at the commotion beyond the door. 'Don't blame yer, child. Not altogether. My young friends can get very tiresome at times. What're yer readin'?'

The abrupt question, the words slurred affectedly in the fashion that had died with the beaux of a generation before, caught her off guard. She blinked.

'Well? Cat got yer tongue? Or can't yer read? Eh?'

'Of course I can!' Indignation came to her aid, 'It's a book of medieval poetry, I think. Troubadour's poems I would guess, though I can't be sure. It's strange –'

'What is?'

'I can't make out the language. It doesn't seem to be French –' Her interest for the moment overcame her embarrassment. 'Robert's – my husband's – family have some like it at home in Suffolk. Robert's father told me that the courtly romances were all written in France – in Provence, I

283

think – in the thirteenth-century. But this –' she hesitated, unwilling to show ignorance to the man who owned this treasure-house of books, '– this looks different somehow,' she finished, lamely.

He straightened, leaning still upon the cane, eyeing her intently with pale, old eyes. 'How?' he barked. 'How – different?' The words were fired like bullets.

She jumped.'The – the language I think. It isn't the same. And, also – the pictures. There's something about them –'

He nodded. 'Very perceptive, child. Right on both counts. The book you've got there isn't thirteenth-century. It's fourteenth. And it isn't French. It's Italian. Tuscan, in fact, written not so many miles from where you're standing. But, oh yes –' he held up a hand as he saw the protest in her face, '– you were absolutely right in your judgement of what it might have been – of what, in fact, it was trying to be. There's many that should know better's been fooled. Your estimable father-in-law was right – the originals were written at the Courts of Love in Provence. But Innocent the Third – what a rogue's name for the Devil! – and his hellish Crusade put paid to the troubadours of the Lange d'Oc, and a lot of them, running for their lives, came here. Very sensible of them if you ask me. Damned Frogs.' He pointed to the book she had been studying. 'That was written by an Italian as the fashion grew here. Good, mind you, it's good. But – if you want to compare it with an original –' he stumped to her side, ran a gnarled, practised finger along the row of ancient leather-bound books and extracted one. 'Try that. Arnaut Daniel. Greatest of them all. Know what the word "troubadour" means?'

Bemused, she shook her head, taking the book. Close up the painted face beneath the balding pate was even more grotesque.

'Derives from the word "trobar" – "*trouver*" d'ye see? To find. To discover. A troubadour was a seeker, and a creator – Look at the book, then gel – look at it!'

She turned the pages. The script was lovely, the illustrations intricate and beautiful, their colours clear as sunshine. 'It's marvellous.'

'Certainly it is. Haven't seen you before. Who the devil are you?'

The autocratically abrupt change of subject made her jump again, but at least it seemed her nervous system was getting a little more used to it. 'Jessica FitzBolton,' she managed, remarkably calmly. 'I'm here with my husband Robert. We were invited by a young man called Arthur. Arthur Leyland, I think. And you must be —?'

'Carradine. Theo Carradine.' An odd shadow of expression that she could not identify had flickered across the painted face at the name of Arthur Leyland. 'So — your husband — he'd be the dark young feller who's bin all evenin' with Arthur?'

She nodded. 'Yes.'

He pursed his lips, watching her. 'I see. Finished with the book?'

Bemused by yet another grasshopper leap of subject she reluctantly handed him the book.

'Don't fret. Don't fret. Look at them any time you want. Not many appreciate them. Tell you somethin' about them one day, if ye'd care to hear?'

'I would. I really would.' To her own mild surprise the words were a matter of honesty rather than good manners.

'Hmm.' He replaced the book. 'Used ter chain 'em to the desk, yer know.'

'Yes.'

He grinned a stained smile. 'Somethin' else yer father-in-law told yer?'

'No. I read it somewhere.'

'Good. Good. Come an' talk to me.'

She followed him to the open windows. On the balcony above the pretty courtyard stood a table and two chairs. He waved her to one, then lowered himself evidently painfully into the other, waving away irritably her half-hearted offer to help. 'How long yer bin in Florence?'

She thought. 'Just over a month.'

'Like it?'

Perversely she was suddenly irritated. She did not care to be

285

cross-examined like a prisoner at the bar. 'Not altogether,' she said, shortly.

He lifted his head, frowning. 'You astonish me, gel. Yer struck me as a gel of sense.'

'I'm a girl who likes to walk alone without being accosted.'

He chuckled at that, his seamed face creasing like crumpled paper.

'I really don't see why you should find that funny?' She was on her dignity.

'Tell me about it.'

She told him of that afternoon on the Ponte Vecchio. ' —and that isn't the only time such things have happened. And yet – I don't understand it – I've seen Italian girls – girls of my own age – walking alone, apparently safely.'

He grinned, the yellow teeth evil. 'Think about it, gel. Work it out for yerself.'

She thought. Shook her head. 'I don't understand.'

He tutted testily. 'What were yer wearin'?'

She shrugged. 'I was perfectly respectable. I've more sense than to go out like this –' She indicated the low neckline of her filmy gown.

'Ah, but what colour? Colour! What colour d'ye wear?' he added, speaking as though she might have been a backward child when she was slow in answering.

Some small bell was ringing in Jessica's head. 'All sorts,' she said, thoughtfully. 'Today I was wearing yellow.'

He snorted.

'They wear black, don't they? Married Italian girls?'

'Now yer've got it.'

'And you mean – honestly – that if I wear black I'll be all right?'

'No question, gel. Look – unmarried girls here don't go out on their own. Not ever. Not unless – they're lookin' fer somethin' or someone –' he winked balefully. 'You see what I mean? Young married women on the other hand have as much if not more freedom that yer do yerself. And they're safe as houses.' He leaned forward, 'Use yer head, gel. Study the local customs. You'll find life a lot easier. You ain't in London now.

Don't try to live like that daft bunch of know-nothings that cluck together and lay eggs at the Embassy. Buy yerself somethin' neat an' fancy in black an' you'll be safe as in yer own parlour. Safer. I promise you.'

She nodded. 'I see. Thank you. I will.' She was genuinely grateful for the advice. The thought of being a prisoner in the apartment until such times as Robert saw fit to squire her had been appalling.

'Good gel.' The awful smile wrinkled again ''Course – if yer really want ter go native –' he winked again, salaciously, 'you could always get yourself a *servente cavaliere* –'

She shook her head, puzzled.

The evil smile broadened. 'Yer must have noticed? Yer surely don't think these handsome, attentive young men that escort some of the pretty ladies in black are their *husbands*?'

Jessica had indeed noticed how many handsome young couples graced the streets of Florence. She flushed a little, suspecting derision. 'Well yes. I suppose I did.'

He snickered. 'No, no, no! Civilized people the Tuscans. Look – it goes like this. Old man marries pretty little piece. Pretty piece – being Tuscan – is quite ready to put up with it for his money. Pretty piece is good as gold and butter-wouldn't-melt until she presents old money-bags with a copper-bottomed, no-question legitimate heir. Then – as a reward for hard labour, so to speak – she gets her handsome little helper. Her *servente cavaliere*. He helps her run the house, manages the servants, buys the wine, escorts her to anywhere she wants to go. He is, you understand, the personification of elegance and good manners, to say nothing of excruciating good looks. In England our second sons go into the church or the army. In Florence they very much more sensibly go into the service of a mistress. Some doting fathers have even been known to demand provision for a *servente cavaliere* in the marriage contract!'

She found herself giggling. 'Not really?'

'On my oath. Now –' He twinkled wickedly, an ancient imp of mischief. 'Should you decide to become a true young

287

Florentine matron I insist – I insist! – that you come to me. I know some very promising young men –'

She bit her lip, her cheeks scarlet, and shook her head.

His smile died. The mischief remained, tinged with sudden and unexpected malice. 'You sure about that? I ain't seen you spendin' much time with that husband o' yours tonight. An' he, sure as damn'it, ain't come chasin' after you, has he?'

She felt as if he had slapped her. Deep colour flooded her cheeks. She looked down at her hands that had clenched to small white fists upon the table. There was a long silence. She lifted her head at last, her face composed. He was watching her, pale eyes alight and thoughtful. 'Thank you for your very good advice,' she said, pleasantly, pushing her chair back and rising, chin up. 'And for letting me look at your lovely books. I'm sorry to have disturbed you.' She was proud of herself. Somewhere within her his words had released a surging rage, that screamed for release like an evil genie from a bottle. Her guts twisted with it, painfully. It was almost all she could do not to show it.

'Don't be daft, gel.' His voice was suddenly mild, even conciliatory, 'It was me disturbed you as I remember it. Sit down fer God's sake – I get a crick in me neck if I look up, even at a slip of a thing like you.'

The unexpectedness of it took her off guard, as he undoubtedly had known it would. For a moment the obscure commiseration in the words brought a painful lump to her throat. After a moment's hesitation she sat down again, with an ungainly thump.

'"Thy love to me was wonderful –"' the old voice was very quiet, '" – passing the love of women –"'

She was stunned by his perception. 'That's David and Jonathan, isn't it?'

He nodded. 'Book of Samuel.' He chuckled suddenly and wickedly, 'Now you can truly say you've heard the Devil quote Holy Scriptures with your own ears!' He seemed to find the idea inordinately funny, quaking with laughter.

She had to laugh with him, and the laughter was genuine.

The strange old man regarded her with twinkling, running

eyes. 'I like you, gel,' he said, briskly. 'Come again. Come often. We can talk about books. No-one else around here's interested in talkin' about books. They're all too busy scribbling pictures. Or choppin' up inoffensive bits of stone. 'Cept Arthur of course – an' he doesn't want to talk about books he wants ter dissect 'em. Thinks he knows better than them as wrote them what they're about –'

She smiled. 'I'd like to.'

'Promise?'

'Promise.'

''Course. Hand me me cane, would yer, gel?'

She handed it to him, watched as he struggled to his feet, knowing instinctively that he neither wanted nor needed her help. When she stood her eyes were on a level with his, so wizened was he. 'I don't suppose –?' she found herself asking.

'Hm?' he eyed her sharply.

'I don't suppose you've ever come across a man called Danilo O'Donnel? Danny O'Donnel? Half Irish, half Italian. A sculptor, I think. He'd be – I don't know – about twenty-eight or twenty-nine now –?'

He did her the courtesy of thinking about it, his painted brow wrinkled. Then he shook his head, positively. 'No.'

Despite all her efforts a bleak flicker of disappointment showed in her face. This had been her last hope.

He held up a veined and corded hand. 'But then – I've a terrible head for names. Always have had. People remember me. Don't have to remember them.' He went off into another wheezing cackle of laughter. 'You leave it more than a couple of days to come back, an' I'll have forgotten yours, I promise you. I'll ask. About your sculptor. Ask some of the others. Come back tomorrow. Your Robert has undoubtedly already received the invitation –' the old voice was suddenly waspish, 'an' if he's goin' ter monopolize Arthur, don't see why I shouldn't monopolize you! Danny O'Donnel. I'll ask. Do what I can.'

'Thank you.'

'Now –' the testiness had not gone, 'p'raps you'd be good enough to prise your husband from our pretty Arthur's side and take him home? Or I daresay they'll be up all night worshipping at the altar of that mountebank Byron. It's too much to hope, I suppose that your Robert doesn't find the man as fascinatingly heroic as soft-headed Arthur does?'

She laughed. 'As a matter of fact he does. And as a matter of fact so do I.'

He shook his head in unaffected gloom. 'The youth of today! Bird-witted and led by the nose by a posturing poet! Oh, you'll have to come back, gel – whether you like it or not. Someone's got ter teach yer ter tell the dross from the gold –!'

Theo Carradine, undoubtedly the most bizarre candidate for bosom friendship that Jessica had encountered turned out to be, to her surprise and his delighted amusement, a most entertaining, engaging and stimulating companion, and one with whom she thoroughly enjoyed spending her time. An unexpected and warm relationship blossomed from that moment of first meeting, the usual preliminaries of friendship disposed of in typical style by Theo's testy reminder that such time-wasting tactics were for the young and not for those unfortunates with one foot in the grave.

Jessica laughed. 'Don't be silly. You aren't that old!'

'You think not?' The shrewd, almost colourless eyes twinkled. 'That's all you know! And – what's more – that's all you're goin' ter know! Needn't think yer goin' ter wheedle me age out of me, so there! Not fer a thousand guineas! My secret. A gel's entitled to her secrets. An' if her age ain't one of them I don't know what is!' He chuckled at the expression on her face. One of the delights of this relationship for him, she knew, was the ease with which his sometimes outrageous conversational tricks could take her off guard. Certainly she found disconcerting this occasional habit of his of referring to himself as a member of the female sex. He pointed with his cane. 'Now – fetch me that book, there's a good gel – the one we were lookin' at yesterday – there's somethin' I want ter show you –'

The man was a positive fount of knowledge. Grotesque, unprincipled, degenerate, debauched, he was most certainly all of those things. But what his detractors had failed to tell her was that he had a mind like a needle, a questing soul and a memory like an encyclopaedia. A professed creedless, godless, atheist, yet he could, if the mood took him, discuss not only the various and fascinating facets of Christianity but the beliefs and ideals of Islam as well with a quite remarkable depth of perception and understanding. If the mood did not take him he dismissed them all, with his yellowed grin, as mindless hypocrites. His knowledge and appreciation of the arts was, he informed Jessica, the product of a lifetime's passionate study and a total lack of any kind of talent. In his company the city's galleries, that she had visited so often, suddenly gave up their secrets and became exciting places of discovery. He discoursed, in his dry, drawling irreverent way upon technique, perspective, colour and form and she suddenly found herself looking at paintings she had seen a dozen times before with new eyes. The pencil sketches of the Master, Michelangelo, which in her ignorance she had hardly noticed before, were a passion with him; indeed he had in the library a priceless original, a series of sketches of a woman's head that he was certain was the model for the sculpture of Dawn in the so-called New Sacristy of the Church of Saint Lorenzo. Together they studied Titian and Raphael, Botticelli and da Vinci. They visited the Laurentian Library, which was to Jessica something of a disappointment. 'Your books are much more interesting.'

''Course they are. But my library wasn't designed by Michelangelo.' His stick tapped hard on the floor. 'Still, you're right. We're wasting time. Come. Come. We'll take another look at the Magi. See if you can remember the faces I pointed out to you in the procession. A glass of champagne for every one you get right –'

Robert was openly amused and, Jessica suspected, even secretly gratified by the favour shown to his wife by the eccentric old man. Certainly he showed not the slightest trace of pique at the amount of time she spent with him, and made no objections to their frequent expeditions into the city; on the contrary, Jessica knew, her absences suited him well since they gave him the opportunity to pursue without guilt his fast-growing friendship with Arthur Leyland. The two young men met every day, either at the via del Corso – where, Jessica deduced, Arthur lived – or in the city where they would spend hours over a jug of wine discussing endlessly whether Homer wrote first the *Iliad* or the *Odyssey*, whether the tragedy of the one outweighed the romanticism of the other, whether the *Iliad* could above all others be considered the most perfect example of the Greek method of constructing a play –

Jessica tried very hard to like Arthur. She wanted to like him – for Robert's sake if for no other reason. But try as she might she could not. She could readily admit to his good looks and his quick and well-educated mind. His voice, when he deigned to use it for the pleasure of Theo's assembled guests was very fine indeed. She could very well see his attraction when he expounded a theory or argued a point, the grey-blue eyes bright within their deep arch of bone, the fair hair tousled across the broad forehead, the narrow, elegant hands gesturing fluently. Yet after very short acquaintance it seemed to her quite apparent that Arthur Leyland's predominant characteristic was vanity, his predominant concern himself and his predominant belief that gifted and talented people such as himself should never, in view of their noble qualities be called upon to dirty their hands, figuratively or actually, by earning their own living – nor indeed to do anything that did not sit well with their well-founded opinion of themselves. Aware of the possibility that her antipathy towards her husband's new friend might well be rooted in the certain feeling that he returned the dubious compliment in full measure, she hoped for Robert's sake that her judgement was perhaps too harsh, but strongly she doubted it. And Arthur, she guessed, knew it. Consequently they were always meticulously polite to one another, but there was little of enthusiasm and nothing of warmth in their exchanges, and it seemed to her that Arthur spent every effort to keep Robert from her company. Perhaps it was perverse of her to resent that, but resent it she did, and the situation was not eased by her growing suspicion that Robert was giving Arthur money.

'Tell me – what does Arthur actually do for a living?' she asked Robert one morning as they breakfasted on the shaded balcony.

'Mm?' Robert barely glanced up from the book he was reading.

'Arthur. What does he do for a living?'

Robert managed not to look too impatient as he laid his book face down on the table. 'I'm not sure. He's had some poems published –'

'So you said. I shouldn't think that would keep him in those lovely shirts he wears, let alone anything else?' Jessica put down her cup. 'I assume he must have money of his own?'

'I don't think so. His father was a wastrel. Led poor Arthur a terrible life. Left nothing when he died.'

Jessica smiled at the hovering maid. 'Thank you, Angelina. You may clear away now. So – what does he live on?'

Robert's lips tightened. He picked up the book again, closed it very precisely, marking the page with a piece of paper upon which Jessica could see some scribbled notes in Arthur's flamboyant hand. 'He's employed by Theo,' he said. 'You of all people know how generous Theo can be.'

She ignored the inference. 'He doesn't work for Theo,' she said gently. 'He just takes his money.'

'Jessica –!'

'Don't you think it a little odd for a grown man to live in a style that he has no apparent means to support?' She truly had no wish to provoke an argument, but Arthur's growing dominion over Robert worried her, as did Robert's total inability to see fault in the other man.

'I really don't think it's my business what Arthur lives on,' Robert said, coldly. 'Nor,' he added, his eyes level and unsmiling, ' – yours.'

'You're absolutely right, of course,' she agreed mildly. 'As long as it isn't our money that pays for those pretty shirts?'

She knew by the quick rise of colour in his face that her suspicions were justified. She shook her head. 'Oh, Robert –!'

Defensively he lifted his head. 'If a man can't lend a few guineas to a friend who's strapped for funds –' he stopped. The money they were living off was Jessica's, her marriage settlement left to her by her father, and they both knew it.

She could not bear to see his embarrassment. She leaned forward quickly and covered his hand with her own. 'Robert, I don't want to quarrel. Least of all about Arthur.'

He looked at their linked hands, then lifted his head, searching her face with his eyes. 'Don't try to come between us, Jessica. Please don't do that.'

She was shaken by the intensity of the words. 'I wouldn't. I promise.' He bowed his head. A small silence fell between them. He turned his hand to grip hers, and the strength of it was painful. Then with an effort he relaxed his grip, and with an unexpected gentleness that almost touched her to tears he lifted her hand to his mouth and brushed it very lightly with his lips. 'I'm sorry,' he said.

'Robert, it doesn't –'

He stopped the words with a sad shake of his head. They sat in silence for a moment. 'I'm sorry,' he said again. 'I've neglected you. You have every right to be annoyed. I'll make it up to you. In fact –' he tried a small smile, '– if you'd like we could ride in the Cascine this afternoon? I know you enjoy that, and I know you can't go alone.'

She nodded. 'I'd like that.'

'Arthur has a special class with the Maestro, so I'm free all afternoon. I'll pick you up at two.'

Thus relegated neatly, firmly, – and despite all her resolutions gallingly – to her rightful place in his life she smiled, very brightly. 'I'll be ready.'

Chapter Eleven

From time to time it occurred to Jessica to wonder if Theo monopolized her time as a small revenge upon Robert for apparently supplanting him in Arthur's affections. She knew certainly that Theo was not altogether happy about the amount of time that Robert and Arthur spent together – not she felt so much that he resented their friendship as that he found intolerable their total absorption in each other and the consequent exclusion of anyone else from their private world, and in this she could not help but sympathize with him. It pleased him to support Arthur in the expensive and privileged lifestyle that the young man considered his due because he liked to have about him attractive and charismatic young people of both sexes who could divert him in his hours of boredom and ornament his life in much the same way as did his books, his exquisite home and his works of art. Arthur's supreme self-confidence in flouting his wealthy and influential patron astonished Jessica, yet still she had to admit that it appeared to be justified. Theo grumbled waspishly about cocksure ingrates, even occasionally threatened to cut the purse strings, but never actually did anything. It was perfectly evident that not only Robert was under the young man's spell.

In the meantime Theo's unexpected and sometimes mischievous attentions were turned to the novelty of an obviously neglected young wife.

Jessica was more than happy to accept his testy friendship. Her feelings for Robert, with the unexpected intrusion of Arthur upon their private lives, were more ambivalent than ever. A fondness that has taken the length of a child's growing years to develop does not die easily and sometimes, despite

Arthur's demands upon Robert's time, their friendship still emerged quite surprisingly strongly. They still rode together in the Cascine – both amused to see how many of their former acquaintances now somehow managed to avoid seeing them as they rode by. Florence in some ways was as enclosed a society as the smallest village and gossip travelled fast as flame in dry undergrowth. Their open association with the coterie of the via del Corso had obviously not escaped notice. On those evenings that they were not at Theo's they always dined together – though very noticeably when at the via del Corso they hardly ever did – and exchanged news and views in the old way, enjoying each other's company as they always had. But Jessica was coming to realize that this could never be enough; there were indeed times when she found herself seriously doubting if such a relationship could last, and when that happened she often, oddly guiltily, found herself recalling Robert's words about the possibilities of an annulment. But then the thought of what such a step would mean, for herself and for him, frightened her from even the contemplation of it. There seemed no way out of the coil. She had discovered too late what a terrible mistake she had made and could no longer deny to herself that simple friendship was not, after all, enough. She knew now why David and Annabel's relationship had so disturbed her – knew that what she had felt was jealousy, pure, simple and destructive. Her young body was maturing. The old terrors were still there – the nightmare of violence that seemed to be the only thing that linked Clara and Giles together still haunted her, as did Caroline's betrayal of Danny and the naked pain in his face as he had realized it – none of it was forgotten. But the Romseys had shown her another, and she was coming to suspect a more natural, face of love, and she envied them with a depth of feeling that was like a sickness. Sometimes now, alone in her bed, she would deliberately conjure up in her mind those sounds of lovemaking in the room above, and that half-shameful wholly confusing excitement would burn in her body again. She ached to know what they had known, but was afraid; and Robert could not help her. For that, for all their friendship, she was terribly afraid she could grow to hate him.

Theo watched, the age-bleached eyes reflecting a cy[nical]
lifetime of experience coupled with an even more cyn[ical]
understanding of human nature.

.They sat one day in the library, coolly shuttered against th[e]
afternoon's heat, in companionable silence, he, wigless, and
with one leg propped on a stool in front of him, apparently
half-asleep, she absorbed in a book.

Theo snorted unpleasantly and shifted his position.

She looked up quickly. 'Are you all right?'

''Course I'm not all right. Stupid question. Hand me that
pillow, gel, will yer?'

She propped him up a little, arranging the extra cushion
comfortably behind him. Then she straightened, tucking a
stray strand of hair behind her ear, 'Goodness, it's hot!'

'Yer lookin' pale, gel. You sickenin' fer somethin'?' he
asked, sharply.

She shook her head. 'It's the heat, that's all. And I'm always
pale.'

'Ain't breedin', are yer?' The blunt words were as much a
statement as a question.

'No.' Taken aback, she blushed furiously.

'You sure?'

'Yes.' She knew as she said it that the word had come too
quickly, too certainly. She turned away to avoid the pale,
shrewd eyes and went back to her chair. She picked up the
book, opened it, stared at it sightlessly.

There was a small, intent silence. Then, 'What yer goin' ter
do about it, gel. Eh?'

She kept her head down for a moment, nibbling her lip.
Then she straightened her back and lifted her head. 'About
what?'

He watched her, unblinking, until she looked away.

'"Thy love to me was wonderful —"' he said, musingly.

She interrupted him, as acidly and lightly as she could
contrive. 'You've used that once. I thought you considered
repeating one's self as a social crime so heinous that it should
be punished by hanging?'

'Did I say that?'

ed. 'I was right.'

hly discomposed she tried to settle herself to read

t should the cause be? Oh, you live at court –"' Theo
eepled his hands before him and raised his eyes to the
ing. From the thoughtful and innocent look on his face he
might have been quoting St Augustine, '"And there's both
loss of time and loss of sport, In a great belly –"'

'Theo!' she said, exasperated.

'I but quote Jonson –'

'You but quote Theo Carradine!'

He cackled like a washerwoman and scratched his bald
pate.

She gave up her pretence of reading and snapped the book
shut, lifting her head.

'That's better,' he said, satisfied. 'Now – at risk of me neck
for repeatin' meself again – what are you goin' ter do about
it?'

She took a long, patient breath. 'Theo – this is none of your
business. You don't understand –'

'Oh, yes, gel. I understand.' He spoke with that sudden
sharpness of tone that could be so very disconcerting. 'Better
than yer think, perhaps, I understand.'

She shook her head, helplessly. 'You're impossible.'

He leaned forward, his eyes suddenly bright and gleeful.

'A lover, gel. That's what yer need. Can't hold on to it fer
ever, yer know!' He laughed, his face crinkling like a satanic
child's. 'Let me sort yer one out. Be happy to –'

She managed not to throw the book at him. 'No, thank
you, Theo.' She held doggedly to her composure. Just last
night the large and friendly Georgie had made a suggestion
that might, a year ago, have scandalized her. A small part of
her still regretted her firm rejection of his advances. He was a
nice young man, not unhandsome and he had been flatteringly
eager. She was not sure herself why she had been so swift and
certain in her refusal. He had been disappointed. Perhaps he
would ask again? Was that what she had wanted –?

Theo was speaking, but she had missed the first part o
sentence. '– Italian lessons,' he said.

'I'm sorry – I beg your pardon?'

'I said – you need some lessons –' he paused for a wicke
moment '– in Italian. And I know just the lad.'

She was exasperatedly confused at the apparently wayward
change of subject, 'I thought you said that you'd teach me?'

The grin widened, the Devil's own mischief glimmering in
his wrinkled, berouged face. 'Not as well as Guido Palca can.'

'Theo –!'

He held up an autocratic hand, preventing the explosion.
'An excellent young man of good family. Handsome. Charming. Not too intelligent. Fortunate that. A *servente cavaliere*
that any right-minded young matron would sacrifice her –
right hand for.' The heavily assumed innocence of the words
brought answering laughter, which Jessica could not suppress.

'Theo – truly – you don't understand! I'm not – I can't –'
Even in laughter, to her own surprise her composure suddenly
all but broke. She looked down at her hands that were
clenched fiercely in her lap, and saw the sheen of sweat on the
smooth skin of her arms. 'It's late,' she said, after a moment's
pause, her voice neutral but at least steady. 'I should go home.'

'Home?'

The single word, and the blunt question laid bare her life.
She swallowed. 'Theo, you are undoubtedly the most abominable person I have ever met, do you know that?'

He nodded. The pale, ancient eyes pierced to her soul,
stripping her of pretence and of defence. 'Perhaps,' he said,
'you should persuade your Robert to stay at home more often?'

'And perhaps,' she found herself snapping back without
thought, lashing out in self-defence, 'you should persuade
your Arthur to do whatever it is you pay him to do instead of
letting him take you for an absolute fool –!' She stopped. 'I'm
sorry,' she said. 'That was unforgivable.'

'And absolutely true.' The dome of a head with its wild and
wispy fringe of hair wagged a little, but the small, light eyes
still regarded her steadily.

She frowned, genuinely puzzled. 'Theo – tell me – why do

it? Why let him take your money, live on your
_____ vantage of your kindness – when he offers so
_____ thing.
_____ ook her head. 'It's hateful. He simply takes every-
_____ ou're ready to offer as if – as if it were his right, and gives
_____ ning whatever in return for it. Why do you put up with it?'
He shrugged.

'It's not my business,' she said, contrite.

'No. It's not.' The voice from the doorway was cool.

Shaken, she turned. Arthur stood, elegant as ever, his eyes
very unfriendly indeed as they flicked across hers. He moved
gracefully into the room towards them. 'Honestly, Jessica, if
you're going to talk behind a man's back at least have the sense
not to do it in his own home and with the door open!'

'I wasn't –!' She stopped.

'Of course you were.' The dismissive contempt in the words
made her cheeks burn with mortification. Arthur turned his
back on her and addressed Theo, who had been watching
them, lively interest in the gaze that moved from one young
face to the other. It crossed Jessica's mind to wonder if he had
known that Arthur had been there by the door listening to her
idiotic indiscretions. She would not put such mischief beyond
him.

'Theo, my dear,' Arthur said crisply, 'that wretched little
man Bonetto absolutely refuses to extend my credit any
further. Would you see to it for me?'

Theo nodded. 'Of course.'

'And – bad judgement again I fear – my trip to the tables last
night left me quite penniless –' He smiled brilliantly, and
tossed the tangled curls from his forehead with a small flick of
his head.

Theo chuckled and dug into his pocket. Gold glimmered in
the shadowed light as he tossed a coin into the air, and was
extinguished as Arthur's long fingers expertly flicked it into
the palm of his hand. 'Thank you.' Without another glance at
Jessica he strode lightly from the room.

'Oh dear,' Jessica said, sighing.

Theo's explosive cackle of laughter must certainly have been heard by Arthur, wherever in the house he was.

The small incident did little to improve her relationship with Arthur, poor as it had been in the first place, and in the long run too it damaged her relationship with Robert since Arthur now made no bones of his dislike for Jessica and avoided her as much as possible. Whether he had told Robert of what he had overheard she did not know, but certainly she saw less and less of her husband and the time she did not spend with Theo she spent alone.

Until the day that, with a benign innocence that Jessica found deeply suspicious, Theo introduced her to the young man he had, without her knowledge, engaged to teach her Italian.

Guido Palca was tall, slim, and dark as a shadow with the most open and handsome smile she had ever seen. It was perfectly evident that his qualifications, if he had any, were certainly not in teaching language, though his English, charmingly accented, was excellent.

'Guido, my dear – *this* is Jessica –' It was dauntingly obvious from the emphasis of the words that the young man had been told all – and she knew that meant all – about her.

Theo's often expressed determination that she should form a liaison with an impeccable charmer chosen for her by him had become a source of amused exasperation to her over the past days. She put on a thunderous look. 'Theo –' she began, warningly.

He lifted disarming hands. '"Gather ye rosebuds while ye may"' he quoted entirely unrepentant, '"Old time is still a-flying."'

'My rosebuds are perfectly happy where they are, thank you,' she said, tartly and offered her hand to Guido who carried it to his lips with a simple grace that was totally and dangerously disarming.

Theo chuckled, delightedly. 'I'll leave you two young things together.'

Guido was, she had to admit, utterly charming. He was

attentive and entertaining. He attached himself to her with a tenacity that could only be admired, declaring himself immediately and irrevocably enslaved. And – most beguiling thing of all – he could make her laugh. With Theo's active approval and encouragement he joined them on their expeditions into the city and what had on the whole been relatively serious exercises became hilarious outings. He was stylish on horseback, cut a fine figure on the dance floor and was, he assured Jessica in one of his few earnest moments, even more skilled in bed. It spoke volumes for the change that had overtaken Jessica in the past few months that she did not bat an eyelid. 'I'm sure you are, Guido dear,' she said, kindly. '– Would you mind passing the tomatoes?'

Robert appeared delighted with the arrangement; philosophically she endured that, telling herself she could hardly expect jealousy.

Time passed pleasantly now, its passing eased by Theo's friendship and charming Guido's company. With Theo's help she was refurnishing the apartment, which had been stylishly decorated by two of the young artists who frequented the via del Corso. Firmly she had refused Theo's offer of money to help purchase the exquisite things he would have her buy. 'No.' The word brooked no argument. 'Once and for all, Theo, I want nothing from you but the things you are already giving me – your friendship, your help. I don't want – I won't take – your money. Don't class me with those that do.'

He smiled a rare, genuinely warm smile. 'There's a second-hand shop on the via de'Panzani. You want ter start there, gel?'

High summer was upon them. Several times they picnicked in the hills beyond the city. They visited Fiesole, with its Roman theatre and its spectacular views. On Theo's whim a group of them visited the fine city of Siena, two days' drive away, travelling in a couple of Theo's opulent and comfortable carriages, some of the men on horseback. Guido rode beside Jessica's carriage making charming conversation with her and equally charming eyes at her fellow passenger, an artist's model of stunning beauty and known easy ways. Jessica was fairly sure from the girl's coy looks the following morning that a bed had been shared that night, and suppressed firmly the faint and absurdly proprietary twinge of envy that the knowledge brought.

Siena enchanted her. The medieval city brooded still within its great walls, the narrow, shadowed streets apparently unchanged by the centuries. The spectacularly lovely square known as the Piazza del Campo, where the famous – and sometimes murderous – horserace, the Palio, was run each year she thought the most beautiful she had ever seen. The bizarrely flamboyant cathedral fascinated her.

Driving back to Florence they stopped to picnic in the hills, beneath a sky of flawless, infinite blue. Jessica perched upon a rock, her skirt tucked about her knees. The vivid sky and brilliant sunshine capped a world of browns and golds so in contrast to the soft greens of England that she still on occasions could hardly believe in it. On a nearby rock a lizard basked, glimmering, a living jewel. She stirred and it was gone in a glinting emerald flash of movement, too fast for the eye to follow. In the near distance Robert sat upon the ground, Arthur beside him, the blond boy's long arm thrown with casual affection across Robert's slim shoulders.

She turned at a footstep beside her. 'What are you thinking so solemnly?'

She smiled at Guido. 'Just how very different this is from home.'

'And is that good? Or bad?'

'Good, I think.' Then she laughed, softly and a little ruefully, 'And a little bad.'

He nodded, understanding. 'Will you go back?'

'Home? Why yes, of course. We shall have to.'

'Why?'

She looked at him in astonishment. 'Because – because that's where we belong. We have obligations. Robert will inherit a house, and land –'

'These things mean much to you?'

She pondered a moment. 'Yes. Old Hall has been in the FitzBolton family for generations. We couldn't just walk away

303

from that. There are the people to consider. They'll need us. We can't stay here for ever.' Faintly and uneasily at the back of her mind came the thought that Robert, his dark head bent close to Arthur's fair one, might not agree with her.

Guido took her hand, brought it, palm up, to his lips. 'Then we must make certain that the time you can spend with us is as memorable as it can be.' His eyes were warm, his soft voice with its attractive accent intimate. His lips on her palm sent pleasant pulses of excitement through her body. For a moment, and not for the first time, she felt herself weaken.

A small whistle shrilled. Theo clapped his hands, sharply and a little irritably, 'Come along, dearies, time to leave. Or we'll not make the city by nightfall.'

Two days after their return from Siena, out of the blue, she had news of Danny.

It was Guido who introduced her to a young man whose name she did not catch, but whose first words all but riveted her to the ground where she stood. 'Theo sent me over. Said you were asking about Danny O'Donnel?'

'Yes. Yes, I was. You know him?'

'Known him for years, on and off. We've worked together –' the young man grinned lopsidedly '– drunk together –' he glanced around '– which reminds me – any wine to be had? I'm as dry as the Sahara.'

'Please. Have mine. I haven't touched it.' She thrust her glass into his hand. 'Do you know where he is now?'

His attention had wandered. He cocked his head. 'Sorry?'

She contained herself. 'Danny. Do you have any idea where he is now?'

'Generally yes. Specifically no. Last I heard they were headed for France.'

It was a blow, but not a mortal one. 'France,' she repeated.

'That's right.'

'Where from? I mean – where did you meet him?'

'Why, here. In Florence.'

'When?' Her voice was weak.

He shrugged. His eyes had wandered to where a very pretty

girl was sitting alone, playing with an empty wine glass with long, thin fingers. 'Er – oh six months or so ago. Perhaps a little less.'

Six months. He had left the city as she had married Robert.

His attention was wandering again. He smiled vaguely at her, his eyes still on the girl, who was pointedly ignoring him. 'Would you excuse me –?'

'Oh, please – wait! First – do you know if he's coming back?'

'Danny?' He grinned broadly. 'Who knows? These days it all depends on that wife of his, doesn't it? Have you met Serafina?' He rolled his eyes, 'What a barrel of gunpowder that one is! Half gypsy, they say. And looks it. Danny always was a lucky devil with the ladies, wasn't he? But he's got his comeuppance now – Serafina goes, Danny follows – seems to be the rule. Can't say I blame him, either. Now – please – you'll excuse me for a moment?' He sidled away towards the seated girl before she could reply.

That night, in the bedroom above the salon, with the windows open to the muggy August night and the best part of two bottles of Theo's best champagne inside her, Jessica, wife of six months, lost her virginity. Guido was everything he had promised: gentle, practised, exciting. And, she thought, a little fuzzily, he seemed to enjoy it, which was a bonus for them both. Three parts drunk and very sleepy she was first surprised, then amused and finally moderately satisfied with the rather odd exercise. No doubt things would improve with practice.

Guido kissed her, and handed her another glass of champagne. She knocked it back at one gulp. 'Guido?'

'Yes, my love?' As latin a lover as anyone could wish he pressed her gently back onto the pillows, took the empty glass from her hand, looked yearningly into her eyes.

'Did you ev–ever know –' she giggled a little at the small belch that had impeded her words '– a lady called Ser-a-fin-a?' She pronounced the name very carefully.

A little puzzled he shook his head.

'She's very beautiful,' she said, soberly. 'Ver-ry beautiful indeed.'

'So are you, my love,' said her dutiful lover, smiling.

Jessica blinked sleepily. 'Never get married, Guido,' she advised him, very solemnly. 'It's a – very – silly – thing to do!'

Guido smiled his charming smile and said nothing.

'Take a lover,' she said, smiling happily at being the source of such a very intelligent thought. 'That's a much – much more sensible arrangement –'

In the weeks that followed, perfectly reasonably, Jessica imagined herself truly in love. This, surely was what she had been waiting for? As his practised lovemaking awakened her body her young, love-starved imagination saw in him the personification of both courtly and physical love. She lived for their meetings. Her infatuation for Danny, as a child, had had no physical outlet; in Guido she found, perhaps because she so desperately wanted to, a satisfying passion that she did not recognize until later as a counterfeit of love. Guido was the ideal object of such fantasy – handsome, attentive, apparently devoted he played the part that Theo Carradine had assigned to him to perfection, even occasionally, Jessica with some affection thought later, convincing himself. Theo watched the puppet show with the sly enjoyment of one who has manipulated the puppets, biding his time. He perceived in Jessica a stylish potential and an intelligence that pleased him. Given, he thought, a little more worldly polish she would make an interesting addition to the small court he had chosen to gather about him. Guido was, in his opinion, essential to her education.

Jessica and Guido met only in the Palazzo on the via del Corso – for, strangely perhaps, Jessica could not bring herself to take her lover to the apartment that she shared with Robert, and he never suggested that she should visit him – indeed it did sometimes strike her as a little odd that she did not even know in which part of the city he lived. There was no doubt that Robert knew what was going on, but he never mentioned it, and Jessica received the distinct impression that his main emotion concerning the affair was relief. He had convinced himself that she was happy at last, and that was enough for him. That she had done the same thing herself it took Theo to show her.

Georgie, his pursuit of Jessica come to nothing, had returned to the girl, an artist's model, with whom he had lived, on and off, for three years and whom he regularly left in pursuit of new game only to return when circumstances, in the form of boredom or an irate husband dictated it.

'I don't understand her,' Jessica said to Theo, one day, frowning. 'Why on earth does she put up with it? He treats her so badly –!'

'What would you do? If it were Guido?'

She thought about that. 'I – don't know.'

'Yes you do.'

She eyed him. 'I wouldn't like it.'

He grinned.

'I wouldn't like it at all.'

'You'd throw him out on his handsome ear.'

'I wouldn't!'

He said nothing. Raised his eyebrows.

'Well I might.'

'You would. Of course you would. Stands to reason.' He paused. 'Wouldn't you?'

She thought about it. Thought of the look on the girl's face when Georgie arrived at the via del Corso with another woman. 'Yes,' she said, thoughtfully. 'Yes. I think I might.'

'And what does that tell you?'

'About what?'

He was unusually patient. 'About yer relationship with Guido, gel.'

'I –' she stopped.

'It tells you yer don't love him,' he supplied, mildly.

She turned on him, horrified. 'That isn't true!'

He lifted a wickedly sardonic brow. She flushed to the roots of her hair, and turned from him. 'I do love him! I do!'

'You want him. You enjoy him. That's a different thing.'

She said nothing, knowing how uncomfortably close to the

307

truth he had come, and obscurely ashamed of it.

'Yer know, of course, that he's got a charmin' wife an' children?' His voice was conversational, the affected drawl exaggerated.

She turned, her unschooled face thunderstruck.

'Ah – yer didn't? How very remiss of him.' He was watching her with sharp, expectant eyes. 'But then – what difference? You've got a husband, haven't you? Fer what he's worth.'

She glared at him, her colour rising. Opened her mouth. He grinned and held up his hand. 'Never speak in temper, gel. There's no tellin' what yer might come out with.'

'Why didn't you tell me?'

'About what?'

'About Guido!'

He was all innocence. 'I just did, didn't I?'

She was almost speechless with anger. 'You – you planned this, didn't you? Guido and me?'

''Course I did.' He was entirely unrepentant, openly amused. 'Don't tell me yer weren't ready for it, gel.'

Her mouth tightened.

He chuckled, enjoying himself.

'Truly Theo you are hateful sometimes!' she snapped.

'I know.' She might have complimented him. He beamed, pleased. 'But good God, gel, you couldn't go round a vestal virgin fer the rest of yer life, now could yer? Someone had ter show yer what it was all about. Now – come on – admit it. Yer don't love him.'

He was right, and she knew it, had been aware of it in her heart from the first, but had stubbornly refused to face it. Guido had touched her heart not at all – even this unexpected news of his wife and children hurt her pride rather than her feelings. She had wanted to love him. He was handsome, and charming. He had taught her the joys of her body in love. She ought to love him –

'Well?' The word was sharp.

She sighed, shook her head.

He put his hand behind his ear in an exaggerated gesture. 'Try again,' he said, encouragingly. 'A bit louder.'

Exasperated, she almost laughed. 'All right! Perhaps I don't actually love him.' She shook her head again, a little ruefully, 'Oh, Theo – perhaps I can't? Supposing I can't? I did want to. You're cruel to –'

'No.' The cracked voice interrupted her. 'Not cruel, gel. Kind. You think about it. Think of what you know. Think of the lessons you've learned. Don't twaddle on about love, gel.' He pointed a crooked finger. 'You're best off without it. Muddles the mind and spoils the temper. What will you do about Guido now?' The question was sharp, the drawl gone.

She shrugged. 'I – don't know. Nothing, I suppose.'

'Exactly. Not half dead with jealousy, are yer? Not dyin' of a broken heart? Love's for fools, gel. Remember that. Remember the lesson old Theo taught yer.'

She watched him for a moment, soberly. 'You are the most devious and cynical man I've ever met,' she said at last.

The grotesque bewigged head nodded, jerkily. 'More than likely, gel. More than likely.'

She picked up the bright head of a flower that had fallen from an arrangement onto the polished surface of the table. The brilliant scarlet of the petals lay upon her fingers like blood. She studied it for a moment, a faraway look on her face. Then, 'I don't care what you say, Theo,' she said, suddenly. 'I want to know. I want to know what it's like. I want to know why that girl lets Georgie treat her so. I want to know what it is that poets write of and singers sing about.' She lifted her head, oddly fiercely. 'I want to know!'

He shook his head, testily, tutting.

'I remember once –' she stopped.

'What?'

She shook her head. 'Nothing.'

He struggled to his feet, painfully, stood looking down at her. 'So – yer want ter fall in love, eh?'

She smiled at the absurdity of the conversation. 'Yes.'

He turned and hobbled towards the door. 'More fool you, gel,' he said over his shoulder, 'More fool you.' He stopped by the door, looking back. 'But – well, who knows? Perhaps old Theo can even arrange that?'

'Theo!'

His laughter echoed back from behind the closing door.

Communication between Florence and Suffolk was not easy, and the exchange of letters between the young FitzBoltons and their families was desultory. Robert's mother was the only one who wrote with any regularity – the weather was good, or bad, old Bess had whelped again, the roof of the Great Hall was leaking, an Oxford don had taken a flattering interest in Sir Thomas' collection of butterflies – Jessica loved her letters, they brought with them in their kindly, gossiping, narrow way a glimpse of home that she treasured. Robert hardly read them at all. Maria, too, wrote occasionally, but her letters were stilted and rather formal and contained very little information and no warmth at all. Jessica remembered that her mother had always detested writing letters. For herself she tried to make sure that each month she wrote: short, cheerful notes packed with much general information – the wonderful weather, the beauty of the city and its treasures – and carefully avoiding the slightest mention of anything personal. The only other person who, surprisingly, kept up a devoted and cheering if sporadic correspondence, was Patrick. He was happy and settling in to his new life. He had a new pony. Next term he was to go away to Harrow. Bran was well, and Lucy sent her love. The childish yet somehow flamboyant scrawl brought a smile to Jessica's lips. Almost she could see the bright head, the merry, mischievous eyes.

No-one mentioned Giles or Clara, and Jessica did not ask.

The Florentine autumn was glorious. Jessica's Italian lessons went well and she was delighted to find that in a very short while she could make herself understood in the city. She also discovered to her own surprise a certain facility for drawing. Encouraged both by Theo and by Robert she attended drawing classes twice a week and was guardedly pleased with the results she achieved. She would never, she admitted readily, be any rival for Michelangelo, but she could produce a pleasing picture, and she enjoyed it. She still spent a good deal of time with Theo and his books. All in all life was full, and very enjoyable.

Winter came as something of a surprise. She had certainly not expected a spell of damp and cold to rival anything she had experienced in England, but as Christmas approached the clouds rolled down from the mountains and a curtain of drizzle drifted in the narrow streets. For the first time she saw the women of Florence with their *scaldini* – earthen pots filled with the ashes of charcoal that women of all ranks carried hooked on their arms for warmth, or on occasion, when sitting, very sensibly tucked beneath the spread of their petticoats. Within doors the fires were lit in the great hearths, shutters were closed against the cold and candles glowed warm and bright about the walls. Masques and balls were held, and the invitations for Jessica and Robert came not just from the via del Corso. As the months had gone by and one five minute scandal had been replaced by another some of the younger members of the established English colony had renewed acquaintanceship – indeed Jessica sensed in some cases some small trace of envy at the FitzBoltons' acceptance into Theo Carradine's wicked charmed circle. She and Robert themselves repaid hospitality and entertained their friends to dinners and to card parties. The apartment, redecorated and completely refurnished, had fulfilled all its promise. Angelina the new maid, competent and cheerful, ran it to perfection with very little help from her young mistress. Life ran smoothly and pleasurably; and if Jessica found herself suffering a few pangs of homesickness as she prepared for the coming of Christmas she suppressed them sternly. Instead of the simple holly boughs that would deck the village church at Melbury she had the gleam of gold and silver in the magnificent churches of Florence. Instead of a morning ride across parkland crisp with frost she sat abed, propped up with pillows, drinking precious coffee in a bedroom that had once heard the laughter of princes. Instead of the balls at New Hall attended by the country gentry – most of whom had known little Jessica Hawthorne from the day she was born – who arrived at seven and were yawning at eleven, she had the entertaining gatherings at the via del Corso and elsewhere, where the wine still flowed, the cards still fell, the arguments still raged at three in the morning, and in the kaleidoscope of that constantly changing circle it was perfectly possible to remain all evening in the company of a familiar face without ever actually remembering the name that was attached to it.

She attended Midnight Mass at the Duomo on Christmas Eve with Theo, Robert having chosen to go to Santa Croce with Arthur, whom Jessica still avoided as much as possible. Theo watched her with delight. It had been a very long time since he had had such innocent material to work upon; and already the results of his efforts could be seen. Small and rather slight she still was, but now, under his influence and after several visits to the Mercato Nuovo she dressed with style and held her head high, aware, if subconsciously, of her own attraction. She was no beauty in the true sense of the word – a stroll down any Florentine street would produce a dozen more obvious charmers – but the bright, mobile face with its intelligent eyes and determined mouth was an attraction and a challenge in one. Even the cloud of mousy hair, gleaming now with the golden touch of a summer in the Italian sun, though unfashionable was as individual as was Jessica herself. Sometimes, within the bright halo of that hair she still looked the child of innocence. But laughing, or angry, or lit with some enthusiasm she was like a small flame, brilliant and warm. Her education complete and her dreams of true love shown for the nonsense they were she would make a handsome addition to his eccentric court. It was a measure of the old man's egotism that it did not occur to him that Jessica might question his plans for her.

She found the Catholic Florentine Christmas all but overwhelming. Her very English upbringing had never prepared her for the soul-stirring pageantry, the colourful extremes of a Christian religion born and nurtured amongst the hot-blooded and flamboyant peoples of the south. Sometimes she found herself wondering – was it this that had captured her brother John? Once exposed to this passionate carnival of Christianity, had he found the dour Protestantism of his fathers pale by comparison? Kneeling in the magnificent Duomo amidst the gleam of precious metals and stones and with the triumphant voices lifted about her she thought she glimpsed something of the fervour and conviction that had given John the strength to defy their father. Of all of them, she wondered, might he not end up as being the happiest? She had never forgotten his courageous and passionate rejection of his material heritage. She had applauded him then, and she applauded him now; but even as she did so she knew that for her the way could never be the same. And in knowing that she accepted too that the life now could not last for ever, however much she might wish that it could. Always, somewhere, behind the pleasure and the undeniable enjoyment of the flouting of convention, the living of a life that could only be termed irresponsible, stood an awareness, a need, that would not eventually be denied. When Guido courted her, when Theo charmed her in his grotesque way with his books and his testy erudition, or when the Tuscan sun turned the mountains to gold, or a Catholic cathedral glittered in the light of a thousand candles the feeling was there, and it would not leave her. She remembered the green of the Suffolk countryside. She remembered her father, booted and hardily dressed for a ride about the estates. She remembered, oddly, the bewildered, determined face of the tenant Peter Arkwright as he had faced her mother asking for his wrongs to be righted. She remembered New Hall and its beauty, Old Hall and its warmth. She remembered St Agatha's – dark, cold, neglected, mysterious. She felt her roots, and for all her efforts could not rid herself of them. She could deny it for now. She could pretend to herself and to others that she did not care for the loss of these things, as she was certain Robert did not; she could pretend, but she knew in her heart that it was not so. She wondered, sometimes – if she and Robert had truly loved, would she have felt differently? If she had experienced that emotion that seemed destined to happen to others and never to her, except as a childish passion, could she be blinded to all other needs, all other memories? The new Jessica, schooled by Theo, though largely unconscious of the fact, doubted it. When it came to love she was beginning to think that the world played a game in which she could not join.

In 1818 the annual carnival, the timing of which was determined by the date upon which Easter fell, was early, beginning on the very first day of the year. There were parades and sideshows in every street and square. Plays and comedies were performed every night in every one of the city's seven theatres. There were masked balls, public and private, and each evening the streets and the banks of the river were thronged with masked and costumed crowds, laughing and flirting, making the most of the permissive pre-Lent atmosphere. The cafés were full, the squares rang with music; Jessica had never experienced such festivities before, and she enjoyed every moment. Cloaked and masked she roamed the city with a group of revellers drawn from the artists who frequented the via del Corso. The weather was cold and clear, and the distant hills gleamed, crowned with snow. Lights were strung in the Boboli Gardens, and lovers strolled beneath them, shadows in the darkness. She and Robert with Theo, Arthur, Guido and anyone else who cared to join them visited the theatres, the concerts, the cafés. As the austere days of Lent grew closer the celebrations grew wilder. There were costumed parades through the streets, and more than one drunken brawl to follow.

It was during one such brawl that she caught a glimpse of a face that stopped her heart and her breath at a stroke.

Two parades had taken place in rival neighbourhoods, and in their wake two opposing bands of young men, one dressed fairly approximately in the style of fashionable young courtiers of the eighteenth-century, the other rather more mundanely in the manner of the rivermen of the Arno had come together in the Piazzo del Duomo and picturesque insults were flying. Much wine had obviously been consumed and what started as a relatively good-tempered confrontation soon and predictably deteriorated into scuffles and wrestling matches. Theo, knowing from experience that the next step would be the drawing of knives very sensibly urged withdrawal. Jessica side-stepped a sprawling pair of brawny young men locked in battle in the gutter and with Robert's guiding hand upon her arm followed Theo towards a side street. At the corner she turned to glance back. The free-for-all had started in earnest. Urged on by cheering onlookers the young men were setting about each other like gladiators. On the near side of the square a burly 'courtier' swung his stave in a vain attempt to unseat a 'waterman' who was clinging astride his back howling like a banshee and beating at his unwilling mount with clenched fists. The crowd loved it. Taking sides they urged on first one and then the other. The bigger man bucked, nearly unseating his tormentor, who clung like a limpet. A roar rose from the onlookers.

And one face stood for Jessica alone in the crowd. A laughing face, lean, dark, strong-boned.

She stopped.

Robert pulled at her arm. 'Come on. There'll be real blood spilled in a minute.'

'Wait –!'

But he was towing her through the crowds, following Theo. Frantically she glanced back. There was no sign of that face, for which she had looked for so long.

Behind them the happy pandemonium grew and a whistle shrieked.

She could not get that face from her mind. Everywhere she went she looked for him. She questioned Theo again about Danny and about the young man who had spoken to her of him.

Theo did not remember him. 'So – who is this Danny O'Donnel you seek with such urgency?' The small, shrewd eyes were inquisitive.

'I told you – I knew him as a child. It was he who first told me of Florence –'

'And – it's important to you to find him?'

'Very,' she said, simply. 'But – perhaps I was wrong. Perhaps it wasn't him. The only person I've spoken to who knew him said he left the city a year ago.'

Theo shrugged. 'Anyone who truly cares for Florence does not stay away for long. Perhaps he has returned?'

She nodded. Perhaps he had. With his beautiful wife. 'Florence is a very big city,' she said.

Four days later, with the end of the month of carnival approaching Theo gave his own masked ball. The great ballroom of the Palazzo was opened for the occasion, and the guests were drawn from all walks of life – for the native aristocrats of the city in no way joined Theo's own compatriots in their condemnation of him. He was rich and he was, or could be in the right circumstances, generous; against that his eccentricities counted for nothing. The whole cast of a play that Theo had particularly enjoyed joined them after the evening performance still in costume that in many cases was less flamboyant – and certainly less provocative – than that of most of the non-theatrical guests. Jessica had resisted Theo's more outrageous suggestions and was dressed restrainedly as a dainty shepherdess, prettily masked. She had just joined a group who stood listening to a young man, well into his cups, whom she had not seen before, and who was evidently fresh from England.

'– and so,' he was saying, 'discretion always being the better part of valour, I left. They got my brother, though. Transported him, the bastards. Beggin' your pardon, Miss,' he executed a decidedly unsteady bow in Jessica's direction.

Someone in the crowd laughed, harshly. 'Good God, man – what did you expect? This is England you're talking about! England! Where you can steal a man's wife – or daughter – from under his nose and be thought a great fellow for it. But burn his crops? A capital offence if ever I heard one!'

Amidst the general laughter Jessica asked, 'Why did you burn his crops?'

The young man fixed her with a drunkenly serious eye. 'Why?' He swayed on his feet, marshalling words. 'They'd cut the wages to the bone an' put up the price of bread. There's no work, an' the village is starving while they feed fat. The parish won't feed the men back from the wars an' there's no way for them to earn a crust –' He raised a thin finger, wagging it, 'Happenin' all over it is.'

'Jessica?'

Absently Jessica turned.

Guido smiled. 'From Theo.' He handed her a note.

She took it, smiling her thanks. Her attention was still on the young man who had been speaking. 'Where was this?'

'Cambri – Cambridgeshire –' He could barely get the word out, 'village of Uppington. Prett'est little village in the world. Ruined.'

Jessica opened the note. It contained a brief half-dozen words. She turned to question Guido, but he had gone. The conversation about her had changed.

'– prettiest damned model I've ever seen in my life and the bugger stole her clean from under my nose –'

She excused herself and, intrigued by Theo's message made her way upstairs to the reception rooms and library. In the lovely reception room that had been her first introduction to this house a few people sat, wine glasses in hand, talking. In a corner behind a vast green palm two lovers kissed. From the ballroom below music lifted. She looked at the note again.

'The library. A present from Theo.'

She walked to the library door and pushed it open.

The room was empty and almost dark. A fire glowed in the vast hearth and a couple of lamps had been lit. The shutters were closed against the January night.

She walked further into the room, glancing around. A present, the note said. She looked at the desks and table, expecting to see something – perhaps a book? – lying there, but she could see nothing unusual.

In an armchair by the fire someone stirred. A long leg stretched, a scuffed boot was lit by the flare of flame. She jumped, startled and embarrassed that she had approached so close and so quietly without the stranger hearing. The man in the chair turned the page of the book he was looking at. His face and most of his upper body was hidden by the large wing of the chair. Beside him on the table a bottle of wine and a glass half-full.

317

Very quietly she turned to leave.

'Who's that?' The words were sharp.

She stopped. Turned. 'I'm sorry. I didn't mean to disturb you –'

He leaned forward, looking up at her, the light from the lamp illuminating his features.

– *The library. A present from Theo* –

She was totally speechless.

He laughed. 'Please don't apologize. I probably shouldn't be here. I've got a strong feeling that the invitation was a mistake in the first place – I don't seem to know a soul here. Are you the lady of the house? If so then it's I who should apologize –' He gestured with the long-fingered hands that she remembered so well at the book that lay on his lap, 'I couldn't find anyone to ask –'

'N – no,' she said. 'I'm not the lady of the house. Actually there isn't one. I'm – a friend.'

He smiled.

There was no doubt now. No doubt in the world. This was Danny. Changed, older, with a harshness about the eyes and a hardness about the mouth that she did not remember, but Danny undoubtedly. Yet still her voice was hesitant as she spoke his name. 'Danny?'

The smile faded and he frowned a little, peering at her. Unsmiling the changes in his face were more marked. Deep straight lines were scored between nose and a mouth that did not seem to smile as readily as it once had. A relatively fresh scar cleft his right eyebrow and another, smaller and older marked his cheekbone. The beautifully modelled mouth was straight as a drawn line and as harshly uncompromising. He stood. He was not as tall as she had imagined him, though long of leg and wide shouldered as she had always remembered. He was very thin. 'I'm sorry,' he said. 'I'm afraid I don't –?' His voice trailed off politely as he gestured at the mask she had forgotten she was still wearing.

She raised her head hesitantly, then with a quick movement unclipped the mask and raised her face to him.

He did not recognize her. Nor was there the slightest flicker in his eyes. His puzzlement had deepened. 'Madam, I'm sorry. I truly don't know you –?'

She swallowed an absurd disappointment. Of course he did not. How could he? She smiled. 'You did once.'

He studied her face for a moment, a little warily, then shook his head in self-mocking amusement. She turned her face to the light, watching him steadily, a half-smile on her face.

He laughed at last, bemused. 'Give me a clue? You have the better of me.'

She thought for a moment. 'A small furry animal that owned a large furry animal,' she said.

That confused him more. He shook his head.

Mischievously she held up her hand, counting on her fingers. 'Your name is Danilo O'Donnel. Your mother was Florentine, your father Irish. You look like your mother and drink like your father. You hate horses. You're a strong swimmer.'

His eyes had widened. 'You're a witch!'

'You like to sing while you're working. Your ambition is – certainly was – to be the best damned sculptor in Florence'

The expression on his face was comical. 'Please! Stop it!' He held up his hands in mock surrender.

She took the plunge. 'You once loved my sister,' she said, very quietly.

That did it. She almost saw the connecting thoughts, the memories that flickered to life behind his eyes. He reached a strong hand and with his finger on her chin turned her face to the light of the lamp. 'Good God Almighty!' he said, softly, 'Mouse!'

She laughed a little at the silly name, so naturally spoken. 'That's right.'

'Mouse!' he said again, and now he was truly laughing, his dark face alight with pleasure. He swept her into a bear hug, crushing her to him, swinging her from the ground. 'I don't believe it! I just do not believe it! What in God's name are you doing here –?'

Breathless, she could not answer him. She flung her arms about his neck and hugged him tight, her smooth cheek next to his harsh one, the male smell of him sweet in her nostrils.

At last they stepped back from each other, still holding hands. 'Mouse!' he said. 'Little Jess. Grown up and beautiful –'

She laughed and shook her head, colouring with pleasure.

'And I didn't recognize you!'

'You can hardly be blamed for that! I was – what? – eleven? – twelve? – when last you saw me –'

'But you recognized me.'

'I'd recognize you anywhere.' The words were straightforward, neither coy nor coquettish. They were followed by a breath of silence, and she saw again the faint, wary look in his eyes. He dropped her hand. Then he was laughing again, pulling another chair up to the fire.

'Tell me everything – absolutely every – single – thing that's happened to you since I left Melbury in such a hurry.'

She hesitated.

He smiled, grimly. 'All right. Let's get it over and done straight away. Caroline?'

'She's married.' She was relieved. 'To Bunty Standish. She's Lady Caroline now.'

'And – the child?' There was a thread of remembered pain in the words that made her flinch. She shook her head. He turned from her and walked to the fire, stood for a long moment looking into the flames. When he turned he was smiling again. She could not tell in the half-light if the smile were forced. 'You, little Mouse – what of you? And your family – tell me everything –'

They sat until four in the morning. In the ballroom below the music died. Doors opened and closed, and voices called their goodnights. The house grew quiet though the occasional burst of laughter still rang out. No-one came to the library. She told him everything – her unhappiness after he had gone, the death of her father, her discovery about Giles, the astonishing arrival of Patrick and its consequences. She told him too, honestly and with neither excuses nor self-pity, of Robert and of the near-disaster their marriage had proved to be. '– You must think me dreadfully stupid. But at the time it seemed the best – the only – thing to do. I didn't know – didn't realize what it would involve –' Not for a moment did it strike

320

her as strange to be confiding so in a near-stranger; sitting here with him it was as if those years had never been, as if no events and no time had ever come between them. This was Danny, and she loved him, as she had loved him from the first moment she had seen him. A different Danny to be sure, and most certainly a different kind of love, but undeniable and over-whelming for all that. The young Jessica had given her heart with no reservations to the young man she had thought of as her dark angel; older and wiser she saw him now with clearer eyes, but was as unhesitatingly ready to love him now as she had been then; she could not have prevented herself if she had tried.

He was shaking his head, his face sombre. 'Don't think you're alone in that kind of mistake, little Mouse. One way or another we all make them. And we all have to pay for them.'

She said nothing, watching him.

He picked up his wine glass and drained it, then smiled a small, bitter smile. 'You of all people know that my choice of women has not always been the most sensible.'

'I heard you were married,' she said, non-committally.

He laughed sharply, reached for the wine bottle. 'That I am.'

'I heard she was beautiful.' She kept her voice even.

He poured the wine very steadily. 'That she is. Very.'

In the silence a small branch crackled in the fireplace. 'And wild,' he added, and shook his head a little, laughing self-mockingly.

'I heard –'

'Yes?'

She shrugged. 'I heard you were devoted to her.' She looked at him directly, searching his face. 'Where Serafina goes Danny follows. That's what I heard.'

He leaned back in his chair, stretching out his long legs. 'That was the way of it for a while.'

'What happened?'

He made a small, rather tired gesture. 'One too many fights. One too many lovers. Enough is enough even for the most besotted of fools.'

'You still live together?'

He nodded. 'After a fashion.'

'You – you have children?'

He shook his head.

She had not realized she had been holding her breath. She let it out, long and slowly.

He held the wine glass in front of him, watching the glimmer of flame through its ruby depths. His eyes moved to Jessica and he smiled, ruefully. 'No great advertisement for the institution of marriage, are we, you and I?' he asked.

She had to laugh. 'Who is?'

He joined her in laughter. 'No-one I know.' He sat up, raising the glass in mocking toast. 'Here's damnation to the whole damned institution!'

As he tossed back the last of the wine the door opened. He looked up, and stilled in the act of putting down his glass. Jessica turned her head. Standing by the door, lit by the soft light of candles, stood the most stunningly lovely girl she had ever seen. Her hair was night black, her skin like cream. The body beneath a brilliant emerald green dress was arrogantly beautiful. She was eyeing Danny with something very close to contempt in her gleaming dark eyes. 'So. Here you are. Amongst the books.' Her Italian was oddly accented, her voice surprisingly harsh.

He stood. Though he made no attempt to introduce her, Jessica knew that this was his wife, and her heart contracted at the other girl's beauty. Behind her, Theo had appeared, like a grotesque gnome, the top of his head, even with its ridiculous wig, barely reaching to Serafina's shoulder. His yellowed grin gleamed in the candlelight.

Danny turned back to Jessica. 'I'm sorry. I've kept you far too late. I really must go.'

She nodded. 'I'll see you again?' Despite the listeners she could not prevent herself from asking the question, as she could not help the eager note in her voice. A small, entertained smile flickered across Serafina's face.

'Of course, if you'd like.'

'I would.' She did not care what they heard, what they thought.

He smiled, the wonderful smile she had never forgotten, and with no kiss, no touch of the hand turned and walked through the door, acknowledging Theo with a polite nod of the head, looking at Serafina not at all. The gypsy girl watched Jessica for a moment, the small, amused smile on her lips before turning to follow.

'Well,' said Theo, advancing into the room. 'What did you think of my present? What did I tell you – old Theo can do anything –' He cackled, watching her with an amusement only a little kinder than that Serafina had shown. 'What's the matter, gel? Moonstruck, are yer?'

Quiet and smiling she stood, smoothed her skirt, picked up her mask. Danny, her Danny had been here with her. She could still hear his voice, still see the sharp lines of his face. As she walked past Theo to the door she paused to drop a light kiss onto the rouged cheek.

'Yes,' she said.

Chapter Twelve

The strength of her feelings for Danny astounded her. From the moment she had seen him, from the moment he had turned his head and smiled at her she had known that here was a man that she wanted in a way and with a force that she had never experienced before. In those few short hours in his company all the infatuation of childhood had returned in tenfold strength – but now, too, she recognized the grace of his body, the challenge of that dark face, the open, attractive sexuality of the man. She wanted him near her. She wanted his touch and the sound of his voice. She could not be happy away from him. That night, alone in the silent darkness of her room she relived each moment of their meeting, each word he had spoken, each gesture he had made. She recalled every line of his face, every expression. She counted the ways he had changed, and smiled at the ways he had not. And as the light of a grey winter's dawn filtered through the shutters and she slept at last it was upon the determination that if she had to die for it she would make Danny O'Donnel want her as she wanted him.

Twenty-four hours later the ever-smiling Angelina laid a note upon Jessica's breakfast plate. Robert looked up from his book as she tore it open.

She looked at it for a long moment before saying, very lightly, 'Oh, how nice – it's from Danny O'Donnel – you remember I told you I met him the other night at Theo's? I knew him at home as a child –'

'The one who renovated St Agatha's for Giles' and Clara's wedding? Yes, I remember.'

She indicated the note. 'He wants to call. This afternoon. Will you be home?'

'What time is he coming?'

Entirely unnecessarily she consulted the precious scrap of paper again. 'Two o'clock.'

'Afraid not.' Robert went back to his book, 'We're going to the matinée at the Opera. Martinelli is singing, and we have an introduction from the Maestro.' No need to qualify the 'we' – it was understood that where Arthur went, there Robert would follow.

'That's a pity. I'd like you to meet him. I think you'd like him.'

'Ask him to stay to dinner. I daresay I'll be back by six. Or get him to come to Theo's tomorrow. We'll all be there.'

'Yes. Perhaps I'll do that.' Her brain was racing. She'd wear the new blue dress. Or perhaps the green? She'd be so damned grown up and sophisticated he'd never call her 'Mouse' again –

The morning was undoubtedly the slowest she ever remembered. If she looked at the clock once she looked a hundred times, and a dozen times she checked that it had not stopped. By the time the hands were at last reluctantly creeping around to show the hour of two she was in a state of utter panic, had changed her clothes three times and the arrangement of the furniture in the drawing room twice. The apartment was empty – shamelessly she had manufactured an errand for Angelina that would take the best part of the afternoon – and very quiet. She had placed teacups on a tray, arranged it prettily upon a small table by the fire, then changed her mind, stacked them back untidily into the cupboard and hunted out the wine glasses.

Two o'clock came. But Danny did not.

The weather had turned milder, though still cloudy. She stood upon the balcony, watching the road, poised to draw back when she saw him turn the corner. It would never do for him to catch her watching for him –

The minutes passed slowly – became a quarter of an hour – half an hour –

The clouds had gathered and the sky had darkened. Fine drizzle began to fall, drifting in a dismal curtain through the wet streets. Her heart was as leaden as the skies with disappointment.

Another miserably slow quarter of an hour dragged past before she reluctantly gave up her watching.

He wasn't coming.

Chilled, she wandered back into the pretty drawing room, that Theo had designated her 'salon' and of which usually she was so proud. The inexpensive but stylish second-hand furniture she had found had been painted and cleverly re-upholstered in palest green and silver by one of Theo's young artists. The walls and curtains were ivory, the curtains trimmed with blue that was reflected in her most extravagant buy, an exquisite pale green and blue Chinese carpet. Sapphire blue velvet cushions were scattered upon the chairs and sofa. Robert's piano stood in the corner. Stealing the willing Theo's idea she had used potted plants and shrubs to great effect, screening the mirrors and creating small interesting areas within the big room. In the summer it would be light, airy and cool; now, with a fire dancing in the marble hearth it was warm and cosy. Normally just the sight of the pretty room would cheer her. Now she hardly noticed it. Disconsolately she wandered to a sofa, perched on the arm, picking with small, angry fingers at the silver piping.

Danny O'Donnel was no different from anyone else. What humiliatingly idiotic, ridiculously romantic notion had made her think otherwise?

The clocks of the city were chiming four when he arrived and she, in a miserable attempt to divert herself from her disappointment had changed into a plain grey day dress and had settled to a sketching exercise set her by her drawing master. As she worked she fiddled abstractedly with her wiry hair, pulling and twisting it about her fingers. When the door bell sounded she all but jumped out of her skin, and dropped her pencil.

'Drat it!' She picked it up. The point was broken. The bell rang again. She must have forgotten to give Angelina the key –

He stood in the open doorway, rain glinting in his hair and

on his shoulders, his dark face contrite, a small sprig of winter jasmine in his hand.

She gawped at him like an idiot.

'I'm sorry,' he said. 'I'm late.'

'I – yes. You are.' She cleared her throat. The most extraordinary things were happening to her insides. She stepped back awkwardly, waving him past her, and shut the door, leaning on it for a moment, watching him, trying to calm the strange racing of her heart.

He looked about him. 'What a charming apartment.'

'Yes, isn't it?' Her voice was falsely bright, too high-pitched. She hated the sound of it, but to her horror simply could not stop talking. 'It was in a terrible mess when we came, last year. But Theo helped me, and we're very pleased with the results. We've tried to use the same colours – or at least related ones – in the different rooms, to give some continuity –' Without pausing for breath, and with no difference in her tone she added in an exasperation she could no longer disguise, 'Oh, Danny, I could kill you! Just look at me!' She had caught sight of herself in the mirror – wild hair, crumpled dress and all – and she could not prevent a small splutter of half-angry laughter. 'What a mess!'

He turned. His mouth was twitching. 'You look marvellous. Just as you used to after you'd run down to St Agatha's through the woods with Bran!'

'But I'm not *supposed* to look like that!' She was still torn between anger and laughter.

He proffered the jasmine with a small, charmingly apologetic smile. 'I'm sorry. It's unforgivable of me to be so late. If you're busy would you rather I left? I could call again some other time –?'

'No!' she could not disguise the urgency in the word. 'No,' she said again, more lightly. 'Please stay. I've been so looking forward to seeing you.' She took the spray of sweet-smelling flowers and bent her face to them, using the moment to calm her jumping nerves. 'Please – go into the drawing room. There's a fire in there, and it's cosy. I won't be a moment. Would you like tea? Or a glass of wine?'

'Tea would be very nice,' he said, solemnly. 'Thank you.'

The spark in his eye alerted her. She eyed him suspiciously. 'You're teasing,' she said, suddenly.

He was all innocence. 'About the tea? Of course not. I'd love a cup.'

'The way you said it,' she said, repressively.

'Ah.' He grinned, and her heart lurched. 'Well – just a little. My Mouse playing house. I never thought I'd see the day.'

'I'm not –' She stopped. The dilemma was clear. To him she was still Mouse, the little girl for whom he had had such affection, and who had demanded nothing in return for her love. The advantage of that was the immediate ease of their relationship; the old bond had been renewed with no strain and no affectation. In view of her rather more basic feelings for him, however, the disadvantage of such an attitude was obvious. She smiled her sweetest smile. 'I'll make the tea.'

She walked away from him composedly. Once in the kitchen, like a whirlwind she rummaged in the cupboard for the cups and saucers, put the kettle, fortunately already full, on the hob. Then she flew silently across the hall to her bedroom, hastily undoing buttons as she ran. With fingers like thumbs she changed her clothes, feverishly hunting through drawers and chests, mislaying one of the slippers that matched the pale green gown, not remembering until after she had dragged the pretty dress over her head that she had lost the ribbon that went with it to tie up her wild hair. Settling for a white one she dragged the brush through the mop of her hair that was made even more unruly by the damp atmosphere of the day, winced in despair as it flew in a cloud about her head. With no time for finesse, and with a grimly humorous recollection of how long she had taken to get ready that same morning, she pulled it back and tied it at the nape of her neck. Then tying the sash of her dress as she ran she dashed into the kitchen, only to find Danny already there, making the tea.

'I came to find you,' he said, eyeing her changed appearance with some surprise. 'The water was boiling –'

She skidded to a halt, smoothed her pretty skirt down

casually. 'The weather seems remarkably close, for all the rain. I thought I'd – put on something a little cooler –'

He was watching her with a very odd expression on his face – tender, half-amused, yet somehow suddenly guarded. She had for an awful moment the feeling that he looked through her eyes straight into her soul, and was wary of what he saw. Holding to the fragile thread of her composure she turned from him. 'I'll bring the cups.'

They drank tea in the drawing room as decorously as two maiden aunts. He apologized again for being late, but gave no explanation; with a stab of fearful and irrational jealousy she wondered if it had been Serafina who had delayed him. They spoke for some time about inconsequentials before he asked her, with an air of such carefully casual interest that it made her suspect that this was perhaps the main reason for his call, to tell him in more detail about Caroline. She told him all she could. '– We don't really see much of her now. But I think – I'm sure – she's happy. As happy as she's capable of being. She has what she wants –' she hesitated, '– what she always wanted –' she added, gently.

He nodded, apparently undisturbed. 'Yes. I see that now. Don't worry –' he smiled a little, '– it's been a very long time since I pined for Caroline. I just wanted – had – to know what happened after I left. It's strange how that summer has stayed so clearly in my memory. You – Caroline – the house, and the lake and that glorious old church – it was all somehow very special, wasn't it?'

'Yes,' she said, her voice low.

'I remember the wild flowers that grew along the river. And the great hole that Bran had dug under the old oak, trying to get at the rabbits –'

She was watching him, unblinking, barely breathing.

'You used to get so worried when I swam in the lake –'

'Yes.'

'Funny little thing you were. So intense. So eager. So very lovable.'

The word fell into a silence.

Danny stirred. 'And then – it all fell apart. I've never

forgotten the way you came —' He stopped, and turned his head to look at her. 'Tell me — do you still believe that your father would have killed me that day?'

'Yes,' she said, flatly.

He nodded, accepting it. 'So. I owe you my life. Brave little thing that you were. Are you still so brave?' The tone of his voice had altered a little. Subtly and suddenly the atmosphere between them had changed. She held his eyes, willing him to see not the small, lonely child he so obviously well remembered but a grown young woman who in that instant would be willing to do anything he asked of her to keep him by her side. 'I don't know.'

He turned away from her, breaking that small, strange communion. 'I owe you my life,' he repeated. 'You're entitled to despise me for what I've made of it.' The scar on his cheekbone shone suddenly white in the light as he moved his head.

She put down her cup very carefully. Not for the world would she let him see the shaking of her hand. 'I don't,' she paused. 'I never would.'

He laughed, a short, harsh sound. 'Don't speak too soon.'

She shook her head. 'I know.'

'You don't. You can't.' He ran a hand through his still-damp hair. 'I'm not what you think I am, Mouse. Don't be fooled.'

'If I'm being fooled,' she said quietly, 'it isn't by you.'

He turned again to look at her, a question in his eyes. Again she felt the tantalizing change between them. And again it was he who drew back, leaning down upon his elbows, looking fixedly at his scuffed shoes. She nibbled her thumb and waited.

'What a bloody mess I've made of things,' he said at last, as much it seemed to himself as to her.

She hazarded a single word. 'Serafina?'

'Serafina.' He smiled a small, harsh smile and shook his head a little. 'Serafina,' he said softly, 'is simply the well-deserved end of the road to degeneracy. A road paved with the carnal sins and leading downhill, very fast. The day that you saved me from your father was neither the first nor the last time that I fled down that road.'

She waited until it was obvious he would not say more. 'And what of your work?' she asked, 'Are you still going to be the greatest living sculptor in Florence?'

He laughed at that, quite genuinely. 'Is there nothing I ever said to you that you don't remember? The arrogant dreams of the young! No – I've found my niche. Had found it at St Agatha's and simply didn't see it.'

'You restore churches?'

'I do. And I do it well. There's something very satisfying in salvaging something beautiful that might otherwise be lost. In working on something that other hands fashioned hundreds of years ago. I still get the odd commission – quite often stemming directly from restoration work. It's not unusual for people to commission something new to take the place of something that's been irreparably damaged. It keeps the wolf from the door –' he smiled that quick, heart-stopping smile that she had never forgotten, '– and it keeps me out of mischief.'

She laughed back at him, half-teasing. 'Always?'

He did not answer for a moment. The smile left his face. He looked at her steadily, and as steadily she held his eyes, feeling again the flash of frightening excitement that flickered between them. 'Do you always stay out of mischief?' she asked, quietly insistent.

In silence they looked at each other, and in that moment she knew certainly that he saw the depth of her desire for him.

Abruptly then he stood up, reached for her hands, pulled her to her feet and held her there, at arms' length, shaking his head firmly. 'I think I'd better go.'

She had no talent for guile or artifice, the arts of the coquette were beyond her. 'Please don't,' she said and then added again, with no attempt to disguise her pleading, 'Please?'

'I must.' The words were gentle.

She stepped back, smiling brightly, the high blood of mortification in her cheeks. There was no doubt in her mind that he had known what she meant. She had offered herself, and – however gently – she had been rejected. 'Perhaps we'll meet again at the via del Corso?' she said, over-lightly.

331

He nodded. 'Sir Theodolphus has kindly offered me an open invitation.'

'Then we're bound to bump into one another again. We're there quite often.' She wanted to scream. Or to throw something. She wanted to beg him to stay –

She followed him in silence to the door. There he turned, bent, swiftly brushed her cheek with his lips and was gone, running lightly down the stairs, his hand lifted in farewell.

She closed the door with a thud and rested her forehead against it, closing her eyes. She had chattered like a child, then thrown herself at him like any trollop. No wonder he had run away as fast as his feet would carry him!

She wandered back into the room where she had been drawing when he came. Picked up the broken pencil. And in a sudden burst of nervous energy and fury at herself flung it across the room. 'Damnation! Oh – double damnation!'

She convinced herself she would not see him again. Tortured herself by imagining his reaction to her awkwardness and inexperience. Perhaps he had laughed, after he had left her? Perhaps – terrible thought – he had told Serafina of the child who had thought to seduce him –? If, that is, her pathetic performance could be classed as an attempt at seduction.

She moped about the apartment until even Robert noticed that something was wrong. '– You aren't sickening for something, are you?' he asked, anxiously. Even at this time of year an epidemic of deadly fever was not unknown.

She shook her head. 'No, no. I'm all right. It's the weather I think. One gets so used to the sunshine that this –' she gestured towards the window where the rain ran like tears down the glass '– can get on one's nerves ridiculously quickly. Funny. I never really minded bad weather at home. I suppose it seemed more natural.'

He did not reply. He was seated at the piano in the corner of the room, a sheaf of notes spread across his lap. Lethargically she wandered across the room and stood looking over his shoulder. 'What are you doing?'

He made an odd, almost unconscious movement with his

332

arm, like a secretive child hiding his work from prying eyes. Then he laughed self-consciously and relaxed, leaning back on the stool. 'You promise you won't laugh?'

Intrigued she shook her head. 'Of course not.'

'I'm writing an opera.'

'An opera!' She stared at him.

He nodded.

'But – how exciting!' And how ambitious. She did not say the obvious. 'What's it about?'

'It's about the Trojan War. Oh, Jess, it could be splendid! I've so many ideas! I can hear them in my head –!' His eyes were shining. He stopped speaking and nibbled his lower lip, obviously fighting down excitement. He played a tentative short phrase, one fingered, on the piano. 'It's such a wonderful story, of course. It has everything – heroes, battles and a beautiful heroine. If only I can do it justice –'

'Of course you can.'

He turned a shining face to her. 'Yes. Do you know – this time I believe I can! This time I think it will work. Jess – just imagine – a first night in Milan – or Rome –'

She laughed, caught up in his excitement.

'The libretto is Arthur's, of course. I shall write the part of Achilles for him – oh he'd make a marvellous Achilles! – but the music will be mine. Entirely mine.' She had never seen him so fired with enthusiasm, so full of energy. She touched him on the shoulder, lightly, and he smiled up at her, his small handsome face positively lit with excitement. 'This time I'm going to try. This time I'm going to stick at it. It's a wonderful story, and the music is all there, inside my head. All I have to do is to get it down on paper –'

She laughed. 'You make it sound very easy!'

He shook his head. 'Oh, no. It won't be easy. I'm not stupid. I know it won't. But it will be good, Jess. I'm determined on it. You'll see.' Touchingly, he was like an eager child, needing reassurance but unwilling to ask for it.

She smiled at him affectionately. 'I'm sure it will.'

She had told herself that she did not want to accompany Robert to Theo's that night. If Danny were there she might

333

only embarrass them both by being unable to keep away from him – and if he were not, the more honest side of her admitted, the disappointment would be so great that she could not face the thought of an evening of card-playing and conversation as if nothing were amiss. But at the last moment the temptation to see him, to be near him, was too much and she went, as she supposed she had always known she would.

Theo was out of sorts. 'Haven't seen yer in days, dammit! Where yer bin, gel? Fair-weathered friend, eh? Bit o' rain an' yer run fer cover?'

She smiled. 'No, of course not.' Her eyes searched the room.

'What did yer think of my little surprise, then?' He cocked his head and looked at her slyly.

Absurdly she was so distrait that she could not for the moment think what he meant. 'Oh – you mean Danny? It was a wonderful surprise. How did you find him?'

He tapped his nose, knowingly. 'Not a lot goes on in this city I don't know about, gel.'

'Is he –' She glanced around again, making an enormous effort to keep the strain from her voice, 'Is he here tonight?'

The old eyes were very sharp. 'Aye. He is.'

Her heart lurched uncomfortably. 'Oh? I don't see him.'

He cackled villainously. 'He's playin' cards, gel. Upstairs. Got a gamblin' streak in him has the lad.'

She nodded, absently. His claw-like hands closed painfully on her arm. 'Come up to the library a minute, gel. Got somethin' ter show yer. Fifteenth-century manuscript. In damn' good condition –'

She passed a half hour with him over the manuscript, then wandered back into the main room where a rowdy and wine-fuelled game of charades was taking place. She watched for a while, only half her mind taking in the quarrelsome entertainment. Danny was here. Here, in the same house. It was as if she could sense his presence, sense his breath and his movement. But she could do nothing about it. She could not – would not! – pursue him in public. He had made it perfectly clear that her advances were not welcome – perhaps even an embarrassment –

'Good evening.' His voice was very quiet in her ear. 'I'd given up. I thought you weren't coming.'

It was utterly beyond her to hide what she knew showed in her eyes as she turned to him. She said nothing.

'Is there somewhere we can talk?' he asked.

'The library –'

She allowed him to take her arm and to steer her to the library door, but then she broke free fiercely and walked swiftly away from him. Irrationally it was as if her anger at herself had spread to encompass him, and she would not look at him. As he shut the door and turned to her she held up her hands brusquely, palms out. 'All right, all right, you don't have to say it. I'm a silly little fool and you don't want me trailing after you like a moonstruck child. Well, I can understand that. So let's just leave it there, shall we?'

'Jessie –!'

'I'm sorry. I made an idiot of myself. It won't happen again, I promise. It's just that I – I've been looking for you for such a long time – and –' She heard the perilous waver in her voice and stopped, biting her lip angrily.

'Jessica –' He held out a hand. There was a mortifying hint of laughter in his voice, 'Come and sit down. You're over-wrought –'

She shook her head.

He extended the friendly hand further, cocked his head a little, waiting.

Reluctantly then she came to him, allowed him to draw her down beside him on the sofa.

'What on earth was all that about?' he asked, mildly.

She was fighting tears, and she was not winning. She shook her head.

'Tell me.'

She lifted her head. He was watching her, very seriously, a look of tenderness in his eyes that almost undermined her strength completely. She looked away, down at the hands that were clenched in her lap. 'I love you,' she said, very very quietly and with her voice tightly controlled. 'I know it sounds ridiculous, but I've always loved you. Ever since the first day I

335

saw you I've loved you. But I was too young, and Caroline took you from me. And then – you had to go away. It was horrible. I thought I'd die. I was so sure I'd never see you again.' She faltered for a moment. He said nothing. She dared not look at him. 'And now I've found you again, and you don't –' she faltered a little, swallowed, ' – don't want me. Why should you? I understand that. And I'm trying to be sensible. But – but I can't help it if it hurts –' All at once she gave up the unequal fight with her tears and buried her face in her hands, sobbing like the child she was trying so fiercely to convince him she was not.

He let her cry for a moment, making no move towards her. Then as her sobs subsided a little he produced a folded handkerchief and offered it, wordlessly.

Without looking at him she took it, mopped her eyes, blew her nose, sniffed like an urchin then sat screwing the damp handkerchief into a ball in her fingers.

She saw his movement a fraction of a second before his fingers caught her chin and, despite her stubborn resistance, turned her face to his. Astoundingly and infuriatingly he was laughing. 'Just look at you, child! What a state you've talked yourself into!' Angrily she pulled back, but he held her. Then, slowly and with gentle deliberation he kissed her, ignoring the small, hiccoughing sobs that still shook her. She sat, shocked to stillness, her eyes wide open, hardly responding to the soft touch of his lips. He drew back, took the handkerchief from her strengthless fingers, wiped her eyes and then kissed her again. This time she kissed him back and it was some long moments before they drew apart.

She watched him, wonderingly, half distrustful.

He held up a schoolmaster's finger. 'That,' he said, 'I believe destroys the best part of your case. Now – perhaps we can get down to talking sensibly?' His voice was light. His expression was not.

'Danny –'

'Not a word.' He stopped her with his finger again, 'You've had your say. And pretty silly some of it was, if you don't mind my saying so. Now it's my turn.'

336

He watched her for a long, unnerving moment in silence. She waited.

'The one thing in the world that I don't want –' he corrected himself, '– that I know I mustn't do is to hurt you,' he said at last, quietly. 'Wait –!' he shook his head sharply as she opened her mouth to protest. 'I've made enough mistakes – caused enough pain, knowingly and unknowingly – to know what I'm saying. So – please – listen to me.' He paused, obviously choosing his words carefully. 'You're unhappy with Robert. That's not a good reason for thinking yourself in love with me.'

'It's not the reason,' she said, immediately and positively. 'I know it. And I'm not thinking it. It's true.'

'Perhaps. But you have to recognize it as a possibility. And as for me – as you must certainly have guessed my own marriage is hardly the happiest union in the world. Whether you care to face it or not that could give me a very good reason indeed for –' he hesitated, '– consoling myself with you.'

'I don't care why you do it,' she said, simply and honestly, 'I just want you to do it.'

'Jessica!' He was exasperated. 'You don't – you truly don't – know what you're saying!'

'I know I love you,' she said, staunchly and certainly, 'I know that I always have. And I want you to love me.'

'Love!' He threw back his head in a small gesture of despair. 'Love?'

'Yes,' she said, stubborn as a child.

He drew a long breath. She watched him intently. 'Jessie,' he said at last. 'You must forgive me if my faith in the power of love – perhaps even my understanding of the word – is a little different than yours. It doesn't stop people hurting each other. Quite the contrary –'

'I don't care! I know what you're trying to say. I know I'm an innocent and you've had hundreds of women –' His eyes widened a little at that, and his mouth twitched, '– but I don't *care*! Danny, please believe me. I'm not as stupid as I seem. I know the risks. And I'm ready to take them.'

'For now. What of later?'

'We'll face that when it comes.'

He shook his head. 'I don't want to hurt you.'

'Why not?' She was becoming bolder.

'What do you mean?'

She forced cool reason into her voice. 'From the sound of what you're saying you've hurt plenty of others. Why not me?'

'Because you're different –'

'How? How – different?'

'I – don't know.'

'Perhaps you should try to find out?'

He half laughed. 'Jessie –'

Impulsively she caught his hands. 'Danny, listen to me. If you're trying to frighten me away for my own good you're simply wasting your breath. I told you, I love you. Nothing you can say will change that. I know. I don't care what you are, I don't care what's gone before. I don't care if you can only give me a part of yourself. I don't care if we're both married. I don't care how impossible it all is –' She paused for breath, then added on a quick spurt of nervous laughter '– damn it, I don't care if the world is going to end next week! I just want you to love me. For now – not necessarily for ever – I'm not asking the impossible. I won't demand a lifetime's devotion if that's not what you're ready to give. But we don't have to think of that now. We're here. We're together. To me, for now, that's all that counts – and I won't have you talking me out of today because you feel some guilt about yesterday or some fear of what you might do to me tomorrow. That's my responsibility, not yours. I'm not a child any more. I'm a grown woman, and I want you. The only thing, the one and only thing, that would send me from you, would be for you to tell me that you don't want me. Are you going to tell me that? If so – do it now. And I promise you I'll never bother you again. But if you are going to say then please say it quickly, before I make a worse fool of myself –'

Their hands were still linked. She felt his grip tighten. Steadily she held his eyes. He said nothing.

'I wouldn't tie you down,' she said, softly. 'I'd never demand more than you're ready to give.' Brave, foolish words.

He drew her to him and kissed her. She put every ounce of her love and her longing into her response. His hands brushed her bare arms, moved to her shoulders, slipped into the bodice of her dress to the naked smooth skin of her breast. When his probing fingers closed over her rigid nipple she gasped, her mouth opening under his. Urgently he pulled her dress from her shoulders, baring her breasts to his hands. As fierce as he she pressed herself to him. Then, suddenly, she found herself put from him very firmly, his big hands competently tidying her clothes.

'Danny –!'

'No.' There was no disguising the urgency of his need – his body proclaimed it, and the look in his eyes. 'Not now. Not here.'

'When? Where?' She was shameless. Had he suggested the Piazza del Duomo at midday she would have agreed.

'Can I come to your apartment?'

'Yes.'

'When?'

She thought for only a moment. 'Tomorrow afternoon. Robert has a lesson from two till four.'

He leaned forward and kissed her, very lightly. 'I'll be there.'

She had recovered enough composure to muster a smile. 'Two hours late?'

'Not two minutes,' he said.

He was true to his word. The clocks and bells of the city were combining their tongues to proclaim the hour of two when he swung, walking quickly, around the corner of the via Condotta. This time she was on the balcony, openly watching for him, and had run to the door and opened it before he had reached the top of the staircase. She had slept hardly at all that night, had lived since the evening before in a whirl of unclouded happiness that had made the world and everything it held a delight. The smallest thing had been a wonder – the pale sunshine of February, the sound of the church bells, the skyline of the city against the breezy sky. The thought of

Danny had heightened her senses more surely than any drug, and she sang as she helped Angelina tidy the apartment.

Robert, working at the piano had grunted at her greeting and not looked up. Absorbed in her own excitement she had left him to his labours. After lunch, still moody, he had left for his lesson with the Maestro and, a half hour later Angelina, happy to be given the afternoon off to visit her family, had left too. When Danny arrived the apartment was empty and quiet. Almost before the door closed behind him she was in his arms. Their lovemaking the first time was urgent and wild, and he hurt her more than a little, but she did not care. The driving strength of his body, the violent surge of her own desire, released at last, brought them to a swift climax that moved Jessica to joyous tears and released from Danny a sharp cry of pleasure and triumph. Afterwards they lay together naked upon her bed and with a gentleness that astounded her he loved her again, stroking and kissing, arousing her with skill and tenderness until, tired as she was, she cried out for him and he took her again. They slept then for a while, and woke in the same moment.

'I'm starving,' she said.

He grunted sleepily and wrapped his long arms about her. 'Little pig. Is that all you can think of in such a moment?'

She giggled. 'It's all I can manage just now.' She struggled through his embrace, surfaced, cheerfully dishevelled and lay propped on one elbow looking down at him, drinking in greedily every small detail of his face – the already familiar curve of the scar on his cheek, the relaxed line of his strong mouth, the lashes that lay curled like a child's against the darkness of his skin.

He made a small, grumbling noise. 'What a fidget you are, child!'

She kissed him; kissed his eyes, his nose, his mouth, his throat, his chest.

'Careful,' he said.

She laughed again, the sound of unflawed happiness. 'Don't be silly. Look at you – you're harmless as a baby –!'

His eyes snapped open, and grinning he reached for her. She

340

squealed, struggling, as he wrestled her beneath him, pinning her down. Then, on a breath of laughter he laid his face upon her breasts, groaning comically. 'You're right – witch! You've drained me!' He relaxed on top of her, a dead weight. For a moment she let her fingers follow the lines of his face, brushing his cheekbone, running along the line of his mouth, laughing as he nibbled her fingertip, then stroking his hair.

'You're squashing the life out of me.'

'Serves you right.'

She pulled his hair, hard.

'Ouch!' He rolled over, with her on top of him.

'A cup of tea, Mr O'Donnel?' she asked, politely. 'And a slice of cake perhaps? I made it myself.'

'What did you put in it?'

She considered gravely. 'Several love potions and an aphrodisiac. I may have overdone it a little – but I've got you now, and I'm not letting you go too easily.'

'God, woman, you'll kill me!'

She ran her hand lightly down his body, laughed as she felt immediately the stir of his manhood. 'Unlikely, Mr O'Donnel,' she said, rolling off him before he could hold her and landing on her feet beside the bed like a cat. 'Very, very unlikely!'

They drank their tea and ate their cake naked in the bedroom sitting crosslegged on the bed, watching each other, laughing like children. Jessica gobbled her second slice of cake and licked the sweet crumbs from her fingers. 'What time is it?'

'Nearly quarter to four.'

She sighed, and the happy look faded a little from her face. 'Robert will be home in half an hour or so. I suppose we should get dressed.'

'It might not be a bad idea, Mrs FitzBolton,' he said, lightly.

She stiffened, laid her plate down upon the bedspread and turned her back to him, swinging her feet to the floor. 'Please. Don't call me that. I'm not his wife.'

He said nothing.

She glanced at him, sharply. 'I'm not!'

341

He stretched a hand and touched her sticky fingers. 'The world says you are.'

'The world can say what it likes.' She stood and turned to face him, her young body shining like pearl in the dull light, her small, rose-tipped breasts moving with her breath. 'I know what I know,' she said, 'and be damned to the world.'

With no word he stood and took her in his arms. They stood so, quite still, for a long moment, her face laid upon his warm chest, eyes tight closed.

'You'd better get dressed, my love,' he said at last, gently. 'Before you take cold.'

He left before Robert came. Jessica tidied the bed, washed the cups and plates then sat lost in thought in front of the drawing-room fire.

'Will you tell Robert?' he had asked as he had left.

'I – don't know. Perhaps – not yet.'

'Why not?'

'I don't know.' The wretchedness of seeing him leave sounded in her disconsolate voice.

He had kissed her, smiling. 'Cheer up, little one. I'll come tomorrow, if you'd like?'

'Oh, yes! Yes!' She had clung to him, 'Danny?'

'Yes?'

'Will you tell Serafina?'

Why had she wanted so very badly that he should say yes? She had felt the slight resistance in him. 'No.'

She had repeated his own question. 'Why not?'

'I won't have to. She'll know.'

'Will she mind?'

'Yes.'

'But – I thought – that is –'

'That we lived our own lives? Went our own way? That Serafina has a lover for each day of the week and two for Sundays?' Softly bitter, his tone had cut her to the heart, 'Oh yes. That's all true. But it doesn't stop her from trying to hold with her greedy little fingers anything that she considers to be her own.'

'What – will she do?'

He had laughed a little grimly and shaken his head. 'Don't worry about it, little Mouse. I've many times faced the worst that Serafina can do and survived.'

And now she sat, alone and experiencing for the first time that strange melancholic reaction that can follow the most ecstatic lovemaking, wondering with unjustified and anguished jealousy just what might be the worst that Serafina could do, and just how Danny had learned to counter it: and realizing as she thought it that the achievement of a heart's desire once accomplished could just as easily complicate the business of life as ease it.

'Oh Lord,' she said out loud, a little dolefully, 'What a muddle life can be!' and for some odd reason almost imagined that she could hear Theo Carradine's laughter.

'Well, gel –' Theo squinted at her knowingly, 'somethin's brought a bloom to yer cheeks. Bin sittin' in the sun?'

She had to laugh. It was a little over a month since she and Danny had come together, and Theo was not the only one to notice a difference in her. It was no surprise to her that she looked different; she felt different. She was different. It was as if until now she had lived in chains that had been struck from her by Danny's love. Robert had been the first to sense it and had guessed unerringly at its cause. To his credit he had been happy for her, she suspected partly because her relationship with Danny eased his feelings of guilt with regard to her. All he asked was that she and Danny should be discreet in their liaison. Serafina's reaction had been rather more violent; for a week Danny had carried a livid scratch on his face and – something that had caused their one and only bitter lover's quarrel – another on his back. He had refused to discuss it, and in the end she had had to accept that, though it still rankled these weeks later. One thing she had learned in this past month; Danny's feelings, though sincere and deep were not the same as hers. As he had tried to warn her he was older and more scarred than she. His life had been different, and he was a man. The world for him would not, she realized, end if their love died. For the moment certainly she was the most important thing in his life; but she was not life itself – that would go on, he knew, though the world crumbled and the skies fell. Jessica had not the experience to know that and for her love was all. But she had learned to accept the differences between them and the knowledge that her passion for him was more single-minded than his for her no longer agonized her. He was as he was, and as he was she loved him. That had been her pledge, and she would keep it no matter what happened. It was enough. In his company the world had become a dazzling place. 'The sun,' she said now, 'has very little to do with it. As you well know.'

Theo chuckled.

They were strolling in the Boboli Gardens, the strengthening March sun warming their backs, she slowing her steps to his. He stood for a moment leaning on his stick, panting a little. She looked at him in some concern. 'Are you all right? Should I send for the carriage?'

'No no!' Testily he dismissed her concern. 'Just a bit breathless, that's all. Good God, can't a gel lose her breath on a slope without the world thinks she's dyin'?'

She knew better than to argue. She waited until his breathing eased, then strolled on with him.

'What's all this I hear about Robert an' Arthur goin' ter Rome?'

'That's right. For a fortnight.' Even as she said it a faint frisson of excitement stirred in her body. A fortnight of utter freedom –

'What they goin' ter that Godfersaken place for?'

'It was Arthur's idea, I think. An old friend of his is visiting Rome and has invited him to stay – and of course, Robert must go too –' She hesitated. 'I'm a little surprised really.'

He glanced at her sharply. 'Oh?'

'Well – when Arthur first mentioned the trip Robert said that perhaps he should stay behind – he's working on this opera of his, and he didn't want to leave it. He even said that it might be a good idea for him to get a fortnight's uninterrupted work in on it –'

'So? Why's he goin' then?' They were climbing the steep

flights of steps to the very top of the gardens and he was puffing again.

A little exasperated she caught his arm. 'Theo! Why climb all the way up here? The sun's very warm, you know –'

He made a small, sharp, very rude noise. 'Don't be impertinent, gel. Answer the question. Why's Robert goin' ter Rome instead of spendin' time on this masterpiece of his?'

Used to his acerbity she ignored it. 'I'm not quite sure,' she said, thoughtfully. 'He seems to me to have changed lately – to have lost interest –'

'P'raps he doesn't care for the thought of his wife cuckolding him at every opportunity with a certain handsome hewer of stone?' He giggled like a prurient schoolgirl.

She chose to treat the comment seriously. 'No. I'm sure it isn't that. He doesn't care what I do. I think it's worse than that.'

'How – worse?'

'I think he suspects that his work isn't – won't ever be – what he hoped. He's losing faith in himself. He was so enthusiastic when he started this project, so sure of himself. But now –' She shrugged. 'He's very moody. And the other day I found a heap of ashes in the drawing-room hearth, half-burned. He'd burned pages and pages of manuscript. And twice over the last couple of weeks he's had far too much to drink. He's never done that before –'

Theo, pausing for breath again, nodded.

'– when I asked him why he was going to Rome after all he said –' she hesitated.

'Said what?'

'He said that a lesser talent should always serve a greater in this world, unselfishly and without stint.'

Theo made a small, eloquent and very rude sound.

'Yes,' she said, 'that's what I thought, rather. But what can I do?'

'Nothin' gel. Nothin' at all.' He turned mildly malicious eyes upon her, 'An' tell me – while the cat's away, what's the Mouse planning to do?'

She laughed aloud. 'Mind your own business, you awful old gossip!'

He hooted with laughter. 'Just what I'm doin' young lady! Ah – here we are.'

They had reached the terrace at the top of the gardens. Behind them lay the city. Beyond the lift of land on which they stood lay a magic landscape of green hills that rolled to the mountains beyond. Nestled in the folds of ground white-walled villas and farmhouses could be seen, and tall cypress dotted the hillsides. Vineyards, tiny patches in the distance, lay fresh and budding beneath the spring sunshine. Theo lifted his stick and pointed shakily. 'Pretty, ain't it?'

'It certainly is.'

He cocked his head. 'Fancy a little trip?'

She smiled, humouring him. 'Why not?'

The carriage bowled along the river bank, through the city gate of San Giorgio and out along the via San Leonardo into the warm, spring-fresh countryside.

'Where are we going?' Jessica asked, the sharp clip at which they were travelling alerting her to the fact that this was no aimless afternoon ride.

Theo, still high-coloured and a little breathless leaned back, looking smug. 'Hold yer horses, gel. Wait an' see.'

The trip was short, no more than an hour, yet the narrow lanes that climbed and fell through the gentle hills might have been a whole world away from the busy city streets. Jessica fell to silence. A country girl born and bred she had not realized how much she had missed the green beauty and the life-restoring quiet of the countryside. Through the dappled light and shade of the woodlands they drove, past neat and pretty vineyards, through scruffy villages where hordes of children and dogs ran beside the carriage, the one with flashing teeth and hands outstretched, the other barking with manic excitement at the horses' heels. They passed one or two grand villas, for the greater part hidden behind walls or hedges, their white walls and terracotta roofs glimpsed fleetingly in passing. Then, unexpectedly, the small carriage turned through a gate and drove down a sanded, rather overgrown drive. Jessica looked at Theo in enquiry. Theo said nothing.

They rolled to a halt outside a small, pretty villa, shuttered and faintly neglected-looking. As the sounds of their passage stopped and the horses stood snorting and blowing in the sunlit quiet, Jessica heard somewhere the sound of a cock crowing and a man's voice lifted in urgent, not to say panic-stricken, tones. Seconds later a plump woman, her girth enshrouded in the inevitable black, the equally inevitable apron as big as a bedsheet, hurried around the corner, talking volubly, her hands expressive in the air. Jessica, good as her working knowledge of the language had lately become, could barely understand a word she said.

'Be still, woman,' Theo said, crustily but by no means unkindly, in Italian. 'We've not come on a tour of inspection to catch you out! Just unlock the door for us – my young friend here would like to see the place.'

Still grumbling fluently the woman produced from the folds of her skirt a great bunch of keys, sorted one from the rest and set off for the villa's front door. More slowly Jessica and Theo followed. With the door open Theo flapped a hand at the woman as if she had been a straying chicken. 'Off with you, off with you. A jug of Marco's excellent wine and a plate of your execrable cake for the young lady in half an hour –'

Muttering the old woman left them.

'Theo –?' Jessica began, but Theo held up a gnarled finger. 'Wait.'

They entered the villa. It was not large, but even in the dim light filtered by the shuttered windows Jessica got an impression of airy, pleasantly proportioned rooms, simply furnished, that immediately enchanted her.

'Open the shutters then, gel. You might have cat's eyes, but damned if I have.'

She opened the shutters. The villa was sited perfectly, halfway up a hillside, southfacing, sheltered and quiet. In the distance Florence in her valley shimmered like a jewel on the silver chain of the river. Nearer at hand, beneath the window, beyond an unkempt garden that was delightful with early wild flowers and butterflies, vineyards and lemon groves clothed the hillside in a patchwork of greens and browns. Dark cypress trees pointed their long, Florentine fingers to the sky. 'Theo – it's lovely! Absolutely lovely!'

She ran from room to room, throwing open shutters and windows, letting in the air and the light of the spring day. The layout was simple, four rooms upstairs and four down, a long verandah fronting the southern side, that overlooked the distant city. The furniture too was simple and practical, a comfortable cut above the basic and fitting into this pleasant rustic setting perfectly. Jessica thought she detected Theo's discriminating hand in the deceptively unpretentious decor and in the few apparently casually displayed ornaments and artefacts that brightened the otherwise fairly austere rooms.

'Good Lord –' She touched with a gentle finger a lovely marble bust of a young boy, the purity of the profile silhouetted against a mirrored reflection of sunlight. 'This looks positively Roman.'

'It is.' Theo was obviously enjoying her pleasure.

A small hopeful idea had implanted itself into Jessica's brain. 'Theo – this is your house?'

'It is,' he said again, with a different inflection.

She turned to him, eyes bright, a question on her lips.

'Go on, gel,' he said, blandly, enjoying himself to the full, 'ask away. Them as don't ask don't get, as they say.'

She hesitated still.

He watched her, mischief in his old face. 'Well?'

'Theo – could we? Could – Danny and I –' she had an odd difficulty in getting the name out, '– could we come here, while Robert's away?'

He turned and stumped from the room. 'I'll think about it.'

They spent a blissful week there, at the Villa Francesca, and for that week it was as if no-one and nowhere else in the world existed. For the first time they spent long days together, and for the first time they went to sleep on their loving and woke with the morning together. Their physical need for each other never seemed to be assuaged, and was stimulated and enhanced by the ease and enjoyment of their companionship. Jessica had never believed in, let alone experienced, such

348

happiness, and she knew that whatever befell them in the future this week would be for them both a shining memory of sheer delight. She lived for the moment, savouring each second, loving as much the two days of unseasonal rain that penned them indoors as the sunshine that enticed them out and into the footways of the hills. She enjoyed dour Lucia's peasant cooking as she might that of a royal chef, and found in Marco's homemade wines a sparkle she had never yet discovered in the vintages of champagne.

With reluctance and the first stirrings of resentment, upon Robert's return to Florence she too returned to the city.

Three weeks later, she knew that she was pregnant.

The timing was not the best it might be. Since his return from Rome Robert had been moody and withdrawn. He no longer spent the hours he had at the piano, and she had not seen him put pen to paper in weeks. His enthusiasm for the project of the opera seemed to have been lost entirely. Indeed she began to suspect that he had abandoned the writing altogether.

Tentatively she questioned him about it.

He jerked away from her irritably. He had been drinking – another sign of the change that had overtaken him in the past weeks. 'Don't nag, Jessica. It's none of your business.'

Hurt, she was silent.

He shook his head. 'I'm sorry. I didn't mean that. It's just –' He ran a hand through his uncharacteristically tousled hair.

'What? Robert – what is it? What's the matter?'

He took a long time to answer. 'It's no good, Jessie,' he said at last, tiredly, 'I have to face it. I'm deceiving myself. Making a fool of myself.'

'In what way?' The defeat in his face struck her to the heart. For a moment she forgot her own dilemma.

'Arthur's friend in Rome,' he said, after a long silence, 'was a musician, and a composer. A real one. He told me the truth. I had known it I think for some time. I simply hadn't faced it.'

'What truth?'

'That I'm mediocre. Worse than mediocre. I will never produce anything of any merit –'

'No! Robert, you mustn't let yourself believe such things! Signor Donatti says –'

'Signor Donatti is a nice old man who wouldn't hurt a fly and who likes an easy life discussing over a jug of wine how much of the known text of *King Lear* is Shakespeare's and how much the product of a sixteenth-century actor's promptbook! It's no good, Jessica. I have to face it. It's true. It's always been true. The only thing I ever could do well was to sing. Now that's gone, and there's nothing I can do, nothing I can find to take its place. Arthur's friend was right – brutal, but right. I have no future either as a composer or as a musician.'

'You should keep trying,' she said, obstinately and unwittingly voicing her own philosophy.

He shook his head. 'No.'

'But – what of your opera? You were so certain that it was a perfect idea – ?'

'It was. It is!' He turned sharply. 'The opera will go on. Arthur's –' He stopped.

Her mouth tightened a little. 'What? What is Arthur going to do?'

'He's going to – help me with it. When he has time.'

The hesitation spoke for itself. 'Help you? Or take it over and write it himself?'

He sighed. 'All right, yes. Arthur will write it, and I'll help him.' Before she could speak he turned from her, stood with his back to her, looking out of the window. 'Don't say what you're thinking, Jessica. Please. I know you don't like Arthur, and it saddens me. I just wish you could see in him what I do. He's a fine man, and a splendid friend. He has courage, insight, talent – and something more – a something that adds a different dimension to everything he does –'

'And his friend in Rome obviously thought he could write the opera?' Jessica's voice was absolutely neutral.

'Jessica, don't talk like that! As if Arthur has – stolen the idea –'

'Well, hasn't he?'

'No! I've offered it to him, freely and without stint. He'll make something of it that I never could. I don't mind. I really don't.' The look in his eyes belied the words, but she could say nothing. 'At least it will live. Arthur will give it the life that I never could.'

'And you? What will you do?'

'I'll help him. Support him in every way I can.'

And that, she knew was the end of that. If she had ever harboured hope that Arthur's domination of Robert might some time wane she gave up that hope in that moment, seeing the fervour in his dark eyes, the stubborn set to his mouth. Robert needed a star to follow, and he had found one. He was by nature a squire rather than a knight, one of the devoted herd rather than the shepherd. In Arthur, for good or ill, he had fulfilled his need for a master, and in his own way he was happy. Nothing would change that now.

Perhaps strangely the first person that Jessica told of the coming child was Theo. She had to tell someone, and she was afraid, for different reasons, to broach the subject to either of the two men closest involved, and so she found herself confiding in the worst gossip in Florence in the absolute certainty that he would not betray her confidence until she was ready. His first reaction did not surprise her at all. Prepared for anything from derision to disgust she got both in full measure – 'What yer thinkin' of, gel? Yer gone mad?' – She was, however, taken aback when he started making plans for the child. 'What yer goin' ter call the little sod, eh? Poor little bugger's got ter have a name, hasn't he? An' where yer goin' ter get a nurse that ain't goin' ter tie the poor wee beast in knots fer the first six months of his life?'

She laughed. 'I haven't thought of a name yet. It might be a girl, you know. And Angelina will make a perfect nursemaid – and I certainly won't allow her to swaddle the child, whatever the silly fashion still is in Florence. I thought you didn't like babies?'

'I don't. Can't stand 'em. Pies is the best place fer babies. You told anyone else yet?'

She shook her head.

He raised sparse brows. 'No-one at all?'

'No.'

He grinned his now spectacularly toothless smile. 'Anyone'd think I was the poor little bastard's father!' he cackled, not without some satisfaction at the improbable idea.

The telling, when it came, as it had to, was not easy. There was no question in her mind but that she would have the child, whatever happened. From the first moment she had known of its conception the thought of it had all but obsessed her, heart and mind. In an uncertain world this small soul would be hers, to love, to cherish, to guide, to protect from all ills, all evils. A small piece of Danny from whom no-one, not even Danny himself, could part her. But for all that she did not underestimate the possible problems.

She told Danny first, on a warm summer's afternoon at the apartment in the via Condotta. She could leave it no longer. The firmness of her breasts and the darkening of her nipples she knew would soon tell their own story. She told him in the quiet moments after their lovemaking, flatly and apparently without emotion, whilst pure panic fluttered in her breast like a frantic captured bird.

'You're sure?'

'Yes.'

'How long?'

'About three months, I think.'

A small silence. 'Why didn't you tell me before?'

She did not reply.

'Jessie?'

'I – was afraid.' She got the words out with some difficulty.

'Of what?'

She turned on her stomach, laying her forehead on her crossed arms. For her life she could not look at him. 'I don't know. I thought you might not be happy. I suppose I thought you might be angry. I was afraid – afraid you might –'

'What?'

'I want this baby,' she said, fiercely, into her arms, her voice muffled.'I want it. I won't – do anything to hurt it –'

He seized her by the shoulder and turned her to face him, leaning above her, his face dark with anger. 'What are you saying?'

Suddenly she was crying. 'I thought you might not want it! I thought you might try – to make me –' She could not go on.

'Good God!' He caught her to him, angry and tender at once. 'What do you take me for? You little fool! You honestly think I'd put you through that? If you want the child, have it. It's your decision.'

She struggled from him. 'Is that all?'

'What do you mean?'

'"If you want the child, have it?" Is that all you can say? What about you? Don't you want it?'

He hesitated. 'Of course I do.'

'You don't! I can tell you don't!'

'For heaven's sake!' He kissed her wet cheek in gentle exasperation. 'What do you expect? Give me time, my little love. Give me time to get used to the idea –'

She told Robert a week later, and if anything that was harder. They had seen little of each other lately, their lives seeming to have separated completely, and she had to make a point of asking him to stay at home to talk with her. After she had told him, stumbling a little over the words, he was silent for a very long time.

'Robert?' she asked, tentatively.

He stirred. 'What do you want me to say?'

'I – I don't know. But we have to talk, don't we? We have to discuss it. In the world's eyes the child will be yours. You must realize that?' He must realize too, she knew, that if he repudiated her and the child, in self-defence she would have to have the marriage annulled, with all the scandal and disgrace for him that might involve. Desperately she did not want to use that threat.

He nodded.

'Well?'

His breathing was quiet. She found that her hands were clenched so fiercely that the fingernails were cutting painfully into the skin. With an effort she forced herself to relax.

He lifted his head, on his face the very shadow of a bitterly sad smile. 'Have your baby, Jessica. I give you my word that it

353

will have my name and my protection. That's the least I can do. To all intents and purposes the child will be ours and I swear I will never go back on my promise to care for it.'

The release from the deadly anxiety she had suffered these past weeks was overwhelming. She bowed her face into her hands, her shoulders shaking, the tension draining from her.

He laid a light arm across her shoulders, the first time he had touched her in months. 'Don't cry, Jessica. I've always hated to see you cry.'

She lifted a tear-stained, smiling face. 'It's just such a relief, Robert! I didn't know what you might say – what you might do. How can I thank you?'

'No thanks are necessary,' he smiled, and for a moment the old Robert sat there, his hand in hers, comforting her after a whipping from MacKenzie, or a squabble with Giles. 'I owe you much that I can never repay,' he said. 'This is my thanks to you. And anyway –' he smiled again, a happier smile, 'what are friends for?'

It was not an easy pregnancy, and the dust and heat of a Florentine summer made it worse. In August, with the heat at its uncomfortable height Theo turned up at her door one morning and insisted with apparently autocratic insensitivity that she accompany him on a carriage ride. Faced with his waspish and adamant refusal to listen to her protests she dressed lethargically and joined him in the shaded carriage.

She could not deny that she felt better the moment they left the dust and the noise of the city. When they turned along the familiar lane that led to the Villa Francesca she smiled her delight, looking forward to a lemonade and a slice of Lucia's excellent cake on the cool verandah. She had not been to the villa since her week there with Danny earlier in the year – the week when the baby about which she felt so passionately had been conceived.

When they turned into the drive, the surprise was immediate. 'But – Theo! How very pretty!'

The wilderness of garden had been tamed. Steps had been laid down the hillside through tumbling rock-plants and shrubs to a paved area shaded by a small grove of lemon trees. A fountain played, sparkling in the sunlight. Beneath it the steps continued to a small brick building, a single-storey summer house from the look of it. The villa itself had been painted and gleamed in the bright sunshine. The shutters were thrown wide and fine curtains drifted in the mountain breeze. As they stepped down from the carriage a small bevy of servants presented themselves shyly at the steps, presided over by a beaming Marcos and a still happily grumbling Lucia.

Jessica looked at Theo in astonishment.

He did not bat an eyelid, but banged his stick upon the ground in counterfeit of peevish impatience. 'In with yer then, gel – in with yer –'

The place had been transformed. From a rustic country retreat it had been turned into a comfortable home. Dining room, drawing room, morning room and library – already well stocked with books – downstairs. And upstairs three bedrooms, beautifully appointed and a nursery suite, complete with tiny cradle. She had completed the tour in a stunned silence. At the door of the nursery bedroom she turned to Theo. He was watching her for once without the evil grin that so often accompanied one of his more unexpected actions. 'Yer like it, gel?'

'Like it? It's wonderful! It's – it's the most beautiful place I've ever seen!'

'Can't have yer livin' in that filthy midden of a city in your condition. Not good fer you, not good fer the poor little bugger yer carryin' –' He turned away.

'Theo!'

The word stopped him. He turned, belligerently. 'What?'

'It's – this – is for me?'

'You know any other breedin' women?'

'But – I can't let you do this?'

'Oh? How you goin' ter stop me? You tellin' me yer want ter stay in that dirty oven of an apartment of yours?'

She overlooked the excusable exaggeration. 'Of course not –'

'Oh –' He interrupted her, limping past her to the window and pointing to where the tiled roof of the summer house could be seen. 'Forgot ter mention – small apartment an' music room at the bottom of the garden. The two dear boys can talk in Greek an' play famous composers down there to their heart's content. Can't have the poor little sod woken up by their caterwaulin' –'

She was overwhelmed. As he stumped back past her she caught his hand in hers. 'Theo – how can I thank you?'

'No need.'

'Of course there's need,' she hesitated a little. 'I don't understand –'

'What?'

'Why you're so good to me? No-one – no friend, no family – no-one! – has ever been so kind.'

For the briefest of moments she thought he would answer seriously. Then the two yellowed teeth that were all that were left to him appeared, gleaming barbarously. 'Never know when me tastes might change, gel. Never know when I might fancy a young female agen –'

Shaking her head in amused exasperation she followed him as he cackled his breathless, difficult way down the stairs.

A predictable problem did arise. Robert did not want to remove himself too far from Arthur; Arthur refused point blank to exile himself to the country. A brief and extremely one-sided interview with Theo, however, provoked a change of mind, and Arthur was persuaded to persuade Robert that a country setting was very conducive to genius. In return – apart from the raising of Arthur's allowance, which was strictly a matter between himself and Theo – two carriages were provided and the narrow road through the mountains improved to make access to the city easier. And so arrangements were reached that suited everyone. Since Theo absolutely refused to accept any rent on the villa they were able to keep on the apartment in the city. Robert spent part of the week there and part in the country, for the sake of appearances. Arthur was a frequent visitor, as was Theo – but not as frequent as Danny. Often as she sat in the pretty garden, her expanding girth tying her close to home she watched Danny as he strode down the hillside coming back from a walk, Marco's small terrier, that had adopted him as soon as he had set foot in the house, following at his heels, and thought that for those times they were together they might indeed have been a happily married young couple looking forward to the birth of their first child. Of those times they were apart she tried not to think. Sometimes days on end would pass without a visit, and when she saw him it was an unspoken rule between them that no questions were asked about where he had been or with whom. He had his work, and that inevitably occupied some of his time. He had his friends, and from them she would not have dreamed of parting him if she could. He had his wife: and the relationship between those two was, Danny had made it quite clear, not to be questioned or discussed. In his own way he loved Jessica, and she knew it. His anticipation of the coming child had become almost as great as hers. That, she told herself, for now was enough.

Theo Carradine, mentor of the irregular menage that he had so deftly manipulated, watched and chuckled at the diverse pleasures of the study of human nature.

On a damp December day in her pretty firelit bedroom in the Villa Francesca Jessica, aided competently by Angelina and Lucia who had developed a fierce and unlikely conspiracy of affection for their young mistress, was delivered of a daughter. Gabriella FitzBolton was a black-eyed coquette from the moment she was born. Her first unfocused glances conquered the men in her life with ease. Danny was fierce with pride. Robert was gentle. Cynical Theo was – absurdly as he was the first to admit – enslaved. Jessica, holding the child, feeling her mouth at her breast as she sucked contentedly, had never in her life been happier.

In the few happy years that followed, watching her daughter grow, Jessica sometimes managed to convince herself that this idyll need never end. The news that filtered more irregularly than ever from England gave her no cause for concern – Patrick after a shaky start at Harrow had perfectly obviously found his feet and was happy. It was not long before, wrapped in his new life and new friends, he stopped writing altogether. Her mother's letters did not change a jot; formal and brief they reminded Jessica of their writer – sharp and to the point, the pillar of the family, never changing. Sarah's gossipy letters were still an occasional delight. Meanwhile in the Italian sun Gabriella grew straight and strong. Robert, though quiet and frequently absent from the villa, seemed content with things as they were. Danny loved her, and she him, fiercely as ever. Theo's health failed a little, as he was bound to do, and she worried about him – but always he rallied and as with everything else she put her fears for him to the back of her mind and refused to think about them. Let tomorrow's worries take care of themselves. For today the sun shone, and she was happy.

Part Four

1823–1826

Chapter Thirteen

The moment she saw the letter Jessica knew, with no need to open it, that the idyll had ended. She recognized at once her mother's neat, handsome writing; recognized even quicker the significance of the directions upon the envelope. Since it was not addressed to her she did not open it, but laid it upon the table in the dining room to await Robert's return. It was February, and snow had fallen on the hills. The distant city was veiled in cloud.

She stood at the window, taking in the familiar view. For four years now this had been her home, and she had been happy. Those years had been a gift from the gods of fortune; she had known for some time that a price would be exacted, knew now without doubt that the time had come.

She walked back to the table and stood looking pensively down at the letter. 'To: Sir Robert FitzBolton, Bart.'

It came to her with a small start of surprise that if the title had indeed come to Robert then she must now be Lady FitzBolton. She wondered, sadly, when Robert's father – that calm, kindly, unassuming man – had died; and why the first news of it should come not from Robert's mother but her own. She wondered too, with some misgiving, how Robert would take the news.

She tried not to think of Danny.

'Mama – Mama –!' Four-year-old Gabriella tumbled into the room, bright-eyed and flushed of face, gabbling in rapid Italian. 'Angelina says she'll take me out into the snow if you say she can – oh, please, please Mama say yes! It isn't very cold and I have my –'

Jessica held up a hand to stop the torrent of words. 'English, Gabriella!' she scolded indulgently. 'Speak English, now!'

The child pulled a comical face. 'Angelina say – says – she will take me into the – the –'

'Snow,' Jessica supplied.

'– snow, if you say yes. Please? May we?' The words were stilted and heavily accented.

'Yes. You may tell Angelina yes, providing that you wrap up well.'

'Thank you, Mama!' In her impulsive way the child flung her arms about her mother and hugged her, then turned and ran from the room, calling excitedly for Angelina.

Jessica watched her go. Of all the blessings this past five years had brought, this small bright child was the greatest. Gabriella was like a ray of sunshine. Jessica found herself looking once more at the letter. She could not say with absolute truth that she had not been expecting it. For many reasons – and not the least of them the child she loved so dearly – she had known for some time that the moment was approaching when they must return home. She had tried to ignore it, but in the past months the conviction had grown. Gabriella ran wild, petted and spoiled, more Italian than English, a little gypsy; untutored and indisciplined. If she were to know and to understand anything of her English heritage she must be introduced to it, and soon. Last summer's sunshine still glowed upon her smooth olive skin, her first language was Italian; another few years and she would never adjust to living in England. And meanwhile their money was running low, and Robert was earning nothing. Sooner or later they would have to go home.

She picked up the letter, stood looking down at it thoughtfully. 'Sir Robert FitzBolton, Bart.' How would Robert take this? In these past years she knew he had dismissed from his mind any thought of the England that for him had held so many unhappy memories. While in some small corner of her heart Jessica had always nursed the knowledge that one day she would return, Robert had in truth eaten the fruit of the lotus-tree, and had obdurately turned his face from any suggestion. His life was here, his devotion to Arthur, far from waning, was stronger than ever. He had given up his own ambitions and aspirations – he no longer attended the Maestro's classes, no longer spoke of a future in the composition of music – he had become Arthur Leyland's acolyte, a willing worshipper at the feet of that talented, handsome and vain young man.

No – Robert would not want to go home.

She turned, the letter still in her hand, and walked back to the window. As she stood there, tapping the crisp envelope with a nervous finger, a rider came from under the trees that shadowed the sandy drive. She smiled to see him; Danny may have conquered his initial fear of horses, but he would never make a rider. His dark head was bare despite the cold, the long mouth smiling as he looked towards the house, knowing that she would be there watching for him. She drew a long breath against the warm and painful rise of emotion that the sight of him always brought. Five years, occasionally stormy as they had been, had not served to change her feelings for Danny O'Donnel. Far from it.

'Dan – nee! Dan-nee!' A small bundle of energy launched herself across the garden. 'Dan-nee!'

Danny slid from the horse's back in time to catch Gabriella and swing her high in the air, squealing with laughter. Their voices came to the watcher in the window. Chewing her thumbnail, her face sombre, she turned away.

He joined her, moments later, still laughing.

'That little tyke!' He tilted Jessica's face to his and kissed her lightly. 'She's got more energy than a barrowload of monkeys! She never stops!' He tweaked Jessica's hair teasingly. 'I really can't imagine where she gets it from, can you?'

Jessica smiled.

He strode to the fire, turned his back to it, lifting his coattails. 'God, but it's cold out there! Do you know, there are three inches of snow in the city? –' He stopped, for the first time aware of her silence. 'Jessie? Is something wrong?'

She nodded.

He came to her swiftly, concern on his face. 'What is it? You aren't ill – ?'

'No. Nothing like that.' She hesitated. 'There's – a letter from home.'

Barely perceptibly his face altered. The only time she had ever spoken of the possibility of a return to Suffolk they had quarrelled, and the subject had never been raised again. 'Bad news?' he asked, his voice level.

'I'm afraid it must be. The letter is from my mother. It's addressed to Sir Robert FitzBolton.'

It took a moment for the significance of that to sink in. 'So – Robert's father is dead?'

'He must be. It's strange that the letter should be from my mother and not his.'

'You haven't read it?'

'No. It's addressed to Robert.'

Silence fell. He walked back to the fire, leaned against the mantlepiece staring sober-faced into the flames. 'You think – she wants you to go home?'

'Almost certainly.'

He raised his head. 'What will you do?'

She did not answer.

He pushed himself away from the mantlepiece, frowning. 'Jessica?'

She shrugged, helplessly. 'I suppose – we'll have to go.'

'No!' He shook his head fiercely. 'No – you don't *have* to go! Why should you?'

She turned away from him, not wanting to see the dawning anger in his face. 'Danny – please – we have to face it. If Robert's father is dead – and he must be – then we have to go back. Please – don't make it harder than it already is –'

'It isn't hard. It's very simple. You don't have to go.'

'But we do!' Her voice shook a little. 'Please Danny – you don't understand –'

'You're right. I don't.' In a couple of strides he was beside her, his hand on her arm, swinging her to face him. It was a long time since she had seen him so fierce. 'You're telling me that you're going to leave? Just like that? Is that all our life together means to you?'

She stood still, swallowing the words that she knew would

infuriate him more than ever. We don't have a life together. Whether you admit it or not your life is still with Serafina, however much you say you hate her. She spoke very quietly. 'Danny, you know that isn't true. You know how much I love you.'

'Then how can you talk of leaving?'

'But – can't you see? – If Robert's father is dead, then we have to! There's Robert's mother – Old Hall – the land – the tenants – we can't just desert them –'

'Why not? What has any of it to do with you? With us?'

'It has everything to do with me!' She obstinately resisted the anger that was beginning to rise to meet his own. 'Danny – I don't want to go – you know I don't! It will break my heart to leave. But there are other things to be taken into consideration apart from my own happiness –'

'Yours? What about mine? What about Gabriella's?'

She caught his hand. 'Danny – please – don't let's quarrel about it! Wouldn't you – couldn't you come with us? Things wouldn't have to change all that much –' She knew as she made the plea how childishly silly it sounded.

He shook free of her. 'Have you taken leave of your senses altogether? "Things wouldn't have to change"? In what way, tell me, can they possibly remain the same if you run back to England? Are you suggesting for a moment that we could live like this –' he gestured, his arms wide, '– at Old Hall? Really, Lady FitzBolton, give me credit for a little more intelligence than that!'

She flushed at his sarcastic use of the title. She stepped back from him. In the silence that followed Gabriella's young voice called, and was answered by Angelina. Outside the horse that Danny had ridden was led away, its hooves scrunching on the gravel.

Jessica watched him for a long moment. 'If this letter says what I think it must say,' she said at last, quietly, 'then Robert and I are going to have to return home. We have obligations. You can surely see that?'

'What about your obligations here? To me? To Gabriella?'

'Gabriella won't suffer by being taken back to England,' she said, evenly, 'I'll see to that. In fact I believe it will be good for her. Danny, we've had this out before. She is, in law and in her own belief Robert's child. He's been a good father to her. Old Hall is her home as much as it is ours. You agreed. At the moment she's running wild. Her English is dreadful. She's more Italian than English –'

'What's wrong with that?'

Her control broke. 'Oh, Danny *stop it*! You know what I'm saying is true! You *know* we have no alternative but to go! Why make it harder?'

He brought his hand down with considerable violence onto the table. 'You don't have to go!'

'We do! We *do*! But – oh, Danny, why not come with us? Please? We'll work something out –'

He flung to face her, his long, tense hands spread before him. 'Go with you? To what purpose? To be a faithful servant to the lord and lady of the manor?'

'No –!'

'To be Lady FitzBolton's kept man? Her ne'er–do–well lover? Don't be ridiculous, Jessica – what kind of a fool's paradise are you living in? We live as we live because we're here! You could no more transport our –' his mouth turned down sardonically '– our menage – lock stock and barrel to Melbury than you could transport the sunshine of Italy to Suffolk! Can you imagine it? You'd be the laughing-stock of the county!'

'I wouldn't care!'

'Oh, yes you would. And so would I, and so would Robert, and so, as she grew, would Gabriella! No, Jessica – there's nothing in England for me. In England I would be nothing. In England I would lose you more surely and more painfully than if I let you go now. And besides –' he stopped.

'And besides,' she finished for him, very quietly, 'there's Serafina.'

'I didn't say that.'

'You didn't have to.' Her voice was suddenly weary. Here indeed was the long-standing cause of friction between them. For all his protestations, for all his bitterness Danny's wife

366

still held him in strange thrall. He hated her, she apparently despised him, yet still their marriage held them captive each to the other. Many, many times over these past years Danny had come to Jessica with livid wounds that could only have been caused by Serafina's raking fingernails. Six months before he had all but lost his life in a bar brawl. Devotedly Jessica had nursed him, night after feverish night she had watched with him as he fought the infection in the knife wound. And all the time she had known what he had never told her – that the injury had been taken defending his wilful and beautiful wife's dubious honour. Unable in her own situation to show too strong a resentment of the situation yet it had cut her to the heart to know that when Danny left her it was to return to Serafina. 'Oh, Danny, please –' she said now, tiredly, 'must we quarrel? We don't even know what's in the letter yet. It might not be what we fear.'

He stood, tense as strung wire for a moment longer, until he relaxed and took the hand she offered. But his face was still sombre. He drew her to him and she leaned against him, her face turned to his chest.

On the table the letter lay, innocent and implacable harbinger of change.

Robert stared at the envelope for a very long while, making no move to open it.

'Oh, for heaven's sake, you might as well read it,' Jessica said at last, more sharply than she had intended. 'Whatever's in it won't cease to be just because you haven't opened the beastly thing.'

He still made no move.

'Robert! Please! Read the damned thing or I will myself!' Her nerves were strung to breaking point.

Reluctantly he broke the seal. In tense silence she watched him. His eyes scanned the page swiftly.

'Well?'

He wiped his mouth with the back of his hand, a small, nervous gesture. 'Father's dead.'

'When?'

He frowned. 'Last July.'

She stared at him. 'Last July? Why didn't someone let us know before? Your mother must surely have written? Did the letter go astray?'

His eyes were running over the letter again. 'Wait. Your mother's writing – it's a little difficult – not as clear as usual – r"Sorry to be the source of such sad news – your mother not herself since the tragic loss of your father – advise a swift return – your father's affairs –"' he trailed off. 'Oh, damn!' he said, bitterly, 'Damn and blast it!'

'Your mother's ill?'

'I don't know. "Not herself" your mother says. And it seems that father's affairs are in a bit of a state.'

A wind had blown up since the afternoon. In the silence it rattled an ill-fitting shutter. Lucia's sharp voice lifted in the kitchen, to be answered by Marco's conciliatory one.

Robert, the letter still in his hand, dropped into a chair and sat with bowed head and slumped shoulders.

'We have to go home,' Jessica said, quietly. Since the emotional scene with Danny that afternoon she had had a chance to adapt a little to the idea and her voice was calm.

He shook his head. 'No.'

'Robert, please. We have to. You know it. We can't possibly leave your mother alone, in God only knows what state to cope with God only knows what kind of mess. There must be something very strange going on that Mother felt she had to write. Why didn't your mother write? Why didn't Clara? Does Mother say?'

He shrugged dispiritedly. 'No.'

She took a long breath. 'We have to go.'

There was a very long silence, then, 'I suppose so,' he said, his voice dull.

She stood up, looking about the pretty room that in the past four happy years had been home. 'Very soon,' she said.

He nodded.

'I'll tell Lucia. We'll have to start to pack.'

Breaking the news to Theo was more difficult than she had

imagined it would be. Because of the particularly bad winter Jessica had not visited the city since Christmas, and so had not seen the old man in two months. Calling at the via del Corso two days after the arrival of her mother's letter she was shocked to find Theo confined to bed, propped up with a mass of pillows, his shrunken frame all but lost in the huge bed, his bald pate with its wispy hair wigless, his unrouged face pale as death. He looked very old indeed, and mortally sick.

'Theo – are you ill?'

'Of course I am, you silly beast! Why else would I be lying here like a helpless infant?' he snapped, querulously. He tilted his head sharply to receive her kiss on his dry, cold cheek, his eyes going past her to the door. 'Where's the child?'

'At home, I'm afraid. I thought it too cold to bring her out.'

He tutted, annoyed. 'Nonsense! Utter nonsense! Child's as strong as an ox. Takes after her silly mother.'

She sat down, taking his hand. 'Theo? What's wrong?'

'What's right's more like it. Tired is all, but the silly quack won't have it. Says it's me heart.'

She frowned, concerned.

He waved a weak, impatient hand. 'All nonsense, of course. Nothin' wrong with me heart.'

She smiled, gently. 'You mean it's as hard as ever?'

He chuckled, caught his breath and coughed, wincing. 'What brings you here? Thought you'd given up visiting poor old Theo?'

'Oh, don't be so silly! You know why I haven't been. The weather's been terrible.'

He cast a meaningful glance at the window. 'Don't look any better to me today.'

She sighed. 'No. It isn't.'

'So. What brings you here?'

She did not for a moment answer. Then, 'We have to go home,' she said, quietly. 'Robert's father died last year, and his mother is apparently ill. We have to go.'

In the silence that followed he watched her, the pale old eyes unusually sympathetic. Finally he stirred. 'So. The carnival is

369

done. Off with the mask and the magical ball gown, child. Real life calls you.'

She was surprised that he had voiced her own feelings so very aptly. 'Yes.'

'Think yerself lucky,' he said. 'Not many have what you've had.'

'I know. But it isn't easy.'

'Apart from farting, what is?'

The tart humour brought a small smile.

'You're takin' the child?' It was only just a question.

'Of course. There's never been any argument about that. Robert thinks of her – treats her – as his own daughter. Old Hall is her home.'

'And Danny?'

She shook her head. 'I haven't seen him since I told him. We quarrelled. I wanted him to come with us –'

'He won't.'

She said nothing, picked with a sharp fingernail at the bedspread.

The grotesque head shook slowly upon the mound of pillows. 'Not in a month of Sundays, gel. Would you expect it? Would he be your Danny if he tamely trailed behind you like a trained monkey?'

She laid a hand upon his gnarled, discoloured one. 'I'll miss you Theo,' she said, apparently inconsequentially. 'Very much indeed.'

'Miss me bad tempered tongue, you mean. Who'll keep yer in order, gel, without me around?'

She smiled. 'I'll never forget you. Never ever. I'll write. Often.'

He held her eyes. 'Don't waste yer energy, gel.' The words were smothered in a sudden bout of coughing. Face scarlet he clung to her hand, choking.

'Theo, you're ill! Let me send for someone –!'

'No!' He caught his breath again. The hand that clung to hers was surprisingly strong. 'Keep them stupid women away from me. Fussin' and frettin'. Can't stand it. Silly bitches.'

'You must take care of yourself.'

His face creased into a parody of his old wicked grin. 'Too late, gel, as usual. The Good Lord's doin' that. He's caught up with me at last, it seems.' He laid back on the pillows, his breath laboured. 'So –' he said at last, 'You're goin' home.'

'Yes.'

'Best place on God's earth.' The words were so quietly spoken she thought for a moment she had misheard them.

'You – you think I'm right? Robert doesn't want to go. I think for two pins he'd stay. But – oh, Theo! – how can we?'

'Yer could if yer really wanted to.'

She shook her head.

He let out a dry rustle of laughter that brought on another fit of coughing. 'Tell me why yer goin'.'

'Robert's mother's ill –'

'That all?' The old eyes snapped open, bright and perceptive as they had ever been.

She held them for a moment with her own, then let out a small explosive breath. 'No. Of course not.'

'What then, yer Ladyship?' he asked, slyly.

'Old Hall. The house, the land, the people –'

'Homesick.'

'A little.'

He nodded, satisfied. 'Lie to the world by all means, gel. But don't try to lie to old Theo. An' don't –' he added, softly '– ever try ter lie ter yerself. Y'er goin' home because the time has come, and yer know it. Y'er goin' home because the place is in yer blood, an' there's nothin' yer can do about it.' He moved his head a little. 'Y'er lucky, gel. Yer know that? Damn' lucky. I envy yer. Just think o' that. Old Theo envies yer!'

She stayed with him for half an hour, during most of which time he slept. As she stood to tiptoe away he opened one eye. 'Bring that scallawag child to say goodbye before yer go.'

She bent to kiss him, gently. 'I will.'

The last and inevitable row with Danny was a bitter one. He could not – or rather she suspected would not – see or accept her reasons for returning to England with Robert. He accused

371

her of faithlessness and betrayal, complained bitterly that she no longer loved him. She, in tears, was adamant. She loved him, she would always love him, but she had to go. He was angrier than she had ever seen him.

'If you go I swear you'll never set eyes on me again.'

'Danny, don't say that! Please don't. You know where I am. I'll wait for you –'

'You'll wait for a very long time.' His voice was hard.

'Why are you so angry? It isn't my fault –'

'*You don't have to go!*'

'I do! Oh, God! – Why can't you understand that?'

He looked for a terrible moment as if he might have struck her. He backed away from her, his hands clenched at his sides, then turned and strode to the door.

'Danny!'

He stopped, his back to her.

'Remember St Agatha's,' she said, very quietly. 'It's still there. It will always be there. And so will I. With Gabriella.'

He left the room with no word of farewell, slamming the door behind him.

She did not see him again before they left. He did not come near the villa and pride prevented her from visiting him at the apartment in the city that he still shared with Serafina. Miserably she oversaw the preparations for their departure. Small Gabriella was at first shocked and then intrigued by this unexpected move to the unknown, any terrors removed from the adventure by the fact that her beloved Angelina was travelling to England with them as her nurse. Tickets were bought, possessions crated. She saw little of Robert who, miserable as she, spent these last precious days with Arthur and left the bulk of the work to Jessica, which at least gave her little time to brood on the sudden and shattering break with Danny. On the day before they left she visited Theo again, taking Gabriella with her. The visit was not a success. The old man was failing, the child overawed by the oppressive atmosphere of the sickroom.

As she took her leave Jessica could not entirely blink away the tears.

'Fer Gawd's sake gel,' he said, with amiable asperity. 'Turn off the waterworks. This is my scene, not yours. Fine thing when a gel's last performance gets upstaged by a silly chit's overactin' –'

She kissed the hand she held. 'Thank you, Theo. Thank you for everything.'

He lay quietly for a moment. Almost any effort seemed to be too much for him now. But when she made to stand the pressure of his hand drew her back down beside him. 'If I'd – had a daughter –' he said, speaking with difficulty.

She waited. 'Yes?'

The pale, tired eyes searched her face. And then, predictably, the gleam of mischief appeared, echoed by the ghost of the old, imp's grin. 'She'd ha' bin well ruined by now, wouldn't she? Off with yer, gel. Go live yer life. Yer doin' the right thing, yer know that don't yer?'

'Yes.'

'Well go on an' do it then, an' stop botherin' me.'

They left Florence at the beginning of March, travelling this time straight up the west coast into a France whose dreams of Imperial glory had finally seen an end on Napoleon's deathbed on Elba the year before. The journey was arduous, made more so by a fretful child and a mildly hysterical Angelina who had never until now strayed further from Florence than the Villa Francesca, and who could not be convinced that every Frenchman she saw was not bent upon rape or at the very least murder. At last in desperation Jessica had to threaten to send her back, and the thought of being parted from her darling Gabriella stiffened her backbone and stilled her tongue marvellously. Reaching Calais at last they boarded one of the new passenger steamers that had the year before begun to ply between the French and English coasts and in the miraculously short time of three hours, in bright spring weather they sighted at last the white cliffs of a Dover that looked at the same time incredibly familiar and ridiculously strange to English eyes that had become so accustomed to foreign cities. They landed on English soil on a lovely May day that might

373

have been sent to welcome them home. Jessica thought she had never seen anything so green as the lovely Kentish countryside. She had forgotten the majesty of oak and elm, the pale and delicate delight of a field of wild flowers blowing in the wind. They rested overnight at Canterbury, and again in London. Then they took the coach at last for Sudbury, and home.

The FitzBolton carriage awaited them at the inn at Sudbury. Stiffly they climbed aboard whilst Blowers the coachman saw to the stowing of what luggage had travelled with them. 'Welcome home, Sir Robert, Your Ladyship –' he had said when they had met, and the titles rang strangely still in Jessica's ears. When at last the loaded carriage, squeaking noisily, rolled into the Suffolk lanes she found herself watching eagerly for landmarks.

'Look, Gabriella – that's the stream that feeds the lake at New Hall –' She had spent hours on the journey speaking to the child of her new home. '– and there are the gates – do you see the big house in the distance? That's New Hall, where I lived when I was a little girl like you. Your Grandmama –' she corrected herself quickly, ' –one of your Grandmamas lives there still.'

The child watched from the window, overtired, overawed and unusually silent. Angelina huddled in a corner shivering in the fresh May air that came through the open window. They skirted the parkland of New Hall and crossed the river.

'Oh, Robert –isn't it lovely? I had almost forgotten!' For the moment the pleasure of homecoming outweighed all else for Jessica. Two swans moved, regal heads high, upon the wide waters of the river. The willows bowed gracefully, drifting in the current and in the breeze. In the distance the sound of the weir made itself heard over the noisy movement of the carriage. In the shadowed woodlands across the water the misty, pale carpet of the budding bluebells delighted the eye. 'Look – oh, look! There's St Agatha's.' Like an eager child Jessica leaned to the window and watched the small, ancient church on the other side of the river as they passed. 'It's more overgrown than ever. Oh, Robert, we must do something about that – it's such a pity to see it so neglected –'

The carriage was slowing. With a hollow rattle it crossed the bridge that spanned the river and rolled to a halt outside the gates of Old Hall. Blowers clambered down and stood tugging at his hatbrim apologetically. For the first time Jessica noticed with some surprise that his worn trousers did not match his livery jacket. 'Beggin' yer pardon, Sir Robert, Your Ladyship – but we can't take the carriage across the old drawbridge. It wouldn't stand the weight. Fallin' to pieces it is.'

It was not, Jessica saw with a shock as she stepped from the carriage, the only thing at Old Hall that was falling to pieces. At first sight unchanged and dearly familiar, a second glance swiftly showed how much neglected was the house itself. Tiles were missing from the roofs, not just singly but in some cases in patches. Several windows were broken and patched with wood. The gates stood open, jammed by their broken hinges. Ever since she had known it the old place had been fighting a battle against the merciless depredations of the years, but never had she seen it looking so pathetically run down. Water plants clogged the stagnant waters of the moat and the growth of weeds in the courtyard as they crossed the creaking bridge and entered the gates was such that it was lifting the flagstones and all but hiding the well from sight. As they stood, nonplussed, in the desolation, a dog came barking from the stables, wagging its tail in greeting. Automatically Jessica bent to pat it, as she looked around. 'Where is everyone?'

Angelina looked about her in disbelieving horror, and even the child was struck to silence by the oppressive quiet of the place.

'Christ!' Robert said, quietly and grimly.

'Who's there?' A very plump figure had appeared at the doorway of the Great Hall and stood, her hand shading her eyes, peering vaguely at them. Her voice was querulous. 'Who is it?'

Robert stepped forward. 'Mother – it's me – Robert. And Jessica.'

'Who?' Sarah put her head on one side, frowning, 'Who did you say?'

'Robert, Mother. It's me –'

'Robert! Good heavens!' She lumbered forward. Her clothes were worn and stained, her hair a bird's nest. 'Of course. I'd quite forgotten. And Jessica, my dear! How are you? How is your mother? I really must pay some calls – there just always seems so very much to do. And who in the world is this? Never mind, never mind. Robert – your father is around somewhere – see if you can find him for me, would you? You know what a very naughty man he is when it comes to time-keeping – I really must get that watch of his mended – Not that he ever thinks to look at it of course,' she added in confidential tones to Jessica.

Robert opened his mouth. Jessica put a quick hand on his arm and shook her head. In the doorway behind Sarah FitzBolton a woman had appeared, small and birdlike, with a kindly face. She hurried to Sarah and took her arm. 'Now, now, Your Ladyship – what are we doing here? We're supposed to be resting, aren't we?'

'Oh, don't fuss Janet! See – Robert's back from university. I had quite forgotten he was coming. And Jessica's come to visit – we must find Father – tell him to come –'

The little woman turned apologetically to Robert. 'I'm sorry, sir. She isn't always like this. Not one of her better days. She's a little confused I'm afraid. I'll take her inside if you don't mind? She'll be right as rain by tea time.'

'Yes – yes, of course.'

'I'll tell Mrs Williams you're here. She's been watching for you all day. But there was some crisis in the kitchen –'

It took less than an hour for the sad state of affairs at Old Hall to become painfully apparent. The near-empty house was decaying, most of the servants were gone. The loss of her husband had affected Sarah very badly; most of the time she lived in a world of her own, a world long disappeared. At supper it was clear that she still thought Robert home on vacation from university and Jessica visiting from New Hall. She smiled vaguely when Gabriella, overawed, was brought in to say goodnight and obediently pecked her upon the cheek. Sarah smiled, vaguely. 'What a very pretty child.'

No-one mentioned Clara until Jessica asked Mrs Williams and was answered by a sharp cluck of the tongue and a tightening of the mouth. 'Miss Clara's otherwise occupied, Your Ladyship. She has no time for us at Old Hall.'

'Do you know why she didn't write to tell us what had happened?'

'Everyone assumed she had. They thought –' She stopped abruptly.

'They thought we wouldn't come home?'

'Yes, Your Ladyship.'

Jessica had to laugh. 'Oh, Mrs Williams – can't you go back to Miss Jessica? I can't get used to this "Ladyship" business at all, and from someone who used to let me steal her biscuits –'

Mrs Williams' plump face creased into a small smile.

'So – Clara never comes to see her mother?'

The smile went. 'No, Miss Jessica, that she doesn't. Neither she nor Mr Giles. They've no time for our troubles, it seems.' Her mouth shut like a trap, and Jessica asked no more.

Sarah and the few remaining servants lived frugally from the rents and tithes of the Home Farm. There was no money, and there were debts. In the small parlour that was almost the only habitable living room in the house apart from the little apartment in the turret wing occupied by Sarah and Janet, Robert threw himself into the armchair that had always been his father's and buried his head in his hands. 'My God! – How can things have got into this state so fast?'

'We've been away six years. And I don't think even before that your father was a very good manager. The house was neglected even then –'

'Neglected? The damned place is falling down!'

'It's certainly in a bad way.' Jessica was tired. The journey had wearied her, she had spent the past two hours coping with a distressed and homesick Angelina and an even more distressed and homesick Gabriella. 'Do you know what the debts are?'

He shook his head bleakly. 'No.'

In the silence the tall, ornate grandfather clock that stood in the corner ticked rhythmically. With a spurt of tired irritation Jessica saw that it was more than two hours slow.

'We shouldn't have come back,' Robert said.

Jessica would not be provoked. She said nothing.

'You hear me? We should never have come back!' He stood up and strode to the table by the window, upon which stood a brandy bottle and glasses. She watched him pour himself a generous tot. 'We should have stayed in Florence.'

'What good would that have done?' She tried to keep her voice calm and reasonable, but a small grating edge of nerves sharpened it despite her efforts. 'We couldn't possibly have left your mother here in her condition and with the roof falling in over her head!'

He shrugged, moodily.

'Robert — it's no good letting ourselves be overwhelmed by it. We have to think. We have to find out what we have and what we owe. We have to find out how much it will take to put the house to rights — or at least to prevent it from decaying further. We have to find out what the land is yielding and —'

'I don't care!' He slammed the glass down so hard upon the table that the brandy splashed and spilled. 'You hear me? I don't damned well care! I won't be buried alive here! I won't have this place bleed me dry! I'm going back to Florence —' He tossed back the remaining brandy in one gulp and nearly choked.

Furious, she was out of her chair and beside him in a moment, catching his arm, almost shaking him in her anger. 'You can't! Robert, you can't do that! You can't run away —'

'Oh, can't I?'

'No! Listen to me — please! If we can sort this out — if we can get the place on its feet again — then in a couple of years perhaps we can go back? Oh, not for ever I don't mean — but for a few months each year?'

The look he turned upon her was pure, blistering scorn. 'And what do we use for money to achieve this fantasy? Buttons? Jessica — this place needs thousands — thousands! —

of pounds spent on it! Where are we going to get that kind of money?'

Jessica opened her mouth. Shut it again.

'– I tell you the place will wring us dry!'

'Don't be so ridiculously melodramatic.' Exhausted she dropped into a chair, picking at the worn upholstery. 'Your family have lived here for generations. I don't care what you say, it's your duty to care for it. It's your duty to try. We're here. We have to do something.'

He poured himself another drink. 'I'll tell you what we'll do,' he said, grimly. 'We'll close the house and go back to Florence. Damn the place! Let it fall to pieces!' He tilted the glass and drained it.

'And your mother? Are you suggesting we take her with us?'

'Clara can have her.' His words were becoming slurred. 'Why not? She can live with Clara.'

Jessica almost laughed. 'What? With Clara? Robert, Clara hasn't been near her for months! If she cared a pin for your mother she wouldn't be living here on her own now, would she?'

His mouth set in a stubborn line. 'I'll go and see her tomorrow. Talk to her about it.'

Jessica stood up. 'I wish you luck. You'll need it. Something tells me that whatever else has changed around here your sister is much the same as ever. I'm going to bed. And Robert – tomorrow we must talk. Really talk. We have to work out what to do.'

He turned his back to her, stood looking out of the window as she left the room.

She spent a restless night and woke with the early May dawn to find the rest of the house still sleeping. She lay for a while listening to the blithe torrent of birdsong beyond the window, then on impulse she slipped from her bed and dressed swiftly. The risen sun gleamed through the trees and reflected, shimmering, from the quiet, clear-rippling waters of the river. Very quietly, reminded irresistibly of childhood escapades, she crept down the stairs. As she passed Robert's open door his rasping breaths were loud and rhythmic. She could smell the brandy fumes from where she stood.

She let herself out into the brilliant morning, crossed the drawbridge and stood for a moment breathing the heady air, fresh and sparkling as chilled wine, and listening to the heartstoppingly beautiful song of a blackbird that was perched high in a fragrantly blooming hawthorn tree. In the distant woodlands a cuckoo called. She turned to look at the old house, and in the golden morning sunshine it was again the fairy castle that she remembered, a place of magic and enchantment. In this light and at this distance the crumbling fabric of the place was not apparent. But the beauty of the ancient brick and timber was there, and the idiosyncratic twist of the tudor chimneys, added when the house was already old. Generations of FitzBoltons this house had sheltered; it deserved better treatment now, she thought sadly, than to be cursed and left to rot.

She shook her head, her mouth set. Not while there was breath in her body would the old place be left to fall down or abandoned to stangers.

She set off along the river bank, each bend and twist of the path so familiar and well remembered that it felt strange not to have Bran sniffing excitedly at each fascinating hole and bush. The old dog had died two years before, but not before siring, according to Patrick, a happy pack of mongrel offspring over several square miles of the county. She wondered if she could find one of his progeny for Gabriella. She stopped for a moment, disentangling her skirt from a grasping bramble. The path that once had been so clear to follow was overgrown. Thorns clawed her skirt again, and a new growth of nettles brushed her unprotected ankles painfully. If the way were not cleared, by high summer it would be impassable. She picked a heavy stick from the ground and beat her way through with it. The small cottages, where Danny had lived, were boarded up and nearly lost in the jungle that had sprung up around them. She stood for a long moment by the broken gate remembering the day that a small girl had crept down this path to watch a dark and handsome stranger wash in water from the well in the middle of a yard that was now so overgrown that the gate would not open. A little further on the church had fared no better. It was as if since her wedding six years before no single soul had been near the place, and jealous nature had reclaimed the churchyard and surroundings swiftly for her own. Jessica edged her way up the path and went in, leaving the door ajar behind her. The air of the small building was exactly as she remembered it – cold and dank, musty with age. The easterly rising sun gleamed through the stained glass windows, flooding the place with glittering patterns of light, like a bright, jewelled shawl flung across walls and floor. She walked to the altar, very quietly, her footsteps light, her breathing shallow. St Agatha smiled still from her niche, restored by Danny's loved and loving hands. With a faint rustle of her clothing Jessica sat in the front pew and tilted her head, looking at the statue. A small, frightened something scuttled away from her feet, the sound loud in the silence.

She sat so for a very long time. Outside the sun rose higher and gained in strength. The cuckoo flew, calling, across the treetops. The flowers shed their dew and spread their pale petals to the warmth of the day.

Still she sat.

The world rose and went about its business. Small animals scurried in the undergrowth, blind babies blinked in the milky light.

She stirred at last. She was stiff, and very cold. But in that long quiet time many answers had come to her and her heart was calm, close even to happiness despite all. Outside the light and the warmth all but dazzled her. She stretched her goose-fleshed arms, rubbing them briskly. Even her nose was cold, and her feet were like blocks of ice. She pushed her way along the familiar path around the lake, stopping for a while to watch the nesting waterbirds and the lovely play of the sun on the water. A flustered moorhen with a small flotilla of young paddled away from her, scolding angrily. She sat on a fallen log and let the sun warm her cold flesh. The bluebells here were in their first bloom, laying their carpet of deep and beautiful blue about the woods.

The mood of the church was still with her. She belonged here. No matter what others did, or thought, or wanted, she belonged here. She wanted Danny – oh, how desperately she wanted him! – but yet she knew she had done the right thing in coming home. And – for better or for worse – that was what this was to her. Home. For her – and for Gabriella. She would make it so.

She picked a handful of twigs from the ground near her feet and threw them into the water, watching them reflectively as they spun and drifted lazily in the water. Then she lifted her eyes to take in the shining span of the lake and suddenly and painfully she remembered Edward's death and its awful aftermath.

The water lay still and brilliant as a sunlit mirror.

She drew a breath, blinking; then stood, shaking out her skirts, and turned to set out along the path through the bluebells that led to the park and New Hall.

Maria Hawthorne was breakfasting when she arrived. Jessica – astounded and a little amused at having to explain to the strange young footman who opened the door to this un-wontedly early caller who she was – declined to be announced and slipped into the morning room quietly. Her mother looked up from the paper she was reading, eyes sharp and bright above the pince-nez she wore. Jessica was a little shocked to see that she had aged quite visibly, a network of tiny lines marring the fine skin, deep furrows in her forehead and about her still firm and well-shaped mouth. Composedly and for all the world as if Jessica had been for an early-morning ride in the park and absent for hours rather than years she extended a graceful hand. 'Jessica, my dear. I heard you were back.'

Jessica came to her swiftly and bent to kiss the cool cheek. 'Mother.'

'Sit down, sit down –' With a small grimace of pain Maria reached for a small silver bell that stood by her hand. 'We'll have more tea. You're well, child? And Robert?'

'We're both well, thank you.'

'And my granddaughter?' Maria smiled. 'Have you brought her with you to meet her rheumaticy old grandma?'

Jessica laughed. 'She was still sound asleep when I left this morning. She's had a long and tiring journey.'

'Of course, of course. But you must bring her to see me directly.'

'I will. Tomorrow, I promise. I just came to say hello, and to thank you for writing to us. We didn't know – about Sir Thomas' death. Or Robert's mother's –' she hesitated, '– illness.'

Maria nodded. 'Poor, poor thing. I hadn't realized, you see, just how bad she was. Or I would have written sooner. I have –' she paused, a shadow on her face, '– some small difficulty with my hands nowadays. It has made writing difficult. And I had of course assumed that –' she stopped.

'– that Clara would write,' Jessica finished for her a little grimly. 'I still don't understand why she didn't. Do you?'

Maria shook her head calmly as the door opened and a small uniformed maid appeared. 'More tea for Miss Jessica, please Maude – ah, I'm sorry –' she touched her forehead in a small, pretty gesture of amused apology, '– for Lady FitzBolton, of course.'

'Yes, Ma'am.' The girl threw an interested glance in Jessica's direction, bobbed a quick curtsey and left.

'I'm afraid,' Maria continued as the door closed behind the maid, 'that I can't help you there.' All amusement had fled her voice. 'Clara and I have little or nothing to do with each other if we can possibly avoid it. I suspect that she was simply too caught up in her own self-interests to bother to tell her brother what had happened. She has, it appears, no interest in Old Hall at all –'

'But – her mother!'

Maria shrugged a little. 'Clara isn't greatly influenced by sentimental ties. And Sarah rather took to Patrick.' She sent a small, oblique glance at her daughter. 'That, as you can imagine, was enough to cause trouble between them. They haven't spoken in two years, even after old Sir Thomas died. As for myself – Giles I see of course – he manages the estate, and does that, at least, well,' her voice held a strange small note of asperity '– but apart from that there's little contact between New Hall and Tollbridge House.' She smiled, with mocking and austere amusement, 'Clara changed the name. She could not be found living in a mere farmhouse –' Her voice was outwardly pleasant but deeply beneath the assumed nonchalance Jessica sensed a bitterness that shocked her a little. Clearly the years had done nothing to heal the rift between Giles and Clara and her mother. Maria stirred her tea, lifted the small cup to her lips and sipped it, then carefully replaced it in the saucer. For the first time Jessica noticed the painful distortion of the joints and knuckles of her mother's delicate hands. Maria saw the flicker of her eyes. 'The rheumatics,' she said, calmly.

'Is it – very bad?'

Maria took a small breath, and her smile was strained. 'Yes. It is. It's beginning to affect my legs as a matter of fact. Oh, don't look so worried, child. Old age is all – who am I to escape it altogether? Now, come – tell me of your travels – there is so very much to catch up on –'

When Jessica, at lunchtime, appeared at Old Hall riding a borrowed horse, her skirts kilted to her knees, she was met by an out-of-temper Robert and a delightfully scandalized Gabriella.

'Why Mama! What are you doing riding a horse so? – and whose horse is it? – and where have you been all the day –?'

'English, Gabriella, English!' She bent to give the child a hug. 'You must learn to speak English!'

The pretty child pouted.

'Where on earth have you been? You've been gone all morning!' Robert looked pale and sickly, his dark eyes shadowed. Jessica correctly assumed that he was paying penance for his unaccustomed drinking bout the night before. She shook out her skirts and brushed the dust from them, smiling thanks at the boy who came to take the horse from her.

'I've been to New Hall to see Mother.'

'You might have told me.'

'You were sound asleep and snoring,' she teased. The old Robert would have capitulated and laughed, she knew.

'What news?' Not an inch did he give.

She pulled a small, childish face at his bad-tempered back as she followed him across the yard. When she did not reply to his question he looked back across his shoulder. 'Well?'

She hesitated. She had mulled over the things that her mother had told her as she rode back across the park, but still had not quite managed to marshall them into coherence. She followed him into the darkness of the Great Hall and up the stairs. 'Mother's in a good deal of pain. She's having some trouble with her joints – in fact can barely walk. Giles and Clara are well, and living at Tollbridge Farm – Tollbridge House, that is. Patrick –' she frowned a little, 'Patrick is still at Harrow – I think – well, Mother didn't say so in so many words but I think the lad has turned out to be a little wild. There were – I don't know – some things she very obviously didn't say. She seemed a little worried about him.' She smiled a little ruefully. 'Like father like son, I suspect. I do vaguely remember the most awful rows, on and off, when Edward was about this age –' She followed him along the passageway that led to the parlour. 'Actually,' she added, a little reluctantly, 'things are not exactly what I expected over there.'

He turned. 'What do you mean?'

'It's hard to say exactly.' She wandered to the window, stood with her back to the room looking out.

Sensing her very real concern Robert watched her, his ill-humour and discomfort giving way somewhat to curiosity. He waited.

Jessica turned from the window, sat on the battered sofa and kicked her shoes off that were still cold and damp from her morning walk in the May dew. 'I didn't realize – I don't think any of us did – that after the war, in '15 and '16, when the price of corn dropped so very rapidly Father lost rather a lot of money. He was ill at the time, if you remember and not himself, and he never made it good. Then Giles took over. And apparently before Patrick came along Giles made one or two rather bad investments. He's a good farmer, but no financier.'

Robert was staring at her. 'You don't mean – your father's fortune is gone?'

'Oh, of course not! Nothing as dramatic as that! But certainly things are not as easy as they were. Even in Florence we heard, if you remember, about the agricultural depression and the disturbances? That doesn't help. Giles apparently is convinced that the answer lies in mechanization. It's making fortunes in industry – Giles thinks the same thing could happen on the land. It's causing a lot of trouble.' Her brow was deeply furrowed.

'Trouble?'

She rubbed her cold foot. 'In the village. Giles is experimenting with a new threshing machine. If it works that means no jobs – and no money. He's already cut wages to the bone. There have been threats – unpleasant threats – but of course, Giles won't be threatened. Whatever else you can say about him he's no coward.'

'Did you see him?'

'No. Things are obviously still very strained between him and Clara and Mother. Giles still runs the estate, I think, simply because he fears it will go to rack and ruin without him. Unfortunately it's beginning to look as if he may be right. Much as Mother still dotes on Patrick she's obviously worried about him –'

'In what way?'

'She didn't say in so many words. He's young – and a little wild – and really much too attractive for his own good. But then the same thing could have been said about both Edward and Giles in their own day, and they both came through it without too much harm –'

'Apart from Edward's unsuitable marriage.'

She looked at him thoughtfully. 'Mm. I don't somehow think Patrick's problem is marriage.' She laughed a little. 'Quite the opposite I shouldn't wonder. Phew!' She laid her head back, breathing deeply and running her hand through her hair, 'I had quite forgotten how exhausting my mother can be!' she said, ruefully.

'So –' Robert clasped his hands behind his back and

walked the floor restlessly. 'There's no help for us there?'

She looked at him in astonishment. 'Help?'

'I had hoped – hadn't you? – that your family might have been able to help us out of our –'

'No!' Her exclamation cut his words short. She scrambled to her feet, tiredness forgotten. 'Absolutely no! Under no circumstances would I take money from them! – Always supposing they'd give it!'

'Jessica – we have to get it from somewhere! What do you suggest? That we mint our own?'

She picked up her shoes. Barefoot, she barely came to his shoulder, small-built as he was. 'We'll get it,' she said, grimly. 'If we have to clear that library shelf by shelf we'll get it.'

He turned, his face blank. 'I beg your pardon?'

She made a sharp, exasperated movement. 'Oh for heaven's sake, Robert – how can you have lived with something all of your life without realizing its value? It surely must have occurred to you? Some of the books in that library are worth a lot of money. Whether it will be enough or not I don't know – but at least we've got something! It will be heartbreaking to see them go, but nowhere near as heartbreaking as to see the house fall down about our ears.' She ignored his silence, and the surprised look on his face. 'The first thing we must do –' she turned and made for the door, '– is to make sure that the hole in the roof is mended before the damned rain ruins our nest egg!'

The gentleman from Sothcby's was guardedly encouraging: Jessica, with the knowledge gleaned from Theo, was indeed right – several of the books and manuscripts in Old Hall's ancient library would very probably be of interest to collectors and might well fetch a handsome sum.

'How handsome?' Jessica asked, bluntly.

The man was flustered. 'Really, your Ladyship – you must realize that I couldn't possibly commit myself to suggesting that. If the right buyers can be contacted –'

'How long will that take?'

'It's hard to tell. The sale next month is too soon. These things cannot be arranged overnight, you know. It will have to be the next one –'

'When's that?'

'November.' He looked a little injured at her briskness. He was a tall young man with a prominent Adam's apple, an already receding hairline and, Jessica suspected, an overestimation of his own importance in the scheme of things. His skin was very pale and the hand he had offered had been soft and a little damp. 'The items will have to be catalogued, of course.'

'I can do that.'

'Lady FitzBolton, I hardly think –'

'I've spent the last four years helping to catalogue one of the most extensive and priceless private collections in Europe, Mr Branston,' she said, coolly, 'I don't think this will be beyond me. It will be much more simple for me to catalogue them here and then for you simply to send someone down to check the work. Don't you think?' She smiled beguilingly at him. 'I have a strong feeling it will be cheaper, too?'

He was not used to such straightforwardness. Colour rose from his high collar to his ears. 'I – yes, I suppose that will be satisfactory.'

'Now –' she took his arm firmly and steered him to the door, 'you're welcome to stay to supper of course – but if you'd rather catch the afternoon coach there's still time –'

She settled to work in the library with a will. It gave her something positive to do and kept her mind fully occupied. They were living for now on what little remained of her marriage settlement, and the small income from the Home Farm. The financial situation was tight, but not impossible. They had even managed to scrape together enough capital to repair the worst hole in the roof, though what worried Jessica most was the thought of the onset of the winter rains and snow before they had managed to acquire the money to have the rest of it done.

'Really, almost everything else can wait,' she said to Robert, a week or so after Mr Branston had come and gone. 'The roof is the most important. It leaks in several places still. The fabric of the place will rot if we can't keep the water out.'

Robert said nothing. He was sitting in the window seat of the small parlour staring into space, his face set.

She looked up from the figures she was studying. 'Robert?'

With an effort he brought his attention to her. 'I'm sorry?'

'Didn't you hear a word I said?'

'No. I'm sorry. I wasn't paying attention. Tell me – isn't it the day for the mail coach?'

Understanding flickered in her eyes. 'Yes. It is.'

'Ah. I thought so.' He turned back to the window.

She watched him for a moment, helpless sympathy in her eyes. At least she did not torment herself by expecting to hear from Danny. Robert had sent two letters a week to Florence since they had returned home, and had received not a single reply. He was pining visibly, his moods erratic. He was not, it seemed, interested in the state of the house, his mother's health or their fortunes. He simply wanted to return to Florence, where he had been happy.

'Someone has to go down to see the tenant of Home Farm,' she said, gently, trying to draw his attention from the window. 'We don't seem to have a detailed copy of the accounts for the past years. I don't think it's the tenant's fault – your father had to let the estate manager go a couple of years ago, and really since then no-one seems to have bothered much. The tithes and rents come in regularly enough, but we really should check what's happening. Could you pay them a visit, do you think? You really should, you know – show your face, so to speak, reassure the tenants –'

He made a small, impatiently negative movement with his head.

'Robert – you really should try –'

He stood up, looked at her coldly. 'Why? Why should I try? What has any of it to do with me? If you care what's happening on some grubby little farm, you go and – show your face –' he

389

spoke the words with scorn. 'What are they to do with me?' he asked again.

'You take their money,' she said, suddenly acid. 'You live off their rent and the sweat of their hands.'

'It isn't their money. It's ours. It's our land. And I still think that we should sell it and go back to –'

'Oh, stop it! Why can't you stop it! You're like a silly child –!' She put her hands over her ears.

They glared at each other in hostile silence.

Then she took a breath and forced her voice to conciliation. 'Robert – think! Who'd buy the place as it stands? It's run-down, neglected – virtually worthless! If we build it up, then it will be worth something, then – perhaps – we'll think again.' Over my dead body added a small grim voice in her mind: but she had to play for time, and if hypocrisy was called for to do it then so be it. 'But we have to work to get the place back on its feet. Please – won't you ride down to Home Farm this afternoon and find out what's going on?'

With the stubbornness that she had grown to recognize Robert shook his head. 'No. I've a letter to write.' He walked past her and out of the room. For a moment the rising frustration of anger gathered like a scream in her throat. It haunted her that Robert would enforce his prerogative and sell the house over their heads. She rubbed her eyes with her clenched fists, sat quite still for a moment, her head bowed. Then, very collectedly, she laid down her pen, closed the ledgers and went to change her clothes.

She was glad in the end that Robert had refused to go, for it gave her a chance of an afternoon in the air. She never tired of the countryside; never tired of the fertile greens of grass and leaf, the call of the birds, the movement of water, the scud of clouds across a wide, pale sky. Depressed as she had felt at Robert's defeatist and unhelpful attitude the gentle ride to the farm cheered her. She smiled to see the small starry faces of the milkmaids that grew in the ditch, at the gold of buttercups opening to the sun. Her brain that had been clogged with anger began to work again. She must decide between the three applicants who had answered her advertisement of the post of governess to her daughter. One of them was Scots. Her mouth twitched. The poor woman did not know the handicap under which she laboured! Of the other two the one seemed a little young, and the other had experience only of boys –

She had come to the track that led to the farm. She chirrped quietly to the horse, a docile beast lent to her by her mother from the still well-stocked stables of New Hall, and turned down the rutted way. To her surprise in the fenced field to her left a small flock of sheep cropped contentedly, their mild, quiet faces turned to her as she rode by. The small farmhouse, dwarfed by its barns and outhouses, stood in a bare earth yard around which pecked a few scrawny chickens. It was neat and tidy but unhomely. Jessica recalled from her childhood when a smiling, buxom woman – she could not remember her name – had given her cakes and frothing milk from a doorway that had been garlanded with sweet-smelling roses. Now there was no welcoming air to the uncurtained windows and the closed door, and the roses had gone. The yard was stacked neatly and tidily, no farmyard clutter, no garden, not one blade of grass let alone a flower.

She dismounted and, the reins over her arm, knocked on the door.

Nothing happened.

She knocked again, sharply. The animal stood with docile good temper, nuzzling her ear.

From one of the barns came the sudden sound of hammering.

She walked towards the sound, the horse plodding behind her. The great barn doors were open, flooding the dusty space with a dim light, shadowing the far corners. She stopped just inside the doors, blinking against the gloom. Bars of sunlight gleamed through the spaces of the boarded walls and the huge tiled roof above its ancient blackened beams. A big man who had, with his back to her, been bending over a great five bar gate that lay upon the earth floor, straightened and turned, a sledge hammer swinging in his hand as if it were feather-light. He was massively muscled, his skin weather-beaten to gold.

He tossed the shock of ill-kempt chestnut hair from his eyes as he peered at her, silhouetted as she was against the light. In the first moment of seeing him she felt certain she knew him, but she could not hold the memory, and she could not place him. She smiled. 'Good afternoon.'

He stood for a moment unmoving. Then he nodded his head and made the vaguest of movements with his hand that might have been taken for the salute of servant to mistress, but, Jessica noted with amusement equally well might not. 'Y're Ladyship.'

She never would – never could get used to that title. 'You're the tenant of Home Farm?'

'Tha'ss right, Y're Ladyship. Took over when Uncle died a few year back.'

'We haven't seen you at the Hall?'

'No, Y're Ladyship.' His voice was noncommittal. 'Tha'ss not time for rent yet.'

The strange feeling of familiarity had returned as he spoke. She looked up at him. 'Forgive me – I've been away for some time – but don't I know you?'

For the first time a smile hovered at the edges of his mouth and the hazel eyes crinkled a little in a nut-brown face. 'That you do, Y're Ladyship,' he said, unhelpfully.

She studied his face, frowning a little. Then, exasperated she shook her head. 'Oh, I'm sorry! I really can't remember –?'

'Charlie Best, Y're Ladyship.'

It took a moment for the name to connect with her memory. Then she smiled, staring in delight at the young man she had last seen when she had danced with him at her sister's wedding. And before that – 'Charlie Best! Oh, no – it can't be!'

'"Tis, so, Y're Ladyship.'

'Oh, Charlie –' She was laughing. 'You'll have to stop calling me that! You bloodied my nose twice when we were children –!'

'Three times, Y're Ladyship.'

They stood, smiling at each other. She sensed that the mildly hostile reserve with which he had greeted her had slipped away. Then he recovered himself, and his smile lost something of its spontaneity. 'You'll excuse me a moment, Y're Ladyship?'

'Yes, of course.'

She watched as he picked up the gate as effortlessly as if it had been made of paper, and stood it against the wall. Then he came back to her, dusting his hands on his trousers, and waited.

'Could you spare me a few minutes, Charlie?'

'Of course, Y're Ladyship. Please come this way.'

She followed him to the house. It was stark, and barely furnished, no curtains at the window, no rug on the floor, simply a couple of stools and one high-backed chair and a table. Old ashes lay dead in the fireplace but other than that the single room was scrupulously clean. A cupboard in the corner was the only other furniture. He gestured a little shamefacedly, and her heart went out to him in sympathy. 'Tha'ss not much, I'm afraid, Y're Ladyship – I've no wife to keep for me, you see –'

'You never married?' she asked, surprised.

His whole body stilled for a moment, then he relaxed, and nodded. 'Aye, I did. Little Betty Morris. You remember her? Pretty little thing she was.'

'Yes. I do remember her.' Her voice was quiet.

'She died. A year to the day after the wedding, it was. She died, and the child.'

'Oh Charlie – I'm so sorry –'

He shrugged. Shook his head. 'It happens. That was three years ago – a bit more. Time passes. That helps.'

She bit her lip, not sure what else to say in face of his calm. The man radiated a strength that was more than physical, something which inspired trust, and liking. She smiled. 'Well, now – I've been going through things at the Hall. Your rent is paid, and the tithes collected, but there are no actual accounts for the past few years?'

He nodded. 'Tha'ss right. Haven't been for years. Old Bill – my uncle – he wasn't one for figures an' such, and Sir Thomas wasn't much of a one for 'em either. Matter of trust I s'pose you might call it –' He lifted his shaggy head and met her eyes with a movement that held pride, and a faint trace of defiance.

'I understand that,' she said, quickly, 'I'm not –'

393

'You'll be wantin' to put in your own tenant I suppose?' he interrupted her abruptly.

'Why no! Of course not! We're perfectly satisfied. It's just that – well – affairs at Old Hall are in a bit of a muddle. They've been left to themselves for rather too long I'm afraid. Old Sir Thomas left debts we have to pay. We have to get things on a more businesslike basis.'

His stance had not changed. 'You'll be for sellin' the place?'

'The farm? Absolutely not. What good would the house be without the land?' Neither of them had noticed that he had stopped his monotonous reiteration of her title. 'But we need to know how it's being used – if the best is being made of it. I noticed –' she added, real interest in her voice, 'that you have sheep in the field out there?'

'A few, yes.'

'Do they pay?'

'Properly handled, yes. I think so. Haven't had a chance to try with a larger flock, or a better breed. Problem is money –'

She smiled a smile that turned into a laugh. 'The problem, Charlie Best, is always money –!'

The encounter with Charlie delighted her. An inspection of the farm had proved, as she had been certain it would, that he was a diligent and careful tenant. But more, in the matter of the sheep he had shown imagination and a willingness to experiment. Most small tenant farmers, especially one with as shaky a right to the land as his – he had worked for his uncle when he had been alive and with the easy-won approval of Robert's father had simply taken over the place on his death – would have been contented simply to scrape a living from the soil and leave it at that. But faced with falling prices and fierce competition he had diversified and invested the small profits he had made and that he spent neither on hired labour nor on the creature comforts of life in the sheep. So far the experiment was just that, and the animals had not proven themselves financially, but at least – he had pointed out to Jessica with sober satisfaction – they reproduced themselves, did not fail in bad weather as the crops had twice done in three years, and provided meat for the table and wool for the back when times were hard. 'Used to be sheep country round here,' he had finished, laconically. 'Could be again.'

She was riding the river path, deep in thought, wrestling again with the intransigent problem of Old Hall's decrepit roof when her mount stopped short and sidestepped, bringing Jessica sharply forward in her saddle. She tightened the reins, bringing the startled horse to a neat standstill, then lifted her eyes to the rider who had appeared on the pathway before her, meeting for the first time in five years the brilliant, unsmiling eyes of her brother Giles.

He had not changed. The bright hair gleamed as brightly, the handsome face was as handsome, the body was supple and easy in the saddle. The feelings that the sight of him spawned had not changed either. She sat rigid, giving him no greeting.

'Well, little sister. I heard you were back.'

She said nothing.

'And with a daughter, I gather.' His eyes showed no expression whatsoever. 'Congratulations.'

'Thank you.'

His horse, a bright bay mare with a wild eye danced restlessly. He brought her to quiet with a hard hand. 'You're staying?'

'Yes.'

The mare moved again, throwing up a mettlesome head. He controlled her with ease, his eyes never leaving hers. 'I'm surprised.'

'Oh?'

He shrugged. 'The old house is finished. A stone around your neck. If I were you I'd get out while I could, before it bankrupted me.'

'Thank you for your advice.' Her voice was cool.

'Think about it. If you want to get rid of it – of the farm – I'd be willing to take it off your hands.'

She shook her head. 'No. Thank you,' she added, carefully, keeping iron control of the revulsion that the very sight of him caused her.

'Perhaps I'll speak to Robert. He, after all, is the master of the house, is he not?' The words were mocking, deliberately provocative.

She lifted her chin and watched him, levelly. 'I shouldn't, if I were you.' She made no attempt whatsoever to disguise the meaning behind the words.

The smile fled his face.

'I'm staying at Old Hall,' she said, quietly. 'It is my home now, and my daughter's. Stay away from us, Giles. Save your mischief for others.'

He glared at her for a moment before swinging his mare violently away.

'Giles!' She called after him, her voice sharp.

He reined in, turned impatiently. His face was black with anger.

'Why didn't Clara let us know about Robert's father? About what was happening at Old Hall?'

He raised fair, straight brows. 'She quarrelled with her mother. Over Patrick. They haven't spoken for more than two years.'

Jessica stared at him aghast. 'And for that she'd leave the poor woman – alone – half-mad – with no attempt to bring help?'

He shrugged. 'She's an unforgiving woman.' He paused, fighting the restless mare, 'I should remember that if I were you.' He stood the beast on its hind legs, dancing her in an ostentatious display of horsemanship before he set her at the path and disappeared into the trees.

Jessica watched the retreating figure in distaste. 'If anyone ever deserved each other, Giles Hawthorne,' she said aloud, 'you and Clara do.'

Chapter Fourteen

A week later a letter at last arrived for Robert from Arthur, a long-awaited event that first brought happiness to Jessica's husband but then, perversely, plunged him into a depression deeper than ever, a mood from which he could be neither coaxed nor bullied. Arthur's letter, Jessica could not help but notice, was very brief, a mere page of scrawled, widespaced writing. The one that Robert wrote in reply was the length of one of Lord Byron's epic poems; but neither to that nor to either of his next two epistles, equally long, did he get any reply. Jessica tried valiantly to ignore his ill-temper, as she ignored the fact that the bulk of the work and organization of Old Hall had fallen upon her shoulders, with little or no support from Robert at all. She did not dare to protest, knowing too well how he would counter any complaint. So whilst poor Sarah drifted about the house like a plump, pale ghost Jessica ran the household on their meagre means, hired the essential governess for Gabriella – she had in the end chosen the very young Jane Barton, since neither of the other two more experienced applicants would accept the pittance that was all she could offer – went through the Home Farm accounts with Charlie Best and continued doggedly with her cataloguing of the medieval books and manuscripts that were to be sent to auction.

The summer, after a promising start, was disappointingly cool and wet, and the crops stood, bedraggled and green in the fields. Several days' thunderous rain flattened the wheat and the barley and with no sun to ripen them they lay in the mud, weedbound and rotting. The rain dripped dismally into the buckets that stood about the floors of most of the rooms of Old Hall.

Jessica, whatever the weather, made a point of riding each afternoon, to get her out of the house. Sometimes she would go up to the Home Farm for a chat with Charlie, sometimes she would ride the New Hall parkland as she had done as a child, often calling in to visit her mother. Sometimes Gabriella was allowed to accompany her on these trips; the child was already showing her mother's fearlessness and natural ability in the saddle and pestered constantly for a pony of her own.

'Of course the child must have a pony,' Maria said. 'There surely must be something in the stables?'

'I don't know. I hardly think Giles –'

'Fiddlesticks! What is it to do with Giles? Gabriella, my pet – ring the bell and John shall take you to the stables. Tell one of the stable lads to help you pick a pony. A small one, mind, and docile. There are two or three lazy ones out there that don't earn their way.'

'Thank you, Gran'mama!' The child deposited a huge kiss upon the soft cheek. Maria winced a little at the enthusiasm of the embrace yet smiled indulgently. It never failed to astonish Jessica that her mother, who had taken little or no notice of her own children at this age, openly adored Gabriella and left to her own devices would indulge the child's every whim.

'You spoil her, Mother,' she scolded, smiling. 'You really shouldn't, you know. I'm not sure we can afford to keep a pony just at the moment.'

'Nonsense.' Maria, as had become her habit, massaged one painful hand with the other, the dry skin rustling. It worried Jessica that her mother's condition seemed to be worsening rapidly. Certainly the damp weather did not help. Maria eyed her a little slyly. 'Anyway – what's this I hear about you coming into a fortune?'

Jessica was startled. 'I'm sorry?'

'The gossip is that you're playing the pirate with Old Hall's library –?'

'Oh, Lord! Has everyone heard?' Jessica rolled her eyes. 'It's hardly going to be a fortune, Mother. And believe me, I hate to let them go. But we're desperate, and the old house needs the money more than it needs the books. So yes, we're selling some of them at auction in November. With a bit of luck they'll make enough to get us back on our feet. Needs must when the devil pushes, as they say.' She stood up. 'We'd better be getting back. I don't like to leave Mother Sarah for too long alone. That little Janet does have a tendency to drop off at the oddest moments – I sometimes suspect that Mrs Williams' scurrilous suspicions are right, and she has a secret gin bottle somewhere! – and unattended there's no knowing where Mother Sarah might end up.' She sighed, softly. 'It's so sad. She spends the whole time looking for Robert's father. She's convinced he's there somewhere – talks all the time as if he's just going to walk in from the garden.'

Maria lifted her cheek for her daughter's kiss, patted her hand. 'Come to supper tomorrow night, my dear. Both of you. Patrick's coming home for the summer. I know he'd love to see you. He finds it dull indeed, I fear, closeted here with no-one but a rheumaticy old lady for company.'

Jessica laughed. 'I'm sure that isn't true, but if you'd like us to, then yes, of course we'll come. It's been such a long time since I've seen Patrick. He must be very changed? He's – what? – sixteen –?'

'Nearly seventeen.' Maria's face and voice were strangely sober, 'And as handsome a lad as you'll ever see. The very image of his father.'

'He's doing well at Harrow?' asked Jessica.

Her mother gave a small, sharp bark of laughter, and flinched at the pain it caused her. 'Well? Good heavens, no! Not if you mean academically, that is. They haven't been able to hammer the first principles of learning into his head! I believe they have despaired of him and left him to his lazy ways. But he's played cricket for the school and is wildly popular, according to his tutor. That seems to be enough both for him and for them.'

'He's happy then?'

'Oh yes. He's happy.' Maria seemed about to add something, but did not.

Jessica eyed her curiously. 'Nothing's wrong?'

Maria shook her head firmly. 'Wrong? Silly child, whatever

could be wrong? The boy's a little wild, that's all. He made some rather odd friends a year or so ago, and got himself into a scrape from which it cost me a considerable amount to extricate him.' She held up a quick finger, 'Not a word to anyone about that, mind. The boy has turned over a new leaf. He gave me his solemn word, and I believe him. There's nothing wrong with Patrick that a few more months of growing up won't put right. He's a splendid boy.'

The following evening, watching the tall young man with the ready smile and engaging, frequent laughter, Jessica remembered her mother's words and dismissed her first slightly worrying impression that she had been talking to convince herself. Patrick even had Robert relaxed and laughing as he told an obviously well-censored but hilarious story involving a Harrow inn-keeper's pretty daughter and a student he swore with innocent face and twinkling eyes was not himself.

'If it wasn't you,' Robert chuckled, '– you seem to know an awful lot about the escape route!'

Patrick inclined the red-gold head that was so vividly reminiscent of Edward's and held his hand to his heart. 'My best friend,' he said, 'I swear it!'

He was one of those rare people, Jessica realized as the evening progressed, who with unthinking ease and no particular intention could capture and hold the attention of those about him without appearing overbearing or causing resentment. His personality was warm, his laughter easy. He had an attractive voice and a handsome face. He had the disarming knack of listening with lively attention to the opinions of others, whilst always, with humour, being ready to advance his own. He had wit, and he had charm. Smiling to herself she shuddered to think of the number of feminine hearts he would flutter. How many, indeed, he already had –

'What are you smiling at, darling Jessica?' He had crept up on her and pounced, clicking his fingers and making her jump. His real delight at seeing her again when they had arrived this evening had warmed her heart. She smiled at him.

'I was thinking how very far removed you are from that

little tinker who climbed out onto the church roof at our wedding!'

He laughed aloud. 'Oh – not so very far!' He pulled a funny, self-deprecating face, 'I can still do some pretty silly things to impress a pretty girl!'

'I'm sure you can.'

'As a matter of fact –' his voice was rueful, and for a moment his smile slipped a little, 'I can still do some pretty silly things altogether.'

She laughed a little. 'Oh? That sounds a little dire?'

He shook his head swiftly. 'Oh no – not really – it's just –'

'Yes?' She had stopped laughing.

He grinned. 'Nothing. Well – nothing that won't wait for another day.' He pulled up a chair. 'May I ride over to Old Hall tomorrow? I want to hear all about your wicked adventures in Florence.' He wagged a long finger under her nose. 'Everyone tells me I get my wild ways from my father – but it seems to me that my old Aunt Jessica has her share!'

She assumed a look of outrage. 'I really can't imagine what you mean, young man!'

He chuckled. 'Then you've got less imagination than I give you credit for!'

'Jessica? Patrick?' Imperiously Maria tapped upon the floor with her stick. 'What are you doing over there giggling in the corner like a couple of silly schoolgirls? Patrick, ring for tea if you please – a poor old woman could die of thirst with such neglect!'

Patrick was true to his word and rode, in the rain, to Old Hall next day where he charmed the impressionable Gabriella into ecstasies of bad behaviour, brought a smile to Robert's face, cajoled a handful of buttery biscuits from Mrs Williams, produced flutters in the inexperienced Miss Barton's heart that took a full day to calm and finally ran Jessica to earth in the library where she was all but hidden behind a mountain of books stretched upon a vast desk.

'S'truth!' he whistled, laughing. 'I've found a little bookworm, no less!'

She came out from behind the desk, stood on tiptoe to kiss his cheek. 'Less of the "little", please,' she said, severely.

The afternoon was dark and despite the early hour Jessica had lit a single lamp, economy dictating that to be sufficient. The light glinted in his hair and gleamed in the vivid blue of his eyes. 'I just made Robert laugh,' he announced, solemnly. 'And for that I deserve a drink.'

She laughed, a little ruefully, 'It certainly isn't easy these days, I have to admit. What would you like? Tea? It's a little cool for lemonade –'

He leaned to her ear, blowing gently to stir the tendrils of her hair. 'Wine,' he whispered, conspiratorially, 'A – very – large – glass!' He exaggerated the words.

She hesitated, then capitulated. She reached for the bell pull, laughing, 'I see you're picking up all the bad habits at good old Harrow?'

He looked at her strangely for a moment, then without answering he threw himself with graceful force into a battered sofa, lifting his booted feet onto the scuffed arm. 'Oh, I do like this place! When Sotheby's make your fortune, you won't change it, will you?'

She tutted. 'Sotheby's aren't going to make our fortune, Patrick! They're going to help us to make ends meet. If we're lucky. Ah, Mary –' the door had opened and a small maid entered, smoothing her black skirt with small hands, eyelashes fluttering at Patrick, '– a glass of wine, if you please, for Mr Patrick.'

'A large one.' Patrick smiled, beguilingly, and the girl blushed to the roots of her hair.

As the maid left Jessica turned and surveyed the tall young man who sprawled on her sofa. 'I used to prefer Old Hall to New Hall,' she volunteered.

He did not show surprise. 'Of course you did. You always were a lady of very great sense. Not,' he added in slightly guilty haste, 'that I'm saying that Grandmama isn't the most wonderful person in the world. Of course she is. She's just – a little difficult to live with sometimes, that's all. She has such very great expectations of a fellow –' He fell to pensive silence for a moment, then lifted his head, grinning and changing the mood. 'Is that why you married Robert?' he asked, slyly.

Taken aback by the easy impertinence of the question she did not reply for a moment. Then she laughed. 'You mean because of Mother's expectations, or because I preferred Old Hall?'

'Both. Either.'

She looked at him for a long moment, half-smiling.

He shrugged. 'Sorry. It isn't my business, is it?'

She shook her head, attempting severity, and failing, as she suspected most people did when faced with the lad's winning ways. He swung his feet to the floor and sat up as the maid returned with a large glass of wine on a tray. Jessica noticed with well-concealed amusement that her hair was tidier and her cap perched at a more becoming angle than it had been a few moments before. Patrick smiled at her with almost unconscious charm as she set the tray carefully beside him and bobbed a graceful and somehow impudent curtsey. 'Thank you.'

'You're welcome, Sir.' She walked with small, quick steps to the door, her wide skirt swaying to the movement of her neat hips. Patrick watched her go appreciatively. As she turned to shut the door he caught her eye and winked, bringing a rosy blush of colour to her face. She shut the door with a click.

Patrick leaned back again, glass in hand, and resumed the conversation, undaunted by Jessica's earlier attempt to repress him. 'He's a duller bird than I remember him. He was always quiet. Now – well he seems downright miserable.'

'He misses Florence.'

'So do you, I daresay. But I'm pretty sure you don't make the rest of the world suffer for it.' He glanced at her astutely and as, colouring, she opened her mouth to speak made an easy gesture of apology and apeasement. 'All right. All right. I'm sorry. I'll change the subject.' He tilted his head and to Jessica's surprise she saw the wine disappear at a gulp. He emerged grinning, 'But only if you send for the rest of the bottle. And have one with me.'

She eyed the empty glass. 'Is that what they teach you at Harrow?'

He shrugged, avoiding her eyes. 'Amongst other things.'

He walked to the window and stood looking out into the dark afternoon as Jessica rang once more for the maid. This time, for all her swinging hips and artfully perched cap he took no notice of her at all. As she left, having deposited the bottle and another glass upon the table she glanced at his back and cleared her throat.

'Thank you, Mary,' Jessica said.

Clearly piqued the girl put her small nose in the air and stalked from the room like an offended duchess.

Jessica poured the wine and joined him at the window. The drizzle had given way to driving rain that hit the glass like flung gravel. The room was very dark, but it was not the physical gloom brought by the low, rain-hung clouds that caused the sombre look she surprised on Patrick's face as she glanced at him. Then he turned, smiling again as he took the wine, and she wondered if she had imagined that look of strain. He toasted her. 'Angel of mercy! Grandmama doesn't approve of strong drink before five o'clock.'

'I'm not sure I do myself.' She sipped her wine, watching him as he took a thirsty gulp then held up the glass to the rain-washed window and studied the play of light in the blood-red depths. 'I wondered –' he said, very casually, not looking at her, '– if you might – well, do me a favour. Help me out a bit – ?'

'Of course. If I can,' she said, readily.

'It's – a little difficult.' He sipped his wine, then went back to his absorbed contemplation of it.

She waited.

'I'm a little – short of the ready. You know? Strapped for funds as you might say.' He glanced at her, a swift, sideways look, and then turned back to the window.

She laughed. 'You aren't alone.'

'No. This is – well, serious. I need the loan of a few guineas.'

'We-ell.' She was doubtful, but wanted to help him, knowing how hard it would be for him to go to Maria, 'We're not exactly rolling in money ourselves, but I'm sure I can manage a little. A few guineas, you say? Exactly how few?'

He did not respond to her lightness of tone. He hesitated for a moment. 'Five hundred.'

The silence rang with shock.

'Five *hundred*?' She stared at him. 'Patrick – five hundred guineas is a small fortune! What in the world can you possibly want that much for?'

'Need,' he said, grimly, 'not want.' He turned and walked to the sofa, sat down, his shoulders slumped, the wine glass hanging in his lax fingers.

'Actually, Jessica, it's more than a bit desperate. I owe it to a chap – a nasty piece of work – he'll break my head if I don't get it for him.'

'But – Patrick! – what have you been doing to get into such debt? You have an allowance, don't you?'

He made a small, impatient gesture but said nothing.

'Patrick!'

He lifted his bright head. His eyes gleamed savagely blue in the light. Then he turned away, and the fierce, frightened expression was gone. 'All the chaps at school have a flutter. It's nothing unusual.'

'A flutter? You mean – gambling?'

He shrugged.

'Patrick? Gambling? *Five hundred guineas*?'

'I had a run of bad luck, that's all.' His voice was defiant. 'I'd have made it all back – I've done it before. It went wrong this time, that's all. Then this bounder started to dun me for the money. The others are willing to wait, I don't see why he –' He stopped.

There was a long silence. 'What others?' Jessica's voice was tight.

He shook his head.

'Patrick – what others?'

'Oh, for God's sake – what does it matter? It's this one that's after me – Jessie – please – I *have* to get hold of this money –!'

'Patrick – my dear – we don't have five hundred guineas!'

He gestured at the pile of books, eagerly. 'You'll make it though, won't you?'

'Not for months yet – and in any case –' The words died. She made a small, helplessly worried gesture.

'Oh, well –' Falsely bright he tossed back the wine and stood up, putting the glass on the table with a hand that was not quite steady. Beyond the window the full-leafed trees bent in a sudden storm-wind. 'I'll just have to go elsewhere. Trouble is these loan chappies strap a fellow for interest rather, and I hoped I could get away without, that's all. Don't worry. I'll get it.' He glanced at her from the corner of his eye, 'You – wouldn't mention this to anyone, would you? I don't want to – worry – grandmama –'

She was looking at him soberly. 'No. I don't think you should. And of course I'll say nothing. But, Patrick –'

He shook his head and held up his hand, a ghost of the old smile flickering on his young face. 'Don't "but", Jessica darling. I couldn't stand it. Sorry I brought the matter up. I'd better go now, or I'll be late for supper. I'll see you soon.' He dropped a perfunctory kiss on her cheek and was gone.

She was still standing at the window, a worried frown on her face, her wine untouched in her hand, when he galloped through the curtain of rain at flat speed down the river path and disappeared from sight towards New Hall.

The sad if not altogether unexpected news of Theo's death reached Jessica in September, in a letter from a Florentine lawyer written in July and telling her of a single bequest left specifically to her and forwarded under separate cover.

Jessica stared at the letter, the florid, stylish handwriting blurred by her tears.

'What is it?' Robert had come in from a walk by the river and unusually his eyes were bright and his pale face flushed with sunshine. Perversely, after the awful summer, the autumn was proving to be glorious – warm and balmy, the colours in the trees and hedgerows like the flames of a triumphal fire.

'It's Theo.' She brushed a hand across her wet eyes. 'He's dead.'

They stood in silence for a moment, each separately lost in thought and sudden recollection. This time last year they had been in Florence, and like children they had believed that nothing need ever change –

Robert put an awkward hand on her arm. It was the first time he had touched her in months. She smiled a small, tearful smile and moved a little away from him. 'I think – if you don't mind –I'd like to go for a walk.'

'Would you like me to come with you?'

She shook her head. 'No. I'll go alone.'

St Agatha's was shadowed as always, but the usual chill was gone. The warmth of the autumn air had seeped through even these grey, defensive walls. There was a strange, faint smell of something evocative of incense, a heady, dream-provoking scent that must be the product of one of the herbs that grew in straggling profusion with the weeds of the churchyard. Jessica sat for a very long time, calmed by the silent peace of the place, small disjointed memories flickering in her mind like the dance of flame, whilst the helpless tears welled and coursed down her face almost unnoticed.

Theo, that first night she had met him: wicked, unscrupulous. And kind.

Despite her tears she almost smiled. How Theo would have hated that word!

Theo, discoursing – gnarled, discoloured hands gesturing impatiently, grotesque wig askew, his passion for the perfection of *David* or the form of the *Pieta* evident in every movement.

Theo causing trouble between a group of earnest young artists too self-absorbed to see his mischief – the small, triumphant wink he would send her once he had got them fighting.

Theo stumping awkwardly through the Boboli Gardens. Theo watching her with bright eyes as she fell in love with the Villa Francesca.

Danny.

Danny in the sunshine, the glorious, endless Italian sunshine, laughing, a glass of wine in his hand. A look that could melt the marrow in her bones sent across a busy room, or a crowded, happy alfresco table. Danny, loving her that first time in the via Condotta. Danny angry. Danny happy. Danny working. And above all Danny's lovemaking, fierce and intense, that reduced her soul to willing slavery.

For months, stubbornly, she had fought the memories. For months she had endured the loneliness of living without him, and hardly once had she cried. But now her grief for Theo had released a flood of memories that would not be denied or ignored.

St Agatha smiled, cool and enigmatic, a hand lifted in blessing.

Danny's hands worked upon you, too. He is as much a part of you as he is of me.

For some reason the thought, absurd as it was, brought a fresh rise of tears. She bowed her face into her hands, sobbing. In the darkness behind her closed lids the memories rolled inexorably on.

Danny, so many years ago, here in this very building. 'So. My little Mouse, in a trap at last.' And then; 'Don't be afraid little Mouse. I won't hurt you.'

'Jessica Hawthorne – little Mouse – I hereby declare a day of rest. I've got bread, and cheese. Let's go and eat them by the river –'

Of such small decisions were tragedy made. She saw, though she fought against it, the look that had passed between Danny and Caroline that day, when her sister had appeared on that same riverbank. The look that had excluded her as surely as a barrier of steel.

And then his face, a mask of confused pain. 'She's expecting my child. We were to leave together. Tomorrow.'

She lifted her head, easing the painful tension in her neck.

Florence, and Theo again: 'So – yer want ter fall in love, eh? More fool you, gel. More fool you!'

Then a note. 'The library. A present from Theo.'

'Oh, Theo,' she said aloud, on a little sobbing catch of breath, 'Devil you were! I feel sorry for Lucifer! He doesn't stand a chance against you! You'll be taking over in no time.'

Overwhelmed with sadness she laid her arms tiredly upon the pew in front and buried her face in them, sobbing bitterly. But this time the storm was brief. In a while she raised her aching head, brushing the tears from her hot face with her fingers.

She tilted her head back and shut her eyes, the soft silence calming her. For perhaps an hour she sat in the lulling, strangely perfumed warmth, mourning Theo, longing for Danny, tempted almost beyond endurance to give up her fight to save Old Hall and to return to Florence and to Danny before it was too late. But when she stood, at last, the decision she had made was clear on her calm face. The sun was sinking. Duty called. The house that had survived for so long would not perish because Jessica Hawthorne mourned the loss of a lover.

The fresh air was very welcome. Her head was aching, her eyes heavy from weeping. It was as if the oppressive, scented air in the church had crept sluggishly into her veins, slowing her blood.

She walked to the gate and stood, a little dizzily, her hand to her head.

'You all right?'

The voice startled her into a near-shriek. Calmly Charlie Best steadied her with a huge, calloused hand. 'I'm sorry. Tha'ss daft of me. I didn't mean to frighten you.' His voice was very quiet.

'I – didn't know you were there. You startled me, that's all.' Slowly her head was clearing. She was suddenly acutely aware of her dishevelled and undignified appearance, her swollen, tearstained face.

'I was passin',' he said. 'I heard you –' he hesitated, then continued, 'I waited. Seemed somethin' might be wrong. Seemed there might be somethin' I could do?'

She shook her head, 'Oh, Charlie, thank you. But – I'm all right. Truly. It's just – I had some bad news. Someone I loved more than I knew has died. I just had to go somewhere and have a good cry.'

He nodded and she remembered that here was a man who knew about grief. 'Best thing. You want me to walk back with you?'

She shook her head. 'No. Thank you, but no. I can manage. And just at the moment I think I'd rather be on my own.'

He nodded again, unembarrassed, understanding. She wondered how long he had stood, patiently waiting for her, wondered too, suddenly and with a tiny spurt of amusement, when he had at last stopped calling her 'Your Ladyship' at every other word. 'As long as you're all right.'

'Truly I am. I just need a walk, that's all.'

He nodded, and with no other salute turned and left her, striding heavily and purposefully back along the path that ollowed the river. Like a shadow his small collie Bess had appeared at his heels, following him.

The dipping sun lit the water to fire where it glittered through the drifting willow-branches, yellow-gold now, but still in full leaf.

Jessica watched Charlie's sturdy form disappear around the curve of the path and then set out slowly after him, a little comforted.

The world was not, after all, an entirely friendless place.

Theo's bequest to Jessica arrived a couple of weeks later. Jessica had been to Home Farm to discuss with Charlie the possibility of putting more land to pasture the following year. Charlie had long since become used to discussing such things with her, rather than with Robert, the true master of the estate, for try as she might she could interest Robert in neither her plans for the house nor in the running of the lands that went with it. He left it all to her, shrugging if she asked his advice, agreeing almost off-handedly to anything she suggested as long as it required no effort from him. But at least lately it seemed to her that he had been a little more settled. He spoke less often and less desperately of returning to Florence, and spent more time outside the dilapidated walls of Old Hall. He had begun taking long, rambling, lonely walks at odd hours of the day, his only companion his battered volume of Byron's poems which he would, Jessica presumed, pore over in solitude in some quiet corner of the estate, lost in a dream from which he did not want to awaken. But the walks brought no colour to his cheeks, and he was still *distrait* and very quiet. He rarely spoke and even more rarely listened to anything going on around him. He was like a man constantly in a reverie and at odd moments in her busy life she wondered a little worriedly what was going on in his mind and where this aimless dreaming might lead him.

She had spent an hour with Charlie and was riding back to Old Hall when she saw Gabriella riding towards her on her fat little pony, heels drumming at the animal's rounded sides as she pushed him as close to a gallop as his dumpling proportions would allow. 'Mama! Mama! There is a package! A package from Italy! And it has your name on it!'

Smiling Jessica reined in. The child's dark eyes were shining with excitement in her pointed, smooth-skinned face. Behind her stood the young groom who accompanied her wherever she rode, his long legs keeping easy pace with the pony's short ones. He touched his cap to Jessica, smiling. 'She would come to find you, Y're Ladyship. That excited she was.'

Jessica leaned down to pat the pony's shaggy head. 'Well — we'd best go to see what the excitement is all about, hadn't we?'

'It's pretty,' Gabriella announced, judiciously, an hour or so later, studying the book her mother held, one of the two that the package had held. 'Is it yours?'

'Yes, it is. Theo gave it to me.' Jessica looked at her daughter fondly. 'Do you remember Theo?'

The child narrowed her eyes a little in thought, then nodded uncertainly. 'I — *think* — so.'

'He was a very good friend.' Smiling with pleasure Jessica leafed through the beautifully decorated pages of the book. 'Is Papa somewhere around? I think he might like to see these.'

Gabriella shrugged. 'He was. He went out I think. Perhaps he came to find you, as I did? Mama —' She turned a bright, momentarily serious face to her mother. '— Miss Barton says that when I grow up I must marry a lord and live in his castle. Is that true?'

411

Jessica turned from the drawing. Gabriella's dark eyes, so heartbreakingly like Danny's were fixed solemnly upon hers. She laughed affectionately, and gathered her daughter to her, hugging her until the child giggled breathlessly. 'Only if you want to, my precious. You may marry a prince, or a beggar, live in a palace or a gypsy's tent. Just as long as you're happy.'

'May I tell Miss Barton that?'

'You may.'

The little girl smiled and tucked a confident hand into her mother's. 'And when I get married, may I stay here? I want to live here for ever and ever.'

Jessica dropped a quick kiss onto the small, tender finger-tips. 'Nothing would make me happier, my darling. Nothing at all.'

It was more than two hours later, with Gabriella abed and supper almost ready that Jessica realized that Robert still had not returned to the house. To her surprise no-one remembered his going nor knew where he might be. Mrs Williams agreed with Gabriella that he had been on hand when the package from Italy had been delivered, and suggested the same thing that the child had. 'Perhaps he went off to look for you, Miss Jess?'

Jessica shook her head, puzzled. 'I can't really see why he'd do that. I'm sure I told him I was going down to the farm. If he had gone that way I'd have passed him on the way back –' The first faint stirrings of unease drew her brows together in a frown. The path to Home Farm followed the river at its deepest almost all the way. 'Mrs Williams – wait supper awhile, would you? I'll ride back to the farm and see if he's there. Perhaps he's got talking to Charlie and forgotten the time?'

'You want some help, Miss Jess? Shall I call young Sam?'

'Oh no. There's no need. I shan't be long. Just ask Sam to saddle Bay Dancer for me, would you?'

She rode fast to the farm, sure now that that was where Robert would be. The sun was dipping below the horizon, sending spears of scarlet and gold into the clear sky as she rode up the track. Charlie came to the door, shading his eyes. She did not dismount. 'Charlie – have you seen my husband? I think he may have come here looking for me?'

Charlie shook his head. 'He hasn't been here.'

'You're sure?'

Charlie nodded. 'Somethin' wrong?'

'No.' She spoke the word a shade too quickly. 'No, I'm sure not. It's just unusual for him to be gone so long.'

'You want me to come help look for him?'

She laughed a little. 'Oh no, Charlie! He'd be furious if he found me sending out search parties!' Bay Dancer backed restively away from the door, eager to be gone. 'I'll go back to the house. He's sure to have come home by now.'

She stopped once or twice on the way back along the river path, calling above the sound of the moving waters. 'Robert? Ro–bert!' Almost certainly, she thought, ignoring the chill that the sight of the dark river brought, he had found some sheltered spot and become so absorbed in Lord Byron's heroic poesy that he had forgotten the time. Perhaps he had even fallen asleep. With the sun gone the evening was cooling very quickly. He'd soon be home.

Mrs Williams was waiting at the gate, watching for her, her own eyes worried. No, Sir Robert had not returned, and there had been no word. No-one knew where he was.

Jessica did not dismount. One more idea had come to her. 'Perhaps he's called in at New Hall, and has stayed to supper with Patrick and Mother?'

'The master has been seeing a lot of Mr Patrick lately,' Mrs Williams conceded, 'so yes, tha'ss very likely what he's done.'

Jessica was astonished. So involved in Old Hall's affairs had she been lately that the information that Patrick and Robert had been meeting was a complete surprise. She felt a twinge of guilt that she should neglect Robert so that he felt it necessary to seek the company of a seventeen-year-old, however charming. 'I'll ride over and see if he's there,' she said on impulse. 'Don't worry about supper, Mrs Williams – feed the rest of the household – I'll probably eat at New Hall.'

'Very well, Miss Jess.'

413

Jessica turned Bay Dancer along the path that led to the lake. The sun had gone now, and the air was chill, though the last colours of a brilliant sunset still washed the sky, tingeing the underbellies of a few clouds that hung like painted patches upon the darkening sky. The sound of the horse's hooves were muffled by a fresh, deep carpet of leaves that gave off the sharp, sweet smell of autumn as they were disturbed. A bird twittered sleepily and was still. About the tower of St Agatha's bats swooped, flickering like swift shadows in the still half-dark. Surprised, she reined the horse to a quiet halt. The door of the church stood a little open, and through it she had thought she detected the faintest rosy gleam of light. She frowned and narrowed her eyes. She must be mistaken. But no, as Dancer moved a little, restively, she saw it again – a narrow slither of lamp light, bright in the growing darkness.

Silently she slid from the saddle and tethered the horse to a tree. Then quietly she moved up the overgrown path to the church porch. As she neared the open door she stopped, sniffing the air. A heavy, unpleasantly sweet smell drifted to her nostrils and caught at her throat. She remembered the faint, strange, incense-like scent she had smelled in the church the last time she had come here. This was the same, but stronger, sickly and cloying, strong enough almost to taste.

It was becoming rapidly darker, and as it did so the gleam of light from beyond the door brightened.

Very quietly she stepped to the door and pushed it.

It took a moment for her eyes to adjust to the darkness of the interior, a darkness that seemed strangely clouded despite the rosy halo of the lamp that stood upon a small table in the centre of the church. The smell enveloped her, sweet and nauseating. She put a hand to cover her nose and mouth. Smoke stung her eyes. There was a faint rustle of movement. A wisp of smoke spiralled and hung in the air like an evil genie escaping from a bottle. Jessica stood rooted to the spot.

Patrick reclined amongst cushions on a pew, his long legs crossed, his bright head, propped upon one hand, glinting in the fitful light. The heavy perfume of the drugging smoke that lifted from the pipe he held drifted eerily in the space above him. He was smiling, the long fair lashes veiling his eyes. Robert sat upon the floor beside him, his back against the end of the pew, his head back, his eyes closed, a look of calm ecstasy upon his narrow, dark face. As Jessica watched he opened his eyes, inclined his head a little and drew deeply upon the pipe he held, the twin of the one that Patrick was smoking. Upon the table with the lamp was a saucepan, something that looked like a sieve and a spoon, beside which, incongruously, lay a lemon cut in half. The smoke from the pipes gathered in the dark air like an evil cloud, carrying with it its sweet, drugging perfume.

Jessica had begun to tremble, and her stomach roiled. She felt as if she were suffocating, the poisoned air catching her throat and choking her lungs. She stepped back. The door creaked. Robert turned his head, looking directly towards the sound. For a moment their eyes met: but she knew with a stirring of horror that lifted the small hairs upon her neck that he did not see her. He did not see anything. He smiled, gently.

She fled. Brambles clawed at her riding-skirt, branches whipped painfully at her skin. Bay Dancer turned his head to her as she stumbled to him. Shivering violently she put her arms about the horse's strong, warm neck and stood for a moment, leaning against the animal, drawing comfort from the simple, uncorrupted strength of the beast. Her eyes were stinging, the opium-smell hung about her hair and her clothes, cloyed her throat. It was full dark now. Somewhere close an owl hunted, crying in the darkness, its great wings brushing the air like the pinions of death. A small, terrified animal shrieked and was silent. With an enormous effort Jessica swung herself into the saddle and turned the horse's head for home.

Robert returned to Old Hall minutes after the clocks of the house had chimed midnight. Jessica sat where she had remained almost unmoving since she had returned, in a deep armchair next to the oriel window of the Old Drawing Room, a single lamp burning at her elbow. She saw the lantern he carried, watched it as it approached, bobbing like a will o' the wisp along the river path, across the drawbridge and over the courtyard. She saw it stop for a moment as Robert caught sight of the lamp burning in the window, and then come on more slowly to the door below.

She heard the opening of the door, and its closing. Heard the hesitancy of his footsteps as he mounted the stairs. Then he stood, lantern still in hand, at the door. As he stepped into the room a faint, sickly-sweet smell drifted in with him.

Jessica did not move.

'Jessica? You're still up?'

She said nothing.

'Is – something wrong?' His voice was wary.

'Yes, Robert. There's something wrong.'

'What's happened?' He came further into the room. She saw that the hand that held the lantern shook. With care he set the light upon a table and turned to her, 'What's the matter?'

She lifted her head. He blinked at the look in her eyes. His own were smudged with tiredness, the pupils unnaturally big.

'I came to look for you tonight,' she said.

He drew a long breath, loud in the silence. 'And –' he asked, carefully, 'did you find me?'

'Yes.'

'In the church?'

'Yes.'

'I see.'

The silence that fell was like a door closing between them.

She shook her head, bitterly. 'Robert, you fool! What do you think you're doing? To yourself? To us?'

He threw his head back, hair flying from his forehead. His mouth was tight. 'Be quiet, Jessica. You don't understand.'

'Understand?' She almost laughed at that. 'Oh, I understand!
Better than you'll ever know! You can't face reality, so you drug yourself into stupidity to escape it!'

He spun on her, took a step forward that was clearly threatening. 'That isn't it! It isn't! When I smoke the dreams come – and the dreams are music – music, Jessica! I compose like a master! I hear it – it releases me –'

She leapt to her feet, facing him, a tired, savage anger overwhelming her. 'You're mad! Opium has softened your brain!'

'No! Opium is my salvation!' he glared back at her, breathing heavily. 'With the dreams I can make music. With the dreams I shall write something truly great at last –!'

She shook her head, her temper dying as quickly as it had flared, a terrible sadness filling the vacuum it left in its going. His face was pallid and thin, the eyes huge and burning. The neatly handsome features that had been familiar to her since childhood were sharp-drawn and anguished. He looked a haunted man, and the chilling depths of fear and misery she saw in his eyes terrified her.

'Robert – please! – can't you see how wrong this is? Can't you see the harm you're doing to yourself? Your music has gone – you have to face it –'

'No!'

'You tried! And – you failed. Opium won't change that –'

'But it does! Jessie – it does!' Eagerly he stepped to her, 'I tell you that in the smoke-dreams I hear the music I could write –'

'And do you write it?' she asked, quietly.

He nibbled his lip.

'Robert?' she prompted, gently, 'Do you write it?'

He turned from her. 'Not yet. When I try it – slips away. But I will! I know I will!'

The depth of her pity for him brought unexpected tears. As she watched him they burned, blurring the lamp-light. She rubbed the heels of her hands into her eyes. If she allowed herself to weep now she suspected that she would not stop for a very long time.

'Don't interfere, Jessica,' his disembodied voice was quiet in the gloom. 'Don't try to stop me. I don't know what I might do if you tried to stop me.'

She lifted her head, shocked. He stood very still, watching her, his white face all but expressionless.

'Patrick is my friend,' he said. 'He showed me the way.'

'The way to hell,' she said, bitterly.

'No. The way to paradise.'

She shook her head in wordless despair. The awful smell still clung to him, revolting her, like the sick-sweet smell of death.

He came to her, seeing her misery, his voice suddenly gentle. 'Jessica – many great people have used opium. Poets. Painters. Musicians. They make no secret of it. It is a benign influence. It's nothing to be afraid of.'

'And the dreams?' she asked quietly. 'Are they never to be feared?'

She saw something flicker in his eyes, and she had her answer, for all that he would not speak.

'The dreams are not always of music,' she said softly, 'are they?'

He turned and walked to the window, stood looking at his reflection in the glass, broken and fractured by the lead lights and the flickering lamp light.

'What of the horrors?' Jessica asked. 'How can you face them?'

He shook his head. 'Stop it.'

'Stop what? Trying to make you see the truth? That in the end this will control you – drive you insane –?'

'No!' It was a muted cry of agony.

She bowed her head for a moment, closing her eyes, suddenly entirely exhausted. 'Sweet Jesus Christ. What are we going to do?'

She heard a rustle of movement, smelled the drug-smoke smell as he paused by her side. 'There's absolutely nothing we can do.' His voice was suddenly, astoundingly normal, apparently perfectly controlled. 'It is gone too far. Jessica – you're tired. You've got everything out of perspective. Wait till morning and you'll see that things are not so terrible. We are a nation of opium-eaters. The lord in his castle, the poor man by his hearth. Why, even your mother takes laudenum –'

She dropped her hands to her side. 'Don't be stupid! How can you compare it? Mother takes laudenum to ease her pain –' she stopped.

He smiled, bleakly. 'Exactly. I could not have put it better myself.' He moved to her as if he might have been going to kiss

418

her cheek. She drew back from him. He shrugged a little. 'Good night, Jessica.'

When he had gone she collapsed into the chair like a stringless puppet abandoned by its master. She sat for a long time, staring sightlessly at the smoking flame of the lamp.

Before she slept, huddled into the chair, one thought came, just one constructive thought. 'Patrick is my friend,' Robert had said. 'He showed me the way —'

Patrick.

Tomorrow she would talk to Patrick. God help the boy.

She rode to New Hall the following morning. She had not seen Robert — he had not come down to breakfast and she had not sought him out to enquire why. She rode across the New Hall parkland fighting to control the anger that rose each time she thought of the events of the previous evening, trying to marshal reasoned argument, to bury deep the too-bitter words that seethed in her tired brain. Her neck was stiff from an awkward night's sleep, and her eyes felt as if the dust of the desert had blown into them. But still she kept a brake upon the impulse to blame Patrick for what was happening to Robert. She recognized that the reasons for Patrick's undoubted wildness were more than the simple and the obvious. She remembered the frightened child, his mother newly dead, his grandmother dying, thrown into a hostile environment like a small martyr into a den of lions. She remembered those early letters from Harrow while she had been in Florence with Danny, too busy then to read between the lines. More than once a shadow of doubt had crossed her mind about a child from a background so chequered holding his own in a bastion of privilege and of petty power. She thought of the boy's facile charm, his easy ways, his readiness to indulge in extremes of behaviour. He was not, she told herself determinedly, too much to be blamed. But this game with fire must be stopped, before it destroyed himself and Robert.

The morning was cold. Heavy clouds massed to the west, and the smell of rain sharpened the wind. Leaves swirled past her as she rode and the grass flattened in the strong breeze. As she rode to the front door of New Hall one of Clara's peacocks, no longer Clara's, stalked away from her, crowned head high, the long, beautiful tail blowing gracefully in the wind as it trailed behind the bird.

She handed her hat, crop and gloves to the footman who opened the door. 'Is Mr Patrick at home?'

'Yes, Your Ladyship. He's breakfasting in the morning room.'

'And my mother?'

He shook his powdered head. 'Has been unwell, I fear, Your Ladyship, and has been confined to her room for two days. Her breakfast has been taken to her.'

'I see. Please let her know that I'm here, and tell her I'll visit her after I've had a word with Mr Patrick.'

'Certainly, Your Ladyship.'

She smiled her thanks and left him. The house was very quiet. A small maid scurried by, dressed in her dark morning work-dress, carrying a bucket and mop. As she acknowledged the child's shy greeting it came to Jessica with some surprise that this was the only servant she had encountered between the front door and the morning room. As a child it had seemed to her that New Hall had always at this time of day been an ant-heap of hurrying servants. It was a surprise too to discover that no footman waited at the morning room door to open it and announce her. For the first time she saw that what her mother had told her was true; times at New Hall might not be as desperate as they were at the old house, but neither were they as easy as they had been in the past.

'Jessica!' As she entered the room Patrick looked up from the paper he had been reading, tossed it on the table and came to his feet in a quick, graceful movement. He looked fresh, rested and bright-eyed as a child. He was wearing pale buckskin peg-topped trousers, neat fitting at slim waist and ankle and a white silk shirt, the cravat loosely tied. He looked delighted to see her. 'What an unexpected pleasure! I always say that the nicest things happen when you least expect them! And here I am, eating a dull-dog breakfast – and in you walk, pretty as a picture. Have you come to take me riding?' He grinned engagingly, his eyes taking in her tailored jacket and flared riding skirt, 'I swear I'm overeating so that if I'm not forced to some exercise soon I shall be as fat as butter!' He slapped his narrow hips, laughing.

She stopped just inside the door. If he noticed her silence, her strained expression, he gave no sign.

'Won't you take some breakfast? We've kidneys and bacon – I think they're still hot. The eggs are gone – but I could order some more?'

'No. Thank you.'

'Why, Jessie –' he smiled, a little cautiously, '– how very ill-tempered you look! Did you get out of the wrong side of the bed this morning? Is something wrong?'

She had already decided that there would be no easy or tactful way to broach her subject. 'I want to talk to you.'

He smiled warmly. 'Talk away. Here I am. Won't you sit down first?'

She shook her head. 'Patrick – last night I rode by St Agatha's. I was looking for Robert.'

The bright eyes narrowed. 'Ah.'

'I saw a light in the church.'

'And you investigated?' His voice was light and pleasant, but all movement of his body had stilled.

'Yes.'

He sucked his lower lip, eyeing her speculatively. There was a small silence.

'Patrick – in God's name – what do you think you're doing? Do you know what you're playing with? It's bad enough for you, but to involve Robert –! Can't you see he's already –'

'What?'

She hesitated. '– not as stable as he might be,' she said. 'You'll drive him insane.'

'Oh, nonsense!' He threw the napkin he had been holding onto the table, smiling. 'Jessica, you don't understand the nature of –'

She shook her head sharply, interrupting him. 'No, Patrick! It's you who don't understand!' She paused for a moment, controlling her anger. 'Please. Listen. I haven't come to argue with you. I haven't come to reason. I haven't even, God help me, come to plead with you to give up the filthy habit yourself. Something tells me that the breath would be wasted. I've come to ask you – to tell you – to stay away from Robert. And don't dare – don't *dare* – to supply him with any more of that – that disgusting drug –!'

He turned away from her, his young face impatient. 'For God's sake, Jessica, that's up to Robert, isn't it? He's a grown man –!'

'Which you are not!' She was holding her calm with difficulty. 'Whether you like it or not, Patrick, you are controllable. You are not yet your own master. If I told Mother of this – or of your gaming debts –'

'I'd deny it!' His voice had risen. 'Grandmama would never believe you over me! Never! Take care, Jessica! Don't cross me! I have Grandmama here –' He tucked a long finger into the palm of his own hand. 'Don't make me use that against you. Oh, Jessica –' Even now he tried to laugh, tossing the hair from his eyes, the anger of a second before replaced by shameless coaxing, 'I thought you were my friend –!'

The fury that Jessica had been so determined to control was flooding her, and she was helpless against it. 'And this is how you repay friendship? To feed Robert some horrible concoction that makes for him dreams that could drive him to addiction and insanity? To game with money that is not yours to gamble? To –' she stopped. Patrick was looking past her, a stricken expression upon his face, every vestige of colour drained from his fine, fair skin.

Very slowly Jessica turned.

Maria Hawthorne, leaning heavily upon her gold-knobbed stick, stood in the open doorway.

'Go on, Jessica,' she said, the trembling of her voice barely discernible. 'Really, my dear, you can hardly stop there.'

'Mother –' Jessica glanced distractedly at Patrick. Of all the things she had wanted this was the last.

Slowly, watched by two young people who seemed to have become rooted where they stood the old woman limped into the room and closed the door behind her, then made her careful way across the shining polished floor to a chair at the head of the table, the irregular tapping of her stick loud in the quiet. With iron determination she allowed no tremor of pain to show in her face as she sat down straight-backed and autocratic, both hands folded upon the gold-knobbed stick that rested upon the floor before her. 'Now. Where were we?' she asked, pleasantly. 'Jessica?'

Jessica stood in silence.

'Let me refresh your memory, daughter.' The old woman paused. Bright colour was stealing into Patrick's face. 'Robert is being fed a horrible concoction that will drive him to addiction and insanity – really, Jessica, I can't help thinking that your reading matter must lately have left a little to be desired! – And Patrick has been gaming with money that, as you quite rightly point out, is not his to gamble. You might add –' apparently speaking to Jessica her eyes were upon Patrick's burning face, unblinking, '– against his sworn word to me. Shall we start there? Or is there more?'

Jessica miserably held her tongue. There seemed nothing she could say that would not do more damage.

Patrick took a step forward, his hand outstretched. 'Grandmama –?' The word was a plea.

'Leaving other matters aside for a moment, Patrick –' Maria's voice was cool, but still held that tremor of tightly-controlled emotion, fire burning beneath a fragile crust of ice. 'Let us first establish something. What are these new debts of yours?'

He shook his head. His face was taut and frightened.

'What – are – your – debts?' The old lady emphasized each quiet word with a rap of her stick upon the floor.

He took a breath as if to speak. His mouth worked. He said nothing.

Maria sighed, and for a brief moment closed her eyes. 'Patrick – this is not the first time we have had this conversation. Is it?'

'No, Grandmama.'

'In three years – how many times? Five? Six? How many times have you cried repentance? Sworn and promised reform?'

He said nothing.

'How many times have I taken your word? Foolishly taken your word that you will curb your wild behaviour?'

'Mother –' Jessica stepped forward, her eyes worried upon her mother's drawn face.

Her mother turned her head. 'Yes, Jessica?'

'This – this is my fault. I lost my temper –'

'So I heard. And for good reason it seems.'

Jessica bit her lip. Angry as she had been with Patrick the last thing she had intended was to precipitate such a scene. 'This – this is between me and Patrick,' she said, 'there's no reason for you to upset yourself so –'

The still formidably bright eyes flickered to Patrick and back again. 'Really?' Maria asked, very gently. 'Are you quite sure about that?' She waited in silence for a moment. Neither of the young people spoke. Maria's gaze transferred to Patrick. He sustained it for a difficult moment then looked away, ducking his head, his fair skin flushed. Maria's rigid control had slipped a little. Her shoulders drooped, her face was tired as was her voice when she spoke. 'What is it you've been doing this time that made Jessica so very angry?'

His long index finger rubbed nervously at the buckskin of his breeches. He neither looked up nor answered.

'Patrick?'

He lifted his head at last. His young face was bright with a kind of guilty defiance. 'Jessica found Robert and me in St Agatha's last night. We were –' he faltered a little '– we were smoking opium.'

Maria did not move, but Jessica saw the swift shadow of distaste that flickered in her face. 'Robert? You induced Robert to smoke opium?'

Patrick shrugged, childishly insolent.

Slowly and with great care Maria stood and tapped her way to the window, where she stood with her back to the occupants of the room, looking out into the park. Patrick stole a glance at Jessica's concerned face then looked quickly away. There was a long silence. At last, with a long sigh that visibly lifted her shoulders Maria turned. 'Patrick – what are your debts?' she asked again, very quietly.

The habit of authority won. Patrick's bravura left him. 'I'm – not sure.'

'But – you can guess, surely?' The words were deceptively gentle.

He sucked his lower lip. 'A thousand – perhaps fifteen hundred guineas –' he mumbled. 'I can't be certain – the interest –'

Jessica gasped. Maria said nothing but her grip on the cane that supported her visibly tightened.

'It was a run of bad luck, that's all,' Patrick said defensively, 'and when I couldn't pay I had to go to the moneylenders again –'

'Last year,' Maria said, ignoring his words, 'the estate settled debts of yours totalling over twelve hundred pounds. The year before '

'Mother, please –' Jessica could not bear the flame of embarrassment in Patrick's face. 'I really think I should leave. This is between you and Patrick –'

'No. Stay. You must stay.' Beneath the sharpness of tone there was a thread of urgency she could not ignore. Maria looked levelly back at Patrick. Her back was to the light and her face was shadowed, but not enough to hide the depth of sadness in her eyes, the tiredness that invested every line. 'Patrick. What is to become of you?' she asked. 'And of New Hall, when I am gone and there is no-one to control you?'

Patrick shifted uncomfortably.

'You have flouted every rule of decent behaviour. You have broken every promise, to me and to others. You are eighteen years old. An inveterate gambler, a compulsive womanizer. And now opium.' A trace of weary bitterness had appeared in her voice. 'What other surprises do you have in store for me?'

'It – it won't happen again, Grandmama. I promise.' The words rang weakly in every ear that heard them, including Patrick's own. He fell to silence.

Maria was watching him, her face intent. 'No,' she said, her voice oddly flat. 'I don't think it will.'

He frowned a little at the tone.

Maria walked back to the table, laid her stick upon it and then leaned forward, palms flat upon the shining surface, supporting her. 'I have something to tell both of you. Something I believed I would never reveal to a living soul.' Her eyes rested upon Patrick's face. 'Something I would have given my life not to have you know.'

A deep foreboding stirred in Jessica. 'Mother –' she began, uneasily.

Maria silenced her with a quick movement of her hand. 'It is necessary, Jessica. I am forced to it. Forced to it by Patrick's weakness. I have deceived myself for long enough. Patrick – if you cannot control yourself then I must do it for you by any means within my grasp. However painful it may be.' She lifted her head to look at her daughter. 'And Jessica must know so that always, when I am gone, there is a check on you.' She paused, then spoke directly to Jessica. 'You are the only one I would entrust with such a burden.'

Jessica shook her head. She wanted nothing of secrets. And she had burdens enough of her own –

The unstable colour had lifted again in Patrick's face. 'Grandmama –'

She would not let him speak. 'When you go to your money-lenders, Patrick – to pay off your gaming debts – to pacify angry fathers and brothers – to purchase your drugs and your alcohol – with what do you secure your loans?'

He frowned a little, puzzled.

'Well?'

'With – with my inheritance. They know what I'll be worth when I'm twenty-one. They know they'll get their money in the end. Specifically, this time, I mortgaged the lands to the east of the village, next to the Lavenham Road. The enclosed commons that haven't been sown yet. Giles himself said he doubted their worth to the estate –'

'I see.' For the first time Maria bowed her head, tiredly, looking down at her spread hands. It seemed to Jessica that all at once she looked unsure of herself and the step she had obviously decided to take. Yet when she lifted her head there was nothing but painful and simple determination upon her face. 'And – if I told you that, legitimately, you have no inheritance? That it has all been built on a lie?'

The boy watched her as if struck to stone. 'What do you mean?'

Maria looked down at her hands again. Jessica's stomach churned uncomfortably.

'Grandmama – *what do you mean*?'

She shook her head, not looking at him. 'Even that is a lie,' she said. 'I am not your grandmother.' She looked at him, clear pain in her eyes. 'Sadly we are not even actually related. Though truly I've loved you as if you were.'

The boy stared at her, uncomprehending.

On a sudden fierce spurt of anger Maria struck the table with her hand. 'Why did you have to force me to this?'

The silence was fretted with tension.

Jessica watched as with an effort her mother straightened and squared her narrow shoulders. 'Patrick, you are not Edward's son. You are a byblow of William, my husband, upon a young Cambridge girl, Anne Stewart, whose mother was the true grandmother that you remember, who brought you to us when she knew she was dying and could no longer care for you. You are not heir to New Hall. You are bastard half-brother to my sons.'

'*No!*'

'I'm sorry, but yes. It's true.'

'You're lying.' Patrick sounded dazed. 'You must be lying –'

She shook her head.

'But – the proof! There was proof –!'

Maria moved to a chair and lowered herself painfully into it, resting her elbows on the table. Her face was haggard. 'Forged,' she said. 'Forged, perjured and bought. Have you not discovered that anything – anything! – can be bought by one willing and able to pay the price? Anything and almost anyone –'

'But – Sir Charles! A reputable lawyer! You surely couldn't have –?'

She made a small, tiredly impatient gesture. 'Of course not. One doesn't have to buy fools. They give themselves away for nothing. I bribed a man of the cloth and the son of a peer. Impeccable witnesses. I don't think it crossed Sir Charles' pathetic, parchment-bound mind to doubt them. The best forger in the land worked for two days and nights to reproduce the Parish Register of St Margaret's. Every entry is absolutely authentic. Except one.'

'I don't believe it.' His voice was flat with shock.

She took a very long breath. 'I'm afraid you must. It's true. Your extraordinary resemblance to your half-brother Edward – the thing that first put the plan into my mind – made it all quite ridiculously easy. Even Giles was fooled by that, and decided not to fight. But, if he had, it would have made no difference. He would have found nothing. With the help of your grandmother – your real grandmother – I was very thorough.'

Jessica saw that she was trembling a little. 'Mother – how could you –?' she asked, softly.

Faint defiance lit the tired face. 'I had my reasons.'

'*You*?' Patrick asked, his voice shaking. '*You* had your reasons? Is that all you're going to say? What about me? *What about me*?'

Maria threw her head back. Her face was anguished. 'You need never have known! I never intended that you should! But you have forced me to it! I have to stop you. You have to understand. Before you ruin us all! You have to know that if you don't curb yourself –' she stopped.

He stepped back, shaking his head.

Jessica reached an urgent hand to him. 'Patrick –!'

He shook her off, roughly. 'Leave me alone!'

'Patrick – please – listen to me –'

'Leave me alone, I say!' He was backing to the door. His face was livid, his wide eyes fixed upon Maria's face. 'You talk about me!' he said, wildly. 'You're the wicked one! Wicked and heartless! You'll go to hell for this!' There was an edge of hysteria in the young voice, 'And you deserve to! You deserve to!'

'Patrick!' Jessica jumped forward as he lunged for the door handle. 'Don't go! Wait – we have to talk –'

He pushed her away with muted violence. 'Talk? What is there to talk about? Leave me alone, do you hear? Leave me – *alone*!' And he was gone, slamming the door behind him, his running footsteps echoing down the corridor.

Appalled, Jessica turned to her mother. The old woman was sitting ramrod-straight, her hands folded before her upon the table. In the light from the window the bright tear-furrows shone on the age-softened cheeks. Jessica stepped forward and stopped, her hand outstretched, as her mother turned her head to face her. It was the first time in her life that Jessica had seen Maria Hawthorne cry. 'I shouldn't have told him,' she said, very steadily. 'I thought it was the right thing to do. But I was wrong. Find him, Jessica. Bring him back to me.'

Jessica hesitated for only a moment longer. Then she turned and ran back to the door.

Patrick was nowhere to be seen.

It was two hours before he was found. Two hours in which Jessica searched every corner of the house she could think of. Two hours in which Maria sat, pale-faced and silent at the window of her small sitting room. Jessica, returning finally to report a fruitless search, to her surprise found Giles with her. He was standing by the window. Something in his stance, the grim look on his face, alerted her. 'What is it?' she asked. 'What's happened?'

'Patrick,' he said.

Her heart was beating with a horrible rhythm, thumping in her chest, drumming in her ears. 'What?'

He turned to look at her, his eyes sombre. 'They've just found him. In the barn.'

Maria, very slowly, bowed her head and covered her face with her hands. Giles stepped back from the window. In the distance Jessica could see the roof of the ancient barn, where once long ago Giles had imprisoned Bran and a child had cried as if the end of the world had come.

Across the park came a small, mournful procession. Bareheaded the estate workers bore their burden. A girl – one of the servants – walked beside them, weeping into her pinafore. She was carrying an empty bottle and a shotgun. Upon the door that the men carried carefully between them lay a long, shapeless mound covered in a blanket. At its head a dark stain spread, black in the bright light of midday.

No-one in the room made a sound as the solemn group crossed the garden and disappeared from sight beneath the window.

Chapter Fifteen

The scandal, Jessica noted bitterly, remembering her mother's words to Patrick, was kept to a minimum. Anything and anyone can be bought, Maria had told the bastard boy who until that moment had believed himself to be her grandson, by one who is able and willing to pay the price; and so it proved again. It was an open secret on the estate and in the village that poor young Mr Patrick had got drunk in the barn and shot himself, and as a suicide should not be buried in hallowed ground. The young man had been popular enough in the district, however, for there to be a more or less charitable acceptance of the fiction that the shooting had been a tragic accident – so said Giles' fellow Justice, and so agreed the Church. The tactful and face-saving suggestion that the boy should be buried at St Agatha's rather than the village church silenced the last of the tongues, and if New Hall's already considerably shrunken coffers were further depleted by an extremely handsome donation towards the restoration of the tower of the parish church no-one complained, least of all Giles and Clara who were now reinstated at New Hall with full authority and honour. Speculation about the cause of the tragedy, however, was rather more difficult to stop – no threat and no amount of money could keep the gossips' tongues from that particularly fascinating subject. But so far as Jessica could tell no-one came near to guessing the truth. Patrick's growing wildness had been known and noted in house and village: that he gambled and drank to excess was also a fact that had not passed unremarked. A family row – a high-strung and over-wrought youngster – it was easy enough for the busy tongues to fit the pieces of the puzzle to make an acceptable whole – a whole, Jessica thought that, ironically, was a lot less bizarre than the squalid truth.

Jessica herself, whilst her mother sat in withdrawn silence in her room, told first Robert and then – after much heart-searching – Giles the truth of what had happened. She was thankful that her mother had not yet recovered enough to instruct her, for she suspected that had Maria Hawthorne been in full possession of her faculties she would have fought tooth and nail to prevent the rest of the family – and especially Giles – from hearing the true cause of Patrick's death. Jessica, however, was not ready to protect such a secret, not even for her mother's sake. Whatever happened now, Jessica was Hawthorne enough to know that family ranks must be closed. What was done was done and to risk it becoming public would do nothing but harm to anyone. To keep such a dangerous secret from Giles, as the head of the family, made no sense. To leave the family ignorant would be to leave the family defenceless if at some time in the future the truth were discovered. And so she told him.

Giles was angry enough to kill. He was making for the door with long angry strides when Jessica, her own nerves strung almost to breaking point, stepped in front of him. 'Where are you going?'

'Where do you think? To see her! To tell her –!'

'No!'

He glared at her. A corded vein in his neck throbbed violently.

She did not budge. 'You can't do that,' she said, only the faint tremor in her voice betraying her. 'I told you because I thought you should know. But I won't – you hear me? – I won't have you make Mother suffer for it. Not now. It's too late, and whatever you may think she's suffered enough. What's been done can't be undone. You'll cause nothing but strife if you try to face her with it –'

'Strife? Jesus Christ! What of me? What of the strife my loving mother and father's bastard have caused me? They've run the place into the ground between them! It'll take years to sort out the mess they've made –'

'Then sort it out! You won't change anything by persecuting Mother. Giles, for God's sake! – You've got what you wanted – what you always wanted. Isn't that enough? 'She paused, and as he savagely made to push past her caught his arm. 'We both know what you did to get it.' He turned on her but she did not flinch. 'When you live in a glass house, Giles, it's extremely unwise to cast the first stone. Don't you think?'

He threw back his head. His colour was high, the bones of his face stark with anger. It took every ounce of will not to shrink from him. But she knew she must not. On the day of Patrick's death Maria Hawthorne had given up her cane and taken to a wheelchair, from which in her doctor's opinion she was unlikely to rise. 'Leave her alone, Giles. She's an old woman, her health is poor, and this has all but broken her. She's failed in what she tried to do and in the most tragic way possible. That's surely enough, even for you. Leave it at that.'

He looked at her for an unnervingly long time. Then 'Or?' he asked, his voice perilously quiet.

She shook her head. 'I'm not threatening you. I'm asking you. For her sake and for the sake of the family.' With an enormous effort she kept the sharp edge of fear from her voice. The rage that she sensed in him had the force of summer lightning, held the same promise of sudden violence and danger. But she faced him and she would not let him see her fear. And somehow – she did not understand herself how – she had won. Giles had slammed from the room and from that day had not spoken one word to his mother nor acknowledged her existence. But at least the confrontation that Jessica had been convinced might have killed the sick woman had been avoided. On the day before Patrick's funeral Maria, with a nurse and small staff, had been moved to Tollgate House, where Giles and Clara had lived in exile on the far side of the estate for six long years. Her dream shattered, her health broken and with Patrick's death to haunt her she had left New Hall for the last time with no farewell and no kind word.

On the warm and windy afternoon that followed Jessica walked, Gabriella's small hand in hers, behind the little dogcart that carried her mother in the sad procession of

433

mourners that wound through the parkland and the bright autumn woodlands and wondered, as she had wondered so often in the past days, at Maria's motives for the terrible deception. She pondered the antagonism between Giles and his mother, exacerbated as it had been by the arrival of Clara and her determination to usurp her mother-in-law's authority. Certainly somewhere there, she assumed, must be the key. Jessica had often wondered how much her mother guessed about the circumstances surrounding her beloved eldest son's death. It was beyond doubt that she had never forgiven Giles for not saving his brother. And then Clara had come and Maria had seen her position truly threatened. Patrick's astounding likeness to his half-brother must have come like a temptation straight from the Devil himself. Jessica remembered all too clearly how much the child had reminded her of Edward when first she had met him in the park with his grandmother. She blinked, recalling the handsome little boy with his marigold head and bright, innocent eyes.

Ahead of them the carriage bearing the coffin had ended its sad journey and come to the church gate. The well-schooled horses stood like statues, the dark plumes upon their harness blowing in the wind. The bearers took the weight upon their shoulders and turned through the gate and down the narrow path. A small army of estate workers had in the past few days cleared the way. The grass was neatly scythed, the weeds and nettles gone. The lake gleamed in sunlight through the trees, the surface rippling like molten gold in the wind.

Jessica's mind was still on that day so many years before. She, Jessica, had sent the woman and the child to her mother. How long had it taken for like to recognize like, she wondered? The one fighting for the future of her grandson who was about to be abandoned alone and defenceless in a hostile world, the other still mourning the death of a son and another loss that had cut almost as deep – the loss of an influence she had wielded all her adult life. The child's uncanny likeness to his father's eldest son must have spawned the conspiracy very quickly in Maria's subtle mind. And the child's true grandmother, who must in desperation have come to New Hall to throw herself and the bastard child upon the mercy of strangers would have been an extraordinary woman indeed to stand against the strength of Maria Hawthorne. For Maria the opportunity to take the child, mould him to her own purposes, must have been all but irresistible in face of Giles' stubborn refusal to bow to her authority.

Jessica sighed and turned her head a little to find her mother's still disconcertingly clear blue gaze fixed upon her face, as if almost she guessed her thoughts. Whatever the truth of the matter, conjecture was all that Jessica had; Maria, quietly but firmly, had made it very clear to her daughter on the only occasion that she had attempted to broach the matter that she had no intention either of excusing or explaining her actions, not now nor at any time in the future. 'I am close enough to death,' she had said, simply, 'not to care what the world thinks of me or of my actions. I will make my case to the final Judge, and not before.' And with that Jessica had had to be content.

They walked the path of the little churchyard, threaded their way through the worn and ancient stones. A serving man gently lifted Maria from the dogcart and another followed carrying a sturdy and comfortable armchair. It had been over the fierce protests of doctor and nurse that Maria had insisted upon attending the service. Jessica, watching her, wondered bleakly how she could bear it.

The rector was waiting, pious hands folded, eyes downcast, robes billowing like rainclouds on a sunny afternoon. '"Man that is born of woman hath but a short time to live, and is full of misery —"'

Jessica tried hard not to listen. She hated the burial service.

The wind was blustering to gale force. It tugged at the heavy black skirts and the veils of the mourning women, lifted the coat tails of the men and tousled the hair of their bared heads. Gabriella's small hand had crept back uncertainly into her mother's. Jessica squeezed it gently and attempted to smile reassurance; and as she turned her eyes were caught by a figure

435

who stood alone beyond the low wall of the graveyard in the shadow of the trees. She frowned a little, trying to focus her eyes through the blowing veil, peering around Robert who stood beside her holding Gabriella's other hand.

'"In the midst of life we are in death —"'

The outlandish figure in its flowing robes could not have been more foreign — yet there was something so familiar about the stance, the straight brown hair that blew in the wind that she could not drag her eyes away. The long dusty black soutane blew, flattened against the wearer's legs, and the wind played with the wide hat, the like of which she had so often seen in Italy, held in a brown hand.

'"Suffer us not, at our last hour, for any pains of death to fall from thee —"'

John.

In the moment she thought his name he caught her eye and smiled a little.

John!

She could hardly believe her eyes, but John, the brother she had not seen and had hardly thought of in so many years it was. She glanced at her mother. Maria's veil was lifted, her face utterly stony. She had not seen the unexpected newcomer. She sat ramrod straight in her chair, her useless legs covered by a blanket, staring with unblinking eyes at the shining mahogany casket with its bright brass decoration.

Jessica turned her head again. John lifted a hand in greeting. He was much thinner than she remembered him, his eyes were steady and his skin was brown.

'"We therefore commit his body to the ground; earth to earth, ashes to ashes, dust to dust; in sure and certain hope of the Resurrection to eternal life —"'

Beside her Gabriella, only half-understanding the sombre proceedings was overcome and sobbed suddenly, burying her face in her mother's skirt. One of the serving girls standing with the staff that was ranked behind the family had also given way to open and noisy tears. Maria's face, harshly disciplined, still showed no flicker of emotion, and her back was straight as an arrow. Jessica drew her daughter to her, a comforting arm about her shoulders. The shining box disappeared, swallowed by the earth, the spray of white lilies that lay upon it stirring in a last sudden boisterous gust of warm wind.

Jessica willed herself not to think of a tall, handsome laughing boy. Her part in his death, innocent as it had been, would haunt her for as long as she lived. The scene, darkened by the cloud of her veil, blurred for a moment and was lost in tears. She heard the dreary sound of earth falling onto hollow wood.

Someone coughed. Feet were shuffled. The servants, mopping their eyes, started to move away. Maria shifted a little in her chair. In that moment Jessica could not look at her, could not speak to or go near her. She turned away. John had moved out from the shadow of the trees and waited for her. Jessica, Gabriella still clinging to her hand, hurried to him. He scrambled over the low wall and opened his arms to her. 'Jessica!'

'John! It's really you?' The tears she had been shedding for Patrick still ran down her face, yet looking into the strong, calm face she smiled. She lifted her veil and he bent to kiss her lightly upon her salty cheek. Other mourners had seen the stranger now and a small ripple of comment ran around the group.

'It's really me. I reached the village last night, and heard the news. I didn't come up to the house – I didn't want to bother anyone –' His eyes had wandered past her. She turned to follow his gaze. Giles and Clara were staring at him with surprised eyes, the expression of unwelcome on Clara's face close to hostility. Maria was still sitting stock still by the open grave, a small sheaf of lilies in her lap. As they watched in silence a serving man approached her, bent and spoke in her ear.

The old lady shook her head, sharply. The man straightened and stepped back, leaving her alone. With immense effort she lifted the flowers and dropped them into the open grave.

'Oh John,' Jessica said, softly and sadly, 'there's so much to tell you –'

At Jessica's eager invitation he came to them at Old Hall in time for supper that evening having accompanied Maria home from the funeral and stayed with her for the day. 'The doctor's given her a draught, though it was the Devil's own job to make her take it,' he said. 'She's asleep.' Gratefully he accepted a glass of wine, smiling ruefully, 'And I somehow didn't get the feeling that I'd be particularly welcome at New Hall.' He obviously had not missed any more than Jessica had, the coolness of the welcome his brother had extended to the unexpected guest, nor the hard and calculating look in Clara's eyes as she offered her cheek to his kiss. Anyone with any claim upon them however small was likely to get short shrift from those two.

Over supper, taken in the small parlour because the ceiling of the dining room had all but fallen in, he told them his news. 'I've come to say goodbye. I've joined a missionary order – Brothers of the Cross – and am being sent to Africa.'

Jessica, absurdly she knew, was dismayed. 'Whereabouts in Africa?'

He shook his head. 'I don't know. Wherever I'm needed.'

'But – isn't it terribly dangerous?'

He shrugged a little, and smiled. 'The Lord will protect me for as long as He wills.' The words were spoken with a simple conviction that defied argument. His thin brown face radiated a calm happiness that for a moment struck Jessica to silence. She was reminded of the thought she had once had that of all of them John was probably the most contented. Seeing now the untroubled tranquillity mirrored in his eyes she knew it to be true. John was a man at peace with himself, with his God and with his world. He wanted nothing but what he had, and the radiance of his faith was a gift from that God he obviously served so well and which he equally obviously would not have exchanged for the ransom of a king. For a brief moment, deeply and painfully she envied him – and at the incongruity of that she had to smile a little.

He noticed and lifted his strong, dark brows in amused enquiry. Robert had wandered to the small piano at the far end of the room and was playing softly, his eyes distant, as far removed from them as if he had been in another world. 'Why do you smile?' John asked.

She laughed wryly. 'Because believe it or not for an idiotic moment I was envying you – imagining myself in my nun's

438

veil working by your side to convert the heathen. Can you imagine it?'

His burst of laughter was genuinely amused. 'No, I can't, little sister!' But his quiet and observant eyes had not missed the grim quirk to her mouth nor the sudden self-questioning doubt in her eyes. He covered her hand with his own. 'We are all called to serve in our separate ways, Jessica,' he said quietly.

'You really believe that?' Her voice was suddenly tired.

'Of course. And it's an unusually lucky man – or woman – who sees the road ahead as straight and clear as I did.'

She shook her head, laughing again, rueful and a little bitter. 'Oh, John! Little do you know! Nothing's straight. Nothing's clear. Not in this life!'

He took her hand in his. 'Tell me,' he said.

And to her astonishment, she did. She told him everything, from her discovery about Giles to the disaster of her marriage, her love for Danny, Gabriella's birth, their return to England and the awful circumstances of poor Patrick's suicide. She nibbled her thumbnail, her face tight with grief. 'Oh, John – if only Mother hadn't decided to come downstairs to see me that morning! – if only I'd held my temper with Patrick! – if only –'

'No.' He spoke almost for the first time, sharply and with authority. 'Stop that, Jessica. It does no good.'

'I know. I know. But I can't seem to help it –'

'Of course you can.' The briskness of the words was tempered by a warm smile, and his hand on hers was kindly. 'You can do anything if you try. With God's help.'

She smiled, weakly. 'To be honest with you I don't think He can much care one way or the other. And who's to blame Him?'

He shook his head gently, said nothing.

She fell to silence for a moment, then lifted her head, looking at him with real curiosity in her face. 'Tell me – do you see some great purpose in all this? Some pattern that none of us can fathom?'

'Who knows? God's pattern? The Devil's? Each can be as obscure as the other.'

439

'And you? You truly don't care about any of this? New Hall? – The land? – The money –?'

He shook his head, laughing. 'Remember what we used to sing as children? Daisies are silver, buttercups gold –'

'And you truly still feel that?'

'Yes.'

From the far end of the room the piano notes fell into the silence, little drops of music like raindrops into a pool. Jessica thought for a moment, brows in a straight serious line. 'It isn't the money –' she said, slowly, only just aware that she had spoken aloud.

He followed her train of thought with remarkable percipience. 'I know that, little sister. For Giles and Clara – for Mother too, and I think for Caroline – the things that are all-important are the things that money can buy – influence, power, the grand life. For you – I think it's the roots. The land. The belonging.'

'The heritage,' she said, quietly. 'I've never forgotten that night you faced Father and told him what you thought of the Hawthorne heritage. I don't – I can't – agree with you – but I thought then, and I still think now that it was the bravest thing I've ever seen.'

He stretched his legs beneath the shabby skirt of his soutane. The piano was gay now, rippling like sunshine on water. 'I was wrong.'

She stared at him. 'Of course you weren't.'

He nodded. 'Oh yes. I was wrong. For I had overlooked something.'

'What?'

He paused, a pensive frown on his face. 'I had overlooked the fact that a heritage is not merely a material possession to be handed from one to another, to be accepted or rejected at will. A house. A plot of land. A purseful of gold. Yes – these things one can accept or despise, take or leave. But, Jessica – if I found the courage to fight Father for what I wanted then ironically that courage was my heritage from him. Perhaps Giles would not hate Mother so much for what she did to him through Patrick if he understood that his own ruthlessness is the mirror-image of hers. Take it further – if Patrick had not, like Edward, inherited Father's looks the deception would not have worked so easily. It's all so very much more complicated than it seems, isn't it? I was a frightened boy who saw things in black and white. I still reject that material heritage that in one way or another seems to mean so much to you all – but I recognize and thank God for that which I carry inside me. Whatever drove some forebear to brave the obscenities of the slave trade and make a fortune will hopefully give me the strength to face whatever awaits me in the jungle continent of Africa – and will stand you in good stead to put Old Hall back on its feet again –'

She laughed, surprised. 'You can hardly speak of the two things in the same breath!'

'But of course!' He was serious. 'You've inherited the courage too. And the strength. Perhaps even some of the ruthlessness –' He was looking at her with calm, assured yet gentle eyes that might have been looking directly into her soul. It occurred to her that her brother was probably a very good priest indeed. 'Be careful, Jessica,' he said softly. 'Be careful how you use that most precious part of your heritage.'

The piano had stopped.

'I won't leave Old Hall,' she said very quietly. 'I won't see it fall to pieces. I won't see its people abandoned to starve. I won't see Gabriella brought up like a wandering gypsy. I want this place for her and for her children. A safe and loving place, where they belong.' Robert played a gentle scale. She lowered her voice, that had risen passionately, 'If that's wrong, then I'm wrong. There's nothing I can do about it.'

John chuckled suddenly. 'Perhaps I should persuade you to come with me, veil or no veil. There'd be a few Zulus who'd think twice about taking you on in that frame of mind.'

She laughed with him. 'It isn't Zulus I want to take on. It's a few more sheep and a few more acres of turnips to feed them. It's more work for the people. It's decent houses instead of hovels, and schooling for the children. Giles won't do any of that –' She stopped, a little surprised at herself. This was the first time she had allowed herself to think further than the simple salvaging of Old Hall, and certainly the first time she had realized that her opposition to Giles might be more than merely personal. She nibbled her thumbnail again, thoughtfully.

He grinned, white teeth in a brown face. 'There speaks a Hawthorne if ever I heard one.' Robert was approaching them. John stood up, stretching, 'Well, if you don't mind – I'm for my bed.'

She stood too, and took his hand. 'How long can you stay?' Her voice was wistful. It had been so very long since she had had anyone to talk to – she was surprised at how clearly this conversation had defined for her things that she had not until now even allowed herself to think about. It's confession, she thought, ruefully, watching her priestly brother, it really is good for the soul –

'A few days only. Then I must go. I truly did come to say goodbye. There's so much work to do –'

'You won't come back? To England I mean?'

'I doubt it very much.' He squeezed her hand. 'Don't look so sad. I'll write, I promise.'

'Will you at least stay for the meeting?'

'Yes. Giles particularly asked me to, and I think I should –' he grinned wryly, '– if only to reassure Giles and his lady wife that I have no designs on New Hall or on New Hall money, now or in the future –'

Jessica had to laugh. She tucked her hand into his arm and walked him to the door. 'That,' she said with feeling, 'will undoubtedly make you the most popular – and unusual! – Hawthorne of all!'

Two days before the family meeting called by Giles, of which she had spoken to John, Jessica paid a visit to Home Farm. Charlie was in the small enclosure behind the barn with three or four black-faced ewes. Jessica dismounted and leaned on the gate, watching as with deft movements Charlie pared the sheep's feet with a small sharp knife before smearing them liberally with an evil-looking paste from a bucket by his side. He nodded a friendly greeting when he saw her, finished treating the last ewe then straightened and came to the gate, carrying the bucket.

Jessica wrinkled her nose. 'What ever is that?'

'Treatment for foot-rot.' He swung the bucket over the gate then followed it, surprisingly athletic for such a big man. 'Copper. Zinc. Charcoal. Eucalyptus. Tha'ss mixed in treacle. Sticky, but it works a treat.'

She nodded. They stood for a moment, watching the sheep. All were black-faced and long-legged, the Norfolk breed that was famous for the quality of its meat, though the wool was of a quality less than fine. Over the past year Jessica knew that Charlie had been experimenting with a Southern Down cross, knew too that so far the results looked very promising.

Charlie walked to the rainwater trough by the barn and rinsed the evil-smelling mixture from his hands. His homespun shirt was grubby and ill-fitting, his broad shoulders straining at the seams, and there were two buttons missing. Jessica smiled and not for the first time reflected that Charlie Best could do with a wife.

'I hear the Ruxtons over at Link Farm have a couple of Merino rams,' she said.

He straightened from the trough, looking thoughtful, absently drying his hands on the seat of his trousers. 'That so?'

She nodded.

'Cost a pretty penny for a season I reckon?'

She fell into step beside him as they crossed the yard to the house. 'More than we can afford at the moment I'm afraid,' she admitted. 'But – I wondered – might it be worthwhile to take a couple of ewes over there? Just as an experiment? Mr Ruxton charges ten guineas a time. We could just about afford that, couldn't we?'

He led the way into the stark, dark interior of the house.

'Charlie? Don't you think it's a good idea?'

He pulled a chair forward for her. 'Hard to tell. Might be. Might not. Rather see any money there is saved for new stock next spring meself.'

'Oh?' She raised surprised brows.

He settled himself opposite her, his square brown face

443

earnest, then, colouring suddenly, he scrambled to his feet again and stood like an embarrassed schoolboy. She smiled. They were so easy together that a total lack of formality had become the hallmark of their relationship. Only rarely now did Charlie suddenly and self-consciously become aware, as now, of a breach of manners or etiquette. She waved him to the chair, smiling scoldingly. 'Don't be silly, Charlie! Sit down, do! Now – what's this about new spring stock? I thought the time to buy was now – in the autumn – while the fairs were on?'

He leaned his elbows on the table. 'Usually – traditionally – aye, tha'ss right. But tha'ss bin a bad year for feed this year. I've – we've – bin luckier than most.'

'You mean you've been cleverer than most.' Jessica knew how well Charlie managed the land. He had a feel for it.

He shrugged a little. 'Turnips are comin' in well. An' the cabbages. We're well off fer winter feed.'

'Then why not buy now – as usual?'

He was slow in answering. 'Ay, tha'ss what they'll all do – or most of 'em. Even though feed's short.'

'So?'

'So there's not a lot of profit in that, is there – buyin' now an' havin' ter see the stock through the winter when feed is low? To me that makes more sense to wait. Prices are high now. So wait – store the feed for the spring – by then there'll be some ready to give their stock away, for they won't be able to feed 'em, 'specially if the winter's hard, an' I've got a feelin' it will be – That gives us the chance of a fair, quick profit over the summer –'

'Isn't it a bit of a gamble? Supposing it's a mild winter?'

'It won't be,' he said, positively. 'Look – we've enough winter feed already for the flock as it stands. If I plant late turnips, kale and winter rye by spring we'll have more feed than we know what to do with –'

'Whilst those who are short of winter feed,' Jessica said thoughtfully, 'will find it difficult to see their flocks through between root and grass and might be willing to sell cheaply –?'

'Tha'ss the idea.' He grinned widely at her easy use of the shepherd's phrase for the months of March to May.

444

She sat back in her chair. 'It certainly sounds a good plan. And with the profits we might make we could perhaps afford a Merino for the following season, to improve the wool?'

He shrugged. 'Far as I'm concerned next year's better than this. Like I said, it's goin' to be a hard winter. I feel it in me bones. An' them Merino crosses might produce fine wool, but tha'ss an animal with no defence against the cold, an' the fleece holds the water like a sponge. Why not let Links Farm find out how their stock overwinter before we try it out?'

She looked at him in mildly teasing astonishment. 'How very crafty you are, Charlie Best! But then you always were, weren't you? You always managed to talk your way out of things when we were children, didn't you?'

He chuckled. 'You'll take a cup of milk?'

'Yes, please.' She watched him, still smiling, as he stood, picked up a small jug and went into the yard. At the pump she saw him stop, swiftly strip off his shirt, pump the handle rapidly and duck his head and his torso under the splashing water. Then, unaware of her eyes upon him, he straightened, hair dripping, pulled his shirt back on and disappeared from sight. She smiled again. She liked Charlie. She liked his warm, quiet voice with its dearly familiar Suffolk accent, she liked his big, square, brown hands, his strong, weather-beaten face, the untidy sun-bleached hair. She liked the uncomplicated honesty of him, and the dependability. He never changed. She liked the way he treated her, with no trace of servility, his respect for her based upon what he knew of her as a person, not her position in the arbitrary and inequal society in which they lived. He had a sharp brain and he was the hardest-working man she had ever met. She trusted him implicitly. And the more she thought about it the more she liked the idea of buying new stock in spring –

'What sort of numbers were you thinking of?' she asked as he came back through the door with the dripping jug in his hand. 'You've planted the back acres with turnip and kale, haven't you?'

'Tha'ss right. An' I'd like to leave the kale till spring – give it

445

a chance to side shoot. We could do with a few more acres for the winter rye –'

'What about the pasture land? Is any of that suitable for crops?'

He shrugged, clattering about the kitchen range. 'Then where'd we put the new stock in the summer?' He hesitated a moment, then turned his shaggy head, 'Your brother –?'

'What?'

'Wouldn't let us use the New Hall parkland, I suppose? I do hate to see that good land goin' to waste –'

She laughed aloud. 'What? Sheep with Clara's peacocks? Oh, no, Charlie, he most certainly wouldn't let us use the parkland. He called our sheep "those damnable beasts" the other day. He thinks they're a waste of time and money. You can't buy a machine that will look after a flock of sheep –' She saw, or sensed, the change in him, put her head on one side, watching him. His smile had gone. He had turned back to the milk jug, reaching for two mugs, but the ease had left him. 'Charlie?' she asked, puzzled. 'What is it?'

He shook his head a little. She sat in silence, frowning, as he poured the milk and brought it to the table. She sipped the rich, frothing stuff, watched as he drained half the mug and with an unthinkable movement that made her mouth twitch with a laughter she would never have allowed him to see wiped his mouth with the back of his hand. He looked worried, his usual clear, uncomplicated expression clouded.

'Charlie – what's wrong? Is it something to do with Giles?'

He took a breath. 'Aye, Y're Ladyship,' he hesitated. Jessica frowned at the use of the title. 'Aye,' he said heavily again. 'Him an' them machines. To tell the truth your brother isn't the most popular man in the world about this part of Suffolk –'

She almost laughed. 'Oh Charlie – is that all? I thought you were going to tell me something I didn't know! I don't think it will surprise – or even bother – Giles if he isn't elected May Queen next year!' She laughed a little, mischievously, at the thought, and teased him with her eyes, expecting him to laugh with her.

He didn't. 'It's no great laughing matter.' He paused, as if weighing his words. 'There's a lot of wild talk,' he said at last.

'What sort of wild talk?'

He looked uncomfortable as if he wished he had not said so much, but she would not leave it.

'You mean – threats?'

He shrugged a little, his eyes on the foaming milk.

She shook her head sharply, disbelievingly. 'The people of the village have known us all our lives. They wouldn't do anything to hurt us.'

'Not you, Miss Jess. Him. Your brother. Him an' his machines. Tha'ss not right, takin' the bread from the people's mouths, starvin' their little 'uns. But you? – you an' your is as safe as houses. Not the worst of 'em'd touch you. 'Sides anythin' else –' he lifted his great brown head and looked directly into her eyes, '– they know they'd have to go through me –'

The tiny silence that followed the words was a strange one, loaded in some way with a meaning that Jessica for the moment could not fathom. There was pride in that sudden lift of the man's head, a perhaps unconscious but deeply disturbing challenge in his direct gaze. Absurdly she suddenly found she could not hold his eyes. 'I'm sure that no-one from the village would dream of harming Giles.' Her voice was cooler and sharper than she had intended it.

He stood up abruptly, scraping his stool with noisy force upon the flagstoned floor, draining the rest of his milk at a gulp. ''Course not, Y're Ladyship.' His voice too had changed, and was level and all but expressionless. She could not avoid the feeling that something, somehow, had gone badly wrong between them. 'Now – if you don't need me for anythin' else I'll get across to Barn Meadow. I'm movin' the flock to the river fields – Here, Bess!' He whistled, shrilly, and the dog appeared like a shadow from nowhere. He stood for a moment towering above Jessica, looking down at her, his usually open face shuttered as a closed window. Then very deliberately he bowed his head and pulled at his brown forelock in a gesture of servility she had never seen him make before, made now in the

447

least servile way possible. Then he turned and strode away, the dog at his heels, the set of his head and the lines of his broad back taut with inexplicable but unmistakable anger.

Jessica could not have been more astonished had he slapped her. She watched the tall, retreating back, puzzled and disturbed; puzzled at his anger, disturbed at the sudden confusion of emotion it had awakened in her. She had of course known all along that Charlie Best was no longer the village boy who had taken her birds' nesting and had tossed one of her best slippers into the river – no more than was she the undisciplined urchin who had launched herself at him and all but sent him into the water after the mistreated footwear. But for the first time now, and with a shock, she saw him as a man, with a man's dangerous pride and – she faced it honestly, her cheeks burning – a man's attraction.

She stood up, brushing down her skirt, walked very quickly to where her mare was tethered by the battered stone mounting block. Mounted, she turned the little horse and set her at a fast pace down the stony track. Down by the river she could see the man's tall form, striding fast and purposefully, the black and white shadow slinking at his heels. He did not turn.

Jessica found herself pondering on Charlie's warning, obscure as it had been, as she rode across the park a couple of days later to New Hall and the meeting she had been dreading for a week. The other and odder aspects of that rather strange afternoon she had put firmly from her mind, had indeed almost managed to convince herself that the curious, electric flash of emotion she had thought she had detected in Charlie had been a figment of her imagination. Yet despite her efforts the thought of Charlie Best had taken to popping into her head at odd times in the most distracting manner. Now, however, with the great house shining in the distance beneath scudding rainclouds her thoughts were more of his warning than of his more personally disconcerting behaviour. Should she perhaps warn Giles that local feeling was running high against him? She pulled a small, sour face: he would probably laugh at her. As she had pointed out to Charlie his popularity with the local people was and always had been the least of Giles' concerns.

She rode to the front courtyard and handed the reins to the lad who waited to take them, walked slowly up the steps to where the door had already been opened by a smiling footman. For some reason she had found herself taking considerable care with her appearance today – her riding habit was her favourite, the russet brown of bright autumn leaves that she knew brought out the best of her own colouring. It was stylishly cut with a full skirt and a mannish jacket set off by her cream silk cravat. Her soft leather boots were of the same shade of red-brown, as were her gloves. Her hair she had caught becomingly at the nape of her neck and fastened it with a small bow. She handed hat, gloves and whip to the footman.

'The family is waiting in the library, Your Ladyship.'

She smiled her thanks. Outside the library door she hesitated for a telling second, then took breath, pushed open the door and walked in.

They were all there but Caroline. Maria sat by the window her back half-turned to the room, her hands folded upon the blanket that covered her lap. Her face was drawn. John stood near her. He had spent the last couple of days at Tollgate House. Clara sat, beautifully disposed, upon a small settee. She was dressed in dark red, a colour which suited her admirably. Her skin was flawless, her profile clear and sharp as a new-minted coin. Giles stood by the fire, a sheaf of papers in his hand. He was dressed for riding and his boots were wet from his morning's inspection of the estate. To everyone's relief Caroline had refused to come. She had sent a politely querulous note delivered by a spectacularly liveried servant pointing out that any unfortunate repercussions arising from Patrick's death were absolutely nothing to do with her. Since Bunty's youngest and prettiest sister had married into new and vast industrial money and the Standish family fortunes had been happily re-established Caroline's interest in her own family had waned considerably.

'Ah, Jessica. Come in.' Giles strode to the door and closed it behind her. 'Is Robert not coming?'

449

Jessica shook her head. There was someone else whose interest in family affairs was minimal. In fact since Patrick's death Robert's interest in almost anything seemed to be non-existent. The only thing that had aroused him even slightly from the brown and brooding study into which the boy's death had thrown him had been the arrival of the draft from Mr Sotheby – and even then after enquiring the amount he had simply grunted, as if in disappointment, and said no more.

Jessica nodded coolly to Clara, smiled at John, dutifully kissed her mother. Maria smiled faintly. Jessica took the chair that Giles indicated and waited.

Characteristically Giles came straight to the point. 'I've called you here for two reasons. First: after the – unfortunate machinations –' His eyes were cold as he looked at his mother. She did not even glance at him. '– of the past few years I want it understood here and now that my title to New Hall and its lands is clear and incontestable.' He lifted his handsome head and glanced at each of them, challengingly, in turn. Maria's eyes were fixed upon her folded hands. John shrugged. 'I shan't dispute it, brother,' and he turned away, stood with his back to the company, looking out of the window. Jessica thought she heard Clara let out a small breath, perhaps of relief. When Giles' cold gaze crossed her own she nodded. Much as she disliked him there was no doubt in her mind as to her brother's right to the position of master of New Hall.

'Very well. That's settled. Now, with regard to Mother – since the land she owns in her own right, on the New Hall side of the river, has no house with it I have decided that she should have Tollgate House until her death.' He spoke as if Maria were not in the room. 'After that it will revert to the estate. She has agreed that she will take no income. Brights Meadows, her land by the river will be farmed with New Hall land as always, and a percentage of the profits made over to her. She has agreed.'

Silence. Beyond the window the rainclouds were building, a great purple mass that oppressed the air and turned the waters of the lake leaden.

'Secondly –' Giles waited until all eyes were upon him, then lifted the papers he held. 'I felt I should tell you what I have done – and what I have not – about the debts that were all that Patrick left.'

Jessica stirred, and sighed. Poor Patrick, even now, was not to be left to rest at peace.

'Some of the debts were personal,' Giles was saying. 'He borrowed, it appeared, from absolutely anyone stupid enough to lend to him. Most of those, as a matter of honour, I have settled. There is one, however, that I have not.' He took the top sheet of paper and held it up. 'This is a demand from a moneylender. A threatening demand, I might add. It seems the money was long overdue. I think you should know that I have absolutely no intention of paying the scoundrel.'

Jessica saw her mother's head move a little, sharply. John turned, frowning. Clara smiled.

'This is Patrick's debt. So far as I'm concerned it dies with him. He was a minor. We have no obligation to discharge his debts.'

'No legal obligation,' John said, gently.

'No obligation whatsoever.' Giles' voice was strong. 'I have paid the personal debts. That is as far as I'm willing to go. I will not deal with this usurer.' He paused. 'There is however one thing I think it only fair to tell you –'

He had all their attention now. Maria had lifted her head sharply and was watching him intently.

'This – moneylender –' the word was spoken with disgust, 'who says that Patrick mortgaged land to him as surety of this debt, is not happy at the situation. Since Patrick was a minor, and since the land did not rightly belong to him anyway he had no right to pledge it, of course, and the lender had no right to accept his pledge. However, he did, and is aggrieved by the loss of his money –'

'How much?' Jessica asked, quietly.

'Nearly a thousand guineas. For the past two years it seems that Patrick has been gambling with every penny he could lay his hands on, honestly or dishonestly. He borrowed to cover his debts, and then borrowed again to cover that borrowing.'

'And – what does the gentleman intend to do about the loss of his money?'

Giles smiled humourlessly. 'The man is no gentleman, Jessica. And he's very angry indeed. He has promised to go to extremes to extract the money from us.'

'What extremes?'

'He threatens us with the courts –'

'He has no case,' John said.

'– and he threatens us with scandal.'

No-one said anything for a very long time. Maria's hands twitched in her lap, and were still. It was John who spoke again. 'What does he know?'

Giles shook his head. 'It's hard to tell. But he has it seems approached some of the servants and has been snooping about the village. He's smelled a rat and intends to start it, unless we pay him.'

'If he begins to make enquiries – serious enquiries –' Jessica said, quietly, '– amongst the servants – in the village – there's no knowing what wild stories might be concocted –' Nor what truths might be uncovered. She did not say the words aloud, but they hung in the air, tensely.

'Quite.'

'We have to pay him.' It was Maria, speaking for the first time.

Giles looked directly at her for the first time. 'No.'

'Why not?' Jessica asked, her eyes worriedly upon her mother. A scandal of the magnitude that this might bring about their heads would undoubtedly kill Maria Hawthorne and destroy her reputation for ever.

Maria sat now, her head turned to her son, her face ashen. And Giles watched her, smiling. He knew precisely who would suffer most if he did not pay. 'I'll not pay blackmail,' he said, 'And besides, the estate can't afford such a sum.'

'I don't believe that!' Jessica was fighting to keep her temper. 'You can't be that short of money.'

His eyes flicked to her and back to his mother. 'I have discharged the other debts,' he said, evenly, '– a considerable sum, I might add. There is no more money. I need it for seed, and to buy new stock. I need it for the new thresher –'

452

Maria's shoulders were rigid. Her hands in her lap were tightly clenched. 'Give him the land,' she said composedly. 'My land. I have no need of it.'

'What are you talking about?' Giles was impatient.

John moved to his mother's side. 'I think that Mother is suggesting that since the usurer took the pledge of land for his money then she is willing to part with her land – Brights Meadows – to settle the debt. The land is hers, you said. She may do as she wishes with it.'

Giles barked with laughter that in Jessica's ears was tinged with spite and triumph. 'He won't take it.'

Jessica hated him. She hated what her mother had done, she hated the destruction of that bright-eyed, scared little boy who had sat in this very room six years before: but in that moment, for his laughter, she hated Giles more. 'Why not?' she asked.

He turned on her in scorn. 'He doesn't want the land! What would he do with it? Hang it in his window for sale to the highest bidder? Mother's land is no good to anyone but New Hall. It is part of the estate. There's no right of way. It's caged between the estate and the river.'

'And you'd deny a right of way?'

'Of course.'

'So the land is unsaleable?'

'Yes.'

'And you won't pay the money to keep this beastly man quiet?'

'Absolutely not.'

'Then I will.'

Clara turned sharply. The expression on Giles' face was almost comical. 'You can't!'

Ignoring him she walked to where her mother sat. Maria lifted bright, sombre eyes to hers. 'Mother? Will you sell Brights Meadows to me? We don't need right of way. The land is opposite Home Farm – we can put a bridge across the river. I'll give you –' she sent a venomous glance at Giles, '– a thousand guineas for it.' She would not think of Robert's anger. She would face that later. She searched her mother's face to make certain that she understood what she was saying, and then added pointedly. 'You may, of course, do anything you like with the money.'

'You're mad!' Giles snapped angrily. 'That land isn't worth two hundred.'

'To me it is.' Jessica threw the words over her shoulder. 'We're extending the flock. We need more grazing. Mother —' she turned back to Maria, '— will you sell it to me?'

Maria's hands were trembling very slightly. The old lady lifted her head proudly. 'You're sure? That you want the land?'

'Yes. We need it. Charlie wants to grow more feed. And some of it can be put to pasture for next year.'

'Then — of course you may have it.'

Jessica stood, still pushing to the back of her mind the thought of Robert's reaction when he discovered that a thousand precious guineas had been impulsively expended so. The books and manuscripts had realized just over two thousand pounds. A small fortune she had thought, when first she had received the draft. To spend half of it on land worth less than a quarter of what she had offered to pay was, as Giles had said, madness, when they needed every penny for the house and the farm. But she did not care. She would not stand by and see Giles — of all people! — engineer their mother's disgrace. She turned. John was standing beside her and the look in his brown eyes warmed her. But as she faced her other brother, master of New Hall, the look in his blue ones might have chilled her had she not been so angry. His face was tight with fury. 'You're a fool, Jessica,' he said, quietly.

'And you're a barbarian!' All the savage disgust she felt was in the quiet words.

The enmity lay between them like a drawn sword. No-one spoke. Clara's hands were clenched white in her lap, dislike and hostility written upon her face. John's calm eyes moved from one to the other. Very composedly, though her heart thumped in her chest like an urgent fist, Jessica bent and kissed her mother. 'I'll come next week and bring the money.'

Maria nodded. 'Thank you, my dear.' She smiled with difficulty, a small grimace as of pain.

Jessica turned to John, refusing to be hurried by the hostility about her. 'You'll come and see us before you leave?'

'I leave tomorrow. May I come today?'

'Of course.' Coolly Jessica nodded to Clara. 'Goodbye Clara. Giles.'

Neither said a word.

Straightbacked she left the room, shutting the door very quietly behind her.

She rode home through the darkening afternoon still lost in anger despite her apprehension about facing Robert. The despicable way that Giles had been ready to use his regained power to punish Maria revolted her. Even if the threat had no substance, even if the moneylender had not been intent upon his pound of flesh, she could not have stood by and let her mother live in such a shadow. In her present state of health it would undoubtedly have killed her: which, she surmised grimly, would have suited Giles and Clara very well. Maria was a thorn in their side. Her death would bring them no grief.

She stabled the mare herself, rubbing her down and bringing her water, murmuring and stroking, soothing herself as much as the beast. As she crossed the drawbridge to the courtyard the rain that had been threatening had finally started, cold and hard, stripping the leaves from the creeper that clung to the old walls.

At the foot of the great staircase she met Sarah, a shawl about her head.'Oh dear, oh dear! Just look at the rain! And Sir Thomas not home yet! Why, hello, my dear –' she smiled vaguely at Jessica. 'Have you come to see young Robert? He's about somewhere. I'm sure I've seen him. But you will excuse me? My husband isn't home yet, and I'm a little worried. It's raining, you see, and I'm sure he went out without his hat. Such an absent minded man he is –!'

'Lady Sarah? Lady Sarah!' Janet came bustling down the stairs. 'My, oh my, we are naughty sometimes, aren't we? Come along now – Mrs Williams shall make us a nice cup of tea. This way, my lady, this way.' With a motherly arm about the old lady she guided her away from the front door. As she did so she threw an apologetic glance at Jessica over her shoulder. 'Good afternoon, Your Ladyship.'

'Good afternoon, Janet.' Jessica tossed hat and gloves onto the table, then stopped, lifting her head and sniffing the air.

Janet nodded, briskly disapproving. 'Lord alone knows what it is, Your Ladyship. But nothing good by the smell of it,' and she bustled after her disappearing charge.

Jessica knew what it was. Too well she knew. Her stomach protested and in vain she tried to blot out the picture that rose in her mind of a dark church, lamp-lit and wreathed in drugging smoke.

She ran up the stairs. The Old Drawing Room was empty, and so was the small parlour. Rain beat against the window, a tattoo to herald winter. The smell was stronger. She ran to Robert's bedroom and pushed open the door. The room was empty, the blinds drawn. In the half-light a lamp burned, set upon the floor, and beside it the same paraphernalia she had seen in the church. A pipe lay discarded and still smoking in a bowl. Beside the bed stood a great trunk, the rug beneath it ruckled as if the huge thing had been dragged carelessly across the floor. Tumbled into it were clothes, books and music manuscripts. More manuscripts were strewn across the bed.

There was no sign of Robert.

It was a sixth sense that took her to the library. The opium smell that he carried with him reached her as she pushed open the door. She stood in silence and watched him. A fire had been lit and the flames danced brightly, throwing shadows in the rain-darkness of the afternoon. He stood by the safe, his feet braced apart as if he had some difficulty in balancing. He was dishevelled, wearing neither jacket nor cravat for all the cold of the day. His cuffs were unbuttoned, his shirt rumpled. His smooth dark hair, that he had grown longer of late, fell across his face. In his hand he held a piece of paper.

She stepped into the room and closed the door behind her.

He looked up, slowly, and as slowly his eyes focused on her face. He said nothing. Then, very precisely, he folded the paper he held and tucked it into the breast pocket of his shirt.

They looked at each other for a long moment in utter silence.

'Robert, you can't take that,' she said at last, very quietly. 'You know you can't.'

'They were my books,' he said, calmly.' The money is in my name. It is legally mine. I can do as I like with it.'

'It's for the house.' She kept her voice even and reasonable.

He shook his head. 'No, Jessica. It's for my music. It's for Florence. I'm going back.'

'No!'

'Yes!' His eyes were well focused now, and his voice was quiet and determined. 'You shan't stop me. I have to go. It is a matter of survival. You want the house, and you want the land. For a reason that is a mystery to me you seem ready to take on the whole Pandora's Box of miseries that goes with them. Take them. I give them to you, freely and without stint. *I'm* going back to Florence.'

She drew a long, shallow breath. 'Please – Robert – you can't simply take every penny we have and leave? You can't! What of your mother? What of Gabriella?'

He shook his head, utterly calm, utterly unreasoning.

Still she kept a rein on her temper and her fear. She stepped towards him. 'All right. Go if you feel you must. Take some of the money. But not all of it. In God's name, Robert – not all of it!'

'I need it more than you do,' he said, 'I'm going to buy a villa. So that Arthur can come and live with me. So that we can look after each other. Try to understand, Jessica. I can't stay here. I can't. There is no hope for me here.'

'So – to feed your own hope you would shatter ours?' she asked, still quietly.

He shook his head, an odd, sad smile on his lips. 'While you breathe, Jessica, you'll have hope. Don't you see the difference between us? You're too strong for me. I can't take your strength. I can't live with it. I need Florence, and Arthur, and music –'

'And opium?' she asked.

He shrugged. There was an unusual stubbornness about the set of his jaw, an obstinate line to his mouth. 'You can't stop me, Jessica.'

'What of your responsibilities here?'

'What responsibilities? What do I do? Who needs me? I'm good for nothing here.'

'That isn't true!'

'Of course it's true. Do you think I'm stupid as well as useless? I'm going back to Florence. Arthur is there. The life that I want is there. You'll be better off without me.'

She said nothing. The enormity of what he was doing had half-stunned her. Florence? Arthur? Did he truly believe that she would rather be here, struggling with the problems of a decaying estate and a warring family than in the sunshine of Italy with Danny?

Danny.

She turned her mind from the thought of him. From the endless ache of his absence.

'Robert,' she said, desperately reasonable. 'Please. Think what you're doing. You *can't* abandon your home and your family –'

'The money is mine,' he said, stubborn as a child.

'I know that! But – what of the house? The land? We're winning – beginning to turn the corner. But Robert we need that money –'

'Not as much as I do.' His eyes held hers, painfully intense.

'You'll destroy us,' she said softly, bitterly. 'You'll destroy Old Hall.'

'No,' he said. 'It would take more than this to destroy you. And Old Hall is lucky. It has you to fight for it. I have no-one.'

The self-pity of it took her breath away. She stepped back from him. Avoiding her eyes he made to move past her.

'Robert!'

The sharp word stopped him. It was a long moment before he raised his eyes to hers.

'I want a promise.' Her voice was steady, though her body trembled, very slightly, as if she had contracted a fever. Yet

458

through the shock a clear thread of anger ran, preventing tears, preventing pleading.

He waited.

'If you go –' she said, 'if you take that money – I want your word that you'll never come back. Old Hall is mine.'

The dark eyes searched her face. 'You have it. For what it's worth – you have it.' He hesitated a moment. 'I'm sorry, Jessica.'

He turned from her, walked steadily to the door. With his hand on the handle, however, he stopped, hesitated for a moment, his back to her. Very slowly he lifted his free hand to the pocket in which crackled the Sotheby's draft. She sensed the battle taking place in him, and held her breath, hope surging. Then, with no word and no glance in her direction he swung the door wide and walked into the darkness of the corridor beyond.

She watched him go with blank eyes. The unexpectedness of the blow had all but paralysed her. A log shifted in the fireplace. A candle guttered and blew.

The rustle of movement by the door startled her.

'It's all right. It's me.' John stepped into the room, his dark habit emerging, ghost-like from the shadows.

She looked at him with no vestige of expression. 'You heard?'

'Yes.'

'He's leaving. Going back to Florence. And he's taking the money. All of it. I never thought – it never occurred to me –' She stopped, making a small, distracted movement with her hands. 'The house is falling down about our ears. Mother needs the money I've promised her. The farm needs investment to make it pay. There are men and women depending upon Old Hall for their livelihood – men and women who have worked for nothing for months, in trust. And he's going to Florence. To Florence!' She turned away with a sudden, angry movement. 'Damn him!' she said, quietly and with bitterness.

He watched her in silence, sympathy in his eyes.

'What am I going to do? How are we going to manage with no money –?' She sat down very suddenly in a small armchair by

459

the fire and stared miserably into the flames. 'I had such plans. So many ideas. And Charlie – how will I tell Charlie there's no money after all? He's worked so hard –' Her voice trailed off. She lifted her head. 'I'll have to sell the place. That's what he wants, isn't it? So why not? I don't suppose it would bring much as it stands – but enough to buy somewhere for me and Gabriella and Mother Sarah to live. Enough for Gabriella's education and future –' She stopped and turned her head, frowning. 'What are you laughing at? I'm serious!'

He made no attempt to disguise the faint, affectionate smile she had surprised on his face. 'No you aren't.'

'And I tell you I am! Why should I stay here and fight alone? Why should I struggle to keep the wretched place together? Robert's doing as he wants. Why shouldn't I?'

'But – Jessica – you are. Aren't you?'

She held his eye for a long moment, and then the anger leeched from her and she let out a pent breath. 'Yes. Of course, you're right. I'll die if I have to sell Old Hall. But – what can I do with no money?'

He shook his head. 'I don't know. All I know is that you'll try.'

She pulled a rueful face.

'You won't leave this place, Jessica,' he said softly. 'You know you won't. It's in your blood. You need it as much as it needs you. And – do you know something –?'

She turned her head. 'What?'

'An awful lot of people would envy you, despite your problems. I'm not saying it isn't going to be hard – perhaps even impossible – but at least you know what you want. You know where you belong.' He paused, watching her. '– Jessica? What is it?' He smiled, puzzled. 'What have I said?'

She was looking at him intently, her eyes oddly abstracted, a small frown on her forehead. 'Something you said reminded me – someone else said something like that – Someone – Theo! It was Theo! Good God! Of course!' She struck her forehead with the flat of her hand. Her face was suddenly alight. 'Oh, what an absolute idiot I am!' She jumped to her feet and ran to the desk, scrabbling amongst the piles of books. 'Theo! Darling, darling man! You'd think he knew!'

John had followed her, was watching her frenetic search with almost comic puzzlement. 'Jessica? What are you doing? What are you looking for?'

'I think I'm looking for the answer to all of Old Hall's problems. Theo won't mind. He'll understand – ah!' She pounced, and picked up a book, brandishing it in triumph.

'What is it?'

She turned to him, bright-faced. 'It's a lovely, lovely thing. A unique treasure.'

'A book?'

'A book. Two books in fact. Written and illustrated in the twelfth-century. In Provence, at the courts of. love. A troubadour's precious offering to his lady. Do you know where the word troubadour comes from?' She did not wait for the shake of his head. 'Troubar – trouver – to seek, to find – to seek stories, and love, and magic – and to find them!' She paused for a moment, her eyes far away, remembering.

'May I see it?'

She handed it to him. He carried it to the light, opened it carefully, turning the pages slowly. She watched him. He whistled a little, under his breath. 'This is exquisite!'

'It's more than that. It's nearly priceless! To a collector it must be worth – oh, I don't know, but possibly – with the other one – more than all the others we sold put together! And they're mine! Not Robert's. Mine!'

He handed the book back to her. The brilliant jewel-colours glimmered in the firelight as she looked at it. Then she closed it and ran a gentle finger over the tooled leather.

He smiled. 'I'm surprised you can bear to part with it.'

She lifted level eyes. 'I'd part with blood if I had to, to get the money to keep Old Hall. Of course I hate to part with it – all the more because it's all I have of Theo. But – it is funny –' She had started to laugh a little, an infectious giggle that wasn't far from tears.

'What is?'

'For five years Theo tried to give me money. And I'd never

take it. And now – the only gift I ever had from him I'm going to sell just as fast as I can!' She hugged the books to her, clenching her eyes for a moment. 'But he won't mind,' she said. 'I know he won't.'

Chapter Sixteen

Charlie's prediction turned out to be absolutely right – it was a very hard winter, and in more ways than one. With Robert gone, responsibility for Old Hall and its occupants fell squarely upon Jessica's shoulders. And although Mr Sotheby himself showed a degree of excitement concerning Theo's book which was in itself promising he regretfully told her that the next auction at which it could be sold was not until March. With such an item, of course, a private buyer could almost certainly be found – but if she wanted to make the most of her legacy she would be well advised to wait.

Jessica, though a little disappointed, had been prepared for such news, and decided to take the advice. This windfall was all that she had and she intended to get the very best price for it that she could. If she had to wait a little longer, then so be it. When she left the auction rooms in Yorke Street she went straight to a pawnbroker's shop that she had marked on her way through Covent Garden, and a little over two hours later was climbing aboard the creaking coach for the journey home with enough money tucked into her reticule to see them through the winter safely, if not in the lap of luxury. The small diamond earbobs that had been Robert's wedding present to her had never been her favourite items in her jewel case; she doubted that she would even bother to embark upon the uncomfortable, bone-shaking journey from Suffolk back to the city in order to redeem them.

Through that long hard winter she heard not a word from Robert – she did not even know for certain if he had arrived safely in Florence. Neither, if she were honest, did she greatly care. Her anger and disgust at what he had done in taking the

463

money and deserting them was this time too deeply rooted. She felt nothing for him, and his absence was a relief. She did not care if she never saw him again.

But she was lonely.

She tried to deny it, tried to ignore it, tried to bury it beneath the bustling activity of a busy life, but loneliness ate at her, cold as the winter wind and comfortless as the deserted cottage that had once held Danny O'Donnel's life and laughter and now stood empty and rotting. She passed that cottage every week as she walked to the churchyard to tend Patrick's grave, and each time she saw it the pang was as painful as ever, a physical pain in her heart. The nights were the worst. With the big old house creaking around her, and the silent darkness made deeper by the small flicker of a night candle's flame she would lie, restless and alone with no-one to talk to, no-one to confide in, no-one to laugh with, no warm body by her side, no strong arms to comfort her.

As an early and bitter cold gripped the countryside, stripping the last leaves from the stark skeletons of the trees and freezing the ground to iron she sought to assuage the nagging ache of loneliness with activity. With the help of the village carpenter she went through every inch of Old Hall discovering and noting the worst of the damage and listing it ready to be acted upon when the money was available. She refused to think of the choice that she might be called upon to make if Theo's books did not make enough to cover her pledge to her mother as well as the repairs to the house. Local workmen were called in to patch those parts of the house where inaction and another winter's attack might cause deterioration too bad to be reversed. Those rooms in best repair were made more habitable, the best and most comfortable of the furniture being moved into them, the draughts stopped, the chimneys swept.

She rode often, too, to Home Farm. Apart from being genuinely interested in the wellbeing and progress of their small flock of South Down crossbred ewes she enjoyed Charlie's company – sometimes found herself asking his advice. He knew the local people and the village craftsmen better than she did, was happy to advise and help when it came to choosing a particular man for a particular job.

Twice a week she visited her mother. Maria was in pain and had not regained the use of her legs, although through what seemed to Jessica sheer force of will she could move her hands a little more freely. She refused, adamantly and with all her old authority to be moved into Old Hall. 'What can you be thinking of, Jessica my dear? You surely know me better than to believe I could live in a house full of females, much as I love you all? And in any case – you have quite enough on your plate with Sarah – I should be hopeless with the poor old thing – you know how impatient I am. You'd be living in a houseful of old women! Horrid thought! No, no – I'm quite comfortable here, thank you.'

'Perhaps next winter?' Jessica suggested. 'After the building work is finished and the Hall is cosy again? I could have a separate suite of rooms made for you at the east end of the house – nobody would bother you –'

Maria laughed. 'How very persistent you are! You get that from me, you know. But no, Jessica, I shan't be needing your rooms in the east wing.' She caught her daughter's suddenly sharp look and held her eyes with her own untroubled gaze. Jessica frowned a little and opened her mouth to speak. Her mother, with difficulty, lifted an imperious, knotted finger. 'Enough, Jessica. Don't fuss, now. You know I can't abide fuss –'

That day, trying not to worry about the clear inference of her mother's words she rode back via Home Farm. It was two weeks before Christmas, and bitterly cold. The sky was leaden and miserable, and the wind that bit viciously at her face as she rode blew down from the north. She found Charlie loading a supply of cleaned and cut turnips into a farm cart to take down to the sheep pens. Bess lay not far from him, her nose on her paws, jealously watching his every move.

He staightened easily, smiling. 'Afternoon.'

'Good afternoon, Charlie. I thought I'd drop in to see if the ewe with the sore udder is improved?'

He leaned for a moment on the cart's tail, brushing his

forehead with his coat sleeve despite the cold. The great Suffolk Punch stood docile as a lamb between the shafts of the cart. 'Aye. She's fine. The treatment worked well.'

The mare danced a little, and in the movement Jessica caught sight of Charlie's tall double-barrelled shotgun leaning against the driving seat of the cart. She frowned a little. 'Why the gun? You don't usually carry it with you, do you?'

He shook his head a little grimly. 'There's a dog about. Great brute of a thing. Wild, I think. It's bin after the sheep.'

'Worrying them?'

He nodded. 'But don't worry. I'll have the bugger before long –' He lifted his head and smiled suddenly, his teeth shining very white in his weather-burned face. 'Beggin' your pardon, Ma'am.' The apology was mischievous.

She laughed a little. He pushed himself away from the tailgate. 'Would you be wanting to pick up some more of that horse liniment while you're here? I mixed it last night. Tha'ss ready if you'd like it.'

'Yes, I will. Thank you. It's by far the best we've tried. Ben was saying just the other day that it worked wonders on Bay Dancer's bad leg.' She kicked her foot free of the stirrup and made to swing down from the little mare. She rarely used the sidesaddle when she rode alone around the estate. The mare moved a little and Charlie stepped forward to hold her head. The great carthorse made to follow him and the huge iron wheels grated noisily on the cobbled yard. The mare, startled, reared and danced away before Charlie could reach her and Jessica, caught by surprise, was flung from the saddle to land with a bruising thump on her left shoulder.

With a sharp exclamation Charlie dropped to his knee beside her. She struggled dazedly to a sitting position, her right hand clasping her painful shoulder. She tried to laugh, succeeded in only producing a slightly shaky squeak. 'Good Lord! I haven't fallen off a horse since I was eight-years-old!'

'Don't stand up. Wait a bit. Let me have a look at you.' Charlie had an arm about her, supporting her. With the other hand he slipped the jacket from her shoulder. She let out a smothered gasp of pain. 'Gently, now, gently.' His voice was softly calming. With deft, probing fingers he explored the damaged shoulder. She had seen him many times handle an injured animal so, gently, firmly, reassuringly. His fingers probed, and she jumped. 'Ah,' he said, and then, a few moments later. 'Tha'ss all right. That'll be bruised an' painful, but tha'ss not broken. Can you get your jacket back on?'

She nodded, and with his help got to her feet and struggled into her jacket. She had banged her knee as well, and it throbbed painfully.

He put a hand firmly under her elbow. 'Come over to the house and rest a while,' he said. 'Tha'ss shaken you up.'

To Jessica's surprise as they approached the door of the house it opened, a girl stood there regarding Jessica with wide, anxious blue eyes. She was painfully thin and frail as a buttercup, a mop of bright yellow hair pushed untidily beneath her small mob cap. Though obviously no child she looked like an undernourished waif, the bones of her shoulderblades showing clearly beneath the shabby homespun of her dress, and there were unhealthy shadows beneath her eyes. Behind her, the room had been transformed. The windows shone, framed by clean and pretty curtains, the range was alight, the small door open to let the cheer of the fire into the room. A pot from which rose an appetizing steam bubbled on the hob. On the table stood a small glass jar in which some evergreen twigs, fir, ivy and holly with its bright berries, had been prettily arranged.

'Minna – get her Ladyship a chair. Hurry.'

Jessica disentangled her arm. 'No – really – I'm all right. Just a bit stiff, that's all.'

'That'll be more than stiff tomorrow,' he said.

'Perhaps I'll try some of your liniment on it.' She had regained the composure that the unexpected appearance of the girl had so strangely disturbed, and her voice was light, though she flinched as she moved and a stab of pain shot through her shoulder. She studied the room, watched the waif-like girl with her promise of beauty.

The girl half-carried, half-dragged the only chair to where Jessica stood. Jessica seated herself, straight-backed, finding that she had to force her smile. 'Hello. I haven't seen you before, have I?'

'Her name's Minna. Minna Newton,' Charlie said. 'She's from the village. She comes up to do for me a couple of times a week. Her brother Peter helps with the sheep.'

And she doesn't have a tongue of her own, Jessica thought, mildly caustic, as the girl stood with downcast eyes, her hands twisting in front of her, half-hidden by her apron.

'I'll get the liniment,' Charlie said. 'Minna – mull some ale. Her Ladyship needs something to warm her.'

With little, nervous movements the girl drew the ale from the small cask that stood in the corner, set the jug upon the range, thrust the poker into the fire to heat. She kept her face turned from Jessica and her bony shoulders were hunched defensively almost to her ears. Her thin hands shook a little.

'You've made the room very pretty,' Jessica said.

'Thank you Ma'am – Y're Ladyship –' It was the barest whisper.

'You come twice a week?'

'Yes, Ma'am. Mondays an' Thursdays. An' Sat'days I help with the sheep with Petie.'

'I see.'

The poker was hot. The girl took it from the fire and plunged it into the ale jug. The liquid seethed and sizzled. The girl looked around for mugs.

'They're in the cupboard in the corner,' Jessica said, and was surprised at the obscure satisfaction it gave.

Silent and downcast Minna took two mugs from the cupboard and poured the ale as Charlie came back into the room. Bess, following him, padded with swishing tail across the room and lifted her nose to Minna, who patted the little bitch, her gaunt face softening. Jessica felt a sudden and absolutely absurd frisson of something very close to jealousy. In all the times she had known Charlie Bess had never come near her, let alone shown affection.

Minna, holding the mug carefully between two hands brought her the drink. Jessica accepted it with murmured thanks. Her shoulder was hurting and so was her knee. She could feel her back stiffening a little. She felt quite ridiculously sorry for herself.

The ale was good, strong and hot. She drank in silence, watched as Charlie took the other mug, with no thanks, from Minna. Neither did he offer that the girl should share it. Minna turned back to the range, busied herself with her back to them. Bess lay close to her feet.

Charlie looked at Jessica. 'How's the shoulder feelin'?'

'Painful.'

'Aye. That will be. For a coupl 'a days or more. Rest's the best thing. Try not to use it.'

She nodded, finished the ale and stood up, supporting herself by the back of the chair, waving away his offer of help with an unconsciously arrogant gesture that brought him up short. 'I'd better get back,' she said, 'before I stiffen up and can't ride.'

He was reaching for his stick. 'I'll walk with you.'

'No. Thank you. That won't be necessary. I'm perfectly all right.'

'But —'

'No, Charlie. I tell you there's no need.' Her voice was sharp, and cool. She turned from him and left the room, facing the wind of the dark afternoon, a strange tide of ill-temper rising within her. She did not give the girl a word or a glance of farewell.

Quietly Charlie followed her. Perforce she had to allow him to help her to mount, for her shoulder was too painful to manage alone. Once in the saddle she jerked on the reins, taking them from his hands. He stepped back, unsmiling. His face was forbidding.

Infuriatingly, for she certainly had had no intention of mentioning the girl, she found herself saying, 'I didn't know you had someone to help you in the house?'

He shrugged. 'She needed the work. Her father and elder brother bin laid off from New Hall. The mother's poorly. The few shillings I pay the two sprats come in handy. The family'd be in the workhouse without.'

'Why were the father and brother laid off?'

He clearly hesitated for a moment. Then he lifted his head, his eyes direct. 'Seems Mr Giles thinks they've bin causing trouble.'

'What sort of trouble?'

'They were tryin' to organize the labour.'

'Organize –? You mean – unionize? On New Hall land?'

Charlie shrugged a little.

'I'm not surprised Giles sacked them. It would be a red rag to a bull!'

'They were only tryin' to do what they thought was right,' he said, very quiet and mild.

Somewhere in the near distance a dog barked. Charlie turned his head, immediately alert. Jessica too lifted her head, listening, but heard nothing more above the bluster of the wind in the trees. 'Was that the wild dog?'

He was still listening intently. 'Could be. Damn' it for a killer. I'd better get down to the pens. You sure you can manage alone?'

'I can manage.'

He handed up the bottle of liniment he was carrying, and she saw the faint glimmer of his teeth in his dark face. 'You could do worse than to try that, Y're Ladyship,' the title was faintly mocking. 'Though you'll stink to high heaven. Tha'ss got no lady's perfume in it!'

She took the bottle, returning his smile. 'I might at that.' She turned the mare and walked her down the track into the wind. Behind her she heard his chirrup to the great, patient carthorse and the grinding of the wheels as the ungainly cart turned in the small yard.

It was some hours later, fussed and bathed and tucked into bed by an exasperatedly solicitous Angelina, before she allowed herself to examine the events of the afternoon and to recognize in honesty that the immediate antagonism she had felt for poor, defenceless little Minna had been something absurdly close to jealousy. Not so much of her, as of the change she had obviously wrought in Charlie's life. At least until now if she, Jessica, had been alone then Charlie had been even more so. The austere and cold little house in which he lived had been eloquent testament to that. But this afternoon the warm room, the appetizing smell that had filled the little house, the small pot of evergreens so lovingly arranged upon the table had made a scene so homely that for a moment she had felt a stranger, an unwanted outsider intruding on another woman's territory, and she had resented that. And what was more she was sure that the girl, for all the downcast eyes and still tongue, had returned her resentment in full. She knew she had not imagined the look in the shadowed blue eyes as they had rested on Charlie – any more than she had imagined Bess' immediate and unquestioning acceptance of the small intruder's presence. As she lay, drowsy from the medicine that kindly, fussing Angelina had administered yet still uncomfortable from the pain in her bruised shoulder she found herself wondering what other services the girl provided for Charlie. Did they do together the things that she and Danny had done? Did he love her with his powerful body, did she cry out in the darkness of that little cottage as his great strength was spent in her? She moved restlessly. No! Surely not! Charlie wouldn't find that pale little shadow of a child attractive! She could not believe it! Charlie was a man, with a man's pride, a man's strength, a man's lust. Such milk and water wouldn't – couldn't! – be to his taste?

The fire that Angelina had built for her flared and glowed, making the room uncomfortably hot. She pushed the bed-clothes back, wincing at the twinge in her shoulder, unbuttoned her heavy nightgown to let the cooler air brush her throat and breasts. Shadows danced upon the tester of the bed, flickered in the dark corners of the room. When she slept it was to dreams that were to shame her when she woke, stiff and sore, in the morning.

The weather worsened. Bad before Christmas it got even wilder in the New Year, with no sign of let up, no mild spell to break the relentless battering of wind and rain. Oddly, though it was bitterly cold it did not snow. The wind cut like a knife, the sky was heavy and the rain drove in constant drenching gusts across the countryside. The river rose, swollen and yellow, sullen-looking as it sucked at the soft banks and tugged at the exposed roots of the trees. The mud was a squelching trap for foot and hoof, and a sheep once fallen could not get to her feet for the weight of rain in her fleece. The ewes, Charlie reckoned, were about six weeks off lambing: and the depredations of the wild dog were getting worse. In the middle of January they lost a valuable cross bred ewe to the animal. Two weeks later young Peter surprised the beast amongst the flock and drove it off, but a ewe aborted and valuable twin lambs were lost. Charlie was in a cold rage.

'I'll kill the bugger with my bare hands! See if I don't!'

'Did Peter see what it looks like?' Jessica asked.

'We've both seen it. Tha'ss like a bloody wolf – prick-eared, bushy tailed, mangy, grey. And fast as the Devil.'

'Where does it live?'

'Tha'ss what no-one knows. Moves about like a shadow. One minute tha'ss here, the next tha'ss over to Melford, or raidin' at Links Farm.'

'Well, let's hope that someone stops it soon. With lambing coming up in a few weeks we don't need a killer dog to contend with –'

Charlie's finger closed over the worn stock of his gun, and he stared grimly into the driving rain. 'Tha'ss not "someone" as is goin' to get it. Tha'ss me. That dog's mine, an' I'll get it if it kills me.'

'Would it?'

'What?'

'Would it attack a human?'

He shrugged. 'Who knows? But if the weather gets worse an' the livin' out there gets harder I wouldn't let a child o' mine out in these woods alone.'

The bad weather made life hard at Old Hall. The roof sprang a new leak a day, or so it seemed to the exasperated Jessica. Wood rotted, water crept under doors and through ill-fitting window frames. The wind battered relentlessly at none-too-sound leaded windows and weakened brickwork. But January did eventually end, and February came, and that meant that the sale, and the money, were closer. And surely – the weather could not stay like this for ever?

Sarah took cold, out looking for the dead Sir Thomas in the rain, and was very poorly for a while, and Gabriella, nurtured in the Italian sun, seemed permanently to be sniffling and led poor Jane Barton, whose catarrh reddened her nose and puffed her eyes, a dance that brought her mother's exasperated wrath upon her head more than once.

The days crept coldly on: two weeks to the start of lambing, six weeks to the sale. Painstakingly Jessica had, at her mother's dictation, written yet another letter to the money-lender asking for another couple of months' grace to pay Patrick's debt. Over the winter the thousand guineas had become a thousand and fifty. In the cold church, sheltering from the rain on the way to put holly and greenstuff on Patrick's grave Jessica suggested forcibly to St Agatha that a good price for Theo's book was now essential – or it was not just the church that would be in danger of falling down.

And then, in February, the change in the weather came at last – but it was too much in such a year to expect that it might be a change for the better.

Jessica woke to darkness and to silence, the only sound the murmuring lap of the risen river. For a moment she could not identify the change, and then it registered. There was no sound of wind, no driving rain. It was as if an enormous dark silence gripped the world, bitingly cold. As dawn broke, reluctant and grey, the atmosphere grew if anything colder. Everything was frozen – the mud into irritating, corrugated, ankle-breaking ridges of brown rock, the puddles into dangerous sheets of slippery glass. As the day wore on the river edges began to clog with ice, and the trees were black with it. The sky hung in dark and heavy billows above the miserable, frozen world. In the afternoon, almost as if by sheer habit, the rain tried to fall but turned immediately to sleet that rattled the windows and bounced onto the hard ground where it lay like a layer of dirty broken beads. With night, it was a relief to draw the curtains and stoke up the fires. In the next couple of days the cold did not abate. And then, on the day that Jessica, tired of being cooped up in the dark and airless house, decided to ride to Tollgate House to see if all was well with her mother, the snow came at last.

It was a day as still as death, and as cold. Winter darkness sat upon the landscape still at noon, the very air leaden with the threat that hung in the clouds above. As she rode across the parkland it seemed that the world held its breath, and each sound was magnified a thousand times. A snapping twig was a pistol shot, the sudden startled rising of a bird enough to unnerve the mare and set Jessica's own pulse racing in momentary and silly fright.

Maria was in peevish mood. 'Truly, Jessica, you never did have any sense at all. What possessed you to ride over on such a day? It's perfectly obvious that it will snow – and heavily.'

'Don't be silly, Mother. Old Hall is less than three miles away. I'll leave before the snow starts. There's no danger. Or if it comes down too heavily, I'll stay until it clears. I've left word to say where I am. They won't expect me home if the weather gets too bad –'

Maria turned her head. Almost any movement caused her excruciating pain now, but an onlooker would have to be very well acquainted with her to know it. 'Well perhaps it's just as well you've come. I've been meaning for some time to have a word with you.'

'Oh?'

Her mother's face was repressive. 'It's in my mind, Jessica, that all the hard work expended upon you was for nothing.'

Jessica was stung. 'What on earth can you mean?'

Her mother, with the perfect timing that was a part of her armoury hesitated for long enough for the now-faded blue eyes to move from her daughter's untidy hair to the worn hem of her heavy and mudstained riding skirt. With no word said Jessica felt colour rising to her face. 'Just look at you!' her mother said at last. 'Slipshod and inelegant! Tell me – do you spend the whole of your life in the saddle, or hobnobbing with farm labourers and workmen? Do you never wear a decent gown, or entertain people of your own station? Jessica, you were wild as a child, and wild you still are. For your own sake you should take yourself in hand. It's bad enough that your husband should have deserted you, and that the whole County knows it. At least don't give them room to believe that he had good reason for going!'

Jessica was so taken aback that she could hardly for a moment speak. When she did though she tried to keep her voice level angry exasperation was clear in it. 'Where Robert has gone and why is no-one's business but his and mine. And as for the way I dress and act – for heaven's sake! – what do you expect me to do? There's work to be done and no-one to do it but me. I don't have time to call on the local gentry and drink tea. Nor, to be truthful do I want to –'

'Quite.' Perfectly unruffled Maria nodded her head, her point proven to her own satisfaction. 'Lady Felworth called the other day,' she continued, inexorably, totally ignoring Jessica's obvious annoyance, 'she tells me that you haven't once called upon her since you came home.'

'Mother! Now stop it, do! You're being perverse. And I won't be treated like a disobedient child! I've no time for such things, both literally and figuratively. You know it. For heaven's sake – if I called on her Ladyship – can you just imagine the conversation? "And how is dear Robert? You've heard from him of course? Such a pity that he should have been called away again so soon – and with you and his poor mother left in that draughty great barn of a house – but then no doubt he'll be home soon? Where did you say he'd gone –?"' Jessica's voice that had been lifted in parody of Lady Felworth's drawling tones dropped to normal, 'The woman is a gossip of the very worst order. A hundred years ago she'd have been ducked in the village pond!'

Her mother regarded her stonily.

'And Patrick – you can't tell me she keeps her tongue from Patrick? Such a juicy morsel that! "Such a lovely boy – wild, of course, I always said he was wild –"' Jessica stopped, brought up short by the look in her mother's eyes at mention of Patrick's name. 'No, Mother! I couldn't stand it,' she said, determinedly. 'If the world doesn't like the way I live my life then it's something for the world to worry about, not me.'

'You are isolating yourself, Jessica,' Maria said quietly. 'Cutting yourself off from your own kind.'

'I'm fighting for survival. Mine. Gabriella's. Old Hall's. I've no time and no money. Pretty gowns and carriages have at the moment to run a bad second to roof tiles and winter feed.'

Her mother picked gently at the blanket that covered her knees. 'Clara, you know, is quite making her name as a hostess.'

'Good for her,' Jessica said, shortly.

'Don't be impertinent, Jessica.' Maria's voice still held that note of authority that could bring Jessica up short.

'I'm sorry.' She was fighting to prevent herself from truly losing her temper. She realized how hard it must be on Maria Hawthorne to see the daughter-in-law she detested take her place in local society whilst her own daughter ignored her social obligations and got herself well and truly talked about. But her mother's criticisms, unfair as she perceived them, cut to the bone. 'You have to understand, Mother. I'm a grown woman. I have the right to make my own decisions, live my own life.'

'And you think you've done that successfully up until now?'

Jessica took a long breath. 'In your terms? I suppose not. In mine? Yes. I'm not a simpering silk-draped dummy who opens her mouth when she's told to and keeps it shut when she's not.'

'I've noticed.'

'The mistakes I've made have been my own, and I'm ready to live with them. I've made no-one else suffer for them, that I know of –'

'Defensiveness, Jessica, has always been one of the least attractive of your habitual attitudes.'

'And –' Jessica ploughed grimly on, '– when I've put Old Hall back on its feet, when the house is safe and the future assured, when the land is well managed and the flocks secure I shall know I had a hand in it – a real influence on what's happened. I've discovered that that's more important to me than the entertaining of the County, the petty gossip, the whispering behind the fans –'

Her mother was regarding her with a tart amusement that reduced her effortlessly to the status of a grubby eight-year-old. 'I don't think anyone whispers about you, Jessica,' she said, mildly. 'I have the strongest feeling that they say what they have to say about you in a perfectly normal tone of voice.'

Jessica found herself laughing at that again as she rode across the park towards the woodland path, the first soft flakes of snow drifting into her face. So her neighbours gossiped about her, did they? Let them. She was surprised to realize that it truly did not bother her – and she suspected in her heart that it bothered her mother less than she would have her believe. For all Maria's sharpness there had been a certain twinkle in her eye. Jessica had the distinct impression that, though her mother would never admit to it, Maria Hawthorne harboured a certain pride in a daughter who, rightly or wrongly, stuck to her guns and did what she wanted to do. Jessica found herself wondering how much her mother guessed of the disaster of her marriage. She had never questioned, not even after Robert had left. Perhaps, Jessica thought ruefully, she simply did not want to know – she stopped, her train of thought suddenly broken as the mare whinneyed and pulled to the right suddenly. It was snowing much harder now, the movement quite dizzying, a little disorientating. She reined in the obviously distressed animal, peered ahead to see what had disturbed her. In the trees to the left a dark shadow moved. She walked the mare forward, softly. The snow was settling, drifting and whirling between the bare branches of the trees, limning the world in white. The flicker of movement came again, and then for a moment she caught a glimpse of a grey and menacing shadow, wolf-like, threatening.

The mare tossed her head, worried.

Jessica held her. The shadow moved closer. She waited, straining her eyes, staring tensely into the moving, swirling wall of white. For a moment she lost the vague shape, and then she found it again. It was ahead of her, cutting across her path.

She held the mare still.

The animal appeared not a stone's throw from her on the path ahead. That it was Charlie's wild dog she had no doubt. It was big, but carried no weight, its wolf-like head hung low between thrusting shoulderblades, its great tail swished menacingly. It looked half-starved and entirely savage. In the darkness of the afternoon its yellow eyes gleamed perilously. For several seconds they stared at each other, the dog with each breath making a venomous growling sound deep in its throat.

Jessica's mount shivered beneath her. The dog took a crawling step forward, and then another.

Blindly Jessica set the horse at it. The smaller beast stood its ground for a moment, snapping with vicious teeth, then it turned and fled, swift and silent as a shadow, through the woods.

Jessica fought for control of the frightened mare. By the time she had brought it to a stand the dog had disappeared, in the general direction of Home Farm.

She patted the mare's neck, calming her, and set off at a gallop down the snowy bridleway.

She found the dog's tracks on the bridge, fresh, only a little smudged by the fast-falling snow. She followed them.

Like an arrow they led directly to the sheep pens.

The dog just beat her in the race. She arrived in time to see the animal leap effortlessly into one of the pens. The ewes, heavy with lamb, scuttled away from it, terrified, huddled into a corner, bleating plaintively.

The dog slavered, crawling towards them on its belly.

'Get away! Get away!' She almost fell from the horse, cast about for a stone to throw. The dog ignored her. As she straightened, a stone in her hand, a terrified sheep broke from the flock. The dog was on it in a second, tearing savagely at the struggling animal as the rest of the flock milled in panic-stricken unison.

Jessica watched in horror, seeing the blood that stained the muddy snow, hearing the desperate cries of the dying ewe. Beside herself with anger she flung the stone. It came nowhere near the dog. The ewe had collapsed, bleating pathetically.

Jessica scrambled back onto the mare, clapped her heels to the frightened animal's sides and set off at a flat run, to Home Farm, Charlie, and his gun.

In the few minutes it took for her to reach the house, shout for Charlie and lead him, running fast, gun in hand back to the fold, the place looked like a slaughterhouse. A ewe lay dead, the blood from her torn throat steaming upon the snow, her still-born lamb dead beside her, its head torn from its body. Another ewe struggled weakly upon the ground, fleece torn and bloody. The slavering dog was in amongst the rest of the frightened flock, snapping and snarling, yellow teeth bared. A ewe went down to her knees, her belly contracting, and the dog pounced.

A black and white streak went past Jessica and Charlie like a flash of light. Snow whirled. Bess hit the stray dog like a thrown hammer. The wolf-like creature staggered and turned, vicious teeth glinting like knives. Bravely Bess went for him again. The fangs slashed. Charlie whistled sharply. The sheep milled, terror-stricken. The wild dog lunged at Bess, snarling its fury. Bess yelped, and blood appeared on her shoulder. Calmly Charlie raised the shotgun to his shoulder and took aim. A frightened ewe blundered across his line of fire. He waited. The grey dog had bellied to the ground, its eyes on Bess, who stood her ground courageously, snarling challenge. Jessica's own fingers tensed as she sensed Charlie's steady pressure upon the trigger. The bullet caught the beast in the throat just as it was about to launch itself upon Bess. The animal reared, blood spraying, and dropped to the ground.

'Stay here.' Charlie, gun at the ready, approached the fallen animal, ignoring for the moment the carnage about him, the desperate bleating of the sheep. As he approached it the dog twitched. He brought the gun to its head. Jessica looked away as he pulled the trigger.

'Mr Best! Mr Best! That you? Wha'ss happened? Mr Best?' Peter Newton, a small replica of his sister Minna scrambled through the snow towards them. Charlie was striding back, reloading his gun as he walked.

'Tha'ss that. It's dead. Petie, go get the wagon. We'll have to get those that are birthin' inside or we'll lose 'em sure. Take Bess. An' see to that shoulder of hers. Then put her in the house. The last thing these poor beasts want about them now is a dog –'

Charlie whistled Bess. Limping a little the dog joined him. He patted her. 'Good girl. Now off! Off with Petie! He'll see to you!'

Peter turned and began to run back towards the house and barn. 'Come on, Bess.'

The dog looked at Charlie.

'Off!' he snapped, and she went.

He looked around, shaking his head, grim-faced. Jessica fought nausea. Near them a half-dead sheep, blood spreading upon the snow, was giving birth. The lamb hung, moving weakly, all but dead, half in and half out of its dying mother. The snow fell, large pretty flakes, settling on the frozen ground, melting into the blood, feathering the carcass of the dead dog. Charlie knelt beside the ewe and eased the lamb from her. Then he picked up his gun.

The flock were settling a little, though they still milled aimlessly. Several had wandered off alone, bleating quietly, their sides heaving in the first contractions of birth.

Jessica jumped at the gunshot. The ewe stopped her struggling. Charlie scooped up the tiny lamb and put it in his pocket, strode to where another ewe was standing, head down, sides quivering. He ran his hands over her, straightened. 'She'll be all right.'

'What can I do?'

'Shut the gate.' He was already moving to another sheep that was in some difficulty. Jessica, as she ran to shut the gate heard him curse viciously beneath his breath, then he called her name, urgently, 'Jessie!'

'Yes?'

'Over here. Quickly!'

She ran back to him. 'Bloody dog got this one too,' he said. 'Hold her forelegs. She's a gonner. We might be able to save the lamb.'

Jessica dropped to her knees in the stained snow. Faintly she could hear the sounds of the cart coming down the track to the folds. Charlie worked swiftly and surely. Jessica felt the spasm that ran through the poor creature whose legs she held as the lamb was released, and then the life went from the mauled ewe, and she stilled. Charlie worked on the lamb for a moment, then shook his head and stood up. The lamb lay, a tiny scrap, dead beside its dead mother.

Charlie rubbed his hands on his jacket and shook the snow from his hair. 'We'd better get the rest of the poor little buggers in.'

They worked, the three of them, in the failing light, for nearly two hours, Charlie and Peter taking the lion's share of the labour, Jessica helping where she could. Snow covered everything like a blanket, making the footing treacherous and chilling Jessica's feet in their inappropriate riding boots, to the bone. It settled in Jessica's hair, melted and trickled down her neck. It crept through the fine leather of her boots and gloves till her hands were as numb with cold as were her feet. But she would not give up. Until the last sheep was in, the last lamb safely delivered she stayed with them, fetching and carrying, holding the lantern in the dark barn, assisting with the animals when she was needed. She watched as Charlie introduced the orphan lamb he had carried in his pocket to a mother who had had a still birth, watched as he rubbed the orphan against the dead lamb, soaking it in the liquids of the ewe's labour before gently presenting it to the mother. The ewe sniffed, licked. The lamb, wobbling on unsteady legs, bleated softly.

'Will it work?' Jessica asked.

'Tha'ss difficult to tell. Sometimes does, sometimes doesn't.' Charlie straightened. 'Well looks as if we've done all we can fer now —'

'I'll stay with 'em, Mr Best. I don't mind.' Young Peter grinned staunchly. 'Stay all night out here, if you like. Tha'ss as comfortable as home, an' a lot less crowded!'

'You'll freeze!' Jessica said. She herself was suddenly shivering violently, and her feet had lost all feeling.

The child laughed and shook his head. The past hours had forged a bond between the three of them that for the moment transcended age and station. Tomorrow, Jessica knew, he would be in awe of her again. For now he had lost his constraint with her, as had Charlie. 'It'll be as warm in the straw with the beasts as in me own bed,' he said. 'Might I ha' a drop of ale an' a bite to eat I'll stay all night an' watch 'em.'

Jessica shivered again. Charlie glanced at her sharply. 'Good God, look at you! You're blue! Petie – you sure you're all right out here?'

'Right as rain, Mr Best. They've settled now, poor beasts. If I need you I'll call.'

'I'll get something warm for you to drink, and some supper. Miss Jessica –' Jessie registered the return to a more formal address with something close to regret, '– you should get something too, an' warm up a bit before you go home. They'll ha' missed you at the Hall, I reckon –?'

She spoke through teeth clenched against chattering. 'They'll probably assume that I'm sitting it out at Tollbridge House.' She shivered again, uncontrollably.

He frowned. 'You'd best get back to the house straight away. I'll be along in a minute.'

She did not argue. Truth to tell she was so cold that she could barely think. On feet that she could not feel she crossed the yard and entered the house. The snow was falling in earnest now, steadily and with purpose, as if it intended to bury the world by morning.

She opened the door to a blissful warmth. The early darkness of winter had fallen, and the glow from the range lit the room. She shut the door and leaned against it, tiredness washing over her. The smell of sheep, of blood and of other things she did not care to think of hung about her ruined clothes. She dragged the chair close to the range. For the moment her fingers were too painfully stiff with the cold for her to attempt to light the lantern that stood upon the table. She struggled out of her heavy cord riding jacket. It was soaked through to the shirt beneath. She looked around. Behind the door hung an old jacket of Charlie's, enormous, tattered, but dry and warm. Taking it down she wrapped it around her shoulders, shivering, then hunched in front of the fire, rubbing her hands. The marrow of her bones felt frozen. Her divided riding skirt dripped with dirty water upon the floor, chafed her skin, the hem soaked and blood-stained. Awful as her feet felt she simply did not have the energy to try to remove her boots. She huddled under Charlie's jacket, rubbing her arms and her damp shoulders. The jacket hung heavy and warm about her shoulders, and she smiled at the smells that reminded her of Charlie – the smell of the outdoors, of sheep, and of woodsmoke. She rubbed her cold face upon the rough, dry material of the collar.

When the door opened to a rush of cold air she jumped. Almost, cold and wet as she was, she had dozed. Her hands were coming to life and her face burned uncomfortably in the warmth of the fire.

Charlie strode to the table and lit the lantern. 'Ale,' he said, filling a large jug from the barrel in the corner and setting it on the range. 'And bread and cheese for the boy. You all right for a moment?'

She nodded. 'Just cold, that's all.' Her hands ached as the warmth crept into them and cruel stabs of pain had begun in her feet.

He set the poker in the fire. 'We'll soon have you warmed up.'

She heard him clattering behind her, opening cupboards, setting things upon the table. She set herself grimly to stop herself shivering and gritted her teeth against the pain in her feet. Charlie did not seem in the least tired or cold. She was not about to show less stamina than he. She watched the poker as it began to glow a little in the heart of the fire.

Charlie mulled the wine, set a pewter mug full in front of her. 'Drink that while I take this out to young Petie. I'll be back in half a tick.'

She sipped the drink, relishing its warmth and the comfort it brought as it slipped down her throat and spread its strength into her shaking body. It was hard to say if the pain of returning life in her hands and feet was any improvement on the frozen discomfort of half an hour before.

When Charlie came back he came straight to her. 'Tha'ss Petie taken care of. An' it looks like the worst is over. A couple are in labour, but are managing all right on their own –'

'How many have we lost?'

'Three ewes and four lambs. It could have been worse. If you hadn't seen that killer –'

She leaned forward, grimacing with pain and rubbed at her painful feet through her wet boots.

'Good God, girl,' he said, softly, 'what kind o' boots are they to be runnin' around in the snow in? Give 'em here –' He knelt before her and held out his big hands. Thankfully she lifted her foot for him to pull off her boot, but could not suppress a sharp cry of pain as he jerked it from her painful foot. The skin was white and bloodless as stone, and as cold. He chafed it gently then set it on his lap and reached for the other boot. She could feel the warmth of his hands on her skin, but oddly at a remove, almost as if her feet no longer belonged to her. He rubbed them in turn, briskly and then gently as the warm blood returned and brought with it a glowing, aching pain. She caught her lip between her teeth. The momentary pain was excruciating. Unselfconsciously he opened his jacket and tucked her left foot inside it whilst he rubbed her right. His face was concerned. 'Tha'ss right daft to have let yourself get as cold as this!' he scolded, not looking at her, his big hands chafing her ice-cold ankle.

Her left foot, tucked close to his chest had almost stopped hurting and she could feel the warmth of his body begin to glow through her skin like the warmth of a fire. She looked at the brown, bent head, the intent face. She fought an impulse to put out a hand and brush away the bright drops of moisture that the melting snow had left upon his thick hair.

He tucked her right foot against his chest and started on the left one, rubbing the foot, chafing the ankle and the calf of her leg. She was warm now, glowing with warmth. Her shirt was uncomfortably damp on her shoulders, and she could feel the wet hem of her skirt against her bare legs.

The movement of his hands had become slower, more gentle. A small, delicious shiver that had nothing to do with the cold rippled through her. The warmth that now glowed in her like a live coal seemed centred somehow dangerously

484

deep, dangerously disturbing. The scene was dreamlike – the kneeling man, the flickering light of the fire, the feel of his strong, work-hardened hands upon her skin. Eyes half closed she watched those big, stained hands against her own white skin, watched the curve of his long lashes against his weather-brightened cheek, the curl of his brown hair against his ears; watched and, dreamlike still, felt the warmth grow and spread to flood those deeper parts of herself that until now only one man had ever touched or known.

He sensed it. She knew he did. His hands ceased their movement, but he did not look up. His big hand closed over her foot, drew it with the other close to his chest. For a long moment neither of them moved. She could feel the calloused hardness of his palm on her delicate skin. Then,. very suddenly, he lifted his head and looked at her. His eyes were narrowed a little, his mouth straight and unsmiling. Her heart had taken on an irregular, almost frightened beat. Neither of them spoke, but the silence was suddenly thick with excitement. His eyes searched her face, unafraid, unsubmissive, fiercely questioning. She could not look away.

He sat back on his heels, setting her bare feet upon the cold floor. The touch of his hand brought fire to her body. He watched her for a moment longer. Then he stood up, easy and unhurried, stood before her, towering above her so that she had to tilt her head far back to keep her eyes on his.

He offered his hands.

She sat absolutely still for a moment, and then almost without thought placed her small hands in his. Quite naturally and with no effort he drew her to her feet, close to his body. The jacket fell from her shoulders. Still holding her hands he bent to her and for the first time in a year she tasted a man's demanding mouth. In that brief, aching moment she was lost. The treacherous demands of her young body opened her lips beneath his. She felt his body tense and harden, thrusting against hers. Then he stepped back abruptly and she was left, trembling and bereft, watching him with eyes that pleaded no matter what her efforts to prevent it.

He took a visible breath. His hands were fisted at his sides.

Sharply, with a movement so violent that it startled her he turned and, striding to a wooden door in the corner of the room threw it open with a crash. Beyond it she could see a neat stark room, its only furniture a rough pine chest, a dresser upon which stood a chipped china jug and bowl, and a bed, neatly made, its cover homespun and rough.

He lifted his chin, his eyes meeting hers in challenge. Stay — or go. I'll not beg your Ladyship. She heard the words in her heart as clearly as if he had spoken them into her ear.

Her head as high as his she walked past him into the tiny room. It was very cold, and the only light was that which fell through the open door from the other room. When she turned he still stood by the door, watching her, the arrogant confidence of him suddenly gone.

She lifted her arms. 'I'm cold, Charlie,' she said softly.

His loving was nothing like Danny's, nothing like the cunning Guido's. It was without subtlety or guile, a straightforward act of physical pleasure tempered by tenderness but brutally forceful and totally satisfying to them both. As she had known it would be. Her climax came almost as soon as he entered her, and then she was able to share with delight his demanding pleasure as he thrust himself to join her. Afterwards she lay, relaxed and tired, against his big, strong-muscled body, refusing to think, at ease and truly happy for the first time in months. Yet thoughts of the world could not be entirely blotted out. What they had done was, in the eyes of most of society, almost as bad as murder. If it ever came to light she would be a laughing-stock, ostracized, sneered at, scorned.

She sighed a little. 'I had better go home. They'll be worrying.'

He leaned on one elbow, looking down at her, his face sombre. As he opened his mouth she put a finger to his lips. 'Don't,' she said. 'Don't spoil it. Don't talk about it. There's nothing to be said. Just — we must be careful. For Gabriella's sake. For my mother's sake, and for Robert's mother's too —'

'And for your own, Your Ladyship —' He smiled, but the words held a tiny, bitter edge.

486

'Yes. And for my own.' No matter what, Jessica was still a Hawthorne.

She rode home through the steadily falling snow. Charlie striding beside her, and not once did they speak. In the darkness beyond the windows of Old Hall she reined in, bent to him and kissed him, long, hard and passionately. Then before he could stop her she chirruped to the little mare and rode across the drawbridge and into the courtyard.

It was, as they had both known it would be, a hopeless affair from the start. But yet, in those first months they could not keep away from each other. As spring brought green to the world at last and then burgeoned into a summer that in its warmth and splendour seemed to be trying to make up for the truly dreadful winter they made love not often but whenever they safely could, almost every time swearing, each in concern for the other, that it must be the last, but never being able to hold to their resolution, always coming together again in that small bare room beside the cottage. For those few short weeks almost everything for Jessica became subservient to those clandestine meetings. She was overjoyed when Theo's books realized almost two and a half thousand guineas between them, thus covering not only most of the money that Robert had taken but the whole of Patrick's debt as well; but as she talked to carpenters and tilers, workmen and bricklayers a part of her was with Charlie in that austere little room that had become their haven. She never tired of his lovemaking, never tired of the beauty and force of his strong, work-toughened body; but yet she knew that if they were to avoid disaster they must break with each other before they were discovered. It was not only Jessica's peers who would be shocked and disgusted by such a liaison – Charlie had to live with the village and its prejudices. He too, were their association made public, or even suspected, would be ostracized by his own kind. Both their lives could be ruined. Yet still they hungered for each other.

They lay one early May afternoon, half-sleeping, warm sunshine slanting through the unshuttered window and falling across their bare legs. Jessica wriggled her toes a little. A cuckoo called as she flew across the woodland that was lush with the year's new growth. The gentle bleating of the sheep was as much a background noise as was the song of the birds, so familiar had it become. They had followed Charlie's plan and enlarged the flock in the spring, when the other farmers were short of feed, and the land across the river had, to Giles' unconcealed chagrin, come to Jessica. Jessica knew from her mother that at the last moment he had offered the money for it himself, hating to see New Hall land returning to Old Hall, but Maria had been adamant. Her bargain had been with Jessica, and she had stuck to it. Thinking of Giles Jessica stirred a little, her dislike of her brother twinging like a touched nerve. Relations with Giles and Clara were certainly at a low ebb, and their latest snub, though she denied it vehemently to herself and to others, had stung.

Almost as if reading her thoughts Charlie, whom she had thought to be sleeping, said suddenly, his eyes still closed, 'Ha' you spoken to your brother this week?'

She turned her head on the pillow, surprised. 'No. Why?'

'I just wondered.'

'Wondered what?'

His eyes opened. 'If he's told you. About the letter.'

'Letter? What letter? Oh —' Jessica grimaced, 'Not another of those stupid threatening things?'

'Tha'ss right.'

'This come as a warnin' for you — iffen you doan get rid those machines you'll ave your stacks burned afore next moon — signed, Cap'n Blood!' Jessica's voice was half-amused. 'Oh, come, Charlie — you don't take these things seriously, do you? Giles must have had at least half a dozen —'

There was a small silence. 'There's bin strangers in the village,' Charlie said, apparently inconsequentially.

Jessica had been stroking his chest, that was furred with hair like the warm pelt of an animal, playing with the nipples that stood erect and dark among the soft brown hairs, watching in mischievous amusement as his tired body stirred to the rhythm of her playing fingers. At his words she stopped, coming up on one elbow, a small frown furrowing her forehead. 'What sort of strangers?'

He pulled a face, deliberately nonchalant, not looking at her. 'Just – strangers. Talkative, like.'

'Talkative about – machines? About New Hall's threshers?'

Again apparently at a tangent he said, 'There's bin some bad trouble north of here.'

'Yes, I heard. Riots. Barn and rick burnings. Machine smashing. Are you telling me there's some connection?'

His face was peaceful. 'No idea. Don't have no threshers meself. But –' he turned his head, '– worth watching, p'raps. Worth tellin' someone – someone who might be at risk, like – to keep an eye –'

She knew the effort that warning her must have taken. In common with the rest of the local population Charlie detested Giles and the regime at New Hall that had impoverished the village and filled the workhouses to overflowing. But Giles was Jessica's brother, and warning had been given.

She smiled a little. 'Thank you, Charlie. I'll pass it on. If I get a chance.'

'What about the big shindy on Saturday? A word in an ear – naming no names –?'

She made a small, rude sound in which amusement was sourly tempered. 'I'm not going to the May Ball. I wasn't invited.'

His eyes, that had closed sleepily, flew open again. 'Why not?' he asked, sharply.

She shrugged a little. 'I'm given to believe because of my delicate position in being a deserted wife. My dear brother and even dearer sister-in-law want to shield me from any unpleasant gossip. Any excuse being better than none at all. I don't care. I didn't want to go to their beastly silly ball anyway.'

He turned his head, looking up into her face. His eyes were sombre. 'You sure tha'ss the reason?'

'Of course it isn't. They just don't want me there.'

'No other reason?' he asked, quietly.

'Of course not. What other reason?'

'Try – you carryin' on with a farm hand,' he said. 'Try – rumours an' gossip an' people that can't keep a still tongue in their head.'

She shook her head, positively. 'No. I'm sure that isn't it. You know that Gilés and I don't get on. And Clara and I have never been exactly bosom friends. Why should they bother to ask me to their Ball? I probably wouldn't have gone if they had. No, Charlie, this is a family affair. Nothing to do with us. No-one knows.'

He tucked an arm about her and drew her to him, close to his side, his other hand reaching to cradle her small head on his shoulder. 'It can't go on, Jessie,' he said. 'We have to stop. For both our sakes.'

Her hand slid down his body. 'Once more,' she whispered, feeling him stir beneath her fingers. 'Just once more. Then we'll stop.'

Chapter Seventeen

But they did not – almost they could not – stop. They were young, their bodies were eager, and both had been alone too long. The summer abetted them – long warm day following long warm day in languorous succession, days and nights that might have been made for dalliance in shadows, days and nights that might have been made for the sharing of pleasure. Charlie's skin browned like a nut. The heat of the sun made the most industrious indolent and susceptible to the temptations of the flesh. It was too hard to give up. When she found him stripped to the waist and scything the fresh-scented grass for winter hay she thought almost anything could be sacrificed to their loving. If they lived in a fool's paradise then so be it. At least for this short summer it was worth it. She would not look further.

With the money available and the good weather holding the work at Old Hall went on at great pace. The roof was made secure and the rotting timbers replaced. The first of the many summer storms that thundered about their heads but did not penetrate the newly-tiled roof was a cause for celebration. Jessica negotiated with a neighbouring farmer at a very favourable price for the return of some of Old Hall's original holdings, sold off by Robert's father a few years previously. Despite the losses from the wild dog the South Downs crosses had proved a great success and they made a respectable profit on their lambs. Charlie still held out on the matter of the Merino ram – royal patronage notwithstanding. He was not convinced that in exposed East Anglia the improved wool justified the producing of less hardy stock, and after the hardships of the past winter Jessica was inclined to agree with him. They sheared in June, and she marvelled at the skill of the men who made the handling of the strong and bulky sheep look like child's play. Charlie well knew the advantages of employing the best – a clumsy shearer could ruin a fleece and reduce the wool to little more than chaff – and a gang from Norfolk, well known in the trade, were taken on for three days at a few shillings more than the going rate. The money was well spent. Jessica watched them work, neatly and deftly, handling the animals with ease and confidence, laughing and chafing as they sheared, the thick fleeces piling up, perfectly cut, the sheep untroubled, relieved to be free of the burden of their wool, walking white and fresh as driven snow through their captor's legs and out into the waiting folds.

In the fields on the other side of the river New Hall's crops grew, golden and straight, a promise of prosperity in this perfect year. The grain stood tall and full-eared, rippling in the summer breezes like a deep, gilded sea. The trees of the parkland cast the familiar pattern of their shadows in the brilliant sunshine and New Hall gleamed as golden as the ripening fields about it. But brewed by the heat the occasional storm broke the peace of the summer's days – and beneath the apparently tranquil surface of the village's day to day life trouble was brewing as surely as the summer storms. Jessica knew it, and it disturbed her. She sensed it in the guarded greetings of people who had never before been anything but open and friendly, felt it in the subtly changed, hardening attitudes of those other landowners with whom she occasionally had dealings. The strangers of whom Charlie had spoken came and went. Questioned about them he was non-committal. Jessica could well understand why. Charlie Best was caught in the middle: a tenant farmer, neither landowner nor hired hand he had to remain neutral. Throughout the summer there were spasmodic outbreaks of violence in and around the area, particularly in Norfolk and Suffolk. Special Constables and in some cases small troops of yeomanry were brought in and billeted in some of the larger villages and towns in an attempt to quell the unrest. One such group of Special Constables was brought in to Long Melford, and Jessica, shopping in the pretty little town, found it very strange and not a little disturbing to see them drilling in a nearby field, sweat running down their faces, badges glinting in the sun as they marched and turned, swinging their truncheons.

On the day that trouble finally came to Melbury village the sultry summer's heat was at its height. Jessica's mare had thrown a shoe and, it having been a very long time since Old Hall could support a smithy of its own as did New Hall, Jessica decided, riding the big Bay Dancer, to take the mare herself down into the village so that Jenson the blacksmith could reshoe her. It was a lovely day and a pleasant ride, in the dappled shade beneath the trees beside the river, whilst in the fields the brassy heat shimmered and the crops stood straight and still beneath a layer of summer dust.

It was late afternoon when she walked the two horses into the village street. Melbury was a straggling place, strung out along a mile of rutted road, the church at one end the ale house at the other and the smithy and its attached livery stables in the middle. Small cottages in various states of repair – or in some cases disrepair – were set singly or in groups upon each side of the road, most of them with small gardens, some well-tended some not. A few more substantial dwellings were built about the Green where stood the village pump and where now the duck pond had been reduced by the heat to little more than a sludgy puddle. The afternoon was still, and unusually quiet. A few children played in the dust of the street but the old bench under the elm outside the ale house was empty and the Green too was deserted. She was even more surprised to discover no sign of life when she reached the smithy, none of the habitual bustle of men and animals about the usually busy buildings. She rode Bay Dancer into the big barn, leading the mare, and tethered both horses. She had never seen the village so quiet and certainly never remembered a working weekday when Jenson had not been at his anvil, swinging his hammer in the easy, skilfully rhythmic way of his craft, surrounded by his cronies who met here for an exchange of greetings and news almost as often as in the ale house. Indeed Mrs Williams swore that more scurrilous gossip had its origins at Jenson's than ever started around the village pump or wash-house, where the village women gathered. Yet now the smithy's shop stood empty and deserted, the fire glowing, the blacksmith's tools discarded. Puzzled Jessica stood in the street outside, her eyes narrowed against the brilliance of light, the sun beating onto her shoulders through the thin, high-necked blouse that she wore with her riding skirt. The only sign of life nearby was a small boy who stood a few yards from her, a filthy thumb in his mouth, regarding her with solemn eyes.

'Hello,' she said, smiling.

He said nothing. His trousers, obviously a bigger brother's cast-offs, were tied at the waist with string and cut off in a ragged line at the calf. His feet were bare, the dirty toes splayed comfortably in the dust.

'Where is everyone?'

He shook his head, not removing his thumb.

'Do you know Mr Jenson?'

A nod.

'Do you know where he is?'

A small, dirty finger pointed, the thumb was removed for the briefest of moments and then plugged straight back the moment the words were out. 'Bonner's Field.'

'Bonner's Field?' She was even more puzzled. The field known as Bonner's lay behind the church and was sometimes used instead of the Green for fairs and other festivities. Had she forgotten the day? She was sure she would have known had a village celebration been taking place. She smiled her thanks to the child and gave him a penny, that disappeared like magic into the voluminous trousers. Then she set off along the path he had indicated, that ran behind the smithy and a row of cottages and cut across a small field to the back of the church and Bonner's Field.

She saw Charlie and Minna almost as she turned the corner of the building. The girl was clinging urgently to Charlie's hand and was all but dragging him along, talking volubly and insistently as she went. She was in obvious distress, her gestures and the sound of her voice pleading, though Jessica

494

could not distinguish the words. Taken aback she stood and watched them. Minna tugged at Charlie's hand again, and they both broke into a run, heading for Bonner's Field.

More slowly Jessica followed.

The field lay between a row of cottages and the churchyard. Jessica stopped by the cottages, in the shelter of a rickety fence over which scrambled a riot of sweet-smelling honeysuckle. For a moment she could not make sense of what she saw. The whole village seemed to be there – certainly all of the men and perhaps half of the women. A farmcart had been dragged into the centre of the field to serve as a platform, and upon this stood a powerfully built man in worn labourer's clothes, his hair grizzled, his skin weather-darkened, his eyes the bright pale blue that were to be seen in so many East Anglian faces. Beside him stood a much younger man, a slighter replica of himself and obviously his son. The older man was talking, a hand raised to emphasize his point. In the roar that was greeting what he was saying Jessica lost the words. She stood stock still at the sound, suddenly chill despite the heat. There was a growl of excitement in it, a thread of violence that lifted the hairs at the back of her neck. It was like the snarl of a roused animal, menacing, frightening.

Charlie, towed by Minna, had reached the edge of the crowd and, dropping the girl's hand, had begun to push his way to the front. Jessica saw men greet him and move aside, letting him through. No-one obstructed his way to the cart. The older man on seeing him grinned and extended a hand to help him up. Charlie shook his head and refused the hand. 'Are you gone clean out of your mind, John Newton?' His strong voice lifted above the noise of the crowd. A sudden hush fell. Heads turned. A man muttered and was shushed to silence.

The older man let his hand fall to his side, and straightened, his face black with anger as he looked down at Charlie. 'Iffen you a'n't with us, Charlie Best, then you'd better leave afore we decide you're agin us.'

'Of course I'm with you, man! Tha'ss why I'm tellin' you you're a fool! You don't stand a chance with all this! There's Specials in Melford. They'll be here at the first swing of an axe!

John, man – all of you! – don't get yourselves mixed up in this –!'

The muttering of the crowd swelled in anger. Hands reached for Charlie. He fought them off. 'You're bein' used! Outsiders, using you to stir up trouble, tha'ss all –!'

'Outsiders?' It was the young man on the cart, the young man that Jessica had realized must be Minna's brother, as the older man must be her father. 'Outsiders, you say, Charlie Best? Is it outsiders that've been kicked off New Hall land to make room for Hawthorne's bloody machines?'

'No!' roared the crowd.

'– Is it outsiders that have to feed their little 'uns on pigswill because they can't afford bread –?'

'*No!*'

Charlie was struggling against the hands that were trying to pull him back from the cart. 'Tommy, stop it! Tha'ss daft, lad – can't you see –?' But the hands had him now, and none too gently he was hauled back, cuffed and cursed to the edge of the crowd. As he emerged from the rough handling he staggered, blood upon his face, and went down onto one knee. Jessica started forward, but Minna was there beside him, an arm about his shoulders, a tender hand to his battered face.

And now another man had climbed onto the cart, a tall thin man with a hawk-like face, eyes coal-black and piercing. His appearance stilled the crowd as if by magic, a moment of held breath and expectancy. 'Good people of Melbury –' His voice lifted easily, the voice of an orator, ringing and clear. Faces were lifted to him, eyes shone. Jessica took a careful step backwards, and then another. There had been riots in Eye and in Diss, machine-smashing and fire-raising around Ipswich and Colchester. But here? Surely not? Most of the faces she saw here she had known all her life. The younger ones, like Charlie, she had run with as a child –

She forced herself to listen to the man. '– They protect themselves with their filthy Corn Laws and deny your children bread –!'

A cloud had covered the sun. The atmosphere was heavy. The stranger's face shone with sweat, and his shirt was stained dark with it.

'– They bring in their machines and they deny you a decent day's work –'

'Smash them! Smash them!'

'They enclose your land and make paupers of you –'

'Burn them out!'

To Jessica's horror she saw that Tommy Newton had a lit torch in his hand and was waving it above his head to roars of approval, dark smoke an evil tail behind it. 'Burn the buggers out!'

The paralysis that had gripped her fell away. She had to stop this. She had to do something. She had to get help.

No-one had noticed her, there by the honeysuckle-hung fence. She moved backwards warily, eyes on the crowd, only now and suddenly becoming aware of possible personal danger. Giles Hawthorne was the name being bandied with hatred about the crowd. And she was Giles Hawthorne's sister. The common knowledge of the bad blood between them might not protect her in this charged atmosphere, with strangers inciting violence. Men were shouting, their faces distorted, another torch had been lit. The man on the cart had an axe in his hand, and Minna's father held a sledge hammer.

She took another step. Another few yards and she would be at the corner of the fence and out of sight. Bay Dancer was in the barn by the smithy. She had to get to Melford – bring help, before something truly terrible happened –

As she turned to run, Charlie saw her.

She caught his eyes as she turned, saw the surprise on his face, saw him open his mouth to utter the shout that would betray her, and then clamp it shut again. And then she was running, flying over the stony ground, unaware of pain as she stumbled and fell, picking herself up and running again, her riding hat discarded upon the ground behind her. Across the field, behind the cottages, down the alleyway beside the smithy's. She could hear him behind her, catching her up, heard him now that the danger was two fields away calling her name.

'Jessie! Jessie, wait!'

She flung herself into the barn. Bay Dancer, great head lifted in expectancy as he heard her step, was tethered at the far end of the building. He whinnied softly when he saw her and pawed the ground. She dragged a bale of hay to him, scrambled upon it, flung herself into the saddle as Charlie, panting, his face fearfully bloodied, came to the door. 'Jessie –!' He stopped.

Dismounted she would have stood no chance against his strength. On the big horse she was his match, and more than his match. She wrenched Dancer's head about to face him. 'Get out of the way, Charlie.'

'What are you goin' to do?'

'I'm going to Melford. To fetch the Specials.'

He stepped forward, his hands outstretched. 'Jessie, no! If you bring the police in there'll be worse trouble than ever.'

'Worse trouble?' She stared at him. Excited, Dancer edged sideways, and she fought him round again. 'Are you mad? Worse than what? Worse than what's happening out there? Worse than a riot? Worse than arson? Murder perhaps? You heard them – they're going to New Hall –!'

'I'll stop them! Give me a chance to talk to them –'

'Stop them? Talk to them? Like you tried to just now? Don't be a fool, Charlie! They'll kill you!'

'No! I'll not believe that! They're decent people!'

'Of course they're decent people! In their right minds! I know that as well as you do. But now? They're demented. If they have their way they'll not stop at Giles' machines, and you know it. They'll burn New Hall to the ground! Do you think I'm going to stand by and see that happen? Get out of the way, Charlie!'

He stared at her. He stood in the open doorway, and the light was behind him, throwing his face into shadow. He was a stranger. A stranger who looked at her across a gulf that yawned suddenly at their feet, a gulf that divided, that had always divided, their two lives. A stranger who would never understand why she did as she did. She truly hated Giles, but she would not see him smoked out and murdered by a mob. She would not see the splendour of New Hall, filled with her mother's treasures and her father's loved possessions, burned. There was an odd, hung moment of silence in the barn, broken only by the distant, ferocious shouts of the mob. Then both moved together. Charlie lunged for the huge door, trying to close it, to prevent her from leaving; and in the same moment she set the big horse at the opening. Charlie threw himself to one side, cursing, and she was through and past him, head down and hair flying, out on the dusty road to Melford.

They came too late to save the fields, or the machines that were Giles' pride and joy. Too late to save the barns, or the ricks. The dark pall of smoke that hung over Melbury on that summer's evening as the forces of law galloped hard along the road to the village told its own story of destruction long before they reached New Hall. Fire had ripped through the dry corn, dancing and blazing, spitting destruction in face of a rising wind. Trees were scorched and hedges destroyed. The machines had been smashed and the barns burned about them. But thanks to the timely arrival of the Specials at least New Hall stood untouched, though surrounded by smoking desolation. Giles, unarmed, had been taken by masked men whilst riding his fields, and no-one – no servant, no labourer – had lifted a hand to protect him. He had been held and made to watch the destruction of his crops and of his dreams. He had fought like a demon, and had been hurt for it. He had defied them, and they had used fists and feet, though some, shamefaced as the bloodlust had left them, had crept away and returned to their homes. The remainder scattered as the police rode in, leaving Giles to stand, filthy, his shirt in ribbons, blood upon his handsome face, to watch grim-faced as the roof of the barn collapsed in a shower of sparks.

'Nothin' we can do, sir, I'm afraid,' the sergeant said.

Giles turned cold eyes upon him. 'Oh, yes, Sergeant. There's something you can do. You can make sure that every man jack that had a hand in this finishes behind bars at the next Assizes. You can make sure the ringleaders are hanged and the rest transported for life –'

And Jessica, unthanked, turning Dancer's head from the smoking ruin of New Hall's prosperity, found herself reflecting ruefully that nothing – absolutely nothing – would ever change Giles Hawthorne.

Charlie Best married Minna three weeks after her father and brother had sailed in chains in the convict hulks to Australia, and her mother and small brother moved into the lean-to at the back of Home Farm, their own almost derelict cottage forfeit to the implacable Giles. Charlie and Jessica had had very little to say to each other since the day of the riot – the day when all that had been between them had slipped away into the gulf that had yawned between them as they had faced each other in the barn. Before he married Minna, stiffly he had offered to leave Home Farm, an offer which, as stiffly, she had refused. He was a good farmer and an excellent stockman. Why should she want to replace him? The farm, thanks mainly to his efforts was doing well and in the future could be expected to do better. She would not hear of his leaving.

He nodded, unsmiling. 'Thank you, Y're Ladyship.'

She had looked at him for a moment, the hurt hostility dropping from her. 'You don't want to go, do you?'

'No,' he said, quietly, and then added again, 'Y're Ladyship.'

'Well then,' She had turned her horse's head, her eyes straying across the fields to where Old Hall sheep grazed, peaceful, plump and mild-faced. 'Stay. Stay and help me make this place the most prosperous working estate in West Suffolk.' Those dream-like, magic summer days of their loving, so abruptly terminated, had seemed a million years away as she had turned and ridden from him, not looking back, knowing that Minna watched from the cottage door.

They bought in more stock again that autumn, and the winter that followed was mild and damp with nothing like the bitter weather of the year before. Just after Christmas Sarah took cold again, and this time it settled upon her chest. Worried,

Jessica tried to coax her to bed, but the stubborn old lady would not be persuaded. She refused, coughing and wheezing, to give up her ceaseless, pathetic search for her dead husband. Pneumonia struck in February, and she died upon the day that Gabriella found the first snowdrops growing by the river. Jessica grieved for the old lady, and it fretted her that she could not let Robert know of her death, but still she had not heard from him, nor had an address where she might contact him. He had dropped from their lives, presumably with intention, as surely as if he himself were dead. Sometimes indeed she found herself wondering if he were, and if she would ever hear, ever know what became of him.

Over the next couple of seasons Old Hall fared well and prospered while across the park Giles doggedly tried to regain lost ground at New Hall. Needing money desperately to stave off the ruin that could have been brought about by the riot he drove a hard bargain over the parkland, that would support Jessica's sheep but would not help him to recoup his lost crops. To put it to arable use would be to lose the magnificent trees and spoil the setting of the house; and even Giles could not bring himself to be vandal enough to do that. So Jessica acquired the parkland from the river to the lakeside and as far as the ha-ha that divided the lawns of the house from the grassland, and Clara's peacocks were confined to the garden of New Hall. Jessica saw little of her brother or his wife; there was no love lost between them. Giles had never even thanked her for her effort in bringing the Specials on the day of the riot, and the omission neither surprised nor distressed her. She could guess how galling it must be to him to be in her debt, however slightly. To admit to it by thanks would be impossible for him. She found herself wondering sometimes what kind of life they led, those two, in that great, isolated house, bound to each other in bitterness; childless and unloving; their dreams of grandeur, that was all they had shared, turned to ashes.

For herself she was, she told herself, happy enough. Old Hall was safe, its future – and Gabriella's – assured. Gabriella grew, it seemed, by the day, a child full of laughter and of love, tall and straight, dark as a gypsy and with a promise of beauty.

It was on a late summer's day in 1826, three years after Robert had left, that Jessica finally had news of her husband.

She returned from a visit to her mother who, pain-ridden but indomitable as ever, still stubbornly refused to leave Tollgate House for what she saw as the doubtful luxuries of Old Hall, to discover a small sealed package, grubby and battered-looking, on the table at Old Hall. It was addressed to her, and marked "By Hand". Intrigued she tore it open. A piece of stiff paper fluttered to the floor. She picked it up.

'I, the undersigned, do hereby certify that –'

She stared at it for a long time, numbly. Dead. Robert was dead. In an epidemic of yellow fever, three months since, in Florence.

Dead.

Strangely, though in some ways it could not be called a surprise, she felt a small contraction of pain in her heart. For a moment she allowed herself to remember not the Robert who had faced her, desperate, drugged and hateful, the money that might have saved Old Hall in his pocket, but the Robert who had been her steadfast friend in an all but loveless childhood. The Robert who had played in the park with her, who had supported her through the death of her father. The Robert who had sworn, on a day that now seemed so very long ago that Robert FitzBolton and Jessica Hawthorne would be friends for ever and ever –

There was a letter with the certificate, addressed to her in a hand that, though as shaky as if it might have been written by an old man, still she recognized as Robert's own. She held it for a long time before she could bring herself to open it.

'My dear Jessica,

Florence has become a city of death, and I die with her, in good company and without regret. You will not grieve for me, and I cannot blame you for that. My one sorrow is that my life has so shadowed yours. You deserve better, and in the name of our friendship I now make amends. My death will set you free. Hermes is my gift to you. Clip his wings if you must, but be happy, for all our sakes.

Your loving friend
Robert.'

She frowned a little. *Hermes is my gift to you.* Hermes?

Still holding the letter she reached to the bellpull that hung by the fireplace. Her summons was answered by a small maid, neat in apron and cap. 'Yes, Ma'am?'

'Mary – did you see who delivered this packet?'

'Yes, Ma'am.'

'Who was it?'

'A –' the maid hesitated for a telling moment, '– a gentleman, Ma'am. A foreign-looking gentleman.'

'Is he still here?'

The maid shook her head. 'No, Ma'am. He wouldn't give his name, nor wait.'

'I see. Thank you, Mary.'

Hermes is my gift to you.

Jessica, the letter still in her hand, stepped out into the September sunshine. The sky was a clear and limpid blue, the rustling trees still heavy with leaf. Spiky green chestnuts hung in bunches, attractively bright against the darker foliage of the spreading trees. The river moved beside her, soft and tranquil. She passed the spot where Caroline had stood that day so many years ago, looking down at Danny, and felt again the pang of pain and loss that the child she had been all those years ago had felt. She passed too the cottage, derelict now, from which she had sent him flying from the wrath of her father. As she neared the church a small figure tumbled towards her, dark tangled hair flying, eyes wide. 'Mama! Mama!' Danny's daughter exclaimed excitedly, 'There's a stranger in the church!'

'I thought there might be.'

Hermes is my gift to you.

She was absurdly calm. 'Wait here a moment, Gabriella. I won't be long.'

'But, Mama –!'

'Wait. I'll be out in a moment.'

The church was dark after the brilliance of light outside and, as always, cold. He stood by the altar, head thrown back, looking at the smiling statue of St Agatha. A dark angel, limned in the light of the stained windows, as she had seen him before, as she had so often conjured him in loneliness and longing. She watched him for a moment in silence. Her heart was hammering now, her calm deserted her. As she started towards him he turned, and she saw clearly the changes that the years had wrought. His dark skin was sallow, as if with ill-health, and his face was gaunt, the scar still showing white upon his cheekbone. His eyes were shadowed and tired, the long mouth no longer smiled so easily.

They stood looking at each other from the space of a few feet for a long, quiet moment.

'Danny,' she said.

He smiled a little at the sound of her voice.

'It was you who brought the packet from Robert.'

'Yes. He asked me. Begged me. He knew he was dying. Half of Florence was dying. The worst epidemic in years. Robert's friend – Arthur? – had died the week before. I think Robert was happy to follow him. But – he was desperate that you should know, that you should have the death certificate. He said he could not bear to think of you tied to a dead man for the rest of his life. And so – he asked me to bring them.'

She looked down at the letter in her hand, her eyes unexpectedly blurring. 'Did he – show you the letter?'

'No.'

She stepped a little closer and offered it. 'Please. I'd like you to read it.'

He hesitated for a moment, then reached a hand to hers. As he took the letter their fingers touched, and for a moment their eyes clung, searching. Then Danny took the paper and opened it. She saw him read it, saw his eyes run back over it. He was frowning a little. 'Hermes is my gift to you,' he read aloud after a moment. 'Clip his wings if you must, but be happy for all our sakes. That's a bit obscure, isn't it? What does he mean? Who or what is Hermes?'

She smiled a little, watching him. 'Hermes was a messenger, who served the Greek Gods.'

He thought about that for a moment, then a flicker of amusement crossed his face. 'Then Robert's gift to you –?'

'Is you. The messenger that bore it.'

He laughed a little, but quickly sobered. She watched him. He had made no move towards her, had not attempted to touch or kiss her. 'It was a gift not his to give,' she said, quietly.

He turned his head from her.

'Danny?' Her questioning voice sounded small, lost in the spaces of the old building.

'I don't know –' He stopped.

She waited, but he said nothing more. 'Serafina?' she asked, quietly.

His head snapped up. 'No! No, it isn't Serafina. Jessie – Serafina's dead. She's been dead for nearly a year –'

She said nothing. Hurt filled her. Dead for a year, and he had not come.

He sat down on the front pew, leaning his elbows on his knees. His bowed dark head was close enough for her to have put out a hand and touch it. She clasped her hands before her, willing them to stillness.

'She betrayed a man once too often,' he said, at last. 'Oh – not me. I was far beyond that by then. A lover. One of many.'

'What happened?'

'He killed her.' His voice was absolutely neutral, absolutely devoid of any emotion.

She caught her breath.

'It was bound to happen. She always knew it. Sometimes it seemed she deliberately provoked the violence that would eventually be her death.'

'And you?'

'I? I got drunk. I got drunk and I stayed drunk until Robert sent someone to find me.' He lifted his head and looked at her then, reaching a hand. 'Jessica –'

It was all she had been looking for, that half-pleading gesture. She dropped to her knees beside him, slipping into his reaching arms, tears running suddenly down her face. He kissed her fiercely; her mouth, her eyes, her wet cheeks, his hands cradling her head. 'See – see what I've done – I've made you cry already!'

She shook her head, half-laughing through the tears.

He held her, her face cupped in his hands, his face passionate with conflicting emotions. 'Jessie – supposing I hurt you? I couldn't bear to do that again! I want to stay – I want to be with you. In all the days and nights of travelling, in all the weeks that I've carried that packet I've known, I've thought of it. But – supposing I can't? Supposing I can't settle? Supposing I leave you –?'

She sat back on her heels, her head tilted to look at him. 'That's what you're afraid of? That you won't be able to settle?'

'Yes.'

She kissed him very hard, then sat back again, her hands in his. 'Listen to me. I love you. I have always loved you. I think I always will. I know I can't tie you down. I know what you are – and that's why I love you. Perhaps you'll go. Perhaps you'll leave me. But we don't have to think about that now. We don't have to think about it at all if it doesn't happen. I won't – I won't! – give up a chance of happiness just because it might not last! Oh, Danny! How silly even to think it –!' She jumped to her feet, pulling him after her. Infected by her happiness he caught her to him, kissed her again. She flung her arms about his neck. 'Danny O'Donnel, do you want to stay with me today?'

'Yes.'

'Then do it. Stay while you can – leave if and when you must – but come back to me, Danny. Always come back to me. Robert was wrong – I wouldn't – I couldn't – clip Hermes' wings. But I'll show you someone who just might – come – quickly! Come and see –' She caught his hand and drew him from the chill darkness out into the warmth of the day to where their daughter, eyes bright with excited curiosity, waited, smiling, in the sunshine.